PROJECT LIVE

William Clark Focht Jr.

With ♡

William Clark Focht Jr.

Graphics by Alexander Gómez

Edited by Jim Martin

"Never doubt that a small group of thoughtful, committed, citizens can change the world. Indeed, it is the only thing that ever has."

— Margaret Mead

Dedication

To my family and friends, without you, my soul thirsts for life.

To all the women and men working in the healthcare field who save lives everyday and improve the well-being of those they touch.

Acknowledgement

Thanks to Alexander Gómez for your knowledge of graphic design and to Dr. J. B. Cannon and Jim Martin for your understanding of the editing process.

Table of Contents

Prologue

The journey for Beth up until this point comes to a fiery intersection as we flash forward to the ending. Here, the fire rose high into the cool night. Each body was lying on its bed, lifeless, as the flames charred flesh. Her life as an agent responsible for carrying out a significant part of the CIA's underhanded experiment, and her life married to an ungrateful and demanding husband abruptly came to a fiery end. She changed from caring and compassionate to hate filled facing the possibility of total ruin. All of Beth's old and newly found anger and internal torment burnt up with the house and with the family. She hadn't planned for it to end like this, but she could not face the consequences. She also couldn't believe how simple the deed was to complete. It took only a little bit of gas and a match. Of course, Beth could not let the family die on an empty stomach. Instead, she cheerfully fed them their last meal, ever.

Laced with a little bit of cyanide, the meal's taste was unchanged. It was a scrumptious soufflé served with a side of death. The first little ingrate took a bite after telling her about a boy who had kicked him at school. Then, her husband took a bite; he took such a large bite that Beth thought that he might just die right then without the subsequent show. With a mouthful of food, he grumbled for her to hand him the salt and naturally she complied. Even now, she would not defy the beast. How could she? She had remained defenseless in the marriage until the very end. Her anger towards him, and her twisted situation, fueled the flames of her actions.

Little Mark took the next bite. Like always, he took his sweet time about it. He poked at the tuna surprise and finally got the courage up to lift the fork to his mouth. He whined that he wasn't hungry, but Beth gently assured him that the dish was tasty - the tastiest. Then her daughter, Sara, raised her fork to her lips. She began coughing and for a moment Beth thought she might taste the cyanide. After she stopped coughing, she took another bite, and the deed was done.

Beth got up from the table, walked over to the oven and removed the bread. In the distance, she heard a faint choking noise from Mark. At first, it was just a little gasp followed by a series of deeper gasps. Unexpectedly, her husband slapped Mark across the face. He had no time for games at the dinner table. This was his time to relax and play king for the day, and he was not about to let this little kid steal his thunder as Mark played with his food. His hand went up again to slap some sense into Mark, but it didn't make it past his own throat.

Beth's husband clutched his neck as if it was going to burst. He blasted out for Beth to bring him some more water, but she did not move. Her eyes fixed on the fat man as he winced in pain. "How lovely," she thought. "How perfect is this night? Die you sack of shit! Die!" Her husband grabbed the tablecloth as he fell to the floor.

Dishes crashed down with him as did the centerpiece. The beast lay on the floor writhing as he lay next to Sara who had fallen moments earlier. Sara wiggled like a slinky next to the fat man, and within three minutes, tonight's dinner had gone from the usual to the sublime. All three of them lay there on the floor, each moaning like a cheap whore. Nothing could have satiated the desire that Beth had harbored for so long as the sight before her. Her frenzied state, erupting from the situation she endured for months prior to tonight, coupled with her seething abhorrence of her husband's heavy-handed ways caused Beth to destroy the life that she created.

Beth's husband slowly turned his head and vomited near where Sara had vomited moments earlier. All bodily functions gave its last parting stench to the earth before each one of Beth's family members ceased to draw any further breath. They lay in their fifth awaiting Beth to collect her thoughts about what her next action should be.

Beth was only five foot six inches tall, but she had the strength of a gymnast. She dragged the fat man through the hall to the foyer. Once there, she turned him around and locked her arms around his shoulders. She pulled the massive body up the stairs with each stair knocking against his unresponsive legs. The strong-willed woman pulled the large man up onto the bed and pulled the sheets up to the neck of his limp body. After the covers were firmly in place, she climbed on top of him and gazed down at his motionless, dull eyes. Her eyes locked on his as she sat there and thought about the way she had been treated by him for so long; she thought about all of the comments he made about how she was not good enough to be with him.

He had told her that he should have married someone else. He even cheated on her with his goddamn secretary. Even though this was not the primary reason for his death, it surely made the deed easier to complete. Beth raised her hand and slapped his flabby face. It was a hard slap and that satisfied Beth immensely. She left the room to retrieve the other three now satisfyingly dead bodies. One by one, Mother Beth placed the children in their respective beds and, at 8:35 PM, all the children were lying in what would become their funeral pyres. She went around to each of the rooms where each one of them lay to check on them.

Pure, golden silence was all that she experienced.

Beth ran down the steps and quickly made her way into the kitchen. There, she opened the door to the mudroom and descended the steps into the garage. She tossed over camping gear and her husband's old empty liquor bottles. Finally, she found the little red gas can she was looking for and sprinted back up the stairs to where the big pig lay. She reached out and ripped the fat man's wallet from his pocket. She took all the money from his wallet and stuffed it into her pocket. Then, Beth doused him with gasoline and the others as well. She grabbed a suitcase and packed it frantically. She grabbed several shirts, undergarments, and all of her jewelry and crammed it in the suitcase. She slammed it shut and reached for the pack of matches lying on the dresser.

Beth looked around and thought, "What am I doing?" She knew damn well; she freed herself from the jail her life had become. She took the life she gave; as for now, life is what she abhorred so much. And with that parting thought, she pulled out a match and struck it. She lit the end of the yellow hose attached to the gas can before throwing the flaming can onto the fat man. She watched the flames roar towards the ceiling. Her body twisted as she hurriedly ran back to the garage and jumped into the car. She started the engine, opened the garage door, and floored the gas pedal whipping the car from the garage. She was going several miles down the highway at 55 miles per hour by the time the first fire engine even arrived.

A few minutes earlier, Beth's neighbor ran over to the house to see what was causing all the commotion. He saw the bright flames shooting skyward as he protected himself from the thick black smoke billowing towards him. The neighbor couldn't believe what was going on in front of him. With a heavy heart and a strained voice, he hung his head and asked to himself, "What could have caused this?"

Chapter 1

JIMMY AND JANICE

What started out as a dare for Jimmy turned into a nightmare. Jimmy dared himself that he could handle the military and should join. But, he thought that somehow he was inadequate or was not up to par to serve his country. Despite his lapse in confidence, he decided to visit the Army recruiter's office around the corner from where he worked. He was tired of his 9 to 5 and decided that today was as good as any to visit the recruiter.

Jimmy walked into the recruiter's office and sat down on the chair in front of the desk. The desk was littered with hundreds of applications from other potential GI's. The recruiter turned his thick gaze towards Jimmy and pushed his beret up with his pencil.

"What can I help you with today?" the recruiter asked.

"I want to join the Army," Jimmy said.

"Good, my name is Sergeant Bernard."

"I'm Jimmy Mayfield."

"Ok, what are you good at, what type of skills do you have?" Sergeant Bernard asked as he folded his arms and leaned back into his leather swivel chair.

"I am currently working for an office doing things like making copies, sending faxes and things like that," Jimmy said in a less than thrilled tone of voice.

"Well, what type of position do you want in the army?" Sergeant Bernard asked.

"I want to do something medical," Jimmy said with a hint of enthusiasm. "I have some experience working at a hospital and want to learn more about the medical field."

His face was aglow with the thought of this new and challenging adventure.

"Ok, here, take this application home with you and read over it. Fill it out and bring it back to me tomorrow," Sergeant Bernard said as he handed Jimmy the papers.

Jimmy was starting to get nervous because this was getting too real. He didn't know if he was ready to make the full commitment this endeavor required. He did like the idea he might be marching in Army dress uniform in front of his family and friends after completing boot camp. But his nerves got the best of him, and he thought that this might be a good time to tell a joke to the recruiter.

4

"That sounds good, but one thing though," Jimmy said with a grin on his face.

"What's that?" Bernard asked as he leaned in towards Jimmy a bit.

"I run like a bitch." Jimmy said flatly.

The recruiter was anything but amused.

"Boy, this is the army, if you are looking for a laugh, the comedy club is right around the corner; join that," Sergeant Bernard said with a scowl on his face.

Jimmy sat there dumbfounded at Bernard's humorless expression.

"Well, I...I will talk with you later then. I need to go home now but will call you later or something," Jimmy said as he slowly got up from the chair. He extended his hand out to Sergeant Bernard. Sergeant Bernard looked down at Jimmy's hand and back up at Jimmy and said, "Boy, you have to be kidding me."

With that, Jimmy turned and walked out of the door.

Jimmy rushed home to look over the application; it was about four pages long and full of small print that Jimmy didn't want to read. He grabbed a pen and thought about filling it out when the phone rang.

"Hello," he said as he laid the application on his dresser.

"Hello, baby," Janice, Jimmy's girlfriend of two years, gushed.

"How are you doing honey?" Jimmy asked.

"Pretty ok, I just finished up on my latest Law School Admission Test."

"So, what does that make it, time number five that you've taken it?" Jimmy wondered.

"Yep, I am truly a masochist. I think that this time I did well. Even if I didn't, I refuse to take that damn test again. I just will not be going to law school then," Janice sighed.

This was indeed Janice's fifth time taking the Law School Admission Test. She had taken it four times, before applying to 12 different law schools. All of the schools were in either the first or the high second-tier rankings according to *US News and World Report*. She was denied admissions to all of them except Hofstra University on New York's Long Island. But Hofstra was an expensive private school, and although it had a decent reputation, she did not want to live so far north. Her goal was to get into her undergraduate school, the University of North Carolina at Chapel Hill. However, they, as well, rejected her application based on her low LSAT score. Competition for admission to law school was certainly stiff, and it was even harder to get into UNC, because it was a good school with in-state tuition rates.

"At least you tried," Jimmy said in a conciliatory tone.

"Yeah, maybe somewhere, it will count for something," Janice said.

She then asked, "Did you stop by the recruiter's office like you said you were going to?"

"Yeah, he was kind of a dick, but he did give me an application to fill out; I'll work on it later." His words, "I'll work on it later," were a blatant lie as the application sat uncompleted for three months. In the meantime, Jimmy continued to put in his time at the office. He was completely bored with his job. Making copies was not by any means his passion, and the humdrum of everyday work, like his coworker's constant, loud nibbling on pretzels at her work station all day, was not a very appealing life for him in any way. The more he worked, the more he wanted the excitement that the military presented to him. He just was not sure if he was up to the challenge and that kept him from working on the application even though the Army was his way out. It was also his ticket to leave his parents house. He was not very happy there, but he was frightened to use the ticket.

Janice once again did all the things that were required to get into law school. She sent all of her transcripts to the Law School Data Assembly Service. Janice got an additional Letter of Recommendation from a Political Science professor she knew in college and sent it into the LSDAS. She was determined to be a lawyer. The idea of serving justice to deserving individuals really appealed to her. Her GPA in college was strong but not as good as she would have liked. She had a 3.4 GPA, which was good enough to get her into some lower-tiered schools, but not the Ivy League, to which she aspired. It was her combined LSAT score of 147 that did the most to keep her out of her top choice schools. The scores for the test ranged from 120 to 180, and she scored closer to the bottom half. But, Janice was waiting for her final LSAT score to complete her file and hoped that this time it would be better.

Jimmy eventually filled out his military application and submitted it to Sergeant Bernard who initiated the process for Jimmy to join the Army. Jimmy went through the Military Entrance Processing Center, or MEPS, where he was questioned, took the ASVAB military exam, had a physical, chose a job as a paramedic, and took the oath required of all military personnel. He excelled past the physical requirements and received a very high score on the ASVAB. He was already physically prepared for Boot Camp according to the research he did beforehand, so he knew what to expect when he got there. Finally, the time had come to depart on what would be a life-changing event for Jimmy. Janice, Jimmy's mother, and Jimmy left Charlotte for Fort Jackson, South Carolina.

The heat of the summer was oppressive as they arrived at the Army's largest training facility in the United States. It was just as Jimmy had pictured it: Fort Jackson, South Carolina was a city within a city, Humvees circled the street, and cargo trucks were hauling their loads. Jimmy and the others pulled up to the building where new recruits were to be registered while basic trainees did jumping jacks in the front yard of the building. Jimmy's mother was nervous as she pulled their black Honda Accord into the visitors' parking lot. She also wasn't sure that Jimmy was military material, but she gave him the benefit of the doubt. This was the first time that he would be so far away from home for so long.

Janice was nervous for him too. She was also sad that she would be leaving Jimmy for just over nine weeks. While Janice could still contact him, her contact would be severely limited; she would just have to wait until his graduation to see him again. While Jimmy was becoming a man in the Army, Janice had to finalize plans of her own to attend school for the coming fall. She would attend to that once she got back home since; now, she had to say farewell to Jimmy.

Jimmy, Jimmy's mother, and Janice all walked into the 120th Adjutant Battalion building where the signs that said "New Recruits" had led them. A sea of camouflage greeted them at the door. Soldiers were sitting at a large table towards the front of the building registering new recruits. Once inside, Jimmy sat down his belongings and gave Janice a hug and kiss. Then, he turned to his mother and gave her a kiss on her cheek. He turned to both of them and said, "Wish me luck."

"Yes, we both wish you the best," Jimmy's mother said. "We know that you will do well."

"I will call you," Janice said.

"No, I will call you. I can call you in a day or two, and once a week after that, but I will be busy most of the time," Jimmy replied. "It's nice that the military allows cell phones now. I heard that it didn't always used to be that way."

"I'll be waiting," Janice said.

"I love you honey, and remember that no matter how bad things get, you have people that love you," his mother assured him.

"Thanks, mom, I love you too. Bye now."

Janice and Jimmy's mother turned and walked out the front door.

Jimmy went over to the table where the soldiers were seated and said, "Hello, I'm Jimmy Mayfield reporting for duty."

A soldier at the table looked Jimmy over. He turned his head toward a fellow soldier at the table and said, "They're really not giving us much to work with here."

"No, not at all," the fellow soldier responded.

Jimmy furrowed his eyes a bit in anger as the soldier gave Jimmy his barracks assignment and told him to be ready for orientation in an hour. The soldier explained where Jimmy's barracks was and then Jimmy took his duffle bag down the breezeway to the room. While he was sitting on his bed in the barracks, one of his fellow recruits came into the room.

"Hi, my name is Todd," he said with a hint of Southern drawl.

Hi Todd, I'm Jimmy. Where are you from?" Jimmy asked.

"Charlotte, NC," Todd responded.

"No way, so am I," Jimmy replied.

"That's cool, where did you go to high school?" Todd asked.

"East Mecklenburg," Jimmy responded.

"I went to Garinger," Todd said with a look of resignation.

"Oh, you were one of those kids," Jimmy said.

"Well, I managed to stay alive, if that's what you mean," Todd said.

"You probably made a good choice coming here," Jimmy said.

"Yeah, I was going nowhere and got stuck in a shitty job working for a bank. I wanted to see if the military could offer the excitement that they always advertise," Todd said.

Jimmy and Todd both walked to the large auditorium in the new recruit building. One of the Sergeants directed recruits on where to sit. So far, the first several rows were filled up, but Jimmy and Todd were able to take seats next to a recruit that looked like he weighed about 300 pounds. He was young and had severe acne and wiped his forehead over and over again in attempt to get all of the sweat from it. The young recruit had several coughing bouts as they sat there. Todd turned to Jimmy and said, "I guess not everyone makes it through basic training."

"It sure looks that way," Jimmy said.

As all the nervous recruits filed in to the auditorium, several officers in front were preparing for their presentations. One was checking the microphone while another was adjusting his uniform as he sat there. There were four in all. One was the Lieutenant Commander as designated by the golden oak leaf that appeared on his jacket. There was a Private, a Commander Sergeant Major, and a Drill Sergeant sitting next to each other in fold out chairs on one side of the podium while the Lieutenant Commander and Private sat on the other side.

The Lieutenant approached the microphone to speak first. He was a tall man, about six foot three, and appeared to be the most well built of the five. He cleared his throat and began his speech.

> I would like to welcome you all here today. By being here, you have already taken a step towards becoming a soldier. You have decided to embark on a course that few undertake and even fewer complete. You have decided to serve your country. To serve is one of the toughest commitments you will ever endure. But by doing so, you can count yourselves among the brave, disciplined, and strong. These next nine weeks will challenge you. You will be challenged both mentally and physically. There will be times were you will want to quit. I implore you not to quit. Be strong and give it your all. Not all of you will make it. That is ok; at least you gave it your best shot. The men and women in this room will become your brothers and sisters. Learn to lean on them for support as well as for their skills. You will also come to respect and befriend your superior officers. They are the ones who will shape you as transform from civilian to soldier. Trust their judgment. Go out there and give it your all and make the army proud.

Jimmy and Todd glanced at one another during the speech. Jimmy's eyes were wide with anticipation.

"What have we gotten ourselves into?"

"Whatever it is, it isn't sitting behind a desk all day," Todd said.

"That's for sure," Jimmy muttered back.

The recruit sitting in front of Jimmy turned around and gave him a dirty look. Jimmy stared back at him and said, "Turn around."

The young, pimple-faced recruit shot the bird at Jimmy and told him to fuck off. Jimmy didn't want to cause a scene in the auditorium and decided to ignore him. He felt a little jittery from what was to come and decided that the other recruit felt it too and was just acting out a bit.

The other officers each approached the podium and made their speeches. Each one described their roles while at basic training and what the recruits should expect from them. The newly minted Private also gave a personal account of his experience while at basic training. He told them that he decided to join the Army, because his father had forced him, and he thought he would hate the experience. The Private said that he had improved physically and had felt a pride grow inside himself. He said that this was one of the most gratifying experiences of his life, and it had built him into a man.

After the Private spoke, the recruits were told to report to their barracks, and they began to file out of the auditorium. As Jimmy and Todd approached the lobby, Jimmy felt a sudden slap across the back of his neck. The recruit who had flipped Jimmy the bird was standing there with his hand over his mouth laughing at Jimmy. Two other scruffy looking recruits surrounded him. One had long hair and the other had a ridiculously thin mustache, while the other one was black with thick glasses. Jimmy ran up to the recruit and got an inch from his nose and said, "You better hope that you aren't in my barracks."

"Why what ya gonna do, punk?" The recruit said with a thick southern drawl.

"You'll see," Jimmy said.

The next day came early as all the lights were flicked on at 5:30 am. The recruits got dressed for breakfast; they wore cloths that they brought with them from home. Breakfast consisted of lukewarm eggs, burnt bacon, cold hash browns, and a rock hard biscuit. Jimmy was very disappointed in the menu but was hungry enough to finish the whole pathetic meal. Once he finished, he cleaned up after himself and made his way out of the door where the newbies lined up to get their uniforms and have their ID cards made. Then, it came time for the dreaded haircut where they would transform from new recruit to grunts.

Freshly trimmed and close to bedtime, Jimmy made his only allowed phone call to Janice.

"How did your day go, baby?" Janice asked.

"Ok, except for the fact that some stupid redneck kid hit me in the back of the head," Jimmy said.

"Oh baby, I'm sorry, but please let it go, I know how you get sometimes," she said.

"Ok, I will let it go for you," Jimmy stated. "He better watch out though."

"I wouldn't worry about it too much; it's not worth losing sleep over," Janice said.

"You're right, you're right - but, I can't let go of the fact that the food is so nasty," Jimmy whined.

"Once you get back, baby, I will personally cook you a juicy T-Bone steak. We will also share a bottle of fine wine from the Bordeaux region of France," she promised.

"You're awesome honey," Jimmy said. "Have you thought anymore about school lately?"

"Yes, I am nervous about starting school in the fall," Janice confided.

"You'll do fine Sugar Lips, you are smart as hell," Jimmy said.

Janice waited all spring for her applications to be processed by the law schools. One after another, week after week, they slowly trickled in. She was rejected from the University of Georgia, Georgia State University, Harvard, Louisiana State University, UNC, and Wake Forest University.

The University of Akron, the University of Arkansas at Little Rock, the University of Miami, and Columbia, accepted her. Janice was devastated that she was rejected by UNC again. She thought that her being an undergraduate there would have helped her to get into the school. She also thought since she improved her LSAT scores so dramatically after her last test that she would easily get into the other schools as well. To her, there was no reasoning behind how admissions committees made their decisions. She thought they were really a bunch of pricks.

Janice was happy to get into the other schools though. She narrowed her choice down to the University of Miami and Columbia. Both schools were private and would be very expensive to attend, so it wasn't a matter of price. The academic reputation of the two schools was much different. Columbia was an Ivy League school while the University of Miami was not. Miami is hot and stays hot while New York can be bitterly cold. More importantly, Janice likes to party, and Miami was the place for partying. She also had some aunts and uncles in Miami. After considering all of the differences between the two scenarios, Janice decided Miami was the school for her. She would find out that it would become the right school for everyone involved.

Chapter 2

BETH

Beth wasn't sure how it fit. Where was she supposed to connect the latest device to her computer? She knew it came with a USB plug but there was more than one slot in which she could insert it. She had never used a scanner before, because her assistants always did the routine office duties for her. Her previous position as director of biotechnology for the National Security Agency didn't require her to perform the basic set up of office computers.

However, Beth could tell you about recombinant DNA, cell fusion, and cures for diseases as well as the intricate details of how cutting-edge medical equipment is developed and built. She had worked on many top-secret assignments and was an expert in the area of anatomy as well as digital body imaging. In 1995, she received her doctorate in human anatomy and physiology from Harvard University. She went on to get another doctorate in electrical engineering from Yale. Her work as director of biotechnology had taken her all over the world to collect information on the latest developments in biometric identification.

The people who sought her for this current project said that her background would be needed. Someone named Marvin, if that was his real name, had called her about a month ago. He would not give many details but did mention that he was from the CIA. Marvin told her that since she was already given such high security clearance, she would be familiar with the protocol for this operation. Her replacement had already been found and operation of the biotechnology unit at the NSA would be uninterrupted. He also told her to report to 115 Coral Way in Coral Gables, Florida on March 31 at 9 a.m.

She arrived at 115 Coral Way a week ago. As usual, Beth dressed up in normal professional attire, on this day a navy blue pantsuit with white shoes. 115 Coral Way was an office within an office building. The building was four stories and white, and it looked like the other buildings typical of South Florida. It had a Spanish influence with lots of stucco, and the edges of the building were rounded. The name on the office was Thompson, Mueller, Kline and Garcia and appeared to be a law office. Beth entered at 9 a.m. on the dot.

A receptionist greeted her from behind his desk.

"Hello, can I help you?" He asked quizzically. He was tall with thick, wavy, black hair.

"Yes, my name is Beth."

"Right this way," the receptionist said with authority as he got up and walked Beth to her office.

Beth was led through a series of cubicles and past two offices with thick wooden doors. The people in the cubicles did not pay any attention to her as she walked past. They were busy typing on their computers or talking on the phone. Mike pointed to an office directly at the back of the main room.

"This is yours," he said. With that, Beth stepped into what became her office and dropped her bag on the floor beside the desk.

"You'll be contacted by Marvin in a week," Mike said from the doorway. "Until then, look busy and read what is in the left-hand drawer of your desk."

Beth opened the drawer and inside were nicely arranged folders labeled at the top. She picked up a folder labeled "Research." She opened the folder to find information on stem cell research. In particular, the report that she held had to do with using embryonic stem cells to cure paralysis. These stem cells were isolated before they grew into respective organs and implanted in the spinal cords of paralyzed individuals to repair damaged nerve tissue. She read over all the files for the week, working 9 to 5, roughly.

"I would have thought that this damn scanner would have been hooked up by now," Beth thought to herself as she tried to use the scanner. The phone rang disturbing Beth from her frustration.

"Hello," Beth said.

"Hello, Beth, how are you?" Marvin asked.

"Good, but I can't figure out how to connect this damn scanner to the computer," Beth groaned into the phone.

"Well, don't worry about that right now; it's not important," Marvin assured her. "Did you read the files?"

"Yes - this is cutting edge stuff they are working on," Beth's enthusiasm was apparent.

"I didn't know that the University of Miami was so far advanced in the stem cell research field," she said.

"What, exactly, is my role in all of this?" Beth questioned.

"I mean, why am I down here in Coral Gables?" She asked.

"The law office is a cover," Marvin stated.

"All the people that are at the office work for the CIA," he said.

"Well, I kind of figured that," Beth said with indignation.

"I have worked on covert operations before," she told him.

"Some of the scientists that are working at the University of Miami's Project to Cure Paralysis also work for the CIA," Marvin explained to Beth.

He said to her, "You are going to meet with one of the scientists tomorrow. He will personally tell you what you need to know to do your job."

"Ok, what time will that be?" She asked him. "Ten o'clock. He is a short guy about five-foot-three and has a thick English accent," Marvin said.

The next day Beth arrived at University of Miami's Project to Cure Paralysis to meet Doctor Cornelius. Beth grimaced as she shook his hand. She tried not to notice the hairy mole that grew out of the left side of his cheek, but she looked right at it as she shook his hand. Marvin was right about the scientist being quite short. Beth was also a short lady, but she was taller than Doctor Cornelius, which made the doctor appear even more vertically challenged.

Doctor Cornelius spoke first,

"Hello, Beth, nice to meet you."

"It is also nice to meet you," Beth said. "I have read about what you have been doing here at the University of Miami's Project to Cure Paralysis. The Miami Project is a model of collaboration for researchers across the globe," Beth said without trying to overly flatter the doctor.

Beth was right that The University of Miami's Project to Cure Paralysis is an exemplary collaboration between scientists and families that have experienced spinal cord injuries. It was founded in 1985, and the founders' goal was to find a cure for paralysis. The Miami Project is the world's largest spinal cord injury medical and research center and has gathered a team of scientists from different clinical and scientific fields in order to reach its goal. The Project is housed in the Lois Pope Life Center, which is also the location of the University Of Miami School Of Medicine's Neuroscience Research Programs.

"I want you to follow me," Doctor Cornelius said.

The doctor and Beth walked through the front doors of the Pope Center. Beth was impressed by what she saw inside. In the lobby, there was a glass piece of art that looked like nerve fibers emanating from a spinal cord. The floors were made out of white marble and the woodwork looked like it was carved from aged oak. The doctor escorted Beth over to the elevators to the left of the lobby. They took the elevator to the third floor. Beth and the doctor exited into a hall full of office doors. Doctor Cornelius took Beth to the third door down the hall on the left. He opened the door and the two of them walked into a conference room where seven people sat around a large wooden table dressed in lab coats. There were three men and four women all staring at Beth and Dr. Cornelius as they entered.

"Have a seat here," the doctor said.

Beth sat at the head of the table. On the opposite end of the room from where she was sitting was an easel holding a stack of diagrams. The diagram displayed was a picture of a human nervous system labeled with all of the various parts. One of the scientists got up from the table and walked over to the easel.

"Beth, we are going to go over what we do here at the Miami Project," the doctor said.

"Ok, but I already have read most of the research that was left for me at the office," Beth stated with some impatience over the possibility of duplicating efforts.

"Good, it will ensure that you understand the information that we are going to present to you," Doctor Cornelius said with a serious look on his face.

"But before I begin, I want to let you know that these scientists here are all CIA," the doctor informed Beth.

"Why is the CIA involved with the Miami Project?" Beth asked.

"That will be explained to you later. For now, I just want you to understand what the Miami Project does on the surface. Do you follow?" the doctor asked.

He gave Beth an intense, piercing stare. Beth looked directly at the mole and glanced away. She knew just to be quiet and see what was in store for her.

The first scientist to approach the easel introduced himself as Doctor Ben. He was a young man which Beth guessed couldn't be over thirty. She found him quite attractive and wished that she wasn't married at the time, which, she thought, had never stopped her before. Dr. Ben grabbed a pointer and held it up to the diagram of the spinal column. He explained that a spinal cord injury occurs when the spinal cord becomes damaged. He continued,

> Often, damage to the spinal cord is the result of motor vehicle accidents, acts of violence, falls, and sporting accidents fracturing vertebrae and severing the spinal cord.

Cervical, or neck, injuries usually cause a loss of function in both the arms and legs, resulting in quadriplegia. Thoracic spinal cord injuries, which are lower down the spine, affect the chest and the legs, and Lumbar and Sacral injuries affect the hips and legs, resulting in paraplegia.

Damage to the spinal cord usually results in impairments or loss of movement and muscle control. The patient can't move their muscles; this results in spastic contractions and atrophy from disuse. The patient also cannot feel sensations like hot or cold, pressure, or pain. Also, the patient may need treatment to help with spinal cord injury related pain, sexual function, and fertility.

According to the National Spinal Cord Injury Statistical Center, there are nearly 11,000 new cases of spinal cord injuries each year. There are an estimated 250,000 people living with a spinal cord injury in the United States. The average age at injury is 38 years old. At more than 50 percent, motor vehicle accidents are the number one cause of spinal cord injuries. The remaining causes are falls that cause nearly 24 percent, violent acts account for over 11 percent, and sporting accidents that cause nine percent of spinal cord injuries. The remaining causes make up the last 6 percent.

Doctor Ben was fidgeting with his shirt button, which was very distracting to Beth. He spoke for a little while longer before one of the female scientists went up to the easel. She repositioned the diagrams on the easel so that a picture of several nerve cells was displayed. Beth couldn't help but notice that this hefty woman occupied a lot of space. The women said that her name is Beatrice, and she drew in a large, wheezing breath and began her segment of the presentation. She started,

Some nerve cells die as a result of a spinal cord injury. Mature nerve cells are unable to divide to replace lost cells. When an accident happens, some cell death takes place, but further cell death continues hours, days, or even weeks following an accident. When cell death occurs, connections that are important to function cannot be re-established if the nerve cells are no longer present.

16

When the long axons, also called nerve fibers, which carry signals up and down the spinal cord are damaged, the parent nerve cells and axons often survive up to the place where the injury happened. The segment of the axon separated from the cell body breaks down and the remainder is removed through natural processes. When this removal occurs, regeneration of damaged axons is a real possibility for reconnecting nerve circuits.

Nerve fibers are insulated with a layer of cell membrane named myelin. Myelin increases the speed of transmission of electrical signals from one nerve cell to another. In the absence of myelin, the signal will weaken so much as it attempts to travel the axon, that the target is not reached. With different kinds of spinal cord injuries as well as several neurological diseases, nerve cells and axons may survive, but because of the destruction of myelin, function is lost. Treatment for the loss of myelin may be possible because reconnecting complex circuits may not be necessary and a cure is known to be feasible.

Nurse Beatrice walked back over to her seat and plopped down in it. She was sweating profusely, her hair wet with perspiration. A scientist to her left poured her a glass of water and handed it to her. While she was dabbing her face with a tissue, another, male scientist got up to speak. He was tall and stood about six-foot-five. He looked nervous, his eyes bolting around the room. When he finished looking around, he stared for an uncomfortable amount of time at Beth. He blurted out that his name was Dr. Hanz. He licked his lips and began his speech.

Due to the fact that stem cell therapies have a great amount of potential to treat both spinal cord injuries and neurological disorders, the Miami Project to Cure Paralysis fully agrees with the National Institutes of Health on the urgency of pursuing, at the same time, all lines of human stem cell research. Stem Cell lines that can yield many tissues of the human body are an important development. The quality and length of life can be improved through stem cell research, and the practice of medicine faces a revolution.

The type of stem cells known as pluripotent stem cells come from embryos and fetal tissue and create nearly all of the cell types of the body. This includes muscle, nerve, blood, and heart cells. Human pluripotent stem cells are a unique resource both scientifically and medically. Health care and research stand to gain significantly with these stem cells. Breakthroughs in the understanding of cell biology continue to create excitement among scientists as well as people suffering from a wide variety of diseases.

Spinal cord injury, Parkinson's disease, burns, heart disease, diabetes, osteoarthritis, rheumatoid arthritis, and stroke are some of the conditions and diseases that pluripotent stem cells, once they develop into specialized cells, may be able to treat. The researchers at the Miami Project are working hard to fully use the potential of these stem cells. Their work has helped to identify proteins that cause cells to differentiate into cells found in a developing nervous system.

The nervous Dr. Hanz nearly leapt to his seat. His erratic gaze met Beth again and she cringed in her chair. Beth seemed somewhat disturbed by what she was hearing. She wasn't sure what her reason for being there could possibly be. She didn't ask any questions though. Instead, she patiently waited for the next scientist to approach the easel. He was an older man of about seventy and was slow changing the diagrams.

"Before you begin, I would invite all of you to have a snack or something to drink," Dr. Cornelius interrupted.

There was a table full of fresh fruit, mini sandwiches, and beverages. Beth walked over to the table and helped herself to one of each. The hefty lady helped herself to two of each. Beth bit into the mini ham sandwich and was surprised by how good it was. Usually the food at these meetings sucked, and she thought whoever was in charge of this operation had a padded budget.

After they spent a few minutes eating, the old, gray, bushy-haired scientist slowly lifted his pointer to a picture of a stem cell. He coughed to clear his throat, said that his name is Doctor Samuel and began speaking. He said,

Mature adult nerve cells are not able to divide to heal and replace damaged spinal cord cells. Scientists have

18

identified cells that could be transplanted into the site of injury and integrated into the host nervous system to replaced wrecked cells. Researchers have been searching for helpful sources of replacement cells. Stem cells are a source of these replacement cells.

The Miami Project is studying stem cells from adult, fetal and embryonic tissue. One of the goals attained from this research is to control how stem cells develop into the desired cell type. As a cell differentiates from the embryonic stage, it becomes more and more specialized. Embryonic stem cells create other specialized stem cells like the neural stem cells.

These neural stem cells can be used as replacement cells. They are precursor cells that then develop into specific cells in the nervous system such as those with longer axons and myelin.

"Ok, I understand what you are saying. Now, will someone tell me why you need an individual with a Top Secret Security Clearance, and a background in biotechnology to be part of your operation? And why the hell is the CIA involved?" Beth demanded.

Doctor Cornelius's face froze as he gave Beth a confrontational look and said flatly, "You need to break a few eggs to bake a cake."

Chapter 3

CARLOS

Carlos wasn't feeling all that great today, and he thought he might be catching something. He was walking home from his job as a martial arts instructor. He lived in New York City for most of his life and felt safe on his walk from work but today was different. Today he would find out he was not safe at all. His stomach did flips inside him as he was walking. He couldn't take anymore and ran behind one of the stores on East 34th Street and heaved his brains out. Several guys walking by saw him in his queasiness.

One of the guys said, "Look at the pussy puking."

"Yea, the little girl is sick," one of the stranger's buddies said.

"I'm going to make you eat that puke," a third figure yelled in a challenging tone.

There were three guys total taunting Carlos. Carlos was not in any mood to be bullied, so he turned and began walking away. The tallest of the three men jumped in front of Carlos. Then all three of them moved in and surrounded Carlos. The skinny boy had a bottle in his hand and broke the top off and waved it at Carlos. The skinny boy lunged at Carlos with the broken bottle and slashed Carlos across the face.

Carlos held his face and looked at the skinny boy with a fierce expression of vengeance. He approached the thin perpetrator, lifted his leg, and did a front kick, which landed right in the face of the skinny man. Blood splattered from the mouth and nose of the attacker. Carlos then did a spinning back kick that landed squarely in the middle of the taller man's neck. The tall man fell backward into a pile of trash lying behind the store. The third thug was the victim of a 180 flip. Carlos's lethal move came down right in the chest of the would-be attacker knocking the air out of him. The three harassers lay there stunned and wishing that they had made better plans for the night. They did not approach Carlos again, and he was able to walk away from the losers.

Within fifteen minutes, Carlos made it back to his small, one-bedroom apartment. He walked through the door and tossed himself on his futon. He thought about calling the police, but it seemed like a waste of time at this point. He had more than shown the attackers a lesson, and the three strangers certainly came away from the encounter with the worse end of the deal. They didn't know they were messing with a 4th degree black belt, and they wouldn't soon forget.

Shaken and in need of counsel, Carlos decided to call his friend Cheryl. He told her about the incident, and she gushed her concern for his well-being.

"I can't believe that you were attacked," Cheryl said. "And I can't believe that you kicked their asses! How do you feel now?"

"Not well. I feel like I am going to throw up again," Carlos said as he held his stomach while sitting on the couch.

"Maybe you should go to the emergency room so they can find out what is wrong with you," Cheryl suggested.

"No, not yet, I'll wait for awhile to see if I get any better. If I don't, then I will go to see a doctor," Carlos said as he took a sip of water.

"Well, do it sooner rather than later, since you never know what could be wrong. Do you think that you will go to work tomorrow?" she asked.

"Not unless I am better. I may just call out sick; it's not everyday that someone tries to kill you," he said.

"You're right about that," Cheryl agreed.

"Well, I'm going to go to bed now," Carlos said, as he was growing tired and needed some rest.

"Ok, call me tomorrow," Cheryl said.

"I will."

"Carlos, you are one of the toughest guys that I know," Cheryl said trying to do her best to hide the love that she truly felt for Carlos.

"Thanks, I'll talk to you later," Carlos said clicking the off button to his cell phone.

Cheryl was right about Carlos being tough. You have to be tough to survive in the neighborhood in which he grew up. The projects will make anyone tough, or, more likely, dead. There weren't many choices growing up in government housing. You could either stay indoors and be bored or hang out with the neighborhood thugs. Carlos chose to hang out with the thugs. Not long after that decision, he was doing drugs, stealing, and causing all sorts of problems. He is truly lucky to be alive.

Since that time, Carlos has really cleaned up his act. After going through Detox for the second time, he began making better decisions for himself. While he was in Detox, he met someone that helped him change his life. His name was Mitch who had done quite a lot of Crystal Meth in his day. He turned his act around when he found Jesus. Mitch taught Carlos about the power of prayer and what Jesus could do for his life. Soon after turning towards the divine, Carlos put his effort into other endeavors; namely, he started his karate classes at a local community college. He practiced karate every chance he got. Three or four times during the week and both Saturday and Sunday, Carlos was practicing. By his 24th birthday, Carlos proudly had his black belt.

His mother was very proud of his accomplishments and told all her coworkers at the Center City Diner, and she often told her customers too. The customers didn't seem to care too much about Carlos. They just wanted their Sunday specials. Carlos was the furthest thing from their minds as Juanita served him up with a cup of coffee. It wasn't just Carlo's Karate that she talked about, she told them how Carlos worked hard to get his GED; then, how he got his Associates Degree at Southeastern Community College.

Carlos was proud of his accomplishments and wished his dad knew about them. But, he didn't even know if his dad was alive. His father left when Carlos was two years old. He had worked as a car salesman in New Orleans before moving the family to New York City. Within three months after moving to New York, he left Carlos and Carlos's mother behind. There wasn't a day that went by that Carlos didn't think of where his dad might be now. Carlos inherited his good looks from his father but not his sense of responsibility. Carlos was dedicated to the little family he had and would kill anyone that dare try to harm them. The thought of someone hurting them drove him into a drinking relapse on more than one occasion. On one such occasion, just last year, Carlos found himself in another round of court-ordered alcohol treatment. His brother and he found themselves at a local church's Alcoholics Anonymous meeting.

"Hello, my name is Trish, and I'm an alcoholic."

"Hello, Trish," the others in the group said.

Carlos's rolled his eyes at his brother Tim.

"I had another relapse last night. I just lost my job at the Pancake House over on 64th Street yesterday morning, and I needed something to take the edge off. My boss said I was late again, but I can't control what the bus driver does or how fast he drives. I don't know what I'm going to do. My husband said he might leave me soon unless I can get my act together. The pain is just too much sometimes. I want a drink now," Trish said with tears in her eyes.

"We'll help you get through this Trish. Your sponsor will help you through this too. Did you talk to John last night?" the Alcoholics Anonymous group facilitator asked.

"No, I called but didn't get an answer. I've been calling him too much lately, and he was probably just too busy last night. There isn't much he could have done, really. I needed a drink and that's all there was to it," Trish was starting to get irritated now. She has been on and off the wagon over the past couple of years, much like Carlos.

Carlos was clean from the hard drugs that he used at one time, but he did enjoy drinking occasionally. The problem with Carlos's drinking isn't that he drinks all the time; his problem is that when he drinks he doesn't know when to stop. This has gotten him into some pretty serious predicaments.

The predicament last year was during Christmas. He, his mom, and his brother Timmy were invited over to Carlos's friend Juan's, place in the Bronx. Juan ran out of tequila and asked Jimmy to go get another bottle a few blocks away at the Happy Package Store. Apparently, Juan didn't realize just how drunk Carlos was, and he let Carlos take his brand new Infinity to get the booze. Carlo's made it to the store, selected the large bottle of Jose Quervo, and headed back out to the Infinity. On his way back to Juan's, Carlos swerved his car into oncoming traffic. He nearly collided with a large truck before he jerked the wheel hard enough to avoid the collision. However, he didn't avoid the collision with the fire hydrant and oak tree.

He had several other accidents over the past couple of years during his relapses. He caused car wrecks, fell down stairs, got into fights, and broke a wooden end table with his head. Each time he had an accident, he would blame it on someone or something else. He blamed hit-and-run drivers for the car accidents. He blamed the dog for getting in his way that caused him to fall down the stairs. He blamed the other guy in the fight for being drunk and hitting him first. He said he tripped coming in the front door and landed head first on the end table.

Several more incidents like this didn't lead Carlos to believe he may need to seek some help. The court system insisted upon it. So, after consulting a directory of Alcoholics Anonymous meetings, he decided to go to several near his apartment at a Presbyterian church. The meetings were all the same to him. The group leader read the AA preamble, conducted a group prayer including the Serenity Prayer, asked about newcomers, and had people explain how their experiences with alcohol related to whichever step they were working on that night.

Carlos participated on occasion, but he felt that he could control his drinking despite the accidents. He was hardheaded, but his mother was happy that he was taking steps to overcome what she considered to be a big problem. His mother didn't think that he was the only one in the family who had a drinking problem. She believed that Carlo's brother Timmy also was too fond of alcohol.

Timmy got caught drinking at school on several different occasions. The first time, he and a group of his friends went to the woods behind their high school during school hours. There, they shot the shit and traded observations on who they thought was the hottest girl in the school. The hooligans did this over a case of beer. They got the beer from Timmy's friend's brother and snuck it into the woods before school that day. They hid the case of Milwaukee's Best under sticks and leaves they found nearby and by the time they had their first brew, it was warm. They didn't care though; it was beer! It was the same beer that was confiscated by the school disciplinarian, Mr. Flo Ryder.

So, Mr. Flo as he was known, took the boys to the principal's office. The principal did not call the police; but rather, he gave the boys In-School Suspension and contacted their parents. Timmy's mom was extremely angry and didn't let Timmy out of his bedroom other than to go to school. She even made him eat his dinner in his room, as she did not want to look at him. She thought it was a good idea to send Timmy along with Carlos to the Alcoholics Anonymous meeting.

"This shit is boring. I am about sick to death that Trish can't get herself together," Carlos whispered to Timmy as they sat listening to Trish spill her guts to the group.

"I mean, what is it going to take for her to realize that her life is going to suck with or without alcohol?" "If I was her, I would be hitting the bottle more, not less."

"I know what you mean," Timmy said with a soft voice as he and Carlos sat on the floor in the meeting room. "She worked a crappy job that didn't pay her anything, and her husband blew the little inheritance that they did have gambling all the time. It is sad to think that someone that had had such a great life growing up, as she said she did, could fall so hard to rock bottom."

"Yeah, but life is strange like that," Carlos was getting angry stares from the facilitator now for talking to Timmy but was unfazed by them.

"One minute, you are king of the world where anything and everything seems possible, and then you fall flat on your ass and lose everything. It happens all the time in the music business and in Hollywood. Just look at Michael Jackson, Vanilla Ice, or MC Hammer. They were getting paid; and then, they crashed. They couldn't sell records anymore. In Michael Jackson's case, he couldn't be looked at as anything but a freak or a pervert after being accused of child molestation."

"Well, it's not just in entertainment either, look at the sports world. A lot of athletes are accused of taking steroids or other performance enhancing drugs. They get a bad rap. They aren't as valuable as team members or players when the dirt starts sticking to them," Timmy said to Carlos as the instructor was shaking his head.

Timmy continued, "There are also athletes that have accidents too, and they aren't able to play anymore. It happens to everyday people too."

Carlos was getting louder now, he said, "It seems that Christopher Reeves had everything: a beautiful wife, a great home, a long stint as Superman; he was Superman damn it, and then that horrible accident left him paralyzed with no hope of recovery. It is sad."

The facilitator had enough and said to Carlos, "Would you care to share anything with the group? I hear you talking over there and would like for you two to share with the rest of us."

"Well," Carlos muttered with his head down while the others were gazing at him, "I haven't had a drink for a couple of days now. My mother says that she is happy with my progress since I don't have to get totally wasted when I do drink. My job as a karate instructor keeps me busy, and I think about that more now than where I am going to get my next beer."

"Good Carlos," the facilitator said relaxing a little. "I want to see if you can go even longer without taking a drink. Challenge yourself to do better by being totally clean. I promise you will feel even better and be able to focus even more on improving your Karate and helping others to improve theirs."

"I will try," Carlos said feebly

"How about you, Timmy? Have you had any more incidents at school or any more problems with alcohol?" the facilitator empathetically questioned.

"Yeah, I have," Timmy said in an incensed tone. "As a matter of fact I got drunk last night. A police officer stopped me jaywalking across the street and gave me a ticket. So, I cussed him out and called him a pig and everything, and I ended up getting thrown in jail. It really pissed me off. I hate cops."

"Does your mother know about this, or did Carlos come and bail you out again?" the facilitator demanded. He was instructed by Timmy's mother to inform her of any problems Timmy may have. The facilitator explained to her that what goes on in the meetings is confidential, but

Timmy's mother always got her way. So, the facilitator said he would do what he could to help.

"My mother probably will figure it out eventually. I didn't go home last night and she will probably see all the advertisements from lawyers once they see that I was issued a citation. It never fails; those damn lawyers get me deeper in trouble every time. Not with the courts, but with my mother," Timmy said with a look of defeat on his face.

"What are we going to do with you Timmy? What are we going to do?" the facilitator said with concern. He didn't realize that Carlos was the one he really needed to watch.

Chapter 4

MARGE

Marge was dealing with the issues that come with being a disturbed troublemaker. Her behavioral problems started at 15, and she was expelled several times from school since she couldn't act appropriately. Her school behavior was described by one of her teachers as disruptive, disrespectful, and altogether unacceptable. Something had to be done, so Marge's mother called a counseling service. Every other week, Marge would go the therapist after school. About once a month, she would see a psychiatrist.

The first time Marge was expelled, it was 97 degrees on one hot summer day. Everyone at her Dallas, Texas high school was miserable from all the heat. Those students who drove convertibles left them shuttered down, because they opted to run the air conditioners in their vehicles instead. So Marge, being a little bit unstable, decided to walk shirtless down the breezeway on her school's campus. She just let her well-developed breasts flop right out in the open. As expected, after the initial shock had worn off, a teacher tried to cover her up, and then he escorted her directly to the principal's office.

The second time she was expelled, Marge had pushed a shopping cart all the way from a neighborhood grocery store to school. She rammed the shopping cart into the sides of some of the other students' cars causing large scratches and dents. Marge not only got expelled, she also had to work at a local Dairy Queen to pay off more than $9,000 in damage. All she did that summer was work.

A psychiatrist diagnosed Marge as being manic-depressive. He put Marge on Lithium, which caused her headaches. The doctor switched to several different medications, but they all caused her some sort of problem. Lithium had the least side effects so she remained on that for a while. Often, Marge would not take her medications and every time she came off the Lithium, she had another episode.

There were times Marge would drive her mother's car into ditches. Other times she would hear and see things that weren't there. Each time she would have a bout of mania or depression her psychiatrist encouraged her to remain on her medication. He told Marge that she was a danger to herself and to others around her without the lithium. But, she couldn't bare the headaches and would come off the bi-polar meds.

The episodes almost always ended with her being taken to the mental hospital in Dallas. There, she was taken into the psychiatric emergency entrance to the hospital where she would sit in a little room so the staff could observe her. Sometimes she was strapped to a bed where she was monitored by a camera. After a couple of hours, an orderly would take her by elevator to one of the hospital's different psych wards. The people in the ward seemed normal enough, except when Marge talked to them. Then, she realized that they had as many, or more, problems then she did.

She felt like she was a science experiment when she went to the mental hospital. Doctors, nurses, and other patients were constantly watching her. The doctors would monitor her to determine the severity of her current condition. They would come up with the recommended treatments, and these were given to the nurses who would administer the drugs and make sure that Marge took them. If she did not comply, then she would stay even longer at the hospital. The patients were watching to see if she would act out as she sometimes did when she was adjusting to the medication.

After Marge was released from the hospital, she returned to school and continued until another episode occurred. For the most part, Marge could function well enough to do her schoolwork. She was an above average student and often got as on her assignments when she was present. However, every time she would miss class, Marge got behind on her work which caused her grades to suffer. The other students and teachers liked her well enough to help her catch up when she was behind. They knew she had problems, and they also knew Marge was in therapy to help her sort out some of her behavior.

The therapy seemed to work, and Marge was able to continue through high school with only a few more minor interruptions. The therapist told her that she was happy with her progress and gave Marge some tools to use when an episode threatened to cause her to break with reality. Marge used these tools more often than she liked, but they were effective. She enjoyed her time with the therapist and seemed to solve some sort of dilemma each time she went.

Marge continued with her therapy after graduating high school. The therapy helped her to be able to graduate at a respectable 97 out of 450 students. Even though her class rank was good enough to get her into college, Marge decided not to continue her education. Instead, she got a job working as a teller at a local bank, and she worked at the bank for over a year until her sister was in a fatal accident.

It was raining one night and Marge's sister, who was 17 at the time, was driving back from a friend's house after a small party. The time was around 11:30 on a Saturday night. Marge's sister, Ruth, was driving when a drunk driver swerved left of the double yellow lines and hit her head on. She was trapped inside her car. Her head had hit the windshield, and her legs were crushed under the steering wheel. She was rushed to a nearby hospital, but it was too late though. Within three hours, Ruth died.

Marge and the rest of her family were devastated. Marge did not go to work for a month; she stayed indoors all the time. And even though she was a tiny girl already, she lost 25 pounds. She was gaunt and sickly. Her psychiatrist put her on an antidepressant medication at a very high dose. This had some positive effect, but the damage was done.

Marge's mother and father, Alice and John, couldn't bear to keep the house where Ruth had grown up, so they sold it. They had two younger children besides Jenny and Marge. Alice, John, and their two younger sons moved to the north side of Dallas. Marge kept her apartment near downtown Dallas but constantly thought of moving back in with her parents. Alice said she wouldn't mind but thought it might be hard for Marge to move back in after being independent for so long. So Marge decided to stay put for the time being and sort out some of her problems.

It was nearly three years before the family was able to overcome the tragedy. Alice and John still often thought of Ruth, but they were able to work on a regular schedule now. They kept a few things of Ruth's but decided to get rid of most of her old possessions. Marge eventually gained back about half of the weight she lost but still looked a little small. It would be several years before she gained all of the weight back.

Things in Marge's life weren't all bad. She was very gifted musically and had several successes in that area. She had started playing the flute at a very young age. Her neighbor down the street gave her lessons and, gradually, she progressed from aimlessly blowing air into the flute to playing two octave scales. By the time Marge was old enough to play in the elementary school band, she was playing the flute well beyond the level that anyone else in her grade played.

The flute was a means of escape for Marge. The soft tones that emanated from the two-and-a-half foot polished metal instrument were very soothing to her. She visualized herself playing in a symphony one day and this was the goal that she strived to obtain. She made every effort to become a professional flutist for the Dallas Symphony Orchestra.

So, Marge continued her lessons all the way to the beginning of high school. By that time, she figured that she was so far ahead of the other students that she could afford to take a break. Marge played in the high school marching band where she was drum major one year. She also participated in band competitions, which included county district bands as well as the statewide band. Marge was the first chair flutist for every competition.

Marge also excelled in track and field competitions. When she wasn't playing the flute during the marching band season, Marge ran the 400 meter in track as well as the mile relay. She ran much faster than the other girls and often would beat her opponents to the finish line. Losing pushed her to work harder, and she would often spend countless hours practicing sprints after school. This exercise got her in superior physical condition, and Marge continued to maintain her physical health until her eventual commitment.

Now, Marge was lying on her bedroom floor listening to Beethoven's Ninth Symphony thinking it had never sounded so good. She stared at the ceiling as she laid there listening to her iPod. The best part of the symphony, the choral section of the fourth movement, was playing stridently in her ear. At the moment, the string instruments were running up and down the notes at a very fast tempo as if someone was running from someone or something. She thought, "This is heavenly; this is one of the best pieces of music ever written." And then, the string instruments came to a halt, and the thundering baritone exploded in her ears. A tear ran down her cheek as she thought about the beautiful sounds, providing an escape from her terrible day.

As the movement reached its end, Marge stood up and walked towards the kitchen. She opened the refrigerator, and then it hit. A crushing wave of anxiety grabbed her and threw her against the wall. She began to hyperventilate and cry uncontrollably. An acute and debilitating feeling that she would be alone forever brought on this most recent panic attack. Marge forgot to take her medicine again. Her thoughts turned black and sour as she milled all the horrible things that happened to her recently; and then, her mind wondered to him.

His name was Jack who was about 40 years old and extremely attractive. Marge met Jack at a Dallas Symphony concert two weeks ago. It was the summer pop concert series at a nearby amphitheater. She was talking to a flute player that she took lessons from earlier in her school days. Jack was blindsided by Marge's beauty, and he approached her. They talked for some time, and Jack eventually got Marge's phone number. Over the next week, they communicated through text messages, but she noticed that Jack was very slow to respond to her.

Jack and Marge eventually went out on a date; and oddly enough, Marge had to pay as Jack said he forgot his wallet. It was no big deal to her, and she brushed it off. But later on, she would find out that this wouldn't be the only time Jack would use her. They had a pleasant conversation, and Marge hoped that she did not reveal too much that was negative about her. She was scared that if he knew everything, he would never talk to her again. Her worry turned out not to be in vain. Jack gave Marge a tender kiss on her cheek, before he left from the concert. Marge called Jack and left him a message asking if he would like to go out again.

They went out on two more dates before they had sex. It was amazing to her at the time; and despite the fact it was against her better judgment to move so fast, she thoroughly enjoyed the night of passion, at least from her end. A few days later, Marge tried to call Jack but there was no response. She tried one or two more times and her attempts fell flat. She would never hear from Jack again.

Marge became enraged. She went to her kitchen cabinet and smashed a large dinner plate hard against the stove. She grabbed a silver coffee cup that an ex-boyfriend got her from his trip to the Cayman Islands and threw it against her front door. She knocked over her music stand, and she threw sheet music everywhere. Marge smashed the glass top of her coffee table with her bare foot deeply cutting it.

Marge's neighbor heard the commotion and ran over to Marge's place and began pounding on the door.

"Are you alright in there?" The neighbor asked in a frightened tone.

"What is going on? Do you need help?" He asked all the while pounding away.

"What in the hell do you want?" Marge screamed at the top of her lungs. "You just want to use me too, don't you? You guys are all the same! You are fucking pigs! Filthy, dirty pigs!"

"I just want to help you!" The neighbor said as he became more frantic in trying to get Marge to come to the door.

"Don't do anything to hurt yourself. I just want to help you!" The neighbor insisted.

Marge grabbed the coat rack sitting in the small foyer. She unlocked the door, and her neighbor opened it forcefully nearly hitting Marge as he did.

"Take this you man pig!" Marge screamed as she thrust the coat rack at her neighbor. "I hate you!"

Her neighbor struggled over the coat rack with Marge and was eventually able to rip the rack from her grasp. Marge's body went limp, and she fell to the ground crying. There were bloodstains splattered around the carpet. As she sat there, blood was pooling near her lap.

"We need to get you some help." The neighbor called 911, and Marge woke up hours later at Charter Pines Mental Hospital.

Marge was strapped to a bed that felt like it was covered in vinyl. It had a wooden frame supporting the padded mattress. There were four restraints with each one attached to one of the corners of the bed. She laid there much calmer now and looked through the open door into the lobby where other patients were arriving. Some were as confused, irate, and irrational as she had been. An orderly was ushering the patients into various rooms. His haircut was very unusual, because his hair was short except for a ball in the back of his head. Then, the orderly walked into Marge's room and escorted her into the main lobby area. There, a homely, unfriendly, bitter old nurse met with Marge.

"Here, take this," the nurse said with a Northern accent as she scrunched up her leathery face.

"What is it?" Marge demanded with a suspicious look on her face.

"Just take it," the nurse forcefully instructed.

"I'm not going to take it unless you tell me what it is," Marge shot back with anger in her voice.

"It's called Lamictal. It will help with your WILD mood swings. Now, take it," the nurse said impatiently.

Marge lifted the little orange pill that looked somewhat like an officer's badge to her mouth. She looked up at the security camera and noticed that a little red light was blinking on it. She knew it was recording, and she wondered if they used the camera to catch criminals that break into the hospital or whether it was used to observe the patients' activities. Since the hospital never closes, she figured it was for the patients.

The nurse then led Marge to a small observation room and sat her in one of the handful of plastic chairs arranged around the sides of the rooms. After being watched through a five-foot by five-foot window for over an hour by a psych tech, Marge was then transported up to one of the hospital's wings. Once she arrived there, she was ushered into a small examining room and helped onto a table covered with thin, white paper. She underwent the usual exams, this time performed by nurse practitioner instead of a doctor. The nurse practitioner took her blood pressure and found that it was abnormally elevated. She took her temperature and checked Marge's pupils as well. The nurse practitioner asked Marge if she took any drugs before she came to the hospital, and Marge informed her that she hadn't. Marge was then lead to her room.

Marge inspected the small bed that looked very uncomfortable. The bed looked like it belonged in a college dorm room or in a sleeping area used at a summer camp. There was also a small closet for her belongings.

"Funny," Marge thought; "like I had any time to grab anything for this visit while I was going through my ordeal."

Marge was getting tired, as it was late when she arrived at the hospital. The staff had instructed the patients that lights out was in fifteen minutes, so Marge brushed her teeth with the little white toothbrush that was provided and went to bed.

Early the next morning, screams awoke Marge. They were very loud and disturbing at first. Marge lay there and didn't say anything, hoping that the girl in the next bed would stop. Ten minutes later, Marge was able to get back to sleep. Her sleep wouldn't last for more than forty minutes though, as a tech awoke her to take her vital signs. After that, it was time for breakfast, and a meeting of the patients in the community room.

As Marge and the others waited for the activity leaders to begin the day's events, Marge spoke to a man in a wheelchair sitting next to her. He appeared to be about 30 with a well-developed upper body.

"Hi my name is Marge, what's yours?"

He looked her up and down with distrusting eyes and a scowl on his face. He turned away and mumbled, "Jermaine."

"Where are you from?" she questioned. Jermaine did not reply. He sat there in silence and stared blankly before him.

"Ok, never mind," Marge conceded.

On her other side of her was a large woman with a cane and hair that darted out in all directions. While many of people in the mental hospital were not too concerned with their appearance, Marge thought it a basic necessity to comb her hair, and even take a shower. She made sure she had on a fresh pair of blue, hospital issued booties to cover her feet. As she was sitting there, wishing hygiene would be the norm rather than the exception, a young, pretty women walked into the room.

"Hello everyone, how are you doing today?" she said to the twenty or so patients with a spring in her voice. The patients responded with an unenthusiastic and disjointed, "Fine."

"Oh, come on, that wasn't very convincing, I know you all can do better than that," she stated with consternation. "How are you all doing today?"

"Fine," the group said a little louder.

"That is better," she said without truly being satisfied with their half-hearted responses.

"Ok guys and gals, I am here to listen to you. We are going to have a little group therapy." The young women spoke with a positive and confident tone.

"Now, I would like everyone to introduce yourself and tell us a little bit about why you are here today. We will start with you." She pointed to Marge.

One by one the patients introduced themselves and told about a little of their troubles. The young group leader then pointed a female patient with short, uncombed, and bleached blond hair. She said that her name was Gwen, and she told her story.

"I am severely depressed," she said in a surprisingly loud voice. "I just lost my cat, and my stepmother, I mean they passed away," she nearly shouted. "I have been receiving ECT. You know, electric shock therapy. It seems to really be helping; I feel a lot better now," she said in her loud, erratic voice. "The doctors say they are going to have to keep me here for awhile. I really miss my dad," she lamented as her eyes welled up.

As each patient told his or her story, Marge wanted to leave the hospital more and more. She thought about her own mother and father and how she missed them. She also thought about her obligations at work. She informed her boss at the bank that she was sick and would be returning to work in a day or two. The boss understood, told her to get better, and said for her to return when she could. Marge did not know that the doctors had other plans for her.

Chapter 5

MARIE AND CANDICE

"God, I can't take this heat much longer; we need to move," Marie whined to her best friend, Candice.

"Well, it is Atlanta, which is in the south, known to be hotter than the north during the summer," the beautiful Candice said with a playful attitude.

"Yea, but damn, does it need to be 95 out? I mean it looks like I've been in a sauna for an hour, and I've only walked four blocks," Candice said with a nasally voice.

"You'll be fine, plus we are almost to the restaurant," Candice assured Marie to prevent her from complaining any further.

"I love The Flying Roll; it has the best food, despite what everyone else says," Marie said with a large grin on her face.

"I love Midtown; there is a ton of shit to do here, and all the gay guys are so hot," Candice said, ogling an attractive man with his shirt off running on the opposite side of the road. They both were enamored with him, as they both shared a similar taste in men. In general, the two shared many of the same tastes as each other even though they came from very different backgrounds.

Marie graduated from Spelman College, a historically African-American Women's college in Atlanta, several years ago. She graduated Summa Cum Laude after studying diligently through the years it took to earn her Bachelor's degree. After college, she went to work in the field of nursing in which she had studied. She got a job at Piedmont Hospital which was known for its Cardiac Care Center. Marie works Mondays, Tuesdays, and Wednesdays on the 7 to 7 shift. This gives her plenty of time to pursue her passion for nightlife.

Marie didn't party too much in college, and she is making up for that now. She loves the club and can't get enough of it. You will find her at one of the hot midtown venues on any given Thursday, Friday, or Saturday night. Her love for the nightlife is directly linked to her love of music, men, and booze. She made many friends in the scene, and they come from different backgrounds, races, and careers. She met her roommate, Candice, at one of the clubs. They have been friends ever since.

However, there was something lacking in Marie's life. She is terribly lonely, even though she surrounds herself with people. Most of the loneliness is due to a string of sour and abusive relationships. Her first relationship in high school left her with a broken arm and a concussion that threatened her life. Her high school boyfriend was a gambler and a drug user that often stole money from Marie in order to support his vices. One cold and rainy night, Marie and her boyfriend were fighting violently in the parking lot of the projects where her boyfriend lived. He was calling her a fat bitch and punching her in the stomach. She was biting and scratching him. Then, she locked him out of his car and left him in the rain. He broke the driver's side window with a brick lying nearby. He opened the door, raised the brick up high, and slammed it down on her left arm causing a compound fracture. He then raised the brick a second time and slammed it on the top of her head.

When she woke up in the hospital, several days later, the doctor told her she was lucky to be alive. The police arrested her boyfriend, and after a short trial, he was sentenced to fifteen years in prison. She never heard from him again, but the scars he left behind causes her pain even today. Marie finds it difficult to trust men. She finds it hard to open up too much with them unless she has been drinking. She mostly uses men for sex. She had tried relationships with women, but does not feel as sexually attracted to them.

Even though Candice and she have never been sexually involved, she leans on Candice for much of her support. Candice is really the only family that Marie has, since Marie was orphaned at an early age. Her mother died due to complications with Marie's birth, and her father committed suicide after his return from Vietnam, before she was born. Marie lived with several different foster families for most of her childhood. The families treated her well and helped her develop life skills as well as studying skills. It was nothing short of a miracle that she was able to attend college and hold a steady job.

"I'll have the Caesar salad with chicken," Candice said to the young, cute waiter.

"Let me have the club sandwich with fries," Marie said as the waiter scribbled on a little notepad. He then swaggered away towards the kitchen.

"So what are you getting into tonight? It is, after all, Friday," Candice wondered.

"I really don't have any plans, but I will probably go out," Marie said in a suggestive tone to Candice.

"Well count me in; I am thinking we should go to Rocco's on Piedmont, because they have the cutest guys," Marie offered.

"Sure, that sounds good, but since we have time before we go, I am going to go running at the park," Candice stated. "Want to come?"

"No, I just ran this morning, and don't feel like doing it again. I am going to go back to the condo for a disco nap before we go, and I will see you later," Marie said confidently. Thirty minutes passed, and the food arrived just as the girls were about to complain. They were angry about the wait, but the food was fresh and tasty. After they finished their meal, Marie and Candice walked back to their condo. Once there, Marie went to take her nap, and Candice changed into her designer jogging suit. Candice then jogged to Piedmont Park.

Candice was in excellent physical condition. She had a sleek, slender body, with curves in all the right places. Her passion for exercise grew from a deep-seated desire not to be the little fat girl she was growing up. Candice hated those days and vowed never again would she be the brunt of another fat joke. So she began jogging in high school. She eventually lost fifty pounds and then joined the track team. She went on to win the high school state track meet in the one hundred yard dash. So now, she continued to jog to maintain a beautiful physique.

As she was jogging through the park, she noticed the approaching dusk. She thought to herself that she could run another forty-five minutes or so and make it back home in time to get ready and go out. She was enjoying the beautiful bodies in the park and thought about the games people were playing there. Throwing Frisbees, tag football, soccer, and playing catch with the dog were all activities people enjoyed as she jogged. Then, her thought wondered to her job.

Candice despised her boss. She worked as an administrative assistant for the Chief Financial Officer of a medical insurance company. Everything that her boss did bothered her. From his inappropriate sexual comments to his horrid laugh and everything in between made her sick. Her alarm clock's piercing, persistent beep was the signaling of another day of misery. She cringed at the thought of seeing him Monday morning. She longed for the day when she would be free from his excessive, unreasonable, and unwarranted demands. Until then, she would continue to look for another job and hope that the next boss won't be so hard to deal with. Just as soon as that thought crept up, another thought popped into her head. It was a one-night-stand of hers named Andrew.

"Andrew!" Candice said. She would regularly see people that she knew from her various exploits around Atlanta. Like Marie, Candice was single and couldn't find the right guy.

"How are you?" Candice asked as she stopped her running to talk to Andrew.

"I'm doing pretty well. How are you?" Andrew asked.

"Ok, I'm just trying to stay in shape. I've got to look good for my future husband," Candice said with a big smile on her face.

"Yea, well good luck with that, I've got to run; I have to get to my girlfriend's house for dinner," Andrew said as he walked away.

"Ok. Bye," Candice said with a snarl. "Damn," Candice thought, "yet another one got away."

"How was your run?" Marie asked Candice as she came through the door into the foyer of their condo.

"It was relaxing, except for the part when I saw Andrew," Candice sighed as a look of disappointment washed across her face.

"I thought you were over him," Marie said, obviously annoyed.

"It's hard to get over the cutest, funniest, and most sensual guy I have ever met," Candice beamed as she reminisced.

"You are severely over-exaggerating. He was cute, but there are plenty of cute guys around here. There are also plenty of nice guys too. Plus, you only knew him for a couple of days; leave it alone," Marie chided Candice as she was putting on her new DKNY blouse.

"I knew him for a hot, intimate, and arousing couple of days. Then, in true man style, he just quit calling and texting, and I was not going to appear desperate by calling him over and over. No man wants a woman that is overly clingy and needy," Candice corrected Marie as she turned on the shower in the large bathroom located between their adjoining bedrooms.

"Well, tonight is your night to have fun and mingle among the single. Who knows, you may even meet someone at Rocco's," Marie said with a smile on her face. It was a smile that Candice knew all too well. Marie flashed it every time a guy broke her heart, and they were going out to search for Mr. Right or, more likely, Mr. Right now.

Forty minutes of plucking and putting on make-up passed, and the girls were ready for the night, but not before they had each had a shot of tequila.

"Here, take this," Marie said to Candice as she held up a shot glass to her.

"Not tonight, I don't want a headache in the morning," Candice whined.

"Oh come on, it will get your courage up," Marie cajoled.

"Ok, what the hell, here's to an interesting and fun-filled night," Candice said as she tossed back the full shot glass.

"Ok, better, let's go!" Marie shouted as the girls walked out of the door.

Marie and Candice looked stunning in their chic clothes and high heels. They began walking the couple of blocks to Rocco's. On the way, several men and a woman or two, called out, "Hey beautiful! Want a ride? Look at them legs!"

The girls were not fazed and even enjoyed the attention. They waved it off and kept on walking toward Rocco's. As they were approaching the rear entrance, they noticed the line to get in was excessively long. They continued walking around the people waiting and passed through an opening in the fence nearby. The girls don't wait. Marie made a call to her friend Alex beforehand. He let them in the side door out of view from everyone else since beauty has its perks.

As they entered Rocco's, the two of them took in all the sights, sounds, and smells that accompanied it. The crowd was attractive at the club that night. The music was loud, and they were playing one of the girls' favorite songs. Rocco's smelled of cigarette smoke, alcohol, and a putrid stench that they couldn't, and didn't want to put a finger on. They had arrived and were free for the night.

The girls approached the long, wooden bar. Candice's favorite bartender was working that night. He was Marie's least favorite bartender. Mark was his name and he had a tattoo of an inverted cross on his uncovered, large bicep. His hair was medium length, blond, and spiked up in all directions.

"Well, if it isn't my favorite girl and my worst enemy," Mark said with a smirk on his face.

"Good to see you Mark," Candice said with delight.

"Go to hell," Marie shot at him

"Love you too, Marie," Mark said with dry sarcasm. "The regular gin and tonic with three limes for you Candice," Mark said as he placed the drink in front of Candice. "And the boiling bat's blood for you Marie," Mark was on a roll tonight.

"Funny," Marie said with her eyes darting around the room. She then walked over to a cocktail table that a group had just left. The bus boy quickly cleared the table for her. Candice remained back at the bar to talk to Mark.

Marie surveyed the crowd. There were some good-looking men there tonight, she thought to herself. If only one of those men wouldn't break her heart and would treat her like the queen she was, Marie would be happy. She put her wine up to her lips to take a sip and then a man, who caught Marie's eye, walked in the rear entrance.

His name was George, and he was not a regular at Rocco's; rather, Marie never saw him there any other time. George was a tall man, and his face looked like it had been chiseled in the likeness of a Greek god. His hair was short, brown, and it framed his face perfectly. His body was thick and muscular, and there were no visible areas where fat may be hiding. His well-tailored clothes hugged his body flawlessly. George was a magnificent sight to behold, Marie thought.

George walked over to bar where Mark was standing and ordered a scotch and water. He noticed that Marie was stealing glances at him, and he found her very attractive. He circled the room and spoke to a friend within eyeshot of Marie's table. Five minutes of Marie and George exchanging glances passed, and then Candice walked over to the table.

"Hey girl, what are you doing?" Candice asked as she took a drink of her gin and tonic with three limes.

"Just sitting here waiting for you to stop talking to that pig of a bartender," Marie scowled at the thought of Mark.

"You leave Mark alone. You need to get over your anger towards him. He made the choice between you and me, and he picked me. That was some time ago. You should leave your bitterness in the past," Candice said with anger in her voice.

"Well, I see someone here that could definitely move me from the past. Look over there next to the column," Marie said as she gave a head nod toward George, pointing out his direction.

"Wow, you're right. He is gorgeous," Candice enthusiastically said with a smile. "I think he knows we are talking about him though."

"I have been staring at him ever since we got here; he seems interested," Marie confessed to Candice.

"Well, why don't you say something?" Candice asked as she slid her purse on the seat next to her.

"Yeah, that's playing real hard to get," Marie rolled her eyes.

"Come on, it's a different time, you can approach him if you want," Candice explained to her.

"Oh shit, here he comes," Marie nearly spilled her drink on the table as George made his way over to her.

"Hello beautiful, what is your name?" George asked as he extended a hand towards Marie.

"Marie," she said almost inaudibly.

"Nice to meet you, Marie. Do you come here often?" George asked with a grin on his face.

"This is one of my favorite places to hang out, when I do go out," Marie said looking towards Candice for support.

"Excuse me, I have to go to the bathroom," and with that, Marie's support was gone.

"Can I buy you a drink?" George asked as he looked at Marie's empty glass.

"Sure, I'll have a Captain and Coke, that is my favorite drink," Marie was starting to feel the fuzzy sensation of an alcohol buzz already. She wasn't a heavy drinker, so when she did drink, the alcohol went straight to her head.

George walked over to the bar and ordered Marie her drink. Mark poured the drink and shot Marie the middle finger as he handed it to George. George wasn't too happy about him treating Marie like that, but he thought it was better that he did not get involved. George handed Marie her Captain and Coke.

"What was that about?" George questioned Marie.

"That guy's an asshole; don't pay any attention to him," Marie said as she gave Mark another dirty look.

Some time passed, and George was able to learn about Marie's job, education, and friendship with Candice. Candice hadn't returned yet. Marie and George had another drink, and Marie decided that she wanted to go back to her condo with him. They talked some more, and then, Candice approached Marie as George was getting another drink from Mark.

"Candice, can you stay with Mark tonight?" Marie begged her.

"Oh, don't we move a little fast? Are you sure that is what you want?" Candice asked Marie with concern.

"Yes, it is definitely what I want," Marie responded with excitement.

"Well, I always have an open invitation with Mark, even though I rarely use it. You'll owe me big though," Candice stated with a look of aggravation on her face. "Be careful, and if you do the duty, use protection."

"Of course, of course, thank you so much! I do owe you one," Marie said appreciatively.

George made his way back over to Marie, who was sitting at the table, as Candice was passing in the opposite direction towards Mark. Candice told George to watch himself. George responded that he would.

Marie and George sat and talked a little while longer. They finished up their drinks, and George closed out his tab. They made their way back to Marie's condo hand-in-hand.

Chapter 6

JIMMY

Jimmy was preparing to leave for his basic training battalion. He completed his week of processing at the reception battalion, where he received inoculations and underwent dental and eye exams. He passed the first Physical Assessment Test with ease, as he was already in great shape. Jimmy learned how to upkeep his barracks and learned how to march like a soldier. He even took time to attend the chapel service, though he wasn't particularly religious. He just thought that a little divine intervention might be something he needed to call on when he was choking on the fumes in the gas chamber. Jimmy was ready for what lay ahead, or so he thought.

Drill Sergeant Smith showed up in an old, white, non-air conditioned bus in front of the reception battalion where the recruits waited with trepidation. He got off the bus and instantly began barking out orders.

"Get down on your hands and knees and give me 50 push-ups, now!" He yelled. The recruits threw their heavy bags on the ground and were quick to comply with his order. As Jimmy and the rest of the recruits were doing their best to execute, Drill Sergeant Smith walked up behind them. He walked over to the pudgy kid from the auditorium.

He exclaimed, "Are you kidding me? You fat sack of shit! Is that what you call a pushup? My 70- year-old grandmother can do a better push-up than you!" He motioned and demanded for the rotund recruit to stand up.

"What is your name?" Drill Sergeant Smith questioned.

"Ralph." He muttered.

"Well Ralph, you are going to hate me by the time you get out of here," Drill Sergeant Smith emphatically stated as spit flew into Ralph's face. Ralph then made a horrible, horrible mistake. He said, "I already do."

With that, Drill Sergeant Smith's eyes got as big as golf balls. "Do not talk back to me! You will address me as sir, say yes sir, and when I grind you into a pulp, you will say thank you sir!" the Drill instructor shouted out with a loud, strained, and incredulous voice.

"Is that clear, Porky Pig?" he questioned.

"Yes, sir," Porky Pig said.

"I can't hear you!" the Drill Instructor said as more spit flew into Ralph's face.

"Yes, sir!" Ralph yelled.

"Is that clear to all you snot-nosed brats?" he questioned.

"Yes sir," they said not quite loud enough.

"I can't hear you!" Drill Sergeant Smith cried out.

"Yes, sir!" the grunts shouted with conviction this time.

"Now, give me 100 jumping jacks!" he demanded.

Jimmy almost wet himself as his arms and legs spread apart and came back together. He thought to himself, what have I gotten myself into? Who is this asshole? I hope that he doesn't hit me. Can he hit me? Can he hit anyone? What can he do to me? I don't like being yelled at. I guess no one does. Is he going to call me a name? Damn, it's hot out. Is he going to work us this hard all summer? Fuck!

Jimmy stopped doing jumping jacks before he reached 100 and before anyone else. The five-foot, eight-inch Drill Instructor immediately turned his attention towards Jimmy.

"What are you doing boy? Did I tell you to quit? You haven't reached 100 yet!"

"Sorry sir!" he offered

"Get back to your exercise," Drill Sergeant Smith instructed.

"I have to use the bathroom sir," Jimmy said

"You will use the bathroom when the rest of us get to use the bathroom!" Drill Sergeant Smith said in disbelief.

"Yes sir!" Jimmy was in pain as he held back his urine. He could barely contain himself as they loaded the bus to go to the barracks.

The recruits entered the confined sleeping quarters. The Drill Instructor was close behind them.

He said, "This will be your home for the next nine weeks. I expect it to be spotless at all times. This is not your mother's house, and I am certainly not your mother. If you get things out of order here, then you fix it up. The only time that your bed will not be impeccably made is when you are sleeping in it, and even then it better look nice. Your footlockers are to be locked at all times when not in use and must be maintained as well. Do I make myself clear?"

"Yes sir!" The newbies blurted out in unison.

"I can't hear you!" The Drill Instructor reiterated.

"Sir, yes sir!" They screamed together.

The newbies were each assigned to a one of the bunk beds in the barracks. They unloaded their gear and placed their necessary items in the footlockers located at the end of their beds. Everyone looked rattled, like they just came within two feet of being run over by a locomotive blasting past at 65 miles per hour. No one was really prepared for this. They had seen movies and had heard stories, but to actually experience the iconic Drill Sergeant was a totally different experience.

"All right folks, we have a long day ahead of us tomorrow. You have an hour of personal time to yourself, and tomorrow we wake up at 5:30 a.m. and will begin physical training promptly at 6:00 a.m. We are going light tomorrow just to get you acclimated to doing physical activity and assess your fitness level. You will have another Army Physical Fitness Test Diagnostic on the day after tomorrow. We will also be doing Drill and Ceremony tomorrow as well. Get a good night's rest." And with that, Drill Sergeant Smith exited the barracks.

Jimmy thought about Janice. He really wanted to talk to her, but he didn't want to concern her with his problems right now. He needed to stay focused and concentrate on making new friends with whom he was sharing the barracks. There would be time later to talk to her, and she would be the first person that he calls.

Jimmy's eyes shot around the barracks. He noticed that Ralph was there. He saw him earlier in the day but was too preoccupied to really notice. Jimmy glared at Ralph and thought about how much he disliked him. Then, the guy, Bobby Lee was his name as Jimmy would find out, gave Jimmy the middle finger, and Jimmy returned the gesture. He knew this guy was trouble and there would be a score to settle, eventually. But, for now, it was back to more physical training.

"What the hell are you doing, Porky Pig?" Drill Sergeant Smith screamed since still couldn't believe that the large recruit thought what he was doing was a push up. "You look absolutely ridiculous! You are pathetic! Push harder! How did you not get held back in fat camp?"

Porky Pig and the others couldn't wrap their minds around the fact that it was six o'clock in the morning, and they were doing exercises before they even had breakfast. Most of the new recruits came from their parents' house or from food-service jobs that allowed them to sleep late into the morning. They were not only half-awake, but they also were not used to exerting their muscles so much so early. This was a shock to the unsuspecting.

"I want you all to look at Porky Pig here. He is giving you a perfect example of how not to do a push up. Go run around the training field, Porky," Drill Sergeant Smith directed. The large boy began running and was clearly out of breath after trying to do the pushups, before he even left the hard surface of the training grounds.

45

"I want that boy to be a clear example of how not to be. To be a soldier, you need to be lean, mean, and ready to handle some physically challenging situations when they arrive. Now, I want the rest of you to sit on the ground and prepare yourselves to do a hundred sit-ups. You need to pull your legs and elbows up until they touch," Drill Sergeant Smith commanded them to begin. They all did their best to comply and were relieved that after several more exercises, it came time for breakfast.

Jimmy's platoon walked into the mess hall together. Each recruit went through the food line and got their assorted proteins, carbohydrates, and fats. Then, Jimmy walked out into the dining area to find a seat. He saw Todd from processing week and was about to sit with him. Jimmy's Drill Sergeant went over to Jimmy and said that he needed to sit with the people in his platoon. He said it was to build cohesion amongst the recruits. "Pure crap," Jimmy thought, but he did as he was instructed. He went over to the table and stood near a muscular guy with scars all over his face. He asked the guy if he could sit there, and the guy said that he could.

Jimmy sat at the table in silence for what seemed like an eternity as he downed his food quickly; he was extremely hungry after all the exercise. Then, he looked over to scar face and asked him his name.

"My name is Tom," he said shortly as if he didn't want to give too much information.

"I'm Jimmy, where are you from?" Jimmy asked but not really caring; he was just trying to make conversation.

"Ohio," Tom said abruptly, taking a break from hurriedly eating his food.

"Nice place up there, Ohio, I know a few people there," Jimmy said with a blank look on his face.

"Not really, it's too cold," Tom said with a grimace.

"Huh, I suppose so. It's almost too hot down here. South Carolina is hot and humid," Jimmy was trying not to whine too much. He didn't want to come across as a complainer.

Jimmy noticed that Tom's face was starting to turn pale. He was sweating a little bit too. He placed his hands on his stomach and rubbed it. Then, Tom opened his mouth and threw up all over his tray. Pieces of eggs hit Jimmy's arms and face. It was the most puke that Jimmy had ever seen.

Drill Sergeant Smith walked over to Tom.

"Boy, what's wrong with you?"

"I just felt a little nauseous," Tom said with amazing composure despite what had just happened.

"By the looks of it, you feel a lot nauseous. Do you need to go to the infirmary?" The Drill Instructor asked with the little bit of concern that he could conjure up - it did not fit him.

"No, I'll be fine; I just need some water," Tom said as he wiped his mouth with a napkin. Drill Sergeant Smith looked at Jimmy and told him to go and get Tom some water.

When Jimmy returned, most of the puke had been cleaned up, and Tom's tray was gone. He gave Tom the water and asked Tom if he needing anything else. He joked that an Alka-Seltzer would be nice. Jimmy didn't know where he could get one off-hand, and Tom told him not to worry about it. Then, Jimmy sat back down as they still had fifteen minutes left for lunch.

Jimmy was trying to shake off what just happened. He thought that the guy must have been over exerted during the exercises or that his nerves got the best of him and that caused him to puke. He didn't feel much like finishing his breakfast after seeing Tom expel his. He sat there for a minute and took a look at who was around him.

He noticed that Bobby Lee was gawking at him. He really didn't like that bastard. There was something about him that he couldn't put his finger on, but he thought that the guy was just looking for trouble. He probably had some dark history behind him that caused him to act like a dickhead. His dad probably abused him or his mother was a drunk. He was also a huge redneck, Jimmy thought. They took all kinds in the military, and one of the bad kinds was now looking to challenge Jimmy.

Jimmy stared back at Bobby Lee, and then he shrugged his shoulders and held out his hands and mouthed, "What?" Bobby Lee stood up. He walked over to where Jimmy was and just stared at him. He lifted his hand up and placed his grimy fingers on Jimmy's forehead. Then, he pushed Jimmy's head. Bobby Lee pushed his head hard enough that it snapped back rapidly.

Jimmy stood up and got about three inches from Bobby Lee's face. The recruits were eye to eye with each other.

"What the fuck is your problem, man?" Jimmy angrily implored Bobby Lee.

"You're my problem, pussy boy," Bobby Lee said in a surprisingly indifferent tone.

"I haven't done anything to you. You are just trying to cause trouble," Jimmy said lividly.

Bobby Lee said, "I don't like you. All you North Carolina boys are da same. You think y'all are better den the folks down here. I grew up in South Carolina and am damn proud of it. We don't need y'all coming down here wit you're cocky-ass attitude making fun of us," his southern draw was thick enough to slice with a meat cleaver.

"What the hell are you talking about?" Jimmy asked in disbelief. He couldn't understand why this guy was actually mad at him for being from North Carolina. He couldn't understand how Bobby Lee could think there is some huge class difference between the two states. Clearly, the boy was as about as smart as the eggs he just ate for breakfast.

"Dude, they aren't much different than each other," Jimmy said.

"Yes they are. You just watch yoself. I hear you say one bad thing 'bout South Carolina and I will kick yo' ass. I'm watchin' you boy." Bobby Lee raised his hand towards Jimmy's face.

"You touch me, and I swear I will beat the living shit out of you," Jimmy said and was certainly not in a joking kind of mood - it was too early in the morning for that.

Bobby Lee paused for minute and then started moving his hand closer to Jimmy's face. Jimmy cocked his fist back high behind his head. He was seriously going to give this boy a severe ass beating. Bobby Lee's hand moved within less than an inch of Jimmy's face. Then, his fingers touched Jimmy's forehead. Jimmy jerked his fist forward - it stopped abruptly.

Drill Sergeant Smith held Jimmy's arm. He twisted it around behind Jimmy's back and pressed his stomach against Jimmy's backside. He leaned his face over Jimmy's shoulder and put his mouth right near Jimmy's ear.

"Boy, if you dare lay one hand on him, I will put my foot so far up your ass that you will be tasting leather for a month," Drill Sergeant Smith said as saliva accumulated in Jimmy's ear.

"He touched me first. He started this whole thing. Bobby Lee doesn't like me, because I'm from North Carolina for Christ's sake," Jimmy said trying not to totally whine as he said it.

"Are you kidding me?" Drill Sergeant Smith screamed. "You little girls are about to have something to really cry about. You finish up your training classes today and, tomorrow, your butts are mine."

Chapter 7

BETH

"I don't understand what you mean," Beth said with a quizzical look on her face. "You have to break some eggs to bake a cake? What the hell are you talking about exactly?"

"Beth, you are familiar with the inner workings of agencies whose job it is to protect this country, correct?" Doctor Cornelius questioned with a serious and unflinching demeanor. "You are well aware that sometimes in order to protect the interests of the United States, you have to go outside the boundaries of prudence and caution, agreed?" He pointedly asked Beth.

"I suppose that there are certain circumstances where an agency or people in the agency may need to bend the rules in the interest of justice or security, or to prevent an epidemic, or to regulate and control its population. Yes, I know it happens more than I care to admit, but that doesn't make it right," Beth said with a guarded stoicism.

"What is right is that people have the ability to feel safe within the borders of the United Sates and that those who wish to cause harm here are stopped before real panic ensues," Doctor Cornelius said as he slowly paced back and forth in front of Beth. "We, the CIA and other governmental agencies, need to protect people in every stage of life, even those unborn. We also need to make sure that advances in the sciences do not end up in the wrong hands. The CIA and other governmental bodies need to be at the forefront on new developments that could have the potential to either help or destroy individuals' lives, to prevent what could be a major human catastrophe."

"Yes, that makes sense, we are almost always one step ahead, that is our job," Beth said assuredly. "So, I deduce from this lecture that we are concerned with developments in stem cell research and what that means to the future of the United States and the human race."

"Precisely," Doctor Cornelius said. "We are concerned with this whole line of medical development. We are alarmed at the destruction of embryos, the possibility of cloning, and the overall meaning that this modification to human life entails. While there is great possibility that stem cell research developments will alleviate some serious health conditions for those people afflicted with them, there is also the possibility that countless lives will be destroyed, and the course of what is considered natural human life could be altered, if this ends up in the hands of malicious and sick individuals."

"I get your point. I have seen *The Fly* and other sci-fi movies that delve into areas like this. I have also witnessed first-hand some of the abnormalities that nature creates in individuals, which are never allowed to leave the hospital, and I would hate to imagine what someone could create if left to their own devices," Beth said with a look of disgust on her face.

"Really?" I have heard of some gruesome anomalies. But, what are some of the things that you have seen that are never allowed to leave the hospital?" Doctor Cornelius said wondering if the things Beth saw where the same ones he had seen.

"Well, for starters, there are babies that are born with both female and male sex organs. The babies are called intersex, which is a nice way of saying hermaphrodites, and they have both ovaries and testicles, and both a penis and a vagina," Beth explained. "It used to be that doctors would perform surgeries without first testing the infant to find out the true sex, and the child would grow up a person with the wrong genitalia. Now, all sorts of tests are done to find out if the baby is going to be a little boy or girl."

"There are also more common birth anomalies like: too many arms, legs, and fingers, calcified and petrified fetuses, malformed heads, over and under growth, and fetuses that grow outside of the mother's uterus." Beth was growing impatient. "I'm sure that you are familiar with the whole host of problems that can develop in newborns; I shouldn't have to elucidate every condition and oddity that exists."

"You are right; I am familiar with these conditions, but thought that you may be able to provide further insight into problems and conditions that can occur with newborns. Of course, these problems occur with naturally conceived newborns. Human cloning and stem cell research presents a host of problems of its own," Doctor Cornelius looked concerned as he spoke with Beth.

"Cloning poses serious risks of producing children who are stillborn, unhealthy, severely malformed, or disabled. Some of the ills can consist of mutation, transmission of mitochondrial diseases, and negative effects from the aging genetic material. It is not a pretty picture," Doctor Cornelius cleared his throat and continued.

"I am sure you are aware of the shortcomings of animal cloning. Like animal cloning, human cloning will result in high failure rates, which will definitely take uncountable lives or embryos to reach the point of success since research cloning requires the death and destruction of embryos," Doctor Cornelius was sweating as he spoke, "Damn its hot in here."

He continued, "One thing is certain, sometime in the future we will have to address human cloning. The government needs to be ahead of the game in order to ensure we are the ones who control the outcomes. But now is not the right time to focus on cloning. There is still plenty of room for research to fill in and deal with the current limitations and problems that researchers faced in animal cloning. Its success rate is almost next to nil and impossible so it's useless to implement this technology on humans right now. Well, it's useless for non-government scientists," Doctor Cornelius said with a look of knowing.

"Ok, if we are not going to focus on the cloning right now, then what is it we need to focus on?" Beth questioned, as she also felt a bit flushed from the heat.

"Yes, well one thing at a time, cloning will be a handled in the future by our agency, but right now we are concerned with some of the same issues found in stem cell research, namely the destruction of embryos. We also need to make sure that we are in command of and have a thorough understanding of stem cell applications and developments. Right now, our understanding of stem cells is significant; however, the application of the research is crude at best," Doctor Cornelius stated matter-of-factly.

"Ok, you have explained some of your concerns with this line of medical science, but you haven't yet explained my role here, and what I will be doing here," Beth said now visibly angry.

"Beth, you are here to use your superior knowledge of human anatomy and physiology in combination with your knowledge of medical imaging equipment. We need both these areas of expertise for what you are about to do," Doctor Cornelius paused and stared straight at Beth as if trying to challenge her to a fight or something.

"And what would that be?" Beth asked in a low and monotone voice without taking her eyes off of Doctor Cornelius.

"Beth, we need you to build a tool for us," Doctor Cornelius said in a slow and deliberate manner.

"You want me to build a tool?" Beth asked incredulously. "What kind of tool?"

"Well, Beth, we need you to build a device that will do two things really," Doctor Cornelius paused for a second as he spoke. "Actually, we need you to design and oversee the production of this tool," he corrected himself. "You will have a group of engineers and scientists that will be responsible for the actual creation of this tool."

"And again, this tool will do what?" Beth was growing weary of keeping Doctor Cornelius on track.

"We need you to build a tool that will both, be able to take a precise image of a human's spinal column, and also deliver an electrical or a laser impulse to sever the spine in a precise location," Doctor Cornelius stated with the utmost seriousness.

"Wait, you want me to build a medical tool that will actually hurt someone?" Beth's voice nearly screeched as she spoke. "Doctor, I think you have the wrong person for this; I mean, what you are suggesting is highly unethical and illegal," Beth was in complete disbelief as she spoke.

"No Beth, we indeed have the right person for this. Your credentials are exactly what we are looking for and your Top Secret Security Clearance gives you access. You have admittance Beth, and you know what goes on here will never leave the confines of this facility. The future of the human species depends on your cooperation with us," Doctor Cornelius was a master at convincing people to give him what he wants.

"I understand that, but I believe there are better ways to get the information you need rather than by what you are alluding to here," Beth objected.

"Sorry Beth, this is the only way. The plan has already been approved by the CIA, and it is a done deal. We have the green light. We know exactly what we are aiming to accomplish, and we will accomplish it. We prefer, rather insist, it be with you," Doctor Cornelius stated dryly. "If it is any consolation, you will only be developing this tool. You will have absolutely no responsibility for its implementation or use. We have agents in place for that mission. It is much like Einstein building the atomic bomb, but without the mass devastation that occurred with that," Doctor Cornelius was laying it on thick, and he could pile it higher and deeper if the need should arise.

"Yes, doctor, but Einstein developed something that protected the US and its citizens not that hurt them," Beth said as she shook her head.

"Beth, I wish it were easier to make these tough decisions. Our ultimate goal is a benevolent one. Our aim is to protect life and to make life better for millions. We will gain knowledge and insight into the possibilities that science has to offer. Please help us on our mission to help others," Doctor Cornelius could tell that he was weaseling his way into Beth's head.

"Well, it is my job to help the agency as required. I am going to have to learn more about what you need though. I mean, what should this tool look like?"

"Thanks for asking. This tool needs to be small. It needs to be small and lightweight enough to be easily transported. We need it to be hand-held," Dr. Cornelius put his hand under his chin as if he was covering a goatee.

"Wait, wait, wait - you might as well ask me to have monkeys fly out of my ass. Hand held? Have you seen medical imaging equipment? It is bulky and cumbersome," Beth said as she thought this was getting better by the minute.

"Your knowledge of how the intricate components and electrical parts fit together will give you what you need. Your team is composed of experts in engineering, specifically, in imaging technologies. There is also a physicist and an expert in lasers. You will have access to the most advanced parts and modern technologies that exist. Some of the parts are not available to non-governmental entities. We know that you can get this done, and that is why we selected you," Doctor Cornelius made a good case.

"I guess all there is to do now is to get started on this anomaly of the medical world. Let's call it, the Devil's Breath," Beth suggested.

"The Devil's Breath it is," Doctor Cornelius agreed.

Chapter 8

MARGE

Marge was in the mental hospital for four days now. She took her medicine as directed, and thought that she had adjusted to it fine with no side effects. She still felt the biting sting of anger in her soul over the way she had been treated lately by the men in her life, but she was not violently acting out and felt ready to go home. She needed to get back to work and get on with her existence.

Group therapy was taking place when a doctor quietly opened the door and asked to speak to Marge. Marge excused herself from the group and walked into the hall.

"I would like to speak to you Marge, please follow me," the doctor said in a cool and collected manner. He led Marge to a little office that was not far from the community room.

"Please have a seat. Now, I called to talk to you about your treatment. It appears that you are adjusting to the new medication that I have prescribed for you, but something concerns me. Your blood pressure is extremely elevated. It is elevated to the point that you are at risk for a heart attack," the doctor explained to Marge with a very clinical and cold demeanor.

He continued, "What is odd about the raised blood pressure is that you are in very good shape. Do you exercise?"

"Yes, I try to run and lift weights every chance I get," she explained. "Physical fitness is very important to me, and I also eat right too." Marge looked very concerned and appeared to be on the verge of crying. She felt very tired from an inadequate amount of sleep. She couldn't understand how her blood pressure could be so dangerously elevated.

"Well, I believe that your blood pressure is elevated from stress factors in your life. Do you have a lot of stress?" The doctor asked as he stared at her with his steely gaze.

"Yes, I do. Between men, pressure at work, worrying about my parents, and financial problems, I am under enormous strain all the time." Marge confided in the doctor.

"Well, we are here to help you deal with your problems," the doctor insisted.

"Marge, we are not going to discharge you. You will stay with us until we decide that you are better, is that understood?" Marge thought the doctor was giving her an order and was being a little too forceful.

"Doctor, I can't stay here," Marge's eyes began to well up again with tears. She was on the verge, and the doctor wasn't making the situation any better. "I have to get back to the bank. If I don't show up soon, I'm going to lose my job. I have other things to take care of that can't wait," She insisted as she began to sob.

"Marge, you need to get better and take care of yourself. I can write a note for your job. Your parents are more concerned that you get the help you need right now," the doctor advised her.

"How do you know what my parents want?" Marge said, lashing out at the doctor now. "You medical people are all the same; all you want is my money! You don't give a damn about me!" Marge was upset but not hysterical.

"Marge, that is not true, we all want to see you get better," the doctor insisted.

"Yeah, right! You all suck! I need to go home!" Marge screamed at the doctor.

"You are staying right here until we say you are better. I suggest you pull yourself together. You are not helping the situation any. Please calm down," the doctor left the office and went over to a nearby nurse.

The doctor nearly whispered to her, "Please administer a strong tranquilizer to the patient in my office over there. She may fight you, so take another nurse or two with you."

Armed with an injectable dose of Thorazine, the nurses made their way over to the confining office. Marge let them have it. She screamed expletives at the nurses, kicked them, bit them, and even pulled one of the female nurse's hair. They were eventually able to subdue her and gave her the Thorazine. Marge was then led to room and strapped to a bed. Within an hour, after more screaming and resistance, she was asleep.

The next day, Marge woke up in a subdued and quiet state. She was given another oral dose of Thorazine and went to breakfast. Afterwards, she was allowed to return to her room to resume her sleep. She returned to the activities of the day after lunch. The first activity was another round of group therapy. She sat there calmly as people told their stories of despair and anguish. Then, a while later, Marge quietly watched a young girl eat her dinner at the same table as her. The skinny girl would lift the spoon full of soup up to her lips and let it fall back into the bowl, without ever taking a sip.

After dinner, the people in Marge's wing of the hospital were led outside to the recreation area. There, the patients could sit at the picnic tables and smoke. They also could play a game for some exercise. The staff encouraged people to play a game of volleyball; hearing this, one kid ran behind a building and sat between it and the chain link fence, out of view from everyone.

One of the staffers saw this and went after the patient. The staff member told the patient that he couldn't be over on that side of the building, because no one could see him there. The staff was responsible for the patients' safety during recreation time, and they took the job seriously. Sometimes, though, the staff members would smoke with the patients and would lose sight of one of the stragglers. On several occasions, a patient was able to slip through a hole in the fence made by some potential thieves or boys causing mischief on hospital grounds. The escapee would eventually return after they became confused or lost or both, but the staffer would get an earful from the charge nurse.

Marge did not participate in the volleyball game and decided to sit with some of the smokers even though she doesn't smoke. She sat next to a girl who had a bad complexion, bleached blond hair, and sunken eyes with dark circles around them. The girl was talking to others at the table, but she focused her attention on Marge as Marge sat down. She extended a hand toward Marge, and Marge shook it.

"What is your name?" The sickly looking girl asked Marge.

"Marge," she muttered.

"So what kind of problems are you having?" The girl asked.

"I am having the usual problems: men, money, and migraines," she said, not wanting to reveal too much to a complete stranger. Marge asked, "What brings you here?"

"My mother died two weeks ago. She overdosed on heroin that she was injecting with some of my friends. I cried for the first week, and then, I began smoking crack again. I was driving around after smoking and hit someone. I lost my shit and went crazy; I was yelling, throwing things, and threatening the cops after they arrived. Rather than taking me to jail, they brought me here," the girl said in short, staccato phrases. She was twitching violently and seemed overly agitated.

"Wow, I'm sorry to hear that," Marge said as she was about to get the hell out of there, but the girl grabbed her arm and leaned towards Marge.

"I am also having excruciating back pain," the girl said in an eerie, almost inaudible voice.

"We all have our problems," Marge told her as she stood up.

"Yeah, but some people's problems are worse than others," the girl stated still holding Marge's arm.

"Let me go, it is time for us to go in now," Marge was visibly upset. She jerked her arm away from the girl.

"Your time is coming soon. You have not experienced pain yet, but you will," the girl's voice was filled with hatred.

"You don't know me. How dare you say that to me," Marge began to cry again.

The group returned to the inner boundaries of the hospital. Marge went to her room and laid in her bed, sobbing over what the girl said to her. She couldn't believe the nerve of that girl to say that she hasn't experienced pain. Marge thought about her for a while, and then realized that she was dealing with a sick individual. The girl did have a lot of problems and maybe she could be a little more forgiving of her; she let it go. She stood up and walked to the bathroom. She stood in front of the mirror, and immediately behind her was the girl.

"Your time is coming!" the sickly girl shouted at her.

Marge was backed into a corner by the unruly patient in her room threatening her. The sickly girl was lead out of Marge's room by one of the orderlies. The well-built orderly took her to a padded isolation room for observation. The girl was screeching like a bat while threatening Marge as she was lead away. Her screams and what she was saying were very disturbing to Marge. The sickly girl kept telling Marge that her time was coming, that she was about to experience pain like she has never experienced it before now. Marge dismissed the girl's comments as the irrational delusions of a crack addict. But she could not help but wonder what the girl was talking about. It was as if she knew something Marge didn't, but Marge put the thought aside as it was time for her to make a personal call. She walked down the hallway, picked up the phone mounted to the wall, and dialed. Someone picked up the phone on the other end and said, "Hello?"

"Hello mother," Marge said with a smile as she nestled the phone under her chin.

"Hello dear," Marge's mother said as Marge sat in a chair in the hallway. "How are you feeling?"

"I feel a little better today. They put me on some strong medicine that makes my head feel fuzzy, but it also calms my nerves," Marge said as she twisted the telephone cord around into a knot.

"Honey, I have some bad news for you. I really wanted to wait until you were out of the hospital to tell you this, but I thought you needed to know now so you can start making plans for the future," Marge's mother said with concern in her voice.

"What's that mom?" Marge said.

"Well, your boss from work called," Marge's mother said nervously.

"Yeah, what did he want?" Marge asked sounding a little frightened.

"He wanted me to tell you that your services at the bank will no longer be needed. He said that he couldn't hold your job open any longer. He wanted to tell you directly but he was having a hard time trying to contact you in the hospital," Marge's mother sounded upset.

"He can't do that. He can't fire me. I'm in the hospital for Christ's sake. Why would he say that?" Marge was furious and crushed at the same time. She was on the verge of hyperventilating.

"I know baby. He said that it has been too long and he never got a note from you. I said I would get one to him, and he said that it was too late. He had already made his decision. I'm sorry," Marge's mom was trying her best to keep from crying over the fact that her little girl's life was falling apart.

"That asshole bastard!" Marge shouted.

"Marge, we will get through this. You can move back in with us if you need to. I still have the spare bedroom all made up for you. It will be ok," Marge's mother was a good counselor. She had to be to deal with Marge's inconsistent behavior.

"I can't breathe right now. I need to go. We'll talk about this later. I don't know when they are going to let me out of here, so I will call you later when I find something out. Bye mom," Marge said as she tried to control her rage. She couldn't believe that the company she was so dedicated to would stab her in the back like that. She also couldn't believe that they would do it while she was in the hospital. The nerve of them, she thought.

Marge sat in the small white chair near the phone sobbing. A nurse walked by and asked her if there was something she would like to talk about. Marge did not reply. She just sat there with her head hung low as she propped it up with her arms. The nurse asked her again if she could do anything for her. Marge shouted at the nurse, "Get the hell away from me!" The nurse quickly moved along to tend to other business.

A small, young, attractive girl walked by Marge. She had on a shirt that was too large for her, and it was sharply mismatched in color with her baggy pants. She stopped and saw Marge with her head in her hands. She asked her if there was anything wrong. Marge didn't say a word. She looked at the small girl with a blank stare that was devoid of any emotion. Then, Marge jumped up from her seat and leapt on the girl. She pulled the girl's hair and began smacking her in the face. She bit the girl on the neck and drew blood. Marge threw the innocent girl to the ground while the girl laid on the floor screaming in terror. Marge's fury was unstoppable.

It took two orderlies and a nurse to pull Marge from the girl. A large flap of skin from the girl's neck was ripped off, and she lay there motionless. Blood was gushing onto the floor beside her. The girl was fading in and out of consciousness as the nearby nurses applied pressure to the wound. They lifted the girl onto a stretcher and rolled her into a room where she waited for an ambulance to pick her up to take her to a hospital capable of dealing with her injuries.

Marge was quickly led to an isolation room where she threw another fit. Upon the doctor's orders, a nurse again administered a very high dose of Thorazine. Once Marge was under control, she was instructed to take a high dose of Risperdal via oral solution. She fell asleep in the isolation room where she posed no threat to the other patients. Two doctors and a nurse were standing nearby, peering through the small window to Marge's isolation room, and trying to figure out what to do with Marge.

"She has violated another patient's well-being and inflicted severe injuries to her. She must be transferred to another facility," one of the doctors stated.

"No, she can remain here in isolation until we can figure out if the medicine will keep her asymptomatic," the taller doctor suggested.

"She was on Thorazine before she had this outburst, and it failed to prevent the attack," the nurse offered.

"Yes, but we intend to increase the dose, we will give her the maximum recommended amount. The Risperdal will also help to control her manic episodes," the shorter doctor corrected the nurse.

"We need to keep her as sedated as possible until she can work through some of her issues in therapy. She needs to get to the bottom of some of the problems that are causing this frenzy of anger. We are opening ourselves to liability if the other patient's mother decides to sue. We simply can't allow this to happen again," the taller doctor cautioned as the room fell into a tense silence.

"I don't practice defensive medicine. We are here to do what is right for the patient. I shouldn't have to remind you of that," the taller doctor chided the other.

"The patient is a problem," the shorter doctor said.

"Then we will fix the problem, end of discussion," The doctors stormed off in different directions. The nurse peeked into the isolation room; Marge's face suddenly pressed up against the window. She looked possessed.

The next day, Nurse Todd went into the isolation room to administer the prescribed doses of Thorazine and Risperdal. She gave Marge both doses orally this time around. Marge was stoic as she swallowed the medications. She did not move as she lay against the wall. The nurse then led her to her room where Marge showered and dressed. The nurse was instructed to follow Marge for the first several hours after administering her drugs.

Marge cleaned herself up and made her way down to breakfast with the nurse. They moved through the line where the nurse piled her own plate with eggs, bacon, hash browns, and pancakes. Marge mindlessly chose an apple and some milk. The cafeteria worker looked at Marge and said, "Looks like someone had a bad night." Marge said nothing. She was too medicated to force any type of conversation. She mostly was focusing on not falling down.

Marge slowly drank her milk and ate most of her apple. The nurse ate like a hungry wolf. She told Marge that unless she started acting right, she might never get to leave the hospital. No response from Marge. Nurse Todd pointed to a young man with disheveled hair and thick glasses in the corner of the cafeteria sitting by himself. She said that he had acted out a couple of times and even tried to kill another patient. She informed Marge that he was on his second year of involuntary commitment. Moments later, a tear rolled down Marge's cheek; it hung and glistened in the air before striking the stem of the apple core. It was a bittersweet image of a beautiful woman strife with life's problems.

Chapter 9

CARLOS

"You're free to go," the rotund sheriff said to Carlos. "Your brother posted bail for you. If I were him, I would have let you rot in here."

"Yeah, well screw you too," Carlos said.

"Watch it boy, I will throw you back in that cell so fast you'll have whiplash for a month," the sheriff said, clearly not playing around. He had not seen Carlos for a while, but knew that he wasn't really a threat. After some of the fools that he dealt with, Carlos was downright soft. Carlos and Timmy left the jail and traveled back to Carlo's apartment where they each had a strong drink and discussed what happened to Carlos four nights ago.

Carlos was off the wagon again, which only meant trouble. He hadn't attended an AA meeting in over a month. He felt confident that he had his drinking under control but that wasn't the case last night. He had just finished up a karate tournament where he saw his best student choke terribly at the hands of his opponent. In fact, most of his students had done pitifully. He felt that all the moves he was teaching them had been for nothing. He didn't know what he needed to do to get them to perform better. So, he decided he needed a something to drink, anything.

Before he was thrown in jail, he walked to a nearby restaurant and took a seat at the bar. He proceeded to have one Captain Morgan's Spiced Rum and Coke right after another. Within an hour, he had more than four polished off. The bartender handed him his fifth drink of the night and asked him if he was ok. He told the bartender that it didn't matter since he was walking anyhow. So, after two more drinks, Carlos was out the door and drunk as sailor on shore leave.

Carlos walked outside the restaurant and decided that he didn't want to go home right away and took a seat on the side of the building. His head was spinning so much that he had no choice other than to sit down, or he would eventually fall down. So, he sat for a minute to gain his composure.

As he sat there, a smelly, homeless man in a wheelchair rolled up beside him. He asked Carlos for some money. Carlos slapped the cup out of the old, homeless man's hand and told him to get a job. Normally, Carlos would have given him the bum money, but he was far from being in a normal state of mind tonight. The homeless man called him an asshole and rolled on down the street.

Carlos felt hungry and thought that he needed something to eat, so he went around the corner to a hot dog stand and got himself three hotdogs loaded with ketchup, mustard, onions, relish, and sauerkraut. He inhaled the hotdogs as if he had not eaten for three weeks. Ketchup dripped down his shirt and hit his shoes. He had food all over his face and hands. The hotdog vendor was laughing uncontrollably at him as Carlos ate his food nearby. Carlos told him to fuck off as he finished up the last of his hotdog and continued down the street.

He was gaining some composure as he walked aimlessly in the dark. He walked by a couple making out, as they leaned against the side of an empty building. Carlos couldn't see what they looked like, but they got him thinking about his own need for some affection. He had been without anyone of intimate interest in his life for a while now, ever since his last girl broke up with him and left him with a broken heart. The lonely night had him feeling a little desperate.

Carlos noticed two beautiful girls standing on the corner of a side street. They were dressed very seductively. One girl had on a red halter top, black miniskirt, black fishnet stockings, and red boots that came up to the middle of her calf. The other girl was wearing a blue strapless dress that hung mid thigh. She had a gold chain tied around the dress and also had on black and white low-rise boots that looked like a zebra's skin pattern. The girls were just standing there, but they would occasionally walk down the street a little and then back to the corner. Occasionally, a car would drive by and stop near them, and the girls would lean over into the driver's side of the car. They looked like they were having fun with the drivers.

Carlos stood across the street staring at them for a moment. His head was still a little fuzzy from the alcohol. He wondered what they were doing there. He thought that their car might have broken down. He paused and thought about helping them. He summoned up some courage and walked over to the girls, trying to balance himself to keep from staggering.

"Are you two in some sort of trouble?" Carlos asked a little concerned.

"We could be," the blond in the red boots said coyly.

"What do you mean you could be? How do you not know?" Carlos was clueless as to what these girls really wanted - money. He didn't know a hooker when he saw one.

"Well, if we are in trouble, why don't you spank us?" the girl in the blue dress suggested. She was chewing gum like a cow would chew cud.

"What? Are you hookers?" Carlos said, finally catching on.

"It depends. Are you some sort of cop or something?" The girl in the red boots asked with a smile.

"God no, I fucking can't stand cops," Carlos said, feeling insulted by the question.

"Well, what do you like?" The girl in the blue dress said as she pulled out her gum and put it on the tip of her finger. She licked her finger and thrust it in and out of her mouth. "You can have one of us or both of us at the same time." Blue dress girl was quick to discuss business.

"Hold on a minute. You want me to get kinky with you? You want me to make out with you? I've never been with a whore before. On second thought, yes I have, but I didn't have to pay her. I don't know if I'm comfortable with paying for sex," Carlos was hesitant but stood there thinking about how hot the girls looked and how he'd like to ravage their bodies with his tongue. He fantasized about caressing their large breasts and playing hide and seek with his engorged member.

"We could both come back to your place. We'll give you the time of your life, we promise. You will not regret it for one second," the red boot girl said as she placed her hands on his shoulders and began rubbing them down Carlos's back.

"God damn that feels good," the girls were pushing all the right buttons. The fact that Carlos was still half drunk combined with his need for affection got the best of him. "Let's go, my place is only a couple of blocks away," he said as he grabbed the girl in the blue dress by the hand.

"Wait, do you want both of us to come or just me?" the girl in the blue dress wondered.

"Both of you. Hurry up too. I got something you'll both want to feel," Carlos and the girls walked as fast as they could.

"Hold on a minute! Wait up! These boots aren't exactly made for running!" The girl in the red boots screamed as she lagged behind Carlos and the other girl.

"Hurry up!" Carlos shouted back at her. They nearly jogged the couple of blocks back to Carlos's apartment.

The hooker in the red boots took her boots off to keep up. They made it back to Carlo's apartment building and ran up the four flights of stairs to Carlo's place. Carlos frantically searched for his keys and, after what seemed like a month to him, he eventually found them. He slammed the key into the lock and began to turn it.

"Wait," the girl in the blue dress said. "We need to discuss our price." The girl was a savvy businesswoman. She waited until the last minute before bringing up the cost of their rendezvous. She knew she could get more money that way, since the guy would be so horned up he would pay anything. "It's going to be five hundred dollars," She said. Carlos's jaw dropped. "It's normally two hundred dollars for one, but since you are getting the double pleasure package, it's a little more," she said while stroking his leg. "And we need that money up front."

Carlos paused for a second all the while enjoying the soft touch of her hand. The prostitute in the red boots moved in and began feeling his neck. She looked at him and gave him a soft kiss on the cheek leaving behind a blotch of bright red lipstick.

"Ok. I just got paid yesterday and have money here for rent. Let me get it," Carlos went inside and got his money. He returned after a few seconds and handed it to the hooker in the blue dress. Then, they entered the apartment, and Carlos began taking off his clothes as he made his way towards the bed. He began coddling both the girls' legs. He noticed that the girls were just standing there not taking any interest in him. They also made no effort to take off their clothes.

"What's going on?" Carlos asked a little miffed at the girls' lack of passion. "I just paid you!"

"You sure did," the girl in the blue dress said with a smirk. The next thing Carlos heard shocked him completely.

"Open up, this is the police! Open the door now!"

"What? Are you kidding me?" Carlos couldn't believe what he was hearing.

"This is the police, open up or we will bust down the door!"

"What is going on? Are you two in on this? You fucking bitches! How dare you! I should kill you both!"

The girl in the blue dress went over to the door and opened it up. Three police officers in plain clothes burst through the door with their guns drawn. They told Carlos to put his clothes back on. They told him that he was under arrest and read him his Miranda Rights. Carlos spit on the girls, as he was lead out the door. He was taken to the Manhattan's Bernard B. Kerik Complex and jailed. He sat in jail for four days until Timmy came to bail him out.

While Carlos was in jail, he had a lot of time to think. Most of what he had time for was thinking, that, and fighting off the lowlifes that accompanied him in jail. He was completely furious with himself, and the undercover-cop prostitutes, for his being held prisoner in this filthy, godforsaken place. He wondered what was going to happen to him and how he was going to get out of here. He sat on the floor covered in hot dog drippings and smelling like alcohol. Carlos could also smell an assortment of other unpleasant, rancid effects emanating from both the people and the facility. It was unbearably unpleasant.

Carlos sat on the floor in the holding cell waiting to be properly booked. Drunks and other "alleged" offenders were led in and quickly took a seat without too much protest. Most people kept to themselves, most people, except Rodney. Rodney was brought in minutes after Carlos, and he was visibly irritated and shaking violently. He turned his bloodshot, angry eyes towards Carlos.

"Boy, give me your shoes!" Rodney demanded. He was a short, skinny man, and Carlos judged he was probably 35 years old. He was talking excitedly the whole time. He was screaming that the man was beating him down, and that it wasn't fair that he was being treated like a criminal. He was obviously on some sort of drug. Carlos thought it was probably crack or meth.

"What?" Carlos said trying not to pay attention to Rodney hoping that he would go away.

"You heard me! Give me your damn shoes!" Rodney shouted again as he put his finger up to Carlo's face.

"Get away from me right now, before I crack your skull!" Carlos was in no mood to be pushed around. He would defend himself against any man, woman, or child at this point. He barely had his dignity as it was, and he wasn't about to be brought down another notch by having his shoes stolen from him.

"I'll take your damn shoes when you're sleeping then, and I'll take your shirt too!" The skinny man quickly turned his attention to the prison guards. He couldn't focus on anything for very long before bellowing out another rambling statement.

"When the hell are you going to let me out of here, god dammit!?" He shouted.

"Quiet down in there, before I quiet you down!" A large female prison guard snapped.

"Come on big mama! Let me out of here!" His pleads fell on deaf ears as the guard attended to other business. Eventually, he took a seat and began harassing a drunk passed out on the floor. He was searching the guy for any valuables, but the guards had already taken them.

The next morning at around 8 a.m., Carlos was officially booked into jail. He was fingerprinted and advised that he was being charged with Soliciting a Prostitute. He also had his mug shot taken; a photo he didn't want anyone to see. It was not only unflattering, but it was also embarrassing to him.

He was then led before a judge. The judge read him his rights and his charges. The judge set his bond at $4,000. Since Carlos couldn't come up with the bond himself, someone would have to pay a fee of around $400 for a bail bondsman to have him post bond. Carlos also couldn't come up with the $400 for the bondsman, so he would have to ask Timmy. If Timmy could pay the fee, then Carlos could get out of jail until his trial date.

A prison guard took Carlos to his cell where he would stay until he bonded out. There was a pay phone in the cell, and Carlos used it to call Timmy.

"Hey Timmy, this is Carlos; I'm in a little bit of trouble here," Carlos explained, but he was too embarrassed to give Timmy the whole story.

"What kind of trouble are you in?" Timmy asked in a concerned voice.

"Umm, I kind of need your help," Carlos said sheepishly.

"Yeah bro, I'm here to help you. What is it? Are you in the hospital or something?" Timmy was in the middle of eating lunch, but he quickly pushed it aside as the urgency in Carlo's voice grew.

"Umm, worse, I'm in jail."

"What? What the hell happened? What did you do?" Timmy said relieved that he wasn't hurt, but still perturbed as Carlo's problems turned from possible medical concerns to confirmed legal issues.

"Well, I'll tell you about all that later; but for now, I need you to get me out of here," Carlos said. "Do you have $400 for bail?"

There was a slight pause and then Timmy eked out a response. "Ehrrrr, Ummm, No, not really. If you wait a few days, I get paid and can get you out then." His credit was bad and he didn't have any immediate access to cash.

"Shit man, can't you get any money before then?" Carlos said as he mulled over the horrid possibility of his having to stay in jail longer. "It sucks in here! It smells, and the people are disgusting. I don't want to stay here."

"Well, I could ask mom for it," Timmy said not realizing that his proposal was more of a threat than a solution.

66

"No. No, I don't want mom to know about this. She would rip me another asshole; I don't need that right now," Carlos said as he felt the gaze of his cellmate boring into the back of his neck.

"I need to use the phone," his big, burly cellmate bluntly stated.

"I'll be off in just a minute," Carlos snapped back.

"Ok, as soon as you get the money, come to the jail. There is a bail bonds company across the street from here. Go there and tell the bail bondsman that you need to pay for a bond for me. He should walk you through the process," Carlos said into the receiver as he ignored his cellmate. "I'll call you in a day or two to see where you're at," Carlos said.

"Ok, I'll do what I can to get the money before then, but I can't make you any promises right now." Timmy knew he would have to wait until payday before getting the money. Any extra money that he did come up with would be used just to keep food on the table. He really was in no position to lend anyone any money, but this was his brother, and Timmy would do what he could to help him out.

"Thanks, Timmy. Like I said, I will call you in a day or two to see where you're at with getting the money," Carlos whipped his head around violently and shouted at his cellmate, "Look, dude, I told you that I would be off the phone in a minute!" His cellmate backed up and took a seat on the lower bunk.

"Ok. Sounds good," Timmy said. "Take care of yourself in there and remember one thing."

"What's that," Carlos asked

"Don't drop the soap," Timmy quipped.

"That isn't on my list of things to do in here. I just hope that the rotten food doesn't kill me. Breakfast was worse than eating dog chow," Carlos said with a look of revulsion on his face. "My main goal is to stay alive and not become someone's punching bag or bitch."

"Yeah, watch out for yourself. I'll talk to you later."

"Ok, thanks again Timmy. I'll talk with you soon," Carlos's voice trailed off as the feeling of isolation gripped his spirit. He hung up the receiver and sat there for a few seconds. A fly landed on his face; he swatted it away. His cellmate got up from the bunk and stood beside Carlos. He reached down to grab the receiver, and Carlos jumped up and moved to the other side of the cell. "Ok, you can use it now," Carlos said in a poignant voice.

"Yeah, I know I can," the overgrown, unshaven, smelly captive said.

Carlos didn't respond. He had always heard that the best policy in jail is to keep to yourself. He didn't want to cause a scene or get on anyone's bad side; he just wanted to coast through his time there without incident. Carlos hoped that others would abide by the same rules. The skinny man trying to take his shoes was an example of how the best policies could end up being nothing more than a hope. Carlos realized that the policy was about to get flung to the side again, as he was about to invade his cellmate's sense of decency, but Carlos seriously doubted that he had any sense of it. He needed to use the bathroom.

Carlos thought that there are things that you take for granted in everyday life that you come to appreciate when you are in jail. One such thing is privacy when using the bathroom, the shower, or the sink. When the average person is thrust into a situation where other people are constantly watching you perform normally private acts, it creates a sense of anxiety and embarrassment. It took Carlos several minutes before he was eventually able to pee with his grubby cellmate there. As he was pissing he thought, God, please get me out of here.

Carlos finished up his business and took a seat on the lower bunk. His cellmate was in the middle of a heated conversation on the phone.

He roared, "What the hell do you mean Jane took all the money? I made over $75,000 from that last shipment. I'll kill that bitch! Where is she now? Uh huh, yea, I knew that the blue Cadillac was running. Uh, huh, she took it to Fort Lauderdale? You mean that bitch went down to be with Javier - the fucking runner she had a thing for? Oh, you wait until I get out of here. I'll do her like I did that whore that tried to rat us out; except this time, I'll use a bat instead of a knife. Come bail me out now!" He slammed down the receiver.

Moving closer to Carlos, his cellmate was breathing heavily, and sweat rolled down his face as he tried to regain his composure. He turned around and faced the wall opposite of the bunks before punching it with enough force for his knuckles to pop. He let out a guttural howl that startled Carlos.

Carlos remained silent, and again thought to himself, God, please get me out of here. He turned to God in some of his more trying times and was again asking for his help. Even though some of the situations he encountered before were grim and trying, nothing compared to the monster of a man that stood before him. Carlos understood that Jesus mattered more to those in jail than to those that sit in a church.

The seconds became minutes that turned into hours, which passed into days. Much to Carlos's delight, his cellmate was bailed out a day ago, and they didn't bring anyone else in to replace him. Carlos passed the time by reading some donated books. He browsed through the *Purpose Driven Life* but found it too preachy for his taste. He read a great deal of Stephen King's book, *The Shining*. He found that the book was much more dramatic than the movie, and he enjoyed it thoroughly.

He also had time to workout. During his sessions, he completed several repetitions of several different weight lifting exercises. Since he was already in great shape from all the Karate and strength training he routinely completed, he found the weights were almost an inadequate amount to give him the proper resistance on some exercises. He made due though, and it helped him pass the time. Luckily for him, exercise time passed without incident. He got some deadly stares from some of the inmates, but they focused on working out rather than focusing on kicking some ass.

Carlos eventually returned to his cell. He wondered if he would lose his job as a Karate instructor even though he called the dojo. He wondered if his mother would find out about his time there. His thoughts were plaguing him in his confined space; he was ready to get the hell out of there. He went over to the phone and picked it up. Then, he heard the rattle of keys and saw the cell door open as the sheriff said, "You're free to go."

Chapter 10

MARIE AND CANDICE

"Marie, you are so beautiful," George said as he gently kissed Marie's neck as they sat on her bed. "You take my breath away."

George slid his hands onto Marie's shoulders and gently massaged them. He rubbed his fingertips down her back. George carefully unclasped her laced bra and threw it on the floor. He held her large breasts in his hands and stroked his lips and tongue across them.

Marie unbuttoned George's shirt slowly. She placed her hands on his groomed chest and fondled his well-developed abs. She slid her fingers down his inner thigh and back up to his belt and unbuckled it. She tossed his Italian leather shoes into the laundry basket near the bed. She placed her lips on his and passionately kissed them, tenderly biting them a bit.

Marie and George shared a night of complete and total pleasure that neither would soon forget. They enjoyed passionate and caring lovemaking that went on and on. George caressed Marie and took her to a level of ecstasy that she hadn't often experienced with other men she had made love to. After nearly an hour, they reached their release. Tension melted into serenity as they rested. After exchanging a few words, George and Marie were asleep.

The summer sun's rays painted Marie's eyelids in a bath of light the next morning. She slowly left her dream state and awoke to the mid-morning heat that was permeating her comforter. She gradually remembered George as her thoughts cleared, and she turned her head to the left. George was nowhere in sight. Marie called out, "George, are you here?" There was no response. Marie noticed that his clothes were gone. How typical, how damn typical, she thought.

Marie went to use the bathroom. She brushed her teeth and put her hair in up in a scrunchie. She put on her workout attire and prepared some coffee and a light breakfast before her workout. She drank her coffee, ate her meal, and sat for a minute at the table in the kitchen watching the television. The morning news was on. More bad things happening to good people, she thought. She finished up and walked toward the door. She remembered that she needed to get her keys and access card from her purse.

Marie walked back into the bedroom to get the items from her purse. She reached into her purse to retrieve the access card from her wallet. She felt around for a few seconds and couldn't find it. Marie opened the purse wide and dug around some more for her wallet. She looked in the bottom and in the side pockets of the purse, and it was nowhere to be found. She thought she might have left her wallet near the front door. There was nothing there. Marie searched the entire condo for several minutes and still was not able to find it.

"Shit, did I leave it at the bar?" Marie wondered. Then, her thoughts turned to the possibility that her one-night-stand was a multi-night thief. "Damn, if that rat bastard took my wallet, I will cut his balls off," she thought to herself. But, she had to be sure that she did not leave it behind. She walked back to her purse to get her cell phone to call Candice. It was not in her purse either. Marie looked around for her cell phone and couldn't find it. She grabbed her keys, locked the front door, and since the bar wasn't open this early, went to find Candice to see if she knew where her cell phone and wallet were.

Marie knew that Mark lived about two blocks from Rocco's. Since it was relatively close to her condo, she decided to walk to his place. Marie walked up to the small, first-floor condo and began knocking on the door. There was no answer after several attempts. She began pounding the door as hard as she could with her fist. Then, after a few more seconds, she heard the rattling of a chain and a turn of a deadbolt, and then Mark appeared.

"What the hell do you want?" Mark said with contempt, as he stood there shirtless, wearing only boxers that had black and white polka dots against a red background.

"I don't have time for your crap, Mark. Is Candice here?" Marie asked pointedly.

"Yeah, she's here. I'll go get her. Don't you come inside," Mark commanded Marie as if she was an animal.

"Ok. Hurry though," Marie said.

Candice walked up to the door with her hair in disarray, her shirt undone, and her frilly underwear showing. She looked like she was just waking up.

"Hey, what's up?" Candice asked Marie.

"I was just wondering if you have my cell phone and wallet. I looked everywhere in the condo and couldn't find them anywhere," Marie said with worry.

"Well, yeah, I have your cell phone but not your wallet. Mark gave us our drinks, so you wouldn't have needed to pull your wallet out when we first got there. Didn't that George guy pay for your drinks?" Candice questioned.

"He did pay. I don't remember ever taking my wallet out at Rocco's last night. There was really no reason to take it out at all. Now that I think about it, I would have needed my access card to get into our condo building last night," Marie said with growing distress.

"Damn it - I think that George guy stole it," Marie was very upset now. "I can't believe that asshole. I can't believe he would do that, especially after we had sex," Marie began to stomp around in anger. "I will kill that son of a bitch!"

"Oh, Marie, I'm so sorry. This is all my fault," Candice lamented.

"What do you mean this is your fault? You had nothing to do with him being a thief," Marie stated emphatically.

"I tried to call you last night, but when I did, there was no answer. I walked near the table where you and George were sitting and tried to call again, and I could hear your ringtone playing. Your phone was in the windowsill next to the table," Candice explained.

"Why were you trying to call me?" Marie wondered.

"Well, Mark said that he knew George, or at least heard about him," Candice explained. "Mark said that the guy was a hustler and has a reputation of doing girls wrong. He said that George moves from city to city and is an all around liar."

"Why didn't you come and get me?" Marie angrily said while attempting an intimidating pose while placing her hand on her hip.

"I couldn't. I tried to call you, and it was too late for me to try to walk back to the condo by myself. Besides, Mark wouldn't let me leave. We were both a little tipsy from the drinks. You know it gets dangerous around here late at night. Sorry, I just couldn't," Candice said a little indignant over the accusation Marie was making.

"I can't take this anymore. I can't believe that you knew about him. Please get my cell phone so I can leave," Marie was very distraught and was thinking what credit card companies she needed to call to have the cards cancelled. She was also thinking about the $900 she had in her wallet to give to Candice for rent. "Damn, I guess I will have to empty my savings account to pay for rent this month, or maybe, Candice will let me pay half since she is partly responsible for this," Marie thought to herself.

"Here's your phone," Candice said handing Marie her new iphone.

"Yeah, thanks, some friend you are," Marie was pushing her negative feelings onto Candice as she was still trying to shift the blame.

"Marie, I'm sorry that this happened. But maybe in the future, you can be a little more selective about the guys that you bring back to the condo," Candice suggested with a calm and serious demeanor. Mark, still looking as if he just woke up, walked up behind Candice and peered over her shoulder. "What's going on," he asked.

"Yeah, Candice, I'm the one who should be more selective," she said while glaring at Mark.

"Suck it Marie," Mark hurled his insult at Marie like a sledgehammer.

"If I could find it," Marie retorted as she turned and walked away. Their piss-poor relationship was every bit as bad as a couple going through a nasty divorce. Marie left to go back to the condo to get ready for work.

Marie's career was high pressure, but she did find time on occasion to rest a little bit. She was resting her head on her hand trying not to nod off. The constant, steady beeping of the electrocardiogram monitor rang in Marie's ears as she sat at the nurse's station. She was staring at the door to the nearby patient's room while thinking about George having took her wallet. She had cancelled all of her cards before coming to work and would have to wait several days for their replacements. The past weekend was not a good one, she thought to herself.

Marie's coworker, Sally, broke Marie from her thoughts. Sally was an ebullient, larger woman of about 40 years old. She had fiery red hair that curled in all directions. Sally was nice to work with, but she was a hard-nosed nurse who had seen all that the Level 1 Trauma Emergency Room had to offer.

"Marie, come and help me hold this patient steady, will you? He's fighting me and needs to have his blood drawn because of a possible MRSA infection."

"Yea, I'll be there in a second," Marie said as she made a note in the chart for a patient who suffered a broken arm and cuts from a car accident. She closed the chart and placed it back into the slot. She walked into room number six where Sally and the patient waited.

"Grab his arm and hold it," Sally said as she prepared the needle and test tubes for taking the patient's blood. The patient tried to jerk his arm back.

"Hold still, we need to take your blood to see if you have an infection!" Sally yelled at the patient. "Mandy, we could use your help in here too!" Sally shouted at a third nurse.

Marie and the second nurse were able to hold the patients arm long enough for Sally to pierce the vein and fill the test tubes.

"Ok, we are going to send this up to the lab for some tests. Once we find out what you have, we will be able to see if you need to be admitted or not." Sally told the patient in a much softer voice as she put the labels on the test tubes. "I'll be back in a couple of minutes to check on you. In the meantime, settle down and remain calm while I check on my other patients."

"I want to see the doctor!" The patient yelled at Sally.

"The doctor is busy right now. Once we get the lab results back, he will come and talk to you," Sally told the uncooperative young man.

"Hurry up! I need to get out of here!" The patient was sweating profusely from a high fever.

"You're not going anywhere. Now be quiet!" Sally shouted at the patient. "You want to live don't you? You see those pus-filled blisters on your skin? That could have spread to your organs, which means you are in some serious trouble. The blood test will confirm whether or not we are looking at a MRSA infection or something else. So lie here, shut-up, and help yourself get better."

The patient got quiet as a look of shock covered his face. "Since you put it that way, I guess I have no choice; I'm not ready to die," the patient said after he was jolted with a newfound appreciation for the nurse and with a sense of his mortality. He rested his head on the pillow and serenity took over as Sally exited the room shutting the door behind her.

Sally plodded over to the nearby doctor who was busy formulating an action plan for a patient about to be discharged. She said, "You have a live one in Room Six, but I was able to get him to settle down. It looks like he has a MRSA infection."

"I'll be the judge of that," The doctor said in a condescending tone.

"Oh, of course you will sire," Sally said with all the sarcasm she could conjure up. The doctor and she were bitter enemies; Sally relished in the fact that he was on a rotating schedule and was only in the Emergency Room one or two nights a week.

"Umm hmm," the doctor grunted before walking towards a different patient's room. He nearly tripped on the crash cart. Sally burst out laughing at his misstep. Her laughter was cut short by the crackling of the Ambulance radio wave scanner.

"We have a thirty year old, white male. He is unconscious and not breathing on his own. He suffered blunt force trauma to his neck and believe that he has a crushed cervical vertebrae. We have a stable heart rate. We are two minutes away," the paramedic on the scanner relayed to the medical staff.

"Ok, be ready for this patient," a physician said to the rest of the trauma team. The nurses each slipped on a new set of gloves as the respiratory therapists checked the ventilator in the resuscitation area. The X-ray technician loaded a new packet of film into the printer and positioned the X-ray machine out of the way. Marie attended to a patient in the minor emergency area.

The ambulance, with lights flashing, rolled up to the automatic doors for the emergency room, and the paramedics unloaded the patient. One of the paramedics held a large balloon pump to the face of the victim and provided oxygen for him. They wheeled him through the doors, past the triage area and nurses' station, onto the linoleum floor inside the emergency room itself. The trauma team met the paramedics and patient as soon as they came through the automatic doors.

"He was in a car accident, and his neck was pinned between the steering wheel and the car seat. His neck was twisted around at an odd angle. We were able to put a cervical collar on him but believe he is paralyzed," the paramedic said to the physician as they moved the patient into the resuscitation area.

The paramedics and several members of the trauma team lifted the long spine board and slid the patient from the ambulance stretcher to the hospital gurney. They removed the board from underneath him and the patient rolled sharply to his right.

"Careful," the doctor said. "I want a trache in this guy stat," the doctor readied his tools for the procedure while a nurse hooked the patient up to a heart monitor. The doctor made an incision in the skin on the patient's neck, separated some of the muscles, elevated the cartilage with a hook, made a tracheal incision, and inserted the tracheotomy tube. The respiratory therapist connected the tubing to a ventilator.

The heart monitor displayed a steady heart rate. The blood pressure cuff strapped to the patient's arm took a reading indicating that his blood pressure was dangerously low. Blood was seeping from the patient's nose and mouth. The physician instructed the nurse to give the patient blood as well as to give the patient a saline IV drip for the introduction of medication.

"I need X-rays of the patient's neck and abdomen. We are looking for cervical vertebrae damage as well as any free fluid from hemorrhages," the doctor said. The X-ray technician moved the X-ray machine into position to take a picture of the patient's neck and instructed the others to stay clear as she snapped the picture. The tech positioned the machine over the abdomen and snapped several more shots. As she took her last shot, the patient flat lined.

The doctor grabbed the paddles to the nearby defibrillator. The machine was charged up and ready to use. He placed the paddles in position and yelled, "Clear." The patient's chest jumped upon delivery of the electrical shock. The heartbeat didn't return and the monitor indicated that there was no rhythm. Again the physician yelled, "Clear." The patient did not respond. The trauma team eventually accepted that the patient could not be revived.

The patient's wife was in tears when she arrived in the emergency room. She went to a nearby attendant and asked where her husband was. The emergency room attendant walked to the nurse's station and confirmed that the person the woman was looking for was in the emergency room. The attendant returned with the trauma physician in tow. The trauma physician explained to the woman that her husband had died. She fell apart and cried for several minutes. Eventually, the doctor led the woman to see her husband.

"Ma'am, is this your husband?" The doctor asked.

"Yeah, that's my Rickie," she said through her tears.

"He'll be moved to the morgue shortly. The hospital will need to do an autopsy to see what his cause of death is," the doctor said.

"Ok," the woman stated as she went back to the waiting area to wait for other family.

Several minutes later, the X-ray technician approached the trauma doctor. "Here are the pictures from that last trauma patient," she said placing them on the lit viewing wall near the resuscitation room. "You can see that there is massive hemorrhaging from liver," she said. "You can also see from the X-rays of his neck that the vertebrae had shifted several inches in from the others thus severing the spinal cord in his neck completely."

"Wow, you're right," the doctor said.

"Even if he did live, there wouldn't be anything we could do to help him. He would have been completely paralyzed and probably been on a ventilator indefinitely," the doctor said.

Marie walked over to the doctor and X-ray technician. "So he didn't make it, huh? - That makes me want to stop driving and start walking. I would hate to end up like him."

Chapter 11

JIMMY

"Jimmy and Bobby Lee, I want you two to run the parade field for the next hour and a half while the other recruits are out here completing their exercises. If for one second, I see you two slacking off, you will be out of here faster than a Kenyan in a marathon. Do I make myself clear?" the Drill Instructor demanded.

Bobby Lee was quick to reply with a, "yes sir!" Jimmy, unfortunately, was less eager to placate the Drill Instructor. He said, "Don't you need to hold an Article 15 hearing before you give us a punishment?"

"An Article 15 hearing. Did I just hear you say an Article 15 hearing? Are you kidding me? No really, you filthy dog! Did I really just hear you ask me to hold an Article 15 hearing for you? I can't believe this shit!" the Drill Instructor was in complete astonishment at being asked to go through the formal procedures for punishment in basic training. While fighting with another recruit would be grounds for more serious types of punishment, Drill Sergeant Smith took the matter in his own hands, and he felt that administering strenuous exercise would suffice for now.

"Yes, yes sir," Jimmy looked at the ground and kicked a nearby rock as he mumbled the reply.

"Boy, I suggest you start running now, before I show you some real punishment," the Drill Instructor shouted. Jimmy and Bobby Lee turned around and began running at a fast pace.

"Run, boy, run!" Drill Sergeant Smith shouted.

Jimmy and Bobby Lee ran for nearly 45 minutes before they began to hit their physical wall. Both were in excruciating pain, but each pushed themselves as hard as possible; they did not stop, because they were afraid to. Each one slowed to the pace of a moderate jog. Jimmy led the way and did not look back. He wanted nothing to do with Bobby Lee. Bobby Lee was struggling as it was, and neither one had any plans for small talk as they ran. They each kept their distance.

Basic training wasn't turning out at all like Jimmy had imagined it. He knew it would be work, but he didn't think Drill Sergeant Smith would be so unapologetically cruel and demanding. He also thought that he would be getting along better with his fellow soldiers-in-training. He felt alone and isolated as he ran around the training grounds. He wondered about Janice. He wondered if she was preparing for law school, as it was about to start soon. But his thoughts quickly turned to rejoining the pack, as the hour and a half was complete.

When Jimmy and Bobby Lee made their way to the asphalt surface of the training ground, the other recruits were finishing up their last set of push-ups. The Drill Instructor taunted Porky Pig the entire time.

"Porky, let me ask again, how did you not get held back at Reception and complete training with Company Fat?" Drill Sergeant Smith asked in all seriousness.

"Because," he panted, "I could do most of the exercises. I just couldn't get all the push-ups done. They told me that I could move on and for me to pay attention to doing better on my push-ups," Porky said as sweat dripped down his red, glowing face.

"Great," Drill Sergeant Smith sighed, "send me the lemons and expect me to turn them into soldiers," he said.

"You are going to do a good set of pushups, and you are going to do them soon!" Drill Sergeant Smith roared.

"Yes sir!" Porky screamed.

The recruits all made their way back to the Dining Facility for breakfast. Then, they cleaned themselves up as well as their barracks. The rest of the day was dedicated to Drill and Ceremony training. They learned the official procedures for marching, standing at attention, facing right and left, and standing at ease. They also sat through a class on the army's core values including: loyalty, duty, respect, selfless service, honor, integrity, and personal courage. The hot day turned into the warm night as the soft-centered recruits were gradually being shaped into hardened soldiers.

Jimmy and the others returned to the barracks later that night. They were allowed an hour of personal time before lights out. As Jimmy was not permitted to call anyone, especially since he wasn't exactly in Drill Sergeant Smith's good graces, he decided to write Janice a letter. He explained how he felt about his experiences so far. He wrote about his problems with Bobby Lee, and he asked about Janice's plans for school.

Jimmy longed to speak with Janice just to hear the sweet sounds of her voice. Hearing her gave him refuge from the daily stresses he harbored in his mind and body. Jimmy was concerned though. The distance between the two was disheartening, and he felt that the gap between their meetings would only grow wider. He didn't know where he would end up after basic training, and she would most likely move to Miami for school. He didn't care about that now. He just wanted her in his heart for the moment.

Lights out came quickly. Jimmy lay in his bunk still thinking about Janice as he slowly drifted in and out of sleep. He heard the snoring of his fellow recruits that kept him from immediately passing out. But, his body was aching from the strenuous activities of the day, and he was exhausted. After about an hour, he was in a deep slumber from which a roaring lion couldn't wake him.

As Jimmy lay there drooling onto his pillow, Bobby Lee and several other recruits were in the midst of carrying out their well-crafted plans to play a practical joke on Jimmy.

"Do you have the duct tape?" Bobby Lee whispered to another recruit standing near.

"Yeah, it's right here," the tall lanky recruit whispered back.

"Ok, like we planned, I want ya ta slowly slide Jimmy's piller out from beneath his head," Jimmy said as he quietly unrolled a long piece of silver duct tape.

The lanky recruit slowly slid the pillow from behind Jimmy's head. Within seconds it was fully removed. "I got the pillow," Skinny said as he held it up to Bobby Lee.

"Ok, hold and twister it as I put duck tape on it," Bobby Lee said in his hushed country voice. They removed the pillowcase and Bobby Lee let the duct tape wrap around the pillow until there was no longer any white showing through. The pillow was now hard and jagged. They thought it would be very uncomfortable on which to sleep.

Bobby Lee replaced the pillowcase. Skinny gently lifted Jimmy's head and Bobby Lee slid the pillow back underneath it. Bobby Lee rolled out some more duct tape and placed it over Jimmy's forehead and stuck it to the pillow. He placed about four strips over his head. If Jimmy moved his head to the left or right he would be surprised as the entire pillow would move with him.

"Hand me da lipstick," Bobby Lee whispered in his muted voice. Bobby Lee rubbed the bright red lipstick on Jimmy's lips. It was slopped everywhere around his mouth and chin and looked ridiculous.

Bobby Lee and Skinny went back to their respective bunks and lay there. They waited in silence to hear something from Jimmy. There was not one sound other than the snoring of the other recruits. Bobby Lee and Skinny eventually drifted into a sleep of their own.

The lights were flipped on early in the morning. Jimmy lay there with his eyes closed. He twisted his head a little to the right and then a little to the left. He felt a tug on his forehead as he tried to move. He rapidly sat up in his bed. The pillow went with him as it hung onto the back of his head.

The other recruits were mostly awake when Jimmy sat up. One by one, they noticed Jimmy with the pillow strapped to his head and the bright red lipstick smeared on his face. Soon, the whole room was filled with laughter.

Jimmy quickly began peeling the tape from his forehead until the pillow came loose. He didn't know that there was lipstick on his face. He jumped from his bunk and was walking around the barracks looking like a clown. His eyes fixed on Bobby Lee who was undulating with laughter as he rolled in his bed.

"I'll kill you, you son of a bitch!" Jimmy screamed with anger.

"You want ta kiss me don't ya, prostitute!" Bobby Lee could barely get his words out, as he was laughing so hard. The others were laughing louder at Bobby Lee's comment.

"What is going on here?" Drill Sergeant Smith demanded.

"Oh, you all are playing practical jokes! You think this funny?" He said bluntly. "Who is responsible for this?"

No one responded.

"Bobby Lee did it!" Jimmy shouted.

"Did you do this Bobby Lee?" Drill Sergeant Smith questioned.

"No sir!" Bobby Lee lied.

"Who did this, then?" Drill Sergeant Smith asked.

There was just silence.

"Well, until someone comes forward, you all can expect to do double the amount of exercises today." Drill Sergeant Smith threatened.

"You will act like soldiers, and you will act like soldiers soon!"

The previous several days for Bravo Company became a test of human endurance and strength. The soldiers suffered through the punishment brought on by Jimmy and Bobby Lee's antics. Each day they did a serious of jumping jacks, push-ups, sit ups, and leg thrusts and each day there was something a particular soldier or two did that riled Drill Sergeant Smith to the point of becoming irate, causing him to implement more punishment. While some of the exercises the soldiers completed were required, the rapid pace and number of the exercises were significantly elevated to a level that brought on extreme exhaustion.

The soldiers were well into their second week of training and, even though the Drill Instructor would never admit it, they were progressing along better than expected. There were plenty of mistakes made; but in

Basic Training, mistakes are anticipated and corrected. Recruit Porky Pig provided Drill Sergeant Smith with a copious supply of soldiering errors. He was particularly unskilled at marching. Drill Sergeant Smith took Porky aside on several occasions for a one-on-one session on how to march. Porky would march on his left foot when right was being called out. He was slow and clumsy. Drill Sergeant Smith grew tired of correcting him and sent him running. He told Porky to call out which foot he was landing on as he ran.

Drill Sergeant Smith noticed that Porky Pig was shedding some weight, but he didn't think it would be enough to help Porky negotiate the Victory Tower exercises slated for the day. Conversely, he thought many of the other soldiers were in good enough shape to do well in the activity. As soon as that thought entered his mind, reality set in as he realized that anything could happen during these exercises - he's seen poor performance on Victory Tower from some of his best recruits in the past. Jimmy thought he was ready to tackle the challenge whatever the outcome.

The trainees stood on the training grounds facing the Drill Instructor. The Company was near the Victory Tower and was in the midst of being briefed on the day's activity.

"Ok, ladies and gentlemen, we are going to learn to conquer the obstacle course that stands before you. This wooden structure has several different components to it. It has a ropes course, ladders, a rappelling wall, and a net that you must climb down in controlled form. Today we are concerned with rappelling down the side of Victory Tower," Drill Sergeant Smith explained.

Jimmy looked to his left and examined the trepidation on the face of a fellow soldier. Jimmy was filled with his own anxiety. He had never done any type of rappelling before but had seen it in movies and on television. It seemed dangerous, but he knew that he could execute the challenge successfully.

"Ok. We are going to do this six at a time. I will divide you into groups. You will be instructed on the harness and proper way to hold the ropes while rappelling," Drill Sergeant Smith said.

Jimmy's name was called to form the first group. It included Porky Pig, Bobby Lee, and three other recruits. They were instructed by another Drill Sergeant on the proper way to complete the exercise. After about an hour, the recruits climbed the ladder to the platform that served as the beginning point for several different exercises, including the rappelling wall.

Porky Pig was the first to be to be picked to go down the wall. He did his best to hide his fear, but it was apparent to the rest that he was nervous.

"I don't...Umm...I mean...I don't know if I can do this," Porky said to Drill Sergeant Smith.

"You need to do this in order to complete basic training. You will do fine. Just take your time," the Instructor said.

"But sir, the harness doesn't fit well; it is squeezing my stomach and legs. I can barely breathe," Porky was near the edge of the platform looking down the rappelling wall.

"You will complete this exercise now. Is that understood soldier?" The Drill Instructor shouted as he turned from being concerned to being adamant.

"Yes...yes sir," Porky said in a low, monotone voice - almost as if he was pouting.

"I can't hear you!" Drill Sergeant Smith shouted even louder. "Are you ready soldier?"

"Sir, yes sir!" Porky shouted back. "I guess I'm as ready as I'll ever be," Porky said.

As he was taught, Porky grabbed the two black ropes and threaded them through the metal loops on the front of his harness. The ropes were taut as they were firmly anchored to the platform. He held the ropes in front of him while he attempted to place his foot on the six by six beam mounted about two feet from the top of the rappelling wall. He was sitting on the edge of the platform and dangling his leg over the side. He was unable to stand up on the beam.

"No, no, that's not how you do it. Grab the rope, back up, and place one leg on the beam and then the other. Make sure the rope is tight and that you have a firm grip on it," The Drill Instructor said.

Porky grabbed the rope and slid backward on the platform. His legs were sticking straight out over the beam. He wasn't feeling for the beam below with his foot.

"Ok, now roll to your side a little bit and put your leg on the beam," The Drill Instructor was growing impatient with the big buffoon.

After several more attempts, recruit Porky was standing on the beam hunched over the side of the rappelling wall onto the platform, and he was in pain as the harness dug into his legs, stomach, and genitals. He pulled the ropes behind his back with his right hand and pulled the rope tight in front of him with his left. He stood up and almost fell backward before flopping back onto his stomach.

"You got it, Porky!" The other recruits encouraged him. "You can do it!" His group said as others in his company below also yelled encouraging words.

Porky stood back up on the ledge with the rope perfectly in place. He was instructed to lean back holding the rope tight as he did. Little by little he inched his way back until his foot rested on the side of the beam. The Drill Instructor told him to begin lowering himself. As he was moving off the beam, Porky's foot slipped. He slid rapidly down several inches before regaining his stance against the wall. He stood there for a few seconds, and then he pushed his large body away from the wall letting a little rope pass through his hands each time he did. The others at the bottom congratulated him for making it.

One by one the other recruits made their way down the wall. Jimmy, Bobby Lee, and two others completed the exercise in a manner that greatly impressed their Drill Sergeant. The last recruit to go nearly broke his leg as he let out too much rope on his final jump. He lay on the ground in pain for several minutes. His ankle swelled and turned black and blue. After being tended to by the Drill Instructor, he was taken to the medical barracks to heal up. He probably would have to be assigned to a different company since it looked serious.

The recruits headed back to the barracks after a long day of training. Several of them were able to make phone calls. Since Jimmy and Bobby Lee did so well on the rappelling wall, they both were allowed to use their cell phone. The Drill Instructor confiscated them earlier, but he gave Jimmy and Bobby Lee their respective cell phone back. Jimmy was finally able to call Janice. He dialed her number and she answered after the second ring.

"Hey baby, how are you?" Jimmy asked.

"Doing well - oh honey, it is so nice to hear your voice." Janice said as she held back tears and a knot welled up in her throat. "How have you been? What are you doing?" She wondered.

"Janice, I am worn out right now. The classes, the challenges, and the exercises - especially the exercises - have me very tired and occupied all the time. We get breaks; meals are really the main breaks and the times we get before bed, like now, are the only occasions I have to rest. How are you?" Jimmy asked.

"I'm fine. I saw your mother two days ago. She said that she misses you and is proud of you. Both your parents are happy that you are doing something you want to do. They want you to do your best, you know, they love you," Janice said.

"Yeah, I need to call them sometime soon and tell her how things are going. How are all our friends in Charlotte? Do they ask about me? Probably not, huh?" Jimmy asked remembering how shallow some his friendships there were.

"Yes, they do ask about you. Marcie thought that it is awesome that you are going the military route. She said that her brother did it too. Ronnie, you remember, crazy Ronnie with the lazy eye, he said that he is joining the military too. It is hard to imagine him defending our country. He probably won't pass the drug test though." Janice said as she yawned a little. "How are you getting along with your other recruits?"

"That sonofabitch Bobby Lee played some pranks on me. We were all punished because of him. Things have settled down between us a little. I still don't trust him though. There is something weird about him. Besides being a huge redneck, he acts sneaky around the barracks. I don't know what it is." Jimmy said as he flipped the pages of a magazine while he lay on his side in his bottom bunk. "What else is going on with you?"

"Well, I start law school at the University of Miami soon. My mom and I are driving down there next week to get me moved into my apartment. I am getting a little nervous. You wouldn't believe how much they expect us to read - before classes even begin! It's ridiculous," Janice said with a hint of anger.

"You'll do fine. So, does that mean you won't be coming to my graduation?" Jimmy asked in a pleading tone.

"I'll try Jimmy, but I can't make any promises. You know I will be busy, especially the first couple of weeks. We'll talk later though, and I'll let you know for sure." Janice said as she sat in her chair at the computer uncertain about the future.

"I really hope that you can come; it would really hurt if you didn't," Jimmy said sitting there in heartache over the possibility that Janice wouldn't witness him graduating after all his hard work.

"I will try," Janice dryly stated.

"Ok. Well, I need to go now. It is getting late, and I have a full day tomorrow.

"Ok, bye honey." Janice said

"Bye, Janice, I love you," Jimmy whispered into the receiver.

"I love you too, babe. Bye." Janice said and the phone went dead.

Jimmy was worried that Janice wouldn't show for his graduation; assuming he made it that far he thought to himself. Her not being there would probably be the end of their relationship. He just couldn't handle the rejection he would feel if Janice wasn't around to witness what all the hard work was for.

Jimmy rolled onto his other side. He was instantly jolted by fear and anger. Standing at the side of Jimmy's bed, immediately next to him, was Bobby Lee gazing down at Jimmy's face.

"What the hell do you want?" Jimmy demanded.

"Ya' is talkin' to ya' girlfriend ain't ya'?" Bobby Lee asked.

"That's none of your damn business, now get out of here!" Jimmy said as he stood up and got an inch from Bobby Lee's face.

"A' right, a'right, It's too late ta be doin' dis stuff here." Bobby Lee muttered in his broken English as he walked back to his bed.

Bobby Lee had a few calls of his own to make.

Chapter 12

BETH

Meanwhile, Beth was occupied and wouldn't have free time until the job was complete. Beth and her team were in a laboratory at the University of Miami's Lois Pope Life Center surrounded in a sea of electronic imaging parts packaged in hermetically sealed plastic. They were putting their scientific minds together in an attempt to create what Beth termed "The Devil's Breath." They decided that the Devil's Breath would use the basic principles of photoacoustic imaging to take an image of the spinal column. Doctor Cornelius said the images would be needed both at the time of use of The Devil's Breath as well as later in their mission.

Photoacoustic imaging requires a laser pulse to be introduced into the body of a subject. Some of the delivered energy is absorbed and converted into heat. The heat causes expansion in the subject that leads to ultrasonic emissions. Ultrasonic transducers detect the ultrasonic emissions or waves to form images.

Beth thought that they could manipulate the laser in such a way that it delivered the necessary pulses for imaging and also be powerful enough to cut through the surrounding tissues and structures to sever the spinal cord. The Devil's Breath also could include a display that would produce an immediate image that the operator would use to guide the laser.

The necessary parts to build this machine were available. They were created on a much smaller scale than conventional, commercial imaging parts. Using these parts to build the laser, it was small and lightweight enough to be easily carried and could be incorporated into a hand held device. The ultrasound transducers and lenses were small as well. The bulk of the machine would be in the processor, the amplifier, the oscilloscope, the display, and the housing unit for the parts.

Beth was impressed, but not surprised, that the government had access to such parts not available to the general public. Eventually, they would make their way into the mainstream, but for now, only the developers and the team assembled in this laboratory knew about them. The parts were previously tested to make sure they worked correctly, but The Devil's Breath would be one of the first projects to incorporate them into an assembled unit for use.

The scientists worked frantically on The Devil's Breath since Dr. Cornelius said the mission was on a tight deadline. He said that everything needed to be in place within two weeks so that the mission could begin.

Beth led the scientists on the creation of a hand-held unit. The scientists were divided into three teams. The first team designed the device using computer-aided technology that resulted in the schematics for the Devil's Breath. The second team would assemble the device using the proper tools and equipment while adhering to a strict standard of sterilization required in handling the delicate components. The third and final team was responsible for testing The Devil's Breath and making any required adjustments before use.

Beth walked over to her meticulous teammate, Dr. Marshall. "Dr. Marshall, how are those schematics coming along. Are they finished yet?" Beth prodded while resting her head on her hand as she leaned over the workstation where several computers sat. She was on the verge of collapsing from lack of sleep. She had no idea that this project would be so demanding.

"I am verifying the last electronic circuits in the laser using the schematic entry tool. It should be all completed in a matter of an hour," Dr. Marshall as well as the rest of the members of the design team had been working for almost five days straight. There were six scientists designing The Devil's Breath, and they would work in shifts of three. Three would work for 12 hours while the other three slept or tended to other business. They did not leave the facility and slept in beds adjoining the laboratory.

Dr. Marshall finished up the schematics, printed them out, and handed them to Beth. Beth took the schematics to Dr. Cornelius for approval. Dr. Cornelius was satisfied with the plans so Beth handed them off to the assembly team. Prior to the schematics reaching their hands, the assembly team prepared their laboratory, which was located in a room beside the design teams, by sanitizing it and carefully unwrapping the parts. They began work immediately.

The parts were carefully joined together with an intricate array of wires, clasps, and miniature screws. The scientists took several hours to attach each part as they worked in teams of two. Gloves, lab coats, hair nets, goggles, and shoe covers were all used to ensure no stray hairs or dust particles made their way into the guts of the machine.

Despite some difficulty in the attachment of the display monitor to the front of the Devil's Breath, the scientists completed the construction of the device in four days, one day ahead of schedule. The fifth day was used to created a plastic mold, shape plastic into a firm outer cover, and attach the cover to several points on the components of the machine.

Beth and the other scientists were 10 days into the life of the Devil's Breath, and what they created was both pleasing to the team as well as a functional unit that would be the backbone to the mission that the CIA had planned. The Devil's Breath was about the size of a small microwave. The top was dome shaped, and the bottom was wide and flat. Hanging from the flat bottom was a pair of handles with a trigger on each handle. The front of the machine was concave with the top of the powerful laser positioned flush with the bottom center of the concave. Four ultrasound transducers were evenly spaced on the outer edge of the ten-inch diameter concave.

The right trigger would be used to activate the laser for the purpose of taking an image of the spine. When the left trigger was also pressed, it would cause the laser to intensify in strength and allow it to cut just deep enough to sever the spinal column. One person could hold the unit, although it was somewhat heavy. The unit was fully self-contained since it had an integrated power supply with long enough life to last for over an hour.

Dr. Cornelius studied the completed Devil's Breath and congratulated Beth and the team. He picked up the unit and held it by the handles. He pulled the triggers but nothing happened, as the unit was not charged yet. He said it was exactly what the CIA needed.

Dr Cornelius asked, "Now that you have this unit assembled, there is only one thing left to find out."

"What's that?" Beth questioned

"Does it work?" Dr. Cornelius asked rhetorically.

"We will soon have that answer for you. We have four days left, and we intend to do a few tests during that time to see if the machine works properly, and we will make any necessary adjustments," Beth replied behind sagging, tired eyes. "I am handing the Devil's Breath off to the team that will test the machine. We should have some preliminary results after a few days."

"Very well then, please proceed," Doctor Cornelius turned and walked out of the laboratory.

"I really hope that this thing works," Beth said in a hushed voice within earshot of the testing team. "My career depends on it."

"There it is," Beth said to another one of her fellow CIA agents who team is responsible for carrying out the next phase of the mission. She led him into the laboratory where the completed device rested on top of a stand made specifically for it. "The Devil's Breath is ready. This machine is a testament to the capabilities of some of the most skilled scientists in the biomedical field. It shows that the government can get things done, contrary to popular opinion. Now, it is up to you and your team to test this masterpiece."

"Is it operational?" Dr. Goldberg asked.

"The device was hooked up to a standard wall outlet for seven hours to allow the battery to fully charge. It can run either while connected to a power source or through its own battery. You can test it using either method or both methods; we prefer both," Beth explained.

"It looks clumsy and unattractive," Dr. Goldberg criticized as he folded his arms across his small chest.

"It's not a fashion model; it's a tool to use for the CIA's mission. It may not be pretty, but as we hope you will discover, it will be effective for separating the spinal cord into two unattached pieces," Beth was a little perturbed that Dr. Goldberg was less than impressed with the machine the scientists worked so hard to create.

"Could you explain how it is supposed to function? I understand the gist of how it works, but now that I have the device in my hands, it will be easier to comprehend what I need to do to work the machine," Dr. Goldberg said as he and Beth walked closer to the Devil's Breath.

Beth grabbed the handles of the device and lifted it from its stand with a good deal of strain. She said, "Ok, it is somewhat heavy, but it will do the job quick enough that you shouldn't have to hold it for more than a couple of minutes. The device has three settings on the top here. It has an image only setting, a laser only setting, and an image AND laser setting," Beth watched to make sure that Dr. Goldberg was following.

She continued, "You want to set the dial to the image AND laser setting out in the field. Notice the two buttons on the handles. The black button on the right sends out a pulsing laser into the body of your subject in order to capture an image. The image detailing the anatomy of the spine will appear on this screen here. As you move the Devil's Breath around while the pulsing laser is streaming into your subject, a corresponding white target mark will move around on the screen, showing you exactly where the laser beam will hit your target. Do you follow me?" Beth questioned.

"Yes, and what about the other button?" Dr. Goldberg asked as he shifted he stance.

"Once you line up the target mark over your subject and position it where you want the separation to occur, you pull this red button on the other handle at the same time you are holding the other black button down.

That will deliver an intensified laser beam capable of cutting through bones and tissues," Beth said enlightening the doctor. "Does that make sense?"

"Yes, yes it does." Dr. Goldberg said as he itched the back of his head.

"Here, let me show you." Beth stated as she turned the Devil's Breath on and set it to image and laser. It made a high pitched whizzing noise that signified the power was flowing through the device.

"Stand back," Beth cautioned Dr. Goldberg as he moved behind her. She aimed the Devil's Breath several feet in front of her on the linoleum floor. She pressed the black button on the right handle and a red laser beam shot out onto the floor. The brightness of the beam changed in intensity as it crackled in front of her. "Notice that there is no image on the display as there are no tissues around to absorb the heat," Beth said.

A small amount of smoke began to rise from the floor as she held the pulsating beam in the same spot for a few seconds.

"It probably shouldn't make the floor smoke. We may need to adjust the intensity of the beam," She suggested. "Now, I am going to grab the red button," she told Dr. Goldberg.

Beth pressed the red button on the left handle, and the Devil's Breath laser beam became brighter and more intense. Beth nearly lost control of the Devil's Breath as the beam shot across the floor. It left two black lines in the shape of an "X" across the floor as it melted the linoleum.

"Yes, I am guessing that we will have to make some adjustments," She said as she shut the Devil's Breath off and placed it back on its stand.

"Well, there is only one way to find out," Dr. Goldberg said. "Our team must test this on live subjects now."

Beth said, somewhat frustrated, "I was afraid of that."

Dr. Goldberg lifted the laboratory phone handset to his ear and called for his team, which was waiting in a nearby conference room after being briefed by Dr. Cornelius. Within minutes, they had joined Dr. Goldberg and Beth in the laboratory.

"Ok team, are we set to test the Devil's Breath?" Dr. Goldberg asked.

"Yes, the laboratory next door has been prepped and is ready for the test subjects," one of the team members said.

"Then, bring in the dogs," Dr. Goldberg said in a serious and urgent tone.

"What? - Wait a second there pal. What do you mean dogs? No one told me that we were going to run these tests on dogs," Beth said in an unbelieving voice as the team disappeared around the corner.

"What did you think we would use? Rats?" Dr. Goldberg nearly laughed at Beth's naivety.

"As a matter of fact, I did," She said pointedly.

"No - No way. They are too small to get accurate results. It was either monkeys or dogs, and since dogs are cheaper and more readily available, we decided on them," Dr. Goldberg said as he forcefully pulled gloves over his hands. "Actually, Dr. Cornelius decided on the dogs as he is the one ultimately calling the shots here."

"This mission just keeps getting worse by the minute. If word of any of this shit ever gets out, we are going to face some serious repercussions," Beth said as she wiped away sweat from her forehead.

"We don't have to worry about that, now do we Beth?" Dr. Goldberg wryly stated as he looked squarely at Beth.

"I suppose not," Beth conceded, "as long as all the security measures are in place and everyone executes their role properly."

"They are Beth, and they will. Trust me; this mission is too important to let some parasites suck this experiment dry. The people working here are the best and the brightest in making sure that our tracks are covered. They are excellent and experienced in what they do," Dr. Goldberg said.

Dogs were barking in the background. Dr. Goldberg's team came around the corner with three dogs. The dogs were roughly the same size as each other. Beth couldn't distinguish what type of dogs they were, but thought she recognized some Black Lab in them. They were probably mutts, she thought.

Dr. Goldberg and his team corralled the dogs into the laboratory. Once there, the dogs were each strapped into harnesses. They were completely immobilized as they stood side by side to one another. One of the team members placed muzzles over the dogs face to prevent any barking or excessive noise.

Beth wheeled the stand holding the Devil's Breath over to Dr. Goldberg.

"Here you are Dr. Death," she said with enough disdain to rattled Dr. Goldberg from his concentration.

"Watch it, Beth; we are all in this together," he said to her as she was walking away.

"Yeah, don't remind me," Beth said as she was about to slide out of the laboratory's door. "I can't watch this," she said and the door closed behind her.

Dr. Goldberg gripped the Devil's Breath and lifted it from the stand. He switched the machine to image only. He pointed the machine at the back of the first dog and pulled the black trigger on the right. It shot out a pulsing laser and the dog whimpered slightly. Within a minute, an image of the dog's spinal column appeared on the screen. Dr. Goldberg moved the Devil's Breath up and down the length of the dog's spine as the little white target on the screen moved as well. He moved the machine from one dog to another, and an image of each one appeared on the monitor. His team took notes.

"This appears to be working well," he said to his team. "Now, prepare yourself for the next phase," he said as the team scrambled around an examination table.

He turned the knob to image and laser. He held the Devil's Breath above the first dog. He pulled the black trigger to get an image.

"Ok," he said, "We are looking for spinal cord separation in the cervical region of subject number one."

He aimed the pulsing laser over the first dog's neck. He pulled the red trigger, and the laser intensified as Dr. Goldberg made a sweeping motion from one side of the dog's neck to the other. The dog yelped and then fell limp in his harness.

"For subject number two, we are attempting a thoracic spinal separation," he said as he again pulled the trigger and swept the laser across the dog's back. The dog howled as smoke rose from the location of laser penetration. It continued to howl for several seconds before silence ensued.

"Test subject number three will have separation in the lumbar area," Dr. Goldberg advised as he swept the laser across the dog's lower back.

All three of the dogs lay motionless in the harness. They were still alive but unconscious from the shock to their system. The team placed each of the dogs on the examination table. One by one, the sites where the laser entered their bodies were checked.

"We have total separation of the spinal cord in each subject. Part of the vertebrae and cartilage are disfigured as well," he told his team. "However, I see that the intensity of the laser is too great since there is damage to the surrounding organs," he said. "We will need to curtail some of the laser's strength."

Beth re-entered the laboratory. She saw the dogs lying on the tables with blood pooling around them.

"Ok, now that you have your tests completed you can tend to saving these dogs," she urgently stated.

"Who said anything about saving them?" Dr. Goldberg asked. "In fact, my team is about to terminate these subjects."

"May god have mercy on your souls," Beth seethed.

Chapter 13

MARGE

The third week in the mental health hospital found Marge in a calm, serene state of mind. There were no attacks on other patients, and the only incident to report occurred at the end of her second week, where Marge threw a lamp against a mirror in her room causing it to shatter. Since then, she has opened up to her therapists and participated in group therapy sessions much to her benefit.

Marge delved into some of the most disturbing issues in her life. She explained how the death of her sister left her with a large rift in her soul. Marge had felt then that she lost her best friend. Her sister was to be in her wedding as the maid of honor if Marge was ever to get married. She also was Marge's confidant whom Marge could turn to in both good and bad times to laugh and cry with over life's twists and turns. She was taken too early, leaving Marge to find other ways to cope. She looked to men to fill the void.

"Tell me about your last relationship," the therapist said.

"Ummm, where do I begin?" Marge wondered. "His name was Paul. He was a pilot; we met while I was at the airport. I was having a Diet Coke at the counter of a small café in the concourse of the airport when he came up beside me to order. He asked me how I was doing, and we eventually exchanged phone numbers. He was a gorgeous man."

"Yes, and how did you feel about the relationship?" the therapist asked.

"It was great at first. He took me to some really nice places. I would never have been able to go to Paris on my teller's salary. He was also a great lover for awhile. Then, he just stopped calling," Marge said.

"So, you didn't have any more contact with him after that?" The therapist asked as he scribbled some notes down.

"Well, he called one more time. He came over to my apartment. He was drunk and in a very angry mood. He raped me." Marge fell silent and placed her face in her hands.

"I'm sorry to hear that Marge. Tell me about how that made you feel." The therapist said as he was now furiously scribbling notes on the pad.

"It is a horrible feeling. I felt used like I didn't mean anything to him. I felt betrayed and lonely. I just wanted to die." Marge said but was too sad to cry.

"Has this affected your other relationships?"

"Yes, I am not able to trust men now. I feel I have to be tough, and some men have called me bitchy or cold." Marge stated while rubbing her thigh muscles. She was very tense and uneasy.

"Ok, Marge, I want you to try to push yourself to be more receptive in your relationships. I'm not saying to let your guard down when it comes to meeting someone, I just want you to realize that some people are here to help you rather than harm you. Give people a chance before you judge them. Does that make sense?" The therapist was getting through to Marge.

"Ok, I will." Marge said.

Marge and the therapist continued for several more minutes before their time was up. Marge felt better after opening up to him. It was helpful that the therapist was a male and that she was able to confide in him. Maybe things aren't as bad as they seem she thought to herself. Marge was in better spirits as the day went on. She returned to the scheduled activities. She even participated in a game of volleyball.

Marge was ready to play the game. Some of the other patients were less enthusiastic and didn't immediately participate when asked to form teams. Marge took the initiative and explained that it would be fun and that the exercise will make them feel better. Eventually, two teams were formed, and the game began.

Marge served the ball to the other team. After the ball made its way over the net several times, a tall, blond girl spiked the ball getting the first point for the team opposite Marge's team. The game progressed and everyone seemed genuinely engaged in playing his or her best. The game was tied at 9 to 9 and it came down to the last point to win. The opposing team served the ball, and one of Marge's teammates hit it back over the net. A stout, freckled girl hit the ball back over the net. Another one of Marge's teammates hit the ball high into the air. It came down over Marge, and she tapped the ball, which made its way back over the net. One of the boys on the opposite team ran for the ball and skimmed it with his fingers. It hit the ground giving Marge's team the final game winning point. The team cheered, and Marge enjoyed the moment; until, someone grabbed Marge's attention.

The team was still cheering as Marge froze in place. Her gaze met his as he walked around the elevated staircase running parallel to the volleyball court. Marge had not seen him before. She figured that he was a newly admitted patient, and he may be a little apprehensive about meeting the other patients. He stood there peering down at Marge with an unflinching, unsettling, unapologetic look. He remained there for about a minute before the psych tech told the patients to return indoors.

Marge shrugged off the uneasiness she felt and returned to the community room for the evening snack. She had a banana and some Diet Pepsi. She and another girl decided to play a board game before they had to return to their rooms for the night. Since Marge was an excellent speller and the other girl had no objection, they played Scrabble. Marge easily won the game leaving the other girl with a sad look on her face.

Marge said, "It's OK sweetheart. We will play another game soon. We can play a game that you like next time."

"I'll probably lose at that too," The small girl said, on the verge of tears.

"It's only a game honey; don't take it so seriously," Marge stated.

"I guess you're right. I will see you later; I'm going to bed now." The girl said as she stormed off.

Marge went to her room. She brushed her teeth and put her long hair into a ponytail. She looked in the small armoire holding her clothes. It was much fuller now since her mother brought her some more things to wear. She looked over at the bed on the opposite side of the room and sighed. Her last roommate was there only a few days before being released. She was a nice girl and was just trying to adjust to some new medication. The staff got her behavior and the medication's side effects under control quickly, and she was released. Marge thought it to be a both good, and at the same time bad, that she didn't have anyone else there. It got lonely at night with no one else to talk with.

Marge lay down in her bed and pulled the covers high. Loud, violent thunder rumbled around her room as heavy rain began pelting her window. Lighting flashed through the sky and brightly flickered in the room. It was difficult for Marge to sleep; but after an hour, she dozed off. Several hours later Marge was startled from her sleep by loud screams coming from the hallway.

"AHHHHH! Get away from me! AHHHHH!"

Someone in the hall was screaming loud enough to wake a dead horse. Marge lay there for a few moments wide awake now.

"AHHHH! AHHHHH! I will kill you all!"

Marge sat up in her bed as a girl in the hall screamed again. Marge could see through the window in the door that the lights in the hallway had been turned back on. Another scream was let out, and Marge could not take it anymore. She got up from her bed, opened the door, and looked in the direction of the screams.

Standing in the hallway was the sickly, crack-head girl that had recently been allowed out of solitary confinement. She was covered in blood and thrashing about aggressively. She had something in her hands that the orderlies were trying to wrestle from her. Marge thought it was a knife. The girl's forearms were cut multiple times. Three orderlies and a nurse eventually subdued the girl. They strapped her to a stretcher and wheeled her down the hall toward the elevator while blood dripped on the institutional-style carpet. They got onto the elevator, and the doors closed. The raucous turned silent.

Marge closed her eyes, folded her arms, and leaned against to the wall next to her door. She slowly beat the back of her head against the wall. "When the hell am I going to get out of here?" She asked herself. "It won't be soon enough." Marge heard something in the hallway beside her and whipped her head to the left.

Standing in the hallway was the guy whom was on the staircase staring at her after the volleyball game. He stood about six feet away from Marge and seemed to be examining her again as he quietly peered at her. He turned around and walked down the hallway away from Marge without saying a word.

Marge sat in the community room staring blankly at the signs hung around the room. Each sign was white, about two feet wide by three feet tall, each had different colored letters, and there were different pictures of the brain on each one. The signs described different mental disorders to anyone who cared to read it. There was one that described bi-polar disease, one for depression, one for anorexia, one for bulimia, and one for neuroses. Marge thought it was weird that the signs were there. She felt they were kind of cheat sheets for the doctors and nurses, or they were a way patients could self-diagnose their disorder easing up the staffs' workload.

While Marge sat there quietly, the weird guy who was staring at her during the volleyball game and in the hall came up behind her. Marge was not aware that he was standing there. She eventually turned her head to the left a bit and saw him out of the corner of her eye. Marge leaped up and gasped in shock.

"What the hell are you doing there?" She demanded.

The guy stood there for a second and didn't speak right away.

"I asked you what the hell are you doing behind me? What do you want?" She nearly yelled at the stranger.

The guy stuck out his hand and confidently said, "Hi, my name is Cody? What is your name?"

Marge looked him up and down without saying a word. She stood there for a few seconds before telling him her name. She didn't shake his hand, but instead, turned a little to her right in a defiant manner and walked a few steps away from him before turning her gaze back towards him.

"You shouldn't sneak up on people like that, you could give someone a heart attack," she said.

"I'm sorry Marge; I didn't mean to frighten you," he said. "I just wanted to say hello to you."

"What are you doing here? I mean, are you a new patient?" Marge asked.

"Yes. Yes Marge, I am," Cody, as he is now known, lied. Sure, he was going through the whole act of being a patient. But he was on a mission.

"What are you in for?" Marge wondered.

"Well, I have been having some suicidal thoughts lately. My girlfriend recently left me, and my father just died. They are watching me to make sure that I don't do anything stupid, like off myself." Cody said convincingly.

"I'm sorry to hear that," Marge said with a hint of attitude. "Most of us here can relate; I assure you." Marge walked over to a table and sat down. Cody followed her.

"So, where are you from?" Cody questioned.

"Look, I really don't want to talk right now," Marge shot back.

"Marge, you are going to be in here for awhile so you might as well make the most of it," Cody explained in as sincere a voice as he could conjure up.

"How do you know that?" Marge said with anger in her voice. There was something about this guy that she did not like and did not trust.

"How do I know what?" Cody said trying to play dumb to cover up his misspoken words.

"How do you know I am going to be here for awhile?" Marge wondered where this guy was coming from.

"Sorry, I just figured that since you were here before I and you haven't left by now, that you were going to be here for awhile. Is that not the case?" Cody quickly corrected his error.

"I really don't know when the hell I am getting out of here. The doctors won't tell me - it is really pissing me off too," Marge said obviously irritated.

"I guess I am in the same boat too. They put me on some strong antidepressants and are watching my reaction. I really don't know when I am going to get out of here either," Cody was trying to relate to Marge as best he could. His goal was to gain her trust.

"I just don't know how long they can hold me here. I was really having some problems earlier but have been feeling better lately, with any luck I'll be out soon," Marge stated.

"Tell me Marge, do you play volleyball often? Since I'm new, I don't know how often they let people outside to get exercise and take in fresh air. Do they do it every day?" Cody prodded.

"You'll learn quickly that you are on a pretty routine schedule here. Every day is nearly the same. We go to the cafeteria for breakfast and lunch, and then meet here in the community room for a snack between lunch and dinner. There is also group therapy in the morning and afternoon exercises. Sometimes you will meet with a social worker and sometimes you will meet with a therapist individually," Marge explained as Cody shook his head in acknowledgement.

"Yes, but is your time outside given every day?" Cody wondered.

"Yes, we go outside to the fenced area every day," Marge said. "Like I said, it's a brutal routine."

"What time do you - I mean, does the group go outside? Cody questioned.

"We go outside after dinner at around seven p.m." Marge stated wondering why Cody was staring so intently at her.

"Perfect." Cody said.

"What do you mean, perfect?" Marge inquired.

"Well I - I mean, I need to get exercise after I eat dinner." Cody stumbled again on his misspoken words.

"Cody, you are a strange guy, if you don't mind me saying."

"I guess we are all kind of strange or we wouldn't be in here, now would we?" Cody shot back after thinking about the nastiness of her comment for a few seconds.

"I suppose so," Marge agreed while trying to tame a wild patch of hair sticking straight up from her head.

"I've got to go. We all have to go to dinner soon. You may want to get ready yourself," Marge advised Cody.

"You go on ahead. I have something to do," Cody said to Marge with an urgent tone.

"Ok. It's chicken night tonight, so you may not want to be late," Marge said as she turned and walked out of the community room towards her room.

Marge didn't know what to think about Cody. She thought he was handsome, but he was a patient just like her. He sounds like he has a lot of baggage. She also thought that her baggage plus his baggage could probably fill up a suitcase store. She concluded that she couldn't date that guy. Plus, Marge's women's intuition was telling her that something wasn't right about him.

Cody went to his room. He managed to sneak a small cell phone in his underwear into the facility. He picked up the phone and dialed a number. The phone rang twice before someone picked up on the other end and said, "Hello?"

"Hello, Dr. Cornelius."

Chapter 14

CARLOS

"Thanks for getting me out of there," Carlos said to Timmy. "Jail is nasty, filthily and filled with the scum of the earth. I rather someone shoots me than throw me back in there."

"Well, you need to be more careful in the future. You never did tell me why you were in jail. What was the charge?" Timmy wondered.

"Let's just say that was the most expensive blow job that I ever tried to get," Carlos said as he looked out the window onto Manhattan's bustling streets.

"Fucking undercover cops?" Timmy asked as he tried not to hit a cab driver that slammed on his brakes several feet in front of him. "Asshole," he screamed as he shot the cabbie the bird "That really sucks. When is your court date?" Timmy questioned.

"I have to go in two months. I guess I'll have to hire an attorney," Carlos lamented. "Hopefully, he can get the charges dropped or, at least, reduced so I don't have to do anymore jail time."

"My friend, Cruiser, may be able to help you out. He handles all types of criminal cases. He may give you a break on the price since he owes me a favor anyhow. Here's his number," Timmy gave him Cruiser's card.

"Thanks, bro. I'll give him a call in the morning. Right now, I need to figure out if I still have a job or not," Carlos wondered as fret rattled his voice.

Timmy dropped Carlos off at his apartment at six o'clock in the afternoon. Carlos tended to a mountain of mail that greeted him at the mailbox. His cell phone was still sitting on the counter where he left it before the police busted in. He had seven voicemail messages with three of them from his boss at the dojo. Carlos figured he really only missed two days of work since he was arrested in the early morning hours of a Saturday, and he didn't work on Saturdays or Sundays. Tomorrow was Wednesday and he would report to work as if nothing had happened.

The next morning at 10 a.m., Carlos dressed in his Gi and walked over to the dojo. He entered the front door as he had a thousand times before and gazed upon several young students practicing various moves. He noticed that his boss and owner of the dojo, Sensei Ishimoto, was not in the main training area. Carlos walked to the back of the room into the staff area. He approached Sensei Ishimoto's office and saw him sitting at his desk with his back toward Carlos.

"Where have you been?" Sensei Ishimoto questioned in a calm and steady voice. He had a thick Japanese accent but purposely formed his words to speak English well enough for others to understand.

"I was sick," Carlos lied. He knew that Sensei Ishimoto would fire him immediately if he knew the real reason for his absence.

"Why didn't you call me?"

"I lost my phone and wasn't well enough to get a replacement," Carlos said.

"That's not like you Carlos. You missed some important practices here. Do you want to keep your job?" Sensei Ishimoto asked with his back still facing Carlos.

"Yes sensei, very much so." Carlos exclaimed.

"You know I could replace you very quickly, especially with the economy in such bad shape. People are lining up to take your job," Sensei Ishimoto threatened.

"It won't happen again sensei, I promise," Carlos said.

"It better not. I count on your honesty and integrity. I need you to do what is right for me, for the dojo, and for the students. Do you understand me?" Sensei Ishimoto asked.

"Yes sensei. I will try harder," Carlos promised.

"You have a class to teach. Go out there and prove yourself worthy of your position."

"Yes sensei, I will," Carlos said.

Carlos walked back into the practice area. Some students were still trickling in through the front doors while others were warming up. Most parents dropped off their child while some of the others accompanied him or her. Carlos had a chance to meet a lot of the parents in a prior class and recognized those that walked into the dojo. The class today was composed of beginners and Carlos would be focusing on the kihon, or fundamentals, of karate.

"Ok children, line up against the mirrors on the back wall and take two steps forward," Carlos instructed as he pointed to a line on the mats where he wanted the children. They scrambled around and made a less than perfect row. "Make sure that you are standing right next to someone," he said.

"Ok, now, we are going to work on our forward thrust punch today. I want each of you to squat down a little and spread your feet apart, kind of like a crab," Carlos said as he demonstrated for the children. "Now, line up your knees with your shoulders. You should look really bow-legged, like this." He demonstrated as the children took on a range of forms, some correct and some not. Carlos pointed to a kid that was in correct position. "Do it like Chris here," he said. Eventually, the children adjusted into the correct position.

As Carlos was instructing the eager students, someone walked through the front door. It was a man of average height who was dressed in pressed slacks and a button down shirt. He wore a brown hat that was pulled down low on his forehead. He removed his sunglasses as he moved towards the opposite side of the room from where Carlos and the students were standing.

Carlos didn't recognize the man. He asked, "Can I help you?"

"No, I'm just here to watch," the man stated as he took a seat on a wooden bench.

"Ok." Carlos replied. He thought the guy was a little odd since he just wanted to watch and didn't ask to speak to anyone regarding the dojo's services. But, it wasn't uncommon for people to come into the dojo to ask about lessons and the cost of sessions.

Carlos continued with instructing the children on the correct form for the thrust punch.

"Ok, get back into your squatting position like before," he told the children as they regained their stance. "I want you to hold out your hands, make a fist, and make sure that your thumbs are pointed outward...like this," Carlos demonstrated. "Now, pull your fists back and place them beside your chest, almost under your armpits. Good. Good," he said. "Now, I want you to take your right hand and jab it forward while you turn your fist over to the other side so the back of your hands are pointing up," he explained. The children jabbed their right fist forward. "Now, jab your right fist forward then your left fist forward one at a time until I say stop. I want you to give me a 'yah' on each thrust," he instructed as the children began the exercise.

Carlos turned and noticed that the man sitting in the bench on the opposite side of the room was staring at him while talking on his cell phone. Carlos couldn't really make out what he was saying since he was speaking almost in a whisper. The only thing that he did hear was, "he's here." Shortly after that, the man hung up the phone and sat.

Carlos tried to ignore him and got back to his teaching. Sensei Ishimoto walked into the training area. He saw the man sitting on the bench and asked if he could help. The guy asked the sensei for any materials that he may have on the dojo or the instructors. He asked about cost, and he asked about Carlos. The sensei answered all of his questions and gave him a pamphlet. The well-dressed man continued to sit on the bench until Carlos finished his class.

The parents began arriving five minutes before the end of class to pick up their child or their children. The majority of the parents were mothers who tended to the family while the fathers worked, though there were several men that came as well. Within 20 minutes, the dojo cleared out and Carlos was alone in the room, with the exception of the man on the bench.

Carlos asked him, "Did you enjoy the class?"

"Yes," the man said, "you are a good instructor."

"Thank you. My name is Carlos by the way, what's yours?"

"I go by...Slade," he said.

"Well, Slade, are you thinking about taking lessons here?" Carlos wondered as he tightened his black belt.

"Yes Carlos, I want to enroll my entire family here. But I need to know more about you and your background. I have been checking other places in the area and want to see if this place is a better fit first," Slade said with a monotone, deep voice.

"What do you want to know?" Carlos wondered and was happy to oblige him. He liked to flaunt his accomplishment when he could. Carlos was proud of his karate training and the awards he earned over the years in competitions and as an instructor.

"I have an important meeting in a few minutes," Slade said impatiently, "Can you meet me tomorrow for lunch?"

"I don't think that will be a problem. I teach a class at 1:30 and will need to be back by then," Carlos stated. "Here's my card. Call me tomorrow around 11 in the morning to confirm. There is a lunch place a few blocks from here that is really good. It's called Lucky Diner. Let's go there."

"Ok. That will be fine. Thanks. I'll call you tomorrow," Slade said as he exited the dojo.

Carlos thought to himself that Slade was a bit weird, but Slade was about to give the dojo a great deal of business. He couldn't lose to the competitors, and this would be his chance to get back into the good graces of Sensei Ishimoto.

"Lucky, here we come," Carlos murmured to himself.

The next morning, Carlos called Slade.

"Hello...may I please speak with Slade?" Carlos asked.

"This is Slade."

"Hello Slade, this is Carlos from the dojo you were at yesterday. You wanted to meet for lunch today, right?

"Yes, yes. Is it 11 already?" Slade asked.

"It is 10 minutes before 11. Are you ready to meet at the Lucky Diner soon?"

"Yes. I need about 15 minutes to get there. I'm leaving now." Slade stated.

"Do you know how to get to there?" Carlos asked as he walked down the street towards Lucky.

"Yes. I am familiar with it." Slade said much to Carlos' surprise since Slade didn't mention that he knew where it was in their prior meeting.

"Well, then, I'll see you there soon." Carlos said as he slowed down his walking pace. There was no need to rush now.

Slade strapped his pistol into its holster on the side of his chest. He pulled a plain black blazer over his shoulders concealing the weapon. He checked to make sure the battery life on his cell phone was adequate; its display indicated a full charge. Slade exited the unmemorable hotel lobby of the Marriott several blocks from the Lucky Diner. He was walking toward the diner when a young man hurriedly pulled out his car from a nearby driveway nearly hitting Slade in the process.

"Watch out asshole!" Slade screamed.

"No you watch out, mother fucker!" the young man shot back.

Slade pulled out a small switchblade he had hidden under his pants leg and jabbed it into the man's car's tire. It quickly deflated. The man jumped out of the car and was irate.

"You are going to have to pay for that you son of a bitch!" he threatened.

"You're going to learn to respect your elders," Slade said as he stood staring down at the diminutive man. Slade grabbed the boy's arm and smashed it hard against the doorjamb. A loud snap echoing off the buildings next to the car could be heard. Slade turned and kept walking as the young man screamed in pain.

Slade walked several more blocks and turned the corner to find the Lucky Diner. Carlos was sitting on a bench at the entrance to the restaurant waiting on him. They greeted each other and had a seat in a booth separate from the other guests. A few moments passed, and they heard the blaring sirens of emergency vehicles pass which neither commented on. The waitress quickly came over to the table.

"What can I get you two hunks to drink?" She asked while holding her order pad in one hand, a pencil in the other, and fiercely chewing a piece of gum.

"I'll have a milk," Carlos requested.

"Coffee for me. Make it black," Slade said.

"Do you two know what you want to eat?" The waitress asked still smacking her gum like a horse. It was a miracle that she hadn't choked on it yet the way she let it clumsily fly around her mouth.

"I know what I want," Carlos said.

"I do too. Go ahead," Slade offered.

"I'll have the char-broiled chicken breast sandwich with vegetables," Carlos said.

"I'll have steak and eggs with a side of French fries," Slade ordered.

"Wow. You must work out all the time to be able to eat like that and not be hugely fat," Carlos said.

"I do," Slade said.

"So, I assume you wanted to meet here today to discuss more about our dojo's karate program," Carlos stated.

"Well, that and I want to know more about you Carlos. I want to know your qualifications as instructor and how you prepare yourself physically for the demands that karate imposes on you," Slade said.

"To tell you the truth, I do work out a lot. It is important to me to be physically fit. Personal trainers that I know have told me that I have a physique that most people work their whole lives to achieve but never quite get. I am not saying that to gloat or anything. It is just to let you know that I strive to be the best. Whether that is to be the best instructor, the best physically, or the best in karate, I work towards perfecting myself and my calling," Carlos stated.

"Ok. That is good. Tell me about a time you were injured, if you ever were, during karate and what you did to overcome it," Slade asked.

"One time in particular comes to mind. I was doing one of my high kicks trying to break a very thick board and my foot hit the board sideways. I thought I had broken it, but it turned out to be a very bad sprain. I could not walk on it for several days since it was swollen and bruised. The doctor said I needed to stay off of it for a week or two, but I couldn't bear that. After two days of sitting, I gradually began applying pressure to it. It healed pretty quickly and I regained full use of it in five days, much faster than the doctor said I would," Carlos said. "Why do you ask?"

"I just want to make sure that I am not dealing with a wimp." Slade stated.

"I'm certainly not that. I'm pretty hardened to what life has to throw at me, both physically and mentally," Carlos said.

"Good. I need someone tough. Someone that can...um...show my children what...um...what it takes to get ahead in life despite some hurdles that they may come across. They need to know that situations are not always going to be pleasant and...well they will need to deal with it in a calm and rational manner. You do understand what I'm talking about don't you Carlos?" Slade questioned.

"Indeed, I do. There have been times when I want to rage against the system, but I realized it isn't in my best interest or would it be beneficial to those around me. Sometimes you just have to go with the flow, if you know what I mean, Slade."

"Yes. That's right," Slade said as the waitress, still chewing her gum, arrived with their food. Slade cut into his steak and took a big bite of it.

Carlos and Slade got around to talking more about the karate program as they finished up their meal. They also talked further about Carlos' training and attributes, which made him a good instructor. Some of the negative things in Carlos' past never came up, such as his problems with alcohol and his recent stint in jail. Slade's focus was on the future and how Carlos intended to shape his. He had no idea that Slade was about to shape it for him.

Slade finished his meal before Carlos. He sat there for a few moments watching Carlos finish up his vegetables, when Slade's phone rang.

"Excuse me Carlos while I take this call," Slade said.

"Sure, I'll be waiting right here," Carlos mumbled with a full mouth of broccoli.

Slade walked to the rear of the restaurant into a hallway that lead to a solid metal door that opened into the parking lot out back. He exited the door, and once in the parking lot, he answered his phone.

"Hello."

"Hello, Slade. Have you gathered more information on our subject?" Dr. Cornelius asked.

"Yes. The CIA has made the right decision," Slade stated.

"The plan shall carry forward as scheduled." Dr. Cornelius said.

"I'll be here, waiting." Slade said as he made his way back into the restaurant.

Chapter 15

BETH AND DR. CORNELIUS

"Alright, alright, already," Dr. Cornelius shouted into his cell phone. "I know you are ready, but we cannot move forward until everyone on your team is on board. I will be in contact with you shortly. For now, standby and see what you can do to stall the situation."

Dr. Cornelius was frustrated, but he remained calm and in control of the mission. He had just briefed the first of his four teams and was about to begin what he termed phase M1. He walked into the room where team M1 was gathered.

"Team M1, we are about to deploy you on your assignment. I just spoke with agent Cody and we have subject M1 ready for capture. Remember, you will need to be swift in your actions, confident in your abilities, and able to deal with the unexpected. We have practiced how the capture should be executed, but it may not be as simple as you think."

"Also remember that we are on a tight deadline. Delivery of subject M1 in usable and stable condition will require the proper implementation of the medical protocols you were trained to administer after the use of the Devil's Breath."

"Team M1 leader are you ready to deploy?" Dr. Cornelius asked.

"Yes, we are ready," a stocky, well-built, middle-aged man named Tad responded. The team members gathered up their belongings including: their guns, sets of black gloves, and black ski masks. Each one was dressed in tight fitting black clothes.

They walked down a long hall past stainless steel doors that were sealed tightly. The team exited the building into a small parking garage that contained an unmarked, large white van. All five members of team M1 pulled themselves into the van. Inside, the Devil's Breath lay neatly against the wall towards the front.

"There it is," the leader of team M1 said to the others, "I will be the first to use this baby. Hope it does the job" He turned the switch to the Devil's Breath on and it hummed to life. "I can't wait." The rest of the team looked on in awe.

The van sped away from the Miami Project's Louis Pope Life Center without anyone noticing it. It took the team to a small commuter plane waiting for them at Miami's airport. There, they loaded the plane and boarded.

The plane had room for medical supplies and a hospital bed needed in their mission. A CIA special operations agent flew it. He would take them to Dallas, Texas where they would carry out phase M1. There would be no record of the flight, no one to guide them through the air, and no one to threaten their experiment.

After a couple of hours, the plane touched down in Dallas without incident, and it quickly found its way into a small, secluded hanger far from the runway. The team gathered their things, removed the Devil's Breath from the airplane to another unmarked van, and hurriedly left the airport. They called agent Cody as they made their way onto the highway.

Chapter 16

MARGE

"Who are you talking to?" Marge asked Cody.

"No one," he said.

Marge was near the front of the community room while Cody was near the rear door. Marge took her attention off of the small pamphlet on domestic abuse she was reading and glared in Cody's direction.

"I've got to go," Cody said into the phone as he hung it up.

"Doesn't sound like you're talking to no one," Marge said.

"Wrong number," Cody said as he continued to fiddle with his phone. Marge could see that he was typing something.

Marge was getting the sense that Cody was up to no good. His actions were becoming more erratic and urgent in the last several hours. She didn't want to be around him and felt more and more threatened by him as time went by.

"Excuse me," Marge said as she walked past Cody out of the community room towards her bedroom. She could see over her shoulder that Cody had followed her out into the hall and was staring at her as she walked into her bedroom.

She got on her hands and knees beside her bed and looked underneath where the mattress lay held in place by a patchwork of metal wires. Lodged between the mattress and wires was a knife with a three inch long blade. Marge managed to sneak the knife in between her butt cheeks. She grabbed it and put it in her waistband and covered it with her shirt.

She walked back out into the wing where others gathered. She put some distance between herself and Cody; Cody still seemed pre-occupied with his phone. Marge's senses were heightened, and the hairs on her arms bristled. She studied the other patients as they milled about the room. One girl was nervously biting her fingernails in the corner. Another patient uttered nonsense to herself as she flicked at her hair. Marge felt anxious and disconcerted.

"Ok, let's all make our way outside to the recreation area," an orderly instructed the patients.

One by one, the motley crew descended the stairwell onto the cold, gray concrete activity area. The patients formed two large groups. One young man from each group took charge. Each group became a team for a volleyball game.

Marge and a few others sat at a picnic table near the volleyball court. Marge was in no mood for a friendly game of volleyball and instead, opted to have a cigarette with one of the other patients. She puffed away the minutes as she observed the others around her. She caught a glimpse of Cody standing at the top of the stairs overlooking the recreation area while using his cell phone.

There was a loud noise from inside the building and the orderlies ran up the stairs to investigate. The group was startled from their game for a few brief moments, but they soon resumed playing.

"What's wrong with you?" one of the other patients asked Marge.

"Nothing," she said.

"Why did you just smoke two cigarettes? You said earlier you don't even smoke," the patient said.

"Mind your own damn business," Marge shouted at her.

"To hell with you - bitch!" the patient said to Marge as she turned her back towards her.

Marge finished up her cigarette and placed her head in her folded arms on the table. She lay there for several minutes until she felt a tap on her shoulder. Marge quickly jerked her head around to see Cody standing over her.

"What do you want?" Marge asked.

"Marge, I have something to show you. Will you please follow me?"

"I don't want to follow you." Marge said.

"Marge, it is very important that you follow me. It involves your sister." Cody lied.

"My dead sister? How do you know about her? Who are you?" Marge said as she stared at Cody in shock.

"I have information about her that you need to know," Cody said.

"Ok. Ok." Marge said as she stood and began walking with Cody away from the volleyball court around to the corner of the building. It is the same area where patients sometimes manage to sneak out of the hole in the nearby fence. As the two approached the opening in the fence, Cody violently grabbed Marge by the arm and began pulling her.

"What the hell are you doing? Let go of me!" Marge screamed as she tried to pull away from Cody. He just gripped her tighter. Marge was able to free one of her arms and went for the knife in her waistband. She pulled it out and made a fast sweep at Cody, cutting his hand. She made another powerful thrust at him, but he was able to slap the knife away from her. The knife fell to the ground, and Cody kicked it away from them. He regained control of both of her arms and forced her closer to the opening in the fence.

In the distance, Marge could see several figures dressed in black running quickly through the woods towards her. They leapt logs and brush as they zigzagged their way down the embankment. They eventually caught up with her and Cody as he forced her through the opening in the fence. Four of the people dressed in black grabbed and subdued Marge on the ground. They held her legs and arms still as she writhed under their control. She screamed in terror, but no one heard her; the others were making too much noise during their game, drowning her out.

The people dressed in black were the CIA agents sent by Dr. Cornelius on their mission, phase M1. As Marge continued to wrestle in an attempt to break free from their control, the CIA agents flipped her over on her back and stuffed her mouth with a balled up rag. The mission leader, Tad, held the Devil's Breath in his hands. He flipped the "On" switch to the device as he held it over her body. It hummed to life. The others looked on in trepidation as the machine balanced in Tad's stable hands.

Tad pulled the trigger to get an image of Marge's spine. A small pulsing laser radiated from the machine, but no image showed up.

"Hold her still!" Tad said. "I can't get an image of her with her moving around like that!"

"She won't stop moving," one of the others shouted.

"Make her stop!" Tad said.

"Ok!" Another agent shouted as he placed one knee on Marge's upper arm and jammed another against her rib cage. Another agent did the same thing on the other side, creating a human vice grip, while the other two agents continued to hold her legs.

Again, Tad pulled the trigger to get an image of her spinal canal.

"Voila! We have an image!" He stated. "We are looking for a T-8 break on the spine."

Tad pulled the second trigger on the Devil's Breath and an intense laser beam shot out from the machine. Smoke rose from Marge's back as he gently guided the laser beam over her spine at level T-8. Marge, with the rag still in her mouth, let out a muffled scream. Then, her body went limp as she lost consciousness.

Chapter 17

CARLOS

The CIA agents waited patiently in the far corner of the parking lot. They were ready with the Devil's Breath and ready to pounce on their subject when he made his appearance. Slade was still sitting with Carlos at the table drawing out the conversation as best he could.

"Come with me Carlos," Slade said as both men stood up from the table.

"Where are we going?" Carlos wondered.

"I need to show you something in the parking lot out back," Slade said.

"Alright," Carlos said as he wondered what Slade could possibly have in the parking lot that would be of interest to him.

Carlos and Slade exited the rear of the restaurant. Within seconds, the CIA agents surrounded them.

"What is this," Carlos asked. "Is this some sort of joke?"

"Shut up and get down on the ground!" One of the agents screamed at him.

"I will not, you can't do this to me!" Carlos screamed back.

One of the agents approached Carlos and tried to grab his arm. Carlos grabbed the agent's hand and spun him around. He forced his elbow into the agent's forearm causing it to snap. The agent screamed in pain as he nearly fell over.

"You're going to pay for that you little shit." One of the other agents shouted as he lunged towards Carlos.

Carlos tried to run, but a third agent clothes lined him with his arm bringing him to the ground. He tried to get up but was forced back to the ground with a knee. Three of the agents grabbed Carlos's arms and legs and drug him to the van. There, he was forced into the back where he was tied down with thick leather straps.

The Devil's Breath was activated and used on Carlos. An agent severed his spine at level T-9. Within seconds of the severance, the agents began the necessary medical protocols to preserve the life of the nerve cells surrounding the cut area.

"Hand me that vial," a dark-haired, male agent said to one of the female agents as he pointed to a large cylinder resting on a small cart sitting against the wall of the van.

"What is it?" The female agent asked.

"It's going to mitigate some of the damage that the Devil's Breath inflicted to the surrounding tissues," the male agent said as he grabbed the vial from her.

"What's it called?" She wondered.

"Methyprednisolone," he said.

"Methy - what?" the female agent asked.

"Methyprednisolone," he said.

The Methylprednisolone, which is a steroid, was administered through an IV drip connected to Carlos. Its effect will improve sensory and motor recovery following the separation of the spinal column. It needed to be administered within a very short time from the severance to have any effect on Carlos's recovery.

Next, Brilliant Blue G (BBG), a dye that is used to color food as well as to visualize transparent tissues in eye surgery was introduced through the IV drip as well. This has the effect of dramatically reducing secondary damage following the spinal cord's dissection. Other scientists working for the government had tested the dye on rats whose spines were severely injured or cut apart, and within days, they were walking again. There was no guarantee that the compound would work on humans, but this experiment would give Dr. Cornelius the data that he needed.

A catheter was inserted into Carlo's Vena Cava. An ice-cold solution was introduced to cool a metallic portion of the catheter, which would, in turn, cool the core temperature in Carlos's body. Ice packs were also used to bring his temperature down to around 33 degrees Fahrenheit. This also had the effect of preventing cellular tissue death.

At the same time the agents were inoculating Carlos with drugs that would preserve the nerve tissues surrounding his spine, a couple of the other agents also stabilized his vital signs. The van was large enough to accommodate a stretcher and other medical equipment necessary for the medical protocols to be carried out.

"Alright, let's do this," the dark-haired male agent said to the others as he walked to the front of the van to take the driver's seat. He nearly tripped on some of the wires and tubes hooked to Carlos's body.

"Wait, I think we may be in trouble," the female agent, sitting in the passenger seat, said to the dark-haired male agent.

"What do you mean?" he asked.

"The check engine light is on," she said. "Try to start it."

The dark-haired agent turned the key in the ignition and nothing happened.

"This can't happen, not now," he said in disbelief. "Shit!"

"Shit is right, someone is walking towards us!" the female agent screamed.

Panic filled the van. At the same time, Carlos began moaning.

"Inject him to put him back to sleep," the dark-haired agent shouted to a different, gaunt looking agent sitting in the back. The gaunt agent grabbed a syringe filled with Versed and nearly slammed it into Carlos's arm. Carlos shrieked in pain before falling back into a coma-like state.

"Crank it! Crank it!" the female agent said. After several more attempts, the van sputtered to life. "Floor it!"

The van sped away as the onlooker ran towards it. He picked up a rock and threw it at the van. The darkly tinted back window shattered loudly and glass sprayed the floor in the back of the van.

"Damn, that was too close," the dark-haired agent driving the van said as he sighed in relief. The van was cruising down the highway towards Teterboro Airport on the other side of the Lincoln Tunnel in New Jersey.

Chapter 18

MARIE AND CANDICE

"Another Friday night and I have no date," Candice said in disgust.

"I would say that I feel bad for you, honey, but that would be like a lemon telling another lemon that he is sorry that the other one is yellow - I'm in the same predicament," Marie said with the same sadness and resignation in her voice.

"So, are we just going to sit here and feel sorry for ourselves or what?" Candice was always up for a night out. She wasn't a sit-in-front-of-the-TV kind of person.

"Ahhh god, I don't know. It probably isn't a good idea after just having my wallet stolen by that asshole. I don't know if I'm ready to deal with men right now," Marie stated.

"You know, you could keep your legs closed for the night," Candice shot at Marie.

"Oh you're one to talk. You're like a landing strip at JFK. I'm waiting for them to install runway lights on your thighs," Marie fired back. Both girls broke out in chuckles.

"Let's be discriminating tonight. We will only allow ourselves two drinks, and we will not talk to anyone that doesn't just dazzle us," Candice suggested.

"Ok. Also, we are not allowed to go home with anyone. If someone is interested in us, we learn more about them, and they must learn more about us by taking us on a date," Marie said as she walked into her room and prepared to take a shower.

"Where do you want to go?" Marie shouted from her bedroom.

"How about that new dance club, The Leopard," Marie suggested. "I have heard a lot of great things about it from my work friend, Ginger."

"That place is expensive though, isn't it?" Marie was concerned as payday wasn't until next Friday.

"There might be a $10 cover, but remember, we are on a two drink maximum," Candice reminded Marie.

"I guess you are right," Marie shouted as she removed her clothes. "We can walk there right?"

"It is a little far. We should take an Uber there," Candice suggested.

"Ok. I'll be ready in a little bit," Marie said as she walked into the bathroom to get into the shower. Candice went to her bedroom and prepared herself for the evening as well.

After nearly an hour the girls exited their condo and left the building through the modernly decorated lobby. They noticed an attractive man sitting in one of the chairs close to the elevators. He was dressed in an ultra chic looking, form-fitting, gray suit. His medium length black hair was slicked back to give him the appearance of a mobster.

Candice and Marie walked a block to the busy intersection where it would be easier to catch a cab. After a minute or two, the Uber pulled over to the side of the road and let the two beautiful women into the back. Marie pulled the door shut and peered out of the window before the Uber pulled off. Marie noticed that the nice-looking man from the lobby was walking up the street to the corner where Marie and Candice were just standing. As the taxi drove off, Marie saw the man waving his hand for a taxi of his own. Candice was busy talking with the taxi driver.

About ten minutes later the girls arrived at The Leopard. They could see from the cab that a line had formed outside as people waited to be let into the large club. Being the new hot spot in town, it attracted all types. There were some big names in hip-hop music in attendance as well as some local celebrities. Everyone was dressed to make an impression of elegance and high fashion. The club was a luxurious testament to excess, and it was every bit as pretentious as some of the clubs you would find in Los Angeles.

The girls waited in line for four minutes before they caught the eye of the bouncer. He ogled them briefly before waving them to the front of the line. After a little bit of flirting, the bouncer lifted the velvet rope to allow Candice and Marie to pass. They walked to the large wooden door, and Candice opened it. Smoke, music, and lights hurled towards them and engulfed the girls as they were beaconed into the main lounge area. They gracefully made their way to the long oak bar and took a seat on a stool next to several other revelers.

Outside, a yellow taxicab pulled up to the curb. The man inside pulled out his wallet and paid the driver without giving him a tip. It was the guy Candice and Marie saw sitting in the lobby of their condo building. He walked up to the line, which he judged was 40 deep and lit a cigarette. He would have to wait just like the other men and less attractive women.

"I'll have a gin and tonic with three limes, please," Candice said to the cute bartender, "But don't make it too strong."

"I'll have the same thing," Marie said.

"Oh, are you trying something different tonight?" Candice wondered.

"No, I like gin and tonics too. I know the three limes is your thing, but it was easier to tell him the same thing rather than tell him the same thing with one lime only. It's too loud in here to explain that," Marie said as the bartender poured their drinks and handed them over. Candice opened a tab with the bartender. The girls took a tour of the posh environment.

"Wow. This is really nice; I think this lounge is awesome. I love these white, leather couches they have," Marie nearly shouted as they walked a little further into the club.

"Would you look at that dance floor? It is huge! You could get a 1000 people on it," Candice was excited about her newfound hangout. "Look. There is an upstairs," Candice said as they walked towards the steps. They walked up and found a secluded area with large, comfortable chairs.

"You can see the whole dance floor from up here," Marie said.

"Holy shit, is that Kanye West sitting on that couch beside us?" Candice shouted into Marie's ear fighting to be louder than the music.

"Oh my god, I think it is. Look at those girls around him; they look like whores!" Marie said. "I wonder if he is dating one of them or if they are just trying to get him to have sex with them."

"He is married. I wonder what Kim would think." Candice said. "She wouldn't know and probably wouldn't care since he spends all his money on her," Marie said. "Damn, this place is sizzling it's so hot?" Marie said.

"What, do you mean hot as in warm or hot as in amazing?" Candice asked.

"Hot as in amazing, stupid!" Marie shouted.

The man from the girls' lobby finally made his way through the door. He went to the bar and ordered a beer. He wasted no time in trying to locate the girls. He walked through the lounge, but did not see them. Several women noticed him as he passed. He noticed them but did not stop. Eventually, he made his way upstairs and saw the girls sitting in the chairs and approached them. As he did, one of the women sitting near Kanye West accidentally tripped him. He stumbled a bit and lost hold of his beer in the process. It slipped from his hand and landed right in the lap of Kanye.

"What the hell are you doing, man?" Kanye said. "I should beat your white ass right now!"

"Sorry, bro, It was an accident," The guy said.

"Bro, who are you calling bro?" Kanye said extremely irritated.

"Sorry, I didn't mean anything by it, I just slipped," he said.

"Man, get out of here before I whip yo' ass," Kayne threatened.

He gained his composure and walked over to the girls who had already taken notice of him. He introduced himself as Scott. He said that he noticed them in the lobby. He asked them what they were doing afterwards and mentioned that there was a party downtown to which they were invited. After a few more minutes of conversation, he excused himself to the restroom. He told Candice and Marie he would be right back.

He walked through the crowded lounge and into the men's room. The music was still loud in the bathroom but not so loud that he couldn't be heard. He waited for a stall to open. Two men exited one of the stalls. He noticed that they had white powder under their noses and were brushing it away. They also were sniffing excitedly. He walked into the stall and locked the door behind him. Scott reached into his pocket and pulled out his cell phone. He was somewhat nervous and the sweat from his hand caused him to lose grip of the phone. It splashed into the toilet.

Scott cursed himself and looked around before he frantically reached his hand into the toilet. He found the cell phone through toilet paper and urine. He wiped the cell phone off with dry toilet paper hanging nearby. He pressed the button to make the phone turn on, and the display was blank. Fuck, he said to himself. He tried it one more time and the display eventually appeared. He pressed the buttons and nothing happened.

Luckily the number he needed was burned into his memory. Its owner made sure of that. He thought about leaving the club to use a payphone, but didn't want to wait in that line again; he thought there wouldn't be a payphone near the club anyway.

He asked someone in the restroom if he could use his cell phone. "Hell no," was the response he got. He asked another guy who also declined his request. Scott had no other option. He waited for a few minutes until the crowd in the bathroom dwindled down to just two people. Then, against his better judgment, he pulled out his badge.

"CIA, I need to use your cell phone now!" He said to a young black man standing nearby. The other guy in the bathroom quickly ran out and continued running until he was four blocks from the club.

Scott had blown his cover. He stood in front of the young man and dialed the number.

"Dr. Cornelius, Marie and Candice are here at the Leopard Nightclub in downtown Atlanta," Scott said in as much of a subdued manner as he could given the circumstances.

"Good, we'll implement the plan shortly," Dr. Cornelius said almost inaudibly.

"I'll be waiting," Scott said, handing the phone back to the young man.

Scott rejoined Marie and Candice who were still sitting in their overly comfortable chairs. He asked if they would like a drink, and they accepted his offer. He went to the bar for several minutes and returned with vodka and tonic with three limes for Candice, and vodka and tonic with one lime for Marie. The three chatted a bit about their lives and talked about what they were getting into for the week.

The threesome eventually made their way downstairs where they saw the dance floor filling up with people. Marie and Candice felt the bass from the speakers pulsate through their bodies. The beat was irresistible as it lured them into swaying back and forth with their arms raised in the air. They were ready to let loose on the dance floor. Marie ventured out from the side into the center of the floor. Colorful lights flashed bright across her body as she let her hair drape her face, which was pointed towards the floor. Candice was close behind also feeling the electronic dance music radiating through her body. They both were big fans of DJ Paul Oakenfold who was spinning in the club that night.

Scott also made his way into the center of the dance floor where the other two were. He danced as best he could but could tell from the stares and finger pointing from onlookers that he needed some lessons on how to shake it. The girls found it to be cute. He danced awhile longer, but he was quickly startled from his shuffle when he saw someone pressing himself against Marie. He gazed at them wondering how to handle the situation. "I can't let him interfere with our mission," he thought to himself. Eventually, he made his way over to the tall, muscular, young thug grinding on Marie.

"Excuse me, she is with me," he said while nearly being drowned out by the music.

"Say what?" The threatening man said to Scott.

"You heard me; I said she is with me."

"She's dancing with me punk, step off," He said as he nudged Scott on the shoulder.

"Marie, come on, let's get another drink," Scott said.

"But, I'm dancing," Marie said.

Candice walked closer to see what was going on.

"What are you trying to do? She wants to dance," Candice said.

"I want to chat with you two some more. Plus, that guy is bad news. See that sticking out of his back pocket?" Scott said pointing to the man's backside.

"Yea, what is it?" Candice asked

"It's a gun handle. This guy is dangerous." Scott said

"Your right," Candice said as she walked over and grabbed Marie.

"Let's go," Candice said to Marie.

"But, I-"

"Let's go now," Candice said as she yanked on Marie.

"Damn haters," the young thug said as he threw his hands in the air as the girls walked with Scott off the dance floor.

The three of them walked to the lounge area and sat on one of the white leather couches.

"Why did you pull me away from him?" Marie asked.

"That fool has a gun," Candice said.

"Oh my God! Maybe we should tell someone about him," Marie said.

Candice and Marie walked over to the bouncer and reported the guy. Moments later, the bouncers threw the thug out on the street with his gun still in his pants.

"I can't believe that guy would bring a gun in here," Marie said to Candice.

Scott gently felt the butt of his own gun to make sure it wasn't exposed from underneath his blazer.

"I'll be right back," Scott said.

He walked over to the bar and ordered another round of drinks and two shots for the girls. He quickly paid the bartender and returned to the girls while holding the drinks.

"Here you are sweetie," Scott said to Marie as he handed her drink and one of the shots. He handed a drink and a shot to Candice as well.

Candice turned her head to look at Marie who was sitting beside her on the couch.

"I thought we were only going to have two drinks," Candice said.

"Well, that was before we met this generous man," Marie said as she bent her head closer to Candice's ear. "I think he is hot too. Let's do a three way," Marie said.

"Girl, you are crazy," Candice said.

"Damn right, one more drink and you'll really see how crazy I get," Marie said as she nibbled one of Candice's earlobes.

"Wow, that's hot," Scott said as he nearly salivated. "What do you say we go back to my place for a few more cocktails?"

"Sounds good to me," Marie said

"Me too," Candice said.

"Wait here, I have to close my tab." Scott said as he got up to walk to the bar.

"I can't believe we are going to do this." Marie said to Candice.

"We're young. You only live once you know." Candice said.

"I suppose so, I'm ready," Marie said. Her speech was becoming a little more slurred as the alcohol took effect. The same was true for Candice too.

Scott made his way back to the couch.

"You girls ready?" He asked.

"Ready, willing, and able," Marie said.

"Let's go then," Scott said.

The girls started to walk towards the front exit to the building.

"Wait, let's go out this way," Scott said pointing in the opposite direction. "It will be faster."

"Ok," Candice said. All three walked towards the rear of the bar and exited out the back door. The door opened into a full parking lot. There weren't a lot of lights around making it difficult for Marie and Candice to see too far in front of them, especially since they had been drinking. There weren't a lot of people around either. Most everyone was in the club.

"Follow me," Scott said as he walked into the parking lot.

"Where are we going?" Candice asked.

"We can catch a cab easier if we cross the parking lot to the street over there," he said pointing to a street neither one of them could see.

"Well, alright." Candice said as they followed Scott into the parking lot. The three of them walked about a quarter of a mile. They came up to an alleyway that was blocked by two large, green dumpsters.

"Now where?" Marie asked.

"Follow me behind the dumpsters. There is an alley we can take up to the street," Scott said.

"Ok." Marie said to Scott. Scott was several yards in front of the girls. Marie leaned into Candice and whispered in her ear. "I'm not too sure about this, it seems a little sketchy."

"Don't worry about it, we'll be fine," Candice said to her.

Scott disappeared behind the dumpsters. Marie went to the right of one of the dumpsters with Candice immediately behind her. She had to turn sideways to get between the dumpster and the wall of the adjacent building. Marie placed her hand on Candice's shoulder as she passed through. They made it about halfway.

Suddenly, Candice felt a tug at her leg. Someone or something grabbed Marie's hand. The girls were thrown to the ground in the dark alley. They tried to scream but someone quickly shoved a gag into their mouths, which muffled their cries. Marie began kicking at one of the shadowy figures holding her down with all the force she could muster and was successful in causing him to lose his balance and stumble backwards. He quickly regained his composure and hit Marie in the side of her ribcage with a forceful blow knocking the air out of her.

"Hold them still!" A large man shouted from behind his black ski mask. "I can't get an accurate picture unless you dumbasses hold them still!"

One of the masked men tied Marie and Candice's arms and legs together and laid them on their fronts. Several of the other masked men held them still while the Devil's Breath was readied for use. Within several minutes, Marie had a spinal column separation at level T-8 and Marie had a spinal separation at level T-9. Their unconscious bodies were quickly loaded into separate unmarked white vans large enough to accommodate medical equipment and a stretcher. The CIA's Mission's Phase M2 and C1 were nearly complete.

The vans were ready to pull out to go back to the airport where they would load their subjects into planes to fly back to Miami. There was a small problem that kept them from doing so. The thug that was tossed out of the club for having a gun was standing beside one of the vans with his gun drawn, pointing it at one of the masked agents.

"Yea, that's right. I followed you back here. I was following those fine girls you got up in them vans. What the hell are you doing with them?" The thug asked.

"Please put your weapon away. This matter does not concern you. Please be on your way," the agent said to the thug.

"Man, you got some nerve. I ought to bust a cap in yo' ass right now, you damn bitch." The thug said.

"That's not necessary. Please be on your way." The agent said with all seriousness.

"I'm not going anywhere until you let them girls out of the van." The thug said all the while pointing the gun at the agent.

"Sir, this does not concern you, please leave," the agent said.

The thug fell backwards against the wall as blood sprayed from his head. His body fell limp to the ground as life left his body.

"Now that he is taken care of, please get into the van," another agent said as he took the silencer off of his .45 and put it back into its holster.

"Never send a boy to do a man's job." The agent said as he got into the van.

"Thanks, I owe you one," the other agent said as the vans departed for the airport.

Chapter 19

JIMMY

Jimmy lay in his bed staring up at the lights that had just been flicked on. Not again, he thought to himself. The Drill Instructor commanded that the company get ready for the day.

The razor ate at Jimmy's face as he sluggishly drug it up his neck through the thick foam of the shaving cream. His eyes burned red in the institutional florescent lighting as last night's dreams became the day's harsh realities. He dabbed toothpaste onto the mangled bristles of his toothbrush and slowly scoured away the unfortunate accumulation of bacteria that hoped to lay claim to his mouth. Once he made himself presentable, it was off to do daily PT.

At this point in Basic, physical training was becoming pretty mundane Jimmy thought. The exercises were invigorating, but they were repetitive and just plain boring. He wished to do something different in his quest to develop the perfect body, but he was, as always while in Basic, at the mercy of the superior officers and the rigid guidelines set by the Army. He hoped that he would be able to join a gym someday, but he thought it wouldn't be anytime soon.

Once the workout and breakfast were over with, it was time for the real training to begin. Today, it was time to brave the gas chamber. Every recruit had heard the horror stories about the gas chamber, and it was now time to stare down those rumors and handle the challenge as a soldier. Each was determined to lay their fears to rest and come out victorious.

The recruits were each issued a gas mask and instructed on its proper fit and use. Once the masks were secured to their faces in an acceptable manner, the recruits lined up in single file in front of the gas chamber. Their fate was now left in the hands of Drill Sergeant Smith.

"Are you motivated?" Drill Sergeant Smith shouted.

"Yes, we are motivated, huh...huh. We are ready to kill someone...uhhhhhhhh," they shouted in uniform fashion. Everyone clapped as they entered the gas chamber through an unmarked metal door. The energy in the room was electrifying as the recruits braved the unknown with enthusiasm and bravado. Once in the room the Drill Instructor ordered an about face and the recruits turned and stood with the gas chamber wall to their immediate right and each was directly behind another recruit.

126

"All right, when I tell you, I want you to lift your masks with your right hand high into the air, and I want you to place your left hand on the shoulder of the person in front of you. Is that understood?"

"Sir, yes sir!" They shouted in unison.

"Who leads the way?" The Drill Instructor demanded.

"Bravo!"

"Who leads the way?"

"Bravo!" The recruits said with voices muffled through their masks.

"Remove your masks!" The Drill Instructor commanded.

"Who leads the way?"

"Bravo!"

Within a few seconds, the chamber filled with short coughs. Only a few soldiers began coughing at first and after a few more seconds, the entire company was coughing. All the while, the Drill Instructor shouted.

"Who leads the way?"

"Bravo," was the reply for those whose airways weren't completely constricted from the burning irritant. Some of the recruits began hacking up ropy columns of mucous and phlegm. After about a minute, they exited the gas chamber with burning eyes and lungs. Instructors on the other side told the recruits to flap their arms to get fresh air into their lungs. Two of the recruits lost composure and threw up. Jimmy was one of the two.

"You a'right boy?" Bobby Lee asked Jimmy as Jimmy was leaning on his knees.

"No. Not really. That shit burns!" Jimmy said.

"Yea it do. Real good. I couldn't stop coughin a'tall," Bobby Lee said in an almost conciliatory way.

"What do you care? Why are you bothering me?" Jimmy asked with the suspicion oozing from his mouth.

"Now, Now. We are brothas here. We need to be puttin' our differences to da side. We are goin' ta be soldiers soon. Don't let what did happen in da past get in da way. Trust me, Jimmy," Bobby Lee stated.

"Bobby Lee, you are a rat bastard," Jimmy said as he was hunched over with drool still spilling from his mouth, "But I know you are right. That doesn't mean that I have to trust you though or even be your friend. Let's just make it through this without any more trouble. Can we agree on that?" Jimmy asked.

"I 'spose so," Bobby Lee stated as Drill Sergeant Smith approached.

"You two boys aren't causing trouble, are you?" Drill Sergeant Smith asked.

"No sir. Not dis time. I was jest helpin' Jimmy here. He had no good time in dat thar gas chamber. He getting sicker den all of da others," Bobby Lee said.

"You ok Jimmy?" Drill Sergeant Smith asked.

Jimmy coughed up a little more phlegm. He said, "Yes sir. I am getting better. Just give me another minute and I will join the rest of you."

"Alright then." Drill Sergeant Smith said as he walked off.

"Get up. Come on boy. Stand up and shake off yo' gas funk. You wouldn't want for Janice to be seein' what I am seein' now would you. Wit you all hunkered over an dat pukin'. She wouldn't like dat one little bit," Bobby Lee taunted Jimmy.

"How do you know about Janice? You were listening to my conversations weren't you? You son of a bitch!" Jimmy shouted in disbelief.

"Well, shit." Bobby Lee said as he tried to think how he was going to patch over this misspeak. "I was standin' right where you saw'd me. You know I was standin' thar. I heard you sayin' high to yo' girlfriend. It's no secret is it?"

"You just mind your own business and stay out of mine," Jimmy said.

"Ok. Ok. I didn't mean nothin' by it," Bobby Lee said as he held out his hand, "Here, pull yo'self out of dis slump here. I want ta help you."

"I can handle this myself," Jimmy stated as he regained his composure and stood.

"Last one back to da group is getting' no kind of vittles for dinner tonight! You best hurry yo'self," Bobby Lee said as he sprinted back to be with the others. Jimmy walked back to where the group was standing. He made it just in time to hear the Drill Instructor give a recap of the exercise.

"Congratulations to you all for making it through the gas chamber challenge. Let what happened in there be a reminder to you that you may one day come across a situation where you will need to use your gas mask for survival. There are many chemicals that cause severe damage to the body, and they can even cause death. Remember how to wear the gas mask; it may save your life one day."

"I don't feel so good. I am kind of dizzy," Jimmy said to Porky Pig who had asked him if he was alright.

"We'll get you some help. Wait here," Pork Pig said as he ran up to a nearby Drill Sergeant. It was too late though; Jimmy collapsed.

Jimmy remained unconscious for several minutes. He woke up to see Bobby Lee hovering over him with the Drill Instructor nearby.

"Come on Jimmy, we need you," Bobby Lee said without even a hint of an accent.

Jimmy woke up to find himself lying on a bench near the gas chamber. Several medical technicians were administering oxygen to him. He had been out cold for nearly ten minutes. Drill Sergeant Smith made the decision not to have Jimmy transported to the medical barracks on the account that he had seen other soldiers fall out after a round with the gas chamber. He knew that he would recover, especially since the medical technicians knew how to handle such a situation.

"I feel like shit," Jimmy said as he lifted the oxygen mask off of his nose and mouth. He rubbed his eyes as they still burned.

"Do you think you need to go to the medical barracks for additional treatment?" One off the medical technicians asked him.

"No. No. Just let me sit here for awhile. I'll be alright." Jimmy said.

"Ok. But if you start to feel any worse, let us know." One of the technicians said.

"I will," Jimmy said.

Jimmy sat on the bench for several more minutes. The others were taking a break under a nearby shaded area adjacent to the gas chamber. They sat there until it was time to go back to the barracks. Jimmy made a full recovery several hours later and was able to return to the routine of the day without any complications.

Later that night, Jimmy had time to himself prior to lights out. He used the time to call Janice on his cell phone.

"Hi Janice. I miss you. How are you? It's been awhile since we talked," Jimmy said.

"I'm ok, but stressed as hell. I'm trying to make this damn outline for one of my classes - Elements of Law - since the instructors suggest it. It's ridiculous though. My outline is already 25 pages long and it's only the first week!"

"Wow, that sounds like overkill Janice - they couldn't really expect you to do all that, especially for every class. You need to pace yourself or you are going to get burned out quick," Jimmy said.

"I'm already burnt out Jimmy," Janice said nearly crying.

"Hang in there, baby, you'll get through it, then you will be one of those rich lawyers once you get out," Jimmy said trying to quell her nerves.

"Yea, one of those greasy, ambulance chasers is more like it," Janice said.

"Some of those injured people really need the help to get justice. Insurance companies don't want to pay for anything. Insurance companies are a racket and need to have their asses sued," Jimmy said.

"Your right Jimmy," Janice said.

"So, my graduation is nearing, are you going to be able to come?" Jimmy wondered.

"Jimmy, I'm so sorry. I don't think so," Janice said.

"Ouch, that hurts," Jimmy said.

"It's just I can't afford to take the time off from this stuff since it is so early in the semester, and I have a lot to learn," Janice said. "Jimmy...really...I - well, I-"

"What is it Janice?" Jimmy asked.

"Well - I really think that we need to take a break from each other." Janice said with a lump in her throat.

"What? What are you talking about?" Jimmy asked sitting on the edge of his bed, listening intently to what was being said to him. The other recruits clamored about the room without any regard to Jimmy's conversation.

"It's just that I need the time to concentrate on my studies and I don't want to lead you on. I just can't dedicate the time to you that you deserve. Plus, you are going to be stationed somewhere after your basic training is over. We may never see each other again," Janice said.

"Damn it Janice! How could you do this to me? I need you and you are just going to abandon me? Fine. I don't want to see you ever again!" Jimmy shouted as he hung up the phone. After his initial anger subsided, he wondered if he went too far by ending it so abruptly. He knew that she was right though, and it would be difficult for them to maintain a relationship while he was committed to the Army.

The next day came too early. Jimmy was heartbroken and could barely drag himself out of bed. He wondered what the hell was going on with his life and if he should just leave the Army to try to be with Janice in Miami. He was strong though and knew he was doing what is right for his life and for his future.

Jimmy's Company joined others on the parade ground for morning PT. It was still dark outside and the air was a little brisk due to the breeze. Jimmy begrudgingly performed the exercises and was really getting tired of them, the army, women, and himself. He nearly quit, but fought the urge.

As he performed his exercises, Jimmy saw Bobby Lee run behind a storage facility several hundred feet away. Drill Sergeant Smith had been called to the barracks to aid in discharging a Sergeant and a GI being released from the Army due to their having a sexual relationship with one another. The soldier left in charge was a dim-witted guy who couldn't care less if the other soldiers did the exercises or just sat around talking. He stopped the exercises several times himself to chat for a while.

The back of the storage facility butted up against a gate that was unlocked while soldiers were on the parade grounds. The gate opened onto worn pathways that lead to a garage housing several Army vehicles. The path eventually turned into a street that funneled out onto a nearby highway.

Bobby Lee poked his body out from around the corner just enough for Jimmy to see it. He motioned for Jimmy to come join him behind the building. Jimmy had no idea what he could possibly want, and he shook his head no. Bobby Lee held his cupped hands in the air in front of his chest and twisted them as if he was feeling a woman's breasts. Jimmy, in his newly single state, was intrigued by what Bobby Lee was doing.

The soldier leading the exercises was talking to another soldier and had his back turned to Jimmy and the others. Jimmy briskly jogged over to join Bobby Lee behind the storage building. As he rounded the corner, someone smashed Jimmy in the head with a blunt wooden object. Jimmy was knocked out cold.

Bobby Lee stood over Jimmy looking down at his motionless face and without so much as a hint of an accent said,

"You don't fuck with the CIA, asshole."

Bobby Lee and several other agents dragged Jimmy through the gate. A large unmarked military vehicle waited for them on the other side. Jimmy was quickly loaded in, paralyzed, subjected to the same initial medical treatments to preserve nerve tissues as the others, and quickly taken to a nearby airport.

They arrived at the airport, and just like team M1, C1, C2, and M2, had done with Marge, Carlos, Candice, and Marie, team J1 loaded Jimmy onto a small plane. Destination: Miami.

Chapter 20

THE MEET UP

"I can't deal with this right now!" Beth screamed at her husband on the cell phone. "Plus, I told you never to call this number. This is my work number and should never be used."

"I don't care that you need me to be there to cook for you. Do it yourself or order out! I am very busy on a project here in Miami and don't know when I'll be back," Beth said.

"Well if Mark can't act better in school and get better grades, we will have to send him off to military school," Beth said.

"What did you call me? Did you just call me a bitch? You wait until I get my hands on you - you'll regret saying that. You'll regret a lot of things," Beth was nearly hyperventilating as she pressed the end button on the cell phone.

"Sorry, you had to hear that Dr. Cornelius," Beth stated. "My husband is a handful."

"Yes, Beth, it sure sounds like it. We do need your undivided attention at this point. Are you ready to receive our subjects for the experiment?" Dr. Cornelius asked.

"As ready as I could possibly be," Beth stated. "When is subject M1 supposed to arrive?"

"Any time now," Dr. Cornelius said. "I just spoke with team M1, and they are in route from the airport."

"Ok. I did a final check on the subjects' recovery room. All the equipment is in good working order and ready for the testing," Beth said as she faced Dr. Cornelius.

Beth and Dr. Cornelius, along with a handful of other medically trained agents, waited patiently at the Lois A. Pope Life Center for the arrival of their medical subjects. They were nervous with anticipation at what they would find. Dr. Cornelius sipped on a cup of freshly brewed coffee as Beth looked over some of the medical devices that were scattered about the laboratory.

Within several minutes, Dr. Cornelius's cell phone rang.

"Hello," Dr. Cornelius said. "Ok we'll be right down." He hung up his cell phone. "That was the team, Beth. They are on their way up to the building now. Let's go team."

Dr. Cornelius, Beth, and the other agents made their way down the hallway to a large cargo elevator. The elevator took them to a loading dock in the back of the building. The loading dock was secluded from possible onlookers.

The van containing Marge pulled up slowly beside the Pope Life Center. A guard at the gate gave the driver a nod and pressed a button to lift the gate and allow the van to pass. The van made its way to the rear of the Pope Life Center and backed into the loading dock. Dr. Cornelius, Beth, and the others met team M1 at the rear of the van and opened up the double doors. Marge lay unconscious in the back of the van.

"There she is. The little bitch cut agent Brown with a knife," Tad, leader of team M1 said as he grabbed the stretcher and pulled it towards him. The others were helping move Marge out of the van as well.

"Oh my god," Beth gasped.

"What?" Dr. Cornelius asked.

"She's dead!" Beth shouted.

"No. No, she isn't." Dr. Cornelius calmly stated.

"But look at her! Her lips, her ears, her eyes, and her skin - they're all blue!" Beth said.

"Have you ever seen anyone dead turn that blue, Beth?" Dr. Cornelius asked.

"Well, now that you mention it. No I haven't. What is it then? Beth asked.

"It's the Brilliant Blue G dye that was injected into her body. Her color will return once her kidneys filter it out. Don't worry." Dr. Cornelius said.

"Oh, wow, that is amazing. Now that you mention it, I do remember seeing that happen with the rats that had the dye injected into them. It just looks a lot different with a human." Beth said.

"Help me with this IV bag," Dr. Cornelius said to Beth as they, along with several other agents, lowered the stretcher's wheels onto the pavement.

"Team M1," Dr. Cornelius said. "Please go to the conference room on the third floor where we can have our debriefing. I want to know exactly what took place out there in the field. I'll be there just as soon as we drop this subject off."

Dr. Cornelius, Beth, the other agents, and Marge made their way to the seventh floor, while the agents from team M1 made their way to the conference room. Once Marge was on the seventh floor, she was rolled into a laboratory containing medical equipment as well as four other beds.

She was transferred from the stretcher to one of the hospital-style beds. Her bed had a large sign above it that read M1.

Marge was unconscious the whole time due to a powerful sedative as well as the natural shock that her body experienced from the Devil's Breath. Several agents connected a ventilator to her as well as several new IV drips. Her clothes were cut from her in the van on the way to the lab, and an agent wrapped her in a hospital gown. Marge lay in wait for the next phase of Dr. Cornelius's experiment.

One by one, the other subjects arrived; they were nearly an hour apart. Candice and Marie, Carlos, and Jimmy were as blue as Marge had been, and all were unconscious. Dr. Cornelius planned on keeping them unconscious through the first part of the experiment. They were each transported from the medical vans to the seventh floor of the Lois Pope Life Center. Once there, they were placed in their respective hospital-style beds labeled with their respective subject designations.

The teams that captured the subjects were all debriefed, and Dr. Cornelius was informed on the overall effectiveness of the Devil's Breath. While there were problems, the mission was an overall success as they achieved their goals. Once the debriefing was complete, the agents were dismissed to return to the various lives that they came from before being pulled away from them.

It was a Thursday towards the end of the dog days of summer, and Marge, Marie, Janice, Carlos, and Jimmy laid waiting for what would define them for the rest of their lives. They were the first of their kind. They would be the first to undergo a series of treatments to see if stems cells could cure paralysis; truly, to see if our understanding of stem cells could cure all sorts of diseases.

Other experiments involving the use of Schwann cells to cure paralysis have shown that these cells have difficulty reconnecting past the injury site to surrounding nerve fibers, making it impossible for the patient to make a full recovery and walk again. The use of stem cells may avoid this problem, and that is what Dr. Cornelius hoped to discover.

While, without a doubt, the subjects would prefer not to be the guinea pigs for such an experiment, and while, without a doubt, they, along with most other people of the free world, would object to the method by which they were made part of the experiment; this was the way it had to be done.

"Subject M2's blood pressure is dangerously low," the agent said to Dr. Cornelius as the blood pressure monitor beeped rapidly. "I believe she needs more blood."

"Well get it from the cooler where we have it! And Hurry!" Dr. Cornelius said as the agent ran to a nearby cooler to retrieve blood matching Marie's blood type. She ran back and quickly inserted one end into the IV already placed in Marie's hand.

"Dr. Cornelius, I don't know how you plan on beginning the experiment tomorrow. These subjects have experienced extreme shock, and if you begin the experiment on them now, it would endanger their lives."

"You may be right, but that is a risk that we are going to have to take. We have strict instructions from headquarters to begin the experiment as soon as possible. We need those results," Dr. Cornelius said.

"This isn't something that you rush Dr. Cornelius," the agent said, "It takes time to get the results we are looking for."

"We have steps in place to expedite the process. You just tend to the subjects and make sure that they are in stable condition. I will take care of coordinating the rest. Is that understood?"

"Yes, Dr. Cornelius," the agent said.

Marie, Candice, Carlos, Marge, and Jimmy lay in their beds with the pumps in the ventilators slowly moving up and down. The color of their skin began to return to normal as the BBG dye was broken down and removed from their bodies.

Dr. Cornelius checked on the other agents to see if they were thoroughly prepared to begin the experiment. He checked with the team that would inject embryonic stem cells into the spines of the subjects; he checked with the agents who would work to rehabilitate the subjects - even though they would be used later in the experiment. While making his rounds, Marie went into cardiac arrest.

"Quick, get the crash cart!" One of the agents said to another. The agent ran over to the red crash cart and pulled it beside Marie.

"Charge up the defibrillator! Give me max joules!" one of the agents shouted. She placed the jellied paddles on Marie's bare chest.

"Clear!" she screamed as electricity shocked Marie's limp body. There was silence in the room as the screen of Marie's heart monitor jumped sharply and then returned to a flat line.

"Clear!" the female agent shouted again, as she let another shock flow through Marie's body. Her body jumped violently in her bed. Her heart rhythm fluctuated again on the heart monitor. There were some minor tremors on the screen before the distinctive beat returned to normal.

"You see what I mean?" the female agent said to Dr. Cornelius. "These subjects are not ready for the experiment. They need at least two days to stabilize further."

"I suppose you are right," Dr. Cornelius conceded. "I will call the Deputy Director."

Dr. Cornelius hated to bother Joanne, especially when it involved changing the protocols to a mission. She had a short temper and always insisted that everything be on time. Any change in the mission would come at price for Dr. Cornelius. He would have his ass chewed and handed to him once the mission was completed.

"Joanne, this is Dr. Cornelius. I have some developments that I want to inform you of. It seems that the subjects' bodies are in greater shock than we anticipated. There have been some medical complications with two of the subjects. Our fear is that it may weaken our chances of collecting usable data or that we may lose one of the subjects. I suggest that we wait for at least two days before we begin the next phase of our mission."

"Dr. Cornelius. You know that we need that data as quickly as possible. Many other countries including Australia, Spain, and Japan are developing stem cell research at a faster pace than us. They are even taking on human cloning. We need to get with the program. If we are to remain ahead of the game on the world stage, we need this technology, now. Do you realize the implications and destructive effect on life that human cloning will have?"

"Yes, I understand, and you are right. I just want to see that our subjects survive throughout the entire experiment. They would be no good to us if they die."

"Yes, yes, your concern is noted. However, I require you to start the experiment the day after tomorrow, is that understood?"

"Ok. I will make sure that the experiment starts then," Dr. Cornelius said as he hung up the phone and turned to the other agents in the room. He shook his head and mumbled under his breath, "What have I gotten myself into?"

Beth entered the room. She asked, "What is going on here?"

"We start the day after tomorrow, like it or not," Dr. Cornelius said.

"Well, I don't like it. I heard about the complications with the patients and am concerned about their safety. How can you begin the day after tomorrow while they are in such poor shape?" Beth questioned. She was visibly flustered and very irritated as she spoke.

"Beth, we have orders from the top. This is the way it is going to be. Do you understand?" Dr. Cornelius asked.

"Yes, I understand, but I don't think it is right to begin so soon. This whole experiment is just wrong. I mean, it's so unethical."

"Shut up Beth! Shut your mouth now! You know what you were getting yourself into when you began to play the game, and it hasn't changed. You need to do as you're told for self-preservation. Understood?"

Beth grew silent and withdrawn. A stoic look came over her face. She looked up at Dr. Cornelius with a defeated gaze. "I suppose you are right," she said.

"You're god damn right that I am right! Now, quit being a drain on this mission and help to make it run smoothly. Can you do that?" Dr. Cornelius was fuming. He hated being so confrontational, but he had to be in order to get through to the others. His career depended on it.

"Now, I want you other agents to watch the subjects closely for the next 24 hours. I want to be informed of any developments in their health. I will be in my office until then. Do I make myself clear?"

All of the other agents nodded and faintly said, "yes, sir."

Dr. Cornelius turned and exited through the large wooden double doors to the subjects' area. As he left, he gave Beth an icy stare.

Beth mumbled to herself, "asshole."

Chapter 21

JANICE AND VICK

"Janice, stand up."

Fear gripped Janice as her Civil Procedure professor called her name.

"Now, what was the holding in the Supreme Court case of *International Shoe v. Washington?*" The professor questioned Janice while looking over the top of his reading glasses standing behind the podium in the front of the classroom.

"Well, I read some of the case last night and - "

"I did not ask you if you read the case or not. I asked you what the holding was in the case," the professor said as he scowled at Janice.

"I think that it set up a minimum contacts test," Janice said as her legs grew weak and her mouth became dry as if cotton balls had been placed in it.

"You think or you know?" The professor was relentless. He was known as one of the more difficult ones at the University of Miami Law School.

"Yes, I know that the case set up a minimum contacts test for the states," Janice squeaked.

"Well that is part of the holding but, yes, it did set up the minimum contacts test for the states," the professor hated teaching first year Civil Procedure. He thought these new duds would never get it. "And what is a minimum contacts test?"

"It basically means that a state can force a defendant from another state to defend a lawsuit in their state if the defendant has certain contacts with that state," Janice said as she breathed deeply to keep from passing out.

"Good, but what are those contacts that the court mentions?" The professor asked.

"Well the court doesn't really list out what contacts are sufficient. They just said that jurisdiction is permissible based on the quality and nature of the contacts with the state," Janice said as she began to perspire a bit.

"You are correct," the professor stated. "Sit down."

Janice sat down and wiped her forehead. The other students' eyes were still glued to her as she sat. She thought to herself how much she hated this shit. She wasn't the confrontational type and thought that she may be too sweet to be a hard-nosed attorney.

Several other students were called on during the remainder of the class. One of the students admitted to not preparing for class that day and was chastised by the professor. Another student said that he read the material, but from his answers to the professor's questions, it was clear that he had no comprehension as to what he was reading.

Law school was proving to be the steamroller that everyone said it was. She was having her doubts and just wanted to have the material spoon fed to her like it was in undergraduate school, especially since she was paying that outrageous tuition. The professors could at least be friendlier, she thought.

Janice made her way out of the classroom to the courtyard area where many other students had congregated. Today was "beer on the bricks day." The School bought several kegs of beer and let the students drink at the end of classes on Thursdays.

Janice spoke to a few of her fellow classmates as she gradually made her way to the Miller Lite keg. A young, attractive guy was filling up his cup. He offered to fill up Janice's as well. They exchanged glances, and Janice was instantly enamored with his good looks and sexy disposition. The guy seemed to take notice of Janice's good looks and hot body as well. After he filled up his cup, he offered Janice his hand.

"Hi, my name is Vick. What's yours?"

"Janice," she said through a big grin. She took a large gulp of beer.

"So Janice, I take it that you are a student here, huh?" Vick asked.

"Yes. Like it or not, I am," Janice said as she took another sip of her beer. "How about you? I haven't seen you around. But, then again, I've only been doing this for two weeks now. Are you an upperclassman or something?"

"No. No. I don't go to law school. I am in medical school here though. My friend Billy brought me here for the free beer. I never miss an opportunity for free beer - if you know what I mean," Vick said through nervous laughter.

"Well, I'm not much of a drinker - yet. I'm pretty sure that I will be by the end of the semester though," Janice said as she took another swallow of beer.

"Yea, the stress can really get to you. I understand, medical school is no better. I am just trying to get through it. What keeps me going is the hope that one day I can save someone's life and help people overcome some of life's unpleasant diseases," Vick said with a straight face and a serious demeanor.

"That's great. I'm happy for you that you have found something worthwhile. I'm still trying to figure out if I even want to be a lawyer. A lawsuit never saved anyone's life," Janice said.

"Ahhh. You may be wrong there. You don't know how many people would have attempted the stunts they see on TV if there wasn't some type of disclaimer at the bottom of the screen telling them not to try this at home," Vick joked.

"Yea. Maybe they should attempt to do it at home. It may clean up the gene pool a bit. Get the riff raff out," Janice said.

"Ha ha. You may be right," Vick laughed. "So Janice. What do you like to do for fun?"

"Read," Janice said. "That's all I really do anymore. I read, take a shower, go to class, and read some more."

"Hmmm. That doesn't sound like a whole lot of fun. You have to take a break from it sometimes, don't you?"

"I wish I did, or could. I'm just learning here. Once I get a better handle on what's going on, I will probably be able to relax a little."

"Do you eat? I mean - you have to eat, right?" Vick wondered.

"Believe it or not, I do," Janice said. "Probably not as well as I should."

"Well, if you ever have any free time, I'd love to take you to dinner," Vick said with a big smile on his face. "Here is my telephone number," he handed Janice a piece of torn paper.

"I am - well, yes, I am single. I may just want to do that sometime," Janice was beaming. She was really attracted to the guy, but she didn't want to give him the impression that she was too easy.

"I really hope so. We could go to this really great Cuban restaurant that I know of on Miami Beach," Vick said.

"Aren't all of the restaurants on Miami Beach Cuban?" Janice joked.

"Ha ha. It would seem that way. Cuba is really close to Miami. If you go to one of the high rises downtown, you can almost see it in the distance," Vick said.

"Yea," Janice said. "Well, it was nice to meet you. I'm sure I'll see you around. I might even give you a call."

"That would be great. Take care," Vick said as he walked away from the group.

Janice mingled for a while longer and had a few more beers before heading home. Things were looking up for her she thought. Maybe being here in Miami wasn't so bad after all. Maybe she would find what she was looking for here. Maybe the train wouldn't fall off the tracks. Maybe.

Chapter 22

BETH AND DR. CORENLIUS

"It's time to begin the next phase of our mission," Dr. Cornelius said. "We need to get these subjects into the laboratory where they will have the umbilical cord stem cells implanted into their damaged spines."

One of the agents spoke up, "only two days have passed and -"

"Who is in charge here? I know how many days have passed. We have a strict timeline to follow in order to complete this experiment. Now, I would appreciate it if you held your concerns and helped me in transporting subject M1 to the laboratory where the implantation will take place," Dr. Cornelius said as he made his way over to Marge's bed.

"I can't do that," the female agent said.

"What do you mean you can't do that?" Dr. Cornelius was in shock. "You will do that or you will be locked away indefinitely."

"You - you can't do that to me," the agent stammered.

"Like hell I can't. Now get over here and help me push this bed into the laboratory," Dr. Cornelius demanded. The agent hung her head and walked over to the bed. Marge's ventilator pump loudly wheezed up and down as monitors around her beeped.

Dr. Cornelius and two other agents slowly rolled the hospital bed through the double doors leading to an adjacent laboratory. Once inside, Marge was slid onto an operating table. A team of CIA agents surrounded her as she lay there unconscious. They had an assortment of medical instruments surrounding them including syringes and bright overhead lights.

Once it was determined that Marge was stable, the operation began. One of the team members made an incision into the area where the stems cells were to be injected. The agent injected stem cells directly into Marge's spine both above the area where the Devil's Breath made the cut and below it. The procedure took nearly an hour. Once all of the stem cells had been injected, the team sutured Marge's incision and moved her back onto the hospital bed. She was rolled back into the holding area where the others lie.

Marie, Candice, Jimmy, and Carlos were each taken separately into the laboratory and given the same type of injections. The agents injected above and below the cut from the Devil's Breath and then they rolled the subjects back into the recovery room.

"Are we going to give them any anti rejection drugs?" One of the agents asked.

"No, they won't need them," Dr. Cornelius said. "The stems cells are their own. There should be no issue of rejection, and the stem cells are not distinguished enough for their immunity system to identify them. There are also very few immunity cells in the stem cell blood to cause any problems with the host."

"What do we do now?" One of the agents asked.

"We wait." Dr Cornelius said.

"For how long?"

"Until it is safe to bring them out of their comatose state. Their bodies just need to rest for a while to allow some healing to take place. Once we see further stabilization of their vital signs, and make sure there are no unanticipated complications from the surgery, then we will bring them to consciousness."

"Bring them to consciousness? You have to be joking," the agent said to Dr. Cornelius as she stood next to Marge's bed. "Do you realize what the CIA has done to them? They will be outraged! There is no way that they will participate in the study voluntarily."

"You're right. Unfortunately, you're dead right." Dr. Cornelius said as he pretended to once again stroke his invisible goatee. He paced the room back and forth as the other agents looked on. "But, of course, we were expecting that type of reaction from our subjects, and, of course, we have that covered."

"What, exactly, do we have covered?" A second agent asked.

"Do you see that little white bag there - hanging on subject M2's IV pole?" Dr. Cornelius pointed in Marie's direction.

"Yes," the female agent asked. "What is it?"

Dr. Cornelius rolled his head from side to side. He looked a little piqued and said, "it is a drug called propranolol."

"The drug used to treat high blood pressure? The drug actors use to treat stage fright? What is that going to do?" The agent asked.

"There have been studies that have shown that the drug also causes people to forget traumatic events." Dr. Cornelius said.

"Like being forcibly maimed and taken hostage?" One of the agents asked.

"Watch it - but yes, it should erase the memory of their capture," Dr. Cornelius said. "It is experimental, but it is all we have at this point."

"Why not just scramble their brains to make them forget everything?" A male agent suggested.

"That's not an option. If we tried to make it so they would forget everything, they may even forget how to walk. That type of procedure is too risky, even for us. Not to mention, we want them to be able to interact with us and tell us what they are feeling as well. We need to know what type of pain and discomfort they are in so we know the side effects of the implantation," Dr. Cornelius was still pacing back and forth with a look of concern on his face.

"What makes you think that they will tell us anything or even participate in this experiment?" The female agent said as she looked at Marge's pale, inanimate face.

"We have that covered too - but I don't want to get into the specifics of that right now. We have several days before the subjects regain consciousness. You and I - we all will learn more as time progresses. We should know what we are dealing with here in no time at all." Dr. Cornelius said.

"But until that time comes, you all know what to do. You have been informed about the roles you are to play here, and I fully expect that you will do your part to make this a success," Dr. Cornelius said as he gazed at the others around the room.

Dr. Cornelius left the room and sauntered to his office adjoining the recovery room and the laboratory. The agents went about their business of tending to the subjects. IV bags were changed; tourniquets were rewrapped, and excrement was disposed of. They made notes on all of their patients' progress.

Once in his office, Dr. Cornelius called Beth on his cell phone.

"Hello, Beth," Dr. Cornelius said. "I want to ask you for your continued help on our experiment," he said. "I want you to remain a part of this mission in a different capacity. I know I originally said that we would be able to do this without your support, but things have changed. The agent responsible for running the MRI machine was in a fatal accident over the weekend, and since you are familiar with the equipment, I ask that you operate the machine and help me to interpret the images we are seeing."

Beth was screaming on the other end of the phone. She complained that she needed to get back to her family, because her husband was upset with her leaving for so long. She grumbled that her children needed her, and she was not living up to her parental responsibilities. She also insisted that the mission was something that she felt deeply disturbed about. It was morally reprehensible, and she was not able to sleep at night knowing that she took part in it.

"Beth, I don't want to have to constantly remind you of your pledge that you made to the CIA, and to the government of the United States. You know that your involvement with this mission is extremely important. Yes, Beth, I would say it is even more important than your family," Dr. Cornelius said with consternation. "I expect you here bright and early tomorrow morning."

After more protesting, Beth abruptly ended the conversation and hung up the phone. She was lying on the hotel bed, naked, staring up at the ceiling with a vicious scowl on her face. It was the same face she was making when she rolled sideways and stared into Vick's eyes.

Chapter 23

JANICE AND VICK

Vick's cell phone rang as he was pulling his clothes back on.

"Ahh, it can go to voicemail," he said without checking the number. After a few seconds, the phone beeped indicating that a message was left.

"So, am I going to see you again?" Vick asked Beth.

"Who knows? Our paths may cross again, but I'm very busy," Beth said. "But you knew this was just about sex. It was a hook-up and nothing more."

"It sure felt like more than just a hook -"

"It was nothing more!" Beth insisted. "Look, you have to go now."

Vick stumbled over his shoelaces as he made his way to the door. "Ok, ok. Bye," he said as he leaned in to give Beth a kiss. Beth put her hand over his mouth and pushed him away.

"Damn it," Vick said as Beth slammed the door behind him.

Vick drove his old, overused, half-painted Buick Regal back to his apartment near the university. He walked up three flights of stairs, entered, and plopped himself on the couch where he reflected about the night of passionate lovemaking he just experienced. Beth dominated his thoughts as he got up to cook himself some eggs and turkey bacon. Then, he remembered the voicemail that someone had left for him. He reached into his pocket, entered his access code, and placed the cell phone up to his ear. After several seconds, he heard Janice begin to speak.

"Hello, Vick. I hope you remember me. This is Janice. We met last Thursday at the law school. We had beers together. Well, you told me to call you, so I did. I'm just wondering if you would like to go out sometime. Give me a call back."

"Yes," Vick said to himself. "Damn, I'm a stud," was his second thought. Without pause, Vick returned the call.

"Hello," Janice answered.

"Hello, Janice. It's Vick. How are you doing?"

"Hello Vick. I'm well. Believe it or not, I'm reading right now," Janice said.

"Ahh, I'd expect nothing less. You sure are dedicated," Vick said.

"Yea, I'm trying to get my money's worth. I figure with tuition as high as it is, I'm paying about fifty cents per word that I read," Janice joked.

Vick laughed. "What do you say that you take a break for a few hours and come have coffee with me?"

"That would be great. I need something to take my mind off of offer, acceptance, and misrepresentation," Janice said.

"Do you go to Miami Beach much?" Vick asked.

"I've been a couple of times in the short time I lived here," she said.

"Would you like to go there? There is a Starbucks on Lincoln Road Mall that we could hang out at," Vick said.

"I know right where that is," Janice said.

"Do you want to meet there at, say, three o'clock?" Vick asked.

"That sounds good. I'll see you there at three," Janice said.

"Great, I'll see you then," Vick said as he hung up the phone.

"Yes," he said to himself again as he jerked his arm in a downward motion as if he had just won a prize.

Vick ate his steaming eggs and turkey bacon. Afterwards, he took a shower to remove Beth's scent and clean up. He used the razor he kept for special occasions, because it gave him the closest shave. Vick was paying careful attention as he prepared himself for his date. After an hour or so, he looked clean-cut and attractive and was ready for Janice. He sat in some heavy traffic on US1 as he made his way to the beach. Vick drove over the bridge leading from Miami to Miami Beach. He was always overwhelmed by the breathtaking view of Miami from the bridge. All of downtown was visible, and the architecture of the buildings contrasted beautifully against the clear powder blue sky. The water below shimmered in the sunlight as the waves gently rolled towards the shore. Cruise ships docked in the port signified good times to come for many.

Vick made his way through the Art Deco district of Miami Beach. The pastel colored buildings with their rounded edges and kooky windows were odd to him, but he did like the way they looked lining Ocean Boulevard at night from the nearby beach. It was one big party of a good time on South Beach, he thought to himself.

After battling with another driver for a parking spot, Vick had finally reached his destination. His car horn beeped signaling that his alarm was set, even though he knew it was safe from any would-be thieves. He strolled past several cafes and throngs of people hustling about before reaching the Starbucks. He walked inside but didn't see Janice anywhere. He ordered a tall coffee and fixed it up with an assortment of mixers. He preferred two Splenda packets, skim milk, and cinnamon.

Vick chose a table outside despite the heat. Beautiful people were walking closely by him as he sipped his steaming hot caffeine dose. One woman in particular captured his attention. She had the longest, most well toned, tanned legs that he had ever seen. Her breasts were aching to burst out from underneath her skimpy top. Vick thought it was more of a handkerchief than a shirt. He was ogling the blond beauty when Janice strolled up to the table.

"Hi Vick...oh, am I disturbing something?" Janice said as drool practically formed at the corner of Vick's mouth.

"No. No. I was just enjoying my coffee here," Vick said a little embarrassed at having been caught lusting after the beautiful women.

"I see. Well, how are you?" Janice asked.

"Oh, I'm good. It's great to see you again," Vick said as he stood and hugged Janice before sitting down again.

"Sorry, I already went ahead and ordered. What would you like? Can I get you something?" Vick asked.

"I can get it," Janice said.

"No - that's ok, I'll get it," Vick said as he stood up again.

"Ok. I'll have a blueberry muffin and a small coffee," Janice responded.

"Be back in a jiffy," Vick said.

Janice thought it was a little corny since the word jiffy seemed to be out of the 50's or something. She took a seat as Vick went inside to get her order. As Janice sat there, she noted that there was something she already didn't like about Vick. She thought he was a little weasel the way he was staring at that woman's breasts, but she let it go and wrote it off as his raging male testosterone's fault.

Vick returned with Janice's coffee and muffin.

"Here you are," Vick said as he put the goods in front of Janice.

"Thanks, Vick, so how are things going with you?"

"Busy, busy, busy. Like you, I don't have much time to play around. It gets kind of boring really."

"Boring. Ha! You try reading case after case of mind numbing judge's opinions about the finer points of lawsuit service. Then, when you are done with that, try reading the footnotes for those cases. I mean, the footnotes are a book all by themselves," Janice said with a smile on her face.

"Really? I know it's a lot of reading, so say my friends in law school. But we shouldn't compare who is more bored. I mean, I have to keep myself awake by seven to eight cups of coffee a day down at the lab," Vick said.

"The lab, what lab?" Janice asked.

"Well, its downtown. It's on the campus with University of Miami's Jackson Hospital," Vick said.

"What do you do there?" Janice asked.

"It's just a part-time job that I do when I can - several hours a week. It's mostly working with rats and stuff."

"Is it related to the area you are studying in medical school," Janice asked.

"Yea, I'm studying neurosciences. That's my specialty. We are doing tests on the rats' nervous systems," Vick said.

"Interesting."

"I suppose so. It's not fun to work with rats all day. They are a poor substitute for the real thing. I mean, all of the testing we do is on rats. But, I guess a lot of the things we do with rats we can't do with humans. It would be unethical," Vick said as he took a large sip of his coffee.

"A lot of things you do with rats is unethical too, depending on whom you ask," Janice said as she slowly peeled back the wrapper around her gigantic muffin.

"Do you want some of this muffin?" Janice asked Vick.

"No thank you. I've had enough to eat recently. I just want to sip on my coffee."

Janice bit into her muffin. She went after one of the blueberries sticking out from the spongy cake-like surroundings. She became more interested in Vick after finding out he was studying neurosciences. She knew she wasn't messing around with some dopey screw up. You had to have brains to do what he was doing.

The two of them chatted for a while longer and found out where the other was from and what they were doing before coming down to Miami. The more Vick talked, the more Janice became aroused by his good looks and sharp mind, despite her earlier thoughts about him. Vick also felt strongly attracted to Janice.

"Well Janice, I'd like to hang out with you again sometime, if you'd like," Vick said.

"That would be nice. How about I call you sometime?" Janice asked.

"Anytime. I may be busy, but I surely can call you back if you leave a message," Vick said as he got up from the table to give Janice another hug.

"Ok. I'll do it. Take care until we meet again," Janice said.

"You too. And, Janice."

"Yea."

"Don't let what happen between you and Jimmy affect how you think about me," Vick said somberly as he stopped walking away and turned around to face Janice.

Janice nearly choked on her deep gasp as she stared at Vick. She demanded, "How in the hell do you know about Jimmy?"

Chapter 24

BETH

"God damn it," Beth said out loud as the alarm clock screeched next to her head. "I can't believe this shit. I can't believe...Dr. Corn...errr," Beth's voice trailed off as she pulled herself out of bed.

Beth got into the shower and just stood there wondering what the hell she was doing. She wondered how she went from one of the directors of the NSA, to one of Dr. Cornelius's henchmen. As she stood there in the shower watching the water swirl around and go down the drain, she began to cry. Her cries were pockmarked by screams. She thought about her kids. She wondered why she had them at all, since she was always missing from their lives. She thought about her ungrateful husband who never understood her ambition, her need to be connected to something greater than herself. Beth grappled with how miserable she was. She detested the fact that despite her education and success, she still felt like a pawn in the government's dangerous games.

Eventually, Beth got dressed and made her way out of the hotel into her rental car. She drove up US 1 to the Pope Life Center donning her white lab coat and fake nametag. She ignored the security guard, as she strolled past him to the elevators. She made her way to the seventh floor. The doors to the elevator opened, and she walked past the agent posted outside in an attempt to enter the recovery room.

"Stop right there," the agent said. "Where do you think you're going?"

"You. I am in no mood to deal with a dumbass like you," Beth said.

"Excuse me?" the agent said as he placed his hand on the butt of his gun concealed by his blazer.

"You heard me. How many times do I have to walk through these doors before you recognize me?" Beth asked despite the fact that she had only been there once before.

"I'm sorry; I do not recall seeing you before now. Let me see your badge." The agent said still cradling the gun with his hand.

"Dumbass," Beth said as she took off her badge and handed it to the agent.

The agent glared at Beth as he scanned her badge with a handheld device. "Ok. I see you are in the system. Please understand that I am just doing my job."

"You won't be doing it much longer if I have my way," Beth said.

The agent held his tongue, grimaced at her, and opened the door for Beth.

"Where the hell have you been?" Dr. Cornelius asked Beth as she entered the room.

"I'm here aren't I? Traffic on US1 was abysmal," Beth said.

"Well, we have a lot to cover. You have a lot to cover," Dr. Cornelius said.

"What is going on with the patients...I mean...subjects?" Beth wondered.

"They have been injected with the stem cells. We are giving them several days to recover, and then we can bring them back to consciousness," Dr. Cornelius said.

"Yeah. Good luck with that," Beth said.

"Hmmm," Dr. Cornelius grunted. "Beth, I want you to go down to the sixth floor into the room directly below this one, room TG600. The MRI machine is there. Please re-familiarize yourself with it. I know that it is one you have worked with before. We need to take some preliminary pictures of our subjects' spines to have a reference point."

Beth walked back through the doors, gave the agent outside an awful look, and took the elevator down a floor. She walked into room TG600 and then walked into the MRI bay. She surveyed the control panel and recognized the model as a later version of one she had worked on back at Harvard.

She fired the machine up and ran several maintenance protocols. The machine was state of the art. It was brand new and had all of the latest capabilities and some other ones that she was unaware of. The images it could produce were crystal clear and very detailed. She loved controlling it.

As she was finishing up familiarizing herself with the machine, Dr. Cornelius joined her.

"So what do you think?" he asked.

"This thing is great. I don't think I've seen a gantry that big on any machine," Beth said.

"Yes, well they are making the gantry a lot bigger now since people in the US are getting bigger, and they need to fit into the MRI machine," Dr. Cornelius said.

"That's true. But, if they make the machine any bigger, it's not going to fit inside the facility anymore," Beth said.

"Let's hope it doesn't come to that," Dr. Cornelius said.

"Has this machine even been used before? It just looks so new; it's like the plastic covering the machine during transport was just removed," Beth said.

"Of course the installers used dummies to calibrate the machine at first and were able to get everything into good working order," Dr. Cornelius said. "We scheduled several random outpatients, which would have gone over to Jackson Hospital, to come here and have their test done. We executed the testing without any problems. The patients were given their images and left without incident."

"When do I get to run an exam?" Beth asked.

"The subjects will shortly be brought down one at a time," Dr. Cornelius said.

"How about we run a test scan first before the real ones begin?" Beth asked. "Why don't you hop up on the scanning table real quick?"

"Beth, I don't think that's such a great idea," Dr. Cornelius said.

"Why not, it will allow me to familiarize myself with the machine a little more. There is no danger to you," Beth said.

"I know, I know. Ok. But make it quick. Do my ankle or something," Dr. Cornelius said. Beth walked through the door separating the control room from the MRI.

"Come on in," Beth said as she stood by the scanning table inside the room containing the machine.

Dr. Cornelius sat on the scanning table and lifted his feet towards the opening. He eventually came to rest flat on the thin narrow white table.

Beth forcefully pushed the table into the gantry nearly throwing Dr. Cornelius off of it.

"Easy! What are you trying to do?" Dr. Cornelius screamed.

"You'll be fine," Beth said. "You'll be fine" She positioned Dr. Cornelius's ankle in the crosshairs shining from the front of the machine. "Now hold still while I run this scan."

Beth quickly walked back to the control room and plugged in the protocol for an ankle exam as Dr. Cornelius tried to get comfortable without moving his ankle. She pushed several buttons, and the MRI rumbled to life. The magnets inside sounded like a lion loudly growling. Dr. Cornelius laid there for about half an hour while his ankle was scanned.

Beth put the finishing touches on the images and printed them out. She positioned the film on the view boxes hanging in the control room.

"Beautiful," Dr. Cornelius said with a wry smile. "I don't think I have seen a more impressive ankle. Have you Beth?"

"Well, considering that most of the ankles the MRI machine scans are deformed or diseased in some way, I'd say that's a nice ankle. Oh, wait a second, is that, why that looks like it may be attached to a club foot," Beth said.

"Yea, you can take your club foot and shove it up your butt," Dr. Cornelius and Beth were partaking in a rare session of hilarity that wouldn't take place again until a few more blue moons have passed.

"Ha. Ha. That's very funny. Sticking things up butts, wow, you've sunk to a new low," Beth said. "But to change the topic quickly, when will the subjects be brought down for their preliminary scans?"

"Give me half an hour, and I'll bring subject J1 to you," Dr. Cornelius said.

"Ok. I'll be waiting. I'll have the spine protocol plugged in by the time you return," Beth said.

"Good. Do just that," Dr. Cornelius said.

"Oh, and Dr. Cornelius, make damn sure they don't have any metal in or on them," Beth said with an icy gaze.

"Push harder! He is almost on the table," Beth said as a team of agents manhandled Jimmy's paralyzed body. "Come on, pull the sheets towards you."

The team was moving Jimmy from his bed to the table. After a few more seconds of playing tug of war, the agents had Jimmy lying on the MRI's movable examination table. He was still unconscious as the team wanted him that way. Beth positioned him so she could get the best images of his spine. Once in position, they all cleared the room.

Beth began the exam; and soon, images of Jimmy's delicate body tissues and bones were displayed on the MRI's monitor. It was completed without any mishaps. She printed the images of Jimmy's spine, and she and Dr. Cornelius reviewed them. The separation of the spine was exceedingly apparent and required no significant medical training to decipher the break.

"Do you see those?" Dr. Cornelius asked Beth pointing to two small, gray, round pockets on the film.

"Yes. What are they?"

"Those are fluid filled areas containing the stem cells. Notice that they have seeped into the area where the spinal canal is separated and is nearly filling the whole space up." Dr. Cornelius said stroking his non-existent goatee again.

"Wow, so those stem cells will turn into nerve cells? Huh, amazing really." Beth said staring intently at the images before her. How long do you think it will take to completely heal?"

"Your guess is as good as mine, but I would say that there should be some measurable progress in the growth of the cells within several days to several weeks. The subjects could be walking again within a month or two, if what I've learned holds true," Dr. Cornelius said while pacing the small control room. "We are going to take images with the MRI machine every few days or so to measure the progress. We will need you here during those times of course."

"Yea, I figured that," Beth said with the pain apparent on her face. "I'll be here whether I like it or not."

"Thank you Beth, we appreciate it," Dr. Cornelius said. "This is really going to be cutting edge stuff, and you will learn as we learn."

"It's not like you can publish the results of this experiment in any medical journals though. I mean, this will have to remain classified information," Beth's tone of voice was very condescending as she spoke to Dr. Cornelius.

"We'll deal with that once we need to. Right now, we need to find out how effective the stem cells are, the side effects, and how we can use this new science to the benefit as many people as possible."

Dr. Cornelius left the room and returned to the recovery area shortly after several agents returned Jimmy. There, he instructed the other agents to take Carlos to the MRI scanning area. Beth ran the MRI scan on him. Then, a team of agents assembled to record all of the results of the test and made notations in their journals as to the findings of the exam. They were to record everything that was taking place during the experiment.

One by one, each of the subjects was scanned. Their scans took place without incident; the necessary images were taken, and the notations were made. However, Marge's scan - she was the last one to be scanned - was problematic. Several agents made their way into the scanning room with her.

"Get her onto the table," Beth said to the agents as they tugged on the bed sheet to slide her over. "Good, now please clear the room."

The agents made their way into the hallway where they waited for the exam to be completed, before they were needed to place Marge back into her hospital bed. Beth went to the control area.

She began the exam, and the magnets inside the machine hummed to life to take the necessary images. Beth was staring at the control panel when she heard something inside the exam area that startled her to her feet. She looked through the window. Marge's body was jerking around uncontrollably. Her body slammed hard against the wall inside the opening to the machine. Blood sprayed out in all directions as it colored the narrow opening crimson red.

"Shit! Shit! Shit!" Beth screamed out. "God damn it!"

Beth searched around for the kill button on the control panel. While she did, Marge's body continued to beat violently against the MRI machine. After about a minute, which to Beth felt like an eternity, Beth smacked the kill button as hard as she could; it nearly split in two. Beth ran to the hallway.

"You! I need you to get a crash cart as soon as you can, make sure that it has plenty of bandages in it!" Beth ordered. The agent just stood there in shock. "I mean NOW! I need those bandages now!" She screamed as the agent took off down the hall. "The rest of you get in here immediately!"

The group entered the exam area, and Beth quickly removed the table from the gantry of the machine. As she did, she said to herself, "Oh god." Every inch the table moved out revealed gruesome damages to Marge's body.

Marge's face was covered in gashes and blood. Several of her teeth were missing. She had cuts on her arms and knees. Most disturbing of all was the outline of a triangular object protruding from her leg. Parts of her skin were torn around it, and Beth could make out that it was metal.

"Motherfucker," Beth shouted. "Someone get Dr. Cornelius in here now!" One of the agents tore out of the room as another agent ran in pushing a crash cart and carrying several packets of gauze. Beth grabbed a towel that was lying nearby and applied pressure to the biggest gashes. She sopped up the blood and laid gauze over them. She then put large bandages over the gauze. She cleaned her up and sent her back to the recovery area.

Marge was taken to the room where the stem cells were injected, and a team of agents performed emergency surgery on Marge to fix the damage to her leg. Dr. Cornelius joined Beth in the exam area.

"Why in the hell did you not know that subject M1 had a metal implant in her leg?" Beth seethed anger . "She could have died!"

"Calm down Beth - calm down," Dr. Cornelius was blood red from embarrassment. "Look, we had x-rays taken of the subjects before they came down here. The only mistake I can think of that we may have committed is that we only took pictures of their upper bodies. There was nothing in the medical histories that we compiled on the subjects that indicated that any of them would have metal in their leg. There was no history of a compound fracture in subject M1 that would require metal."

"Pretty sloppy if you ask me," Beth said as she stared at Dr. Cornelius.

"I thought this was a state of the art machine, why would this happen in the first place?" Dr. Cornelius wondered.

"Those are powerful magnets spinning around in the machine. The metal rod in her leg was obviously not one that is able to be scanned," Beth said as she tried to wipe the blood from the MRI machine. It just smeared into the textured plastic. "You better hope that she doesn't die, or we have some real deep shit to kick around."

"Cover up is my specialty," Dr. Cornelius said in a hushed tone of voice.

"Let's just hope that we don't need your specialty," Beth grunted.

Marge was in surgery for a little more than an hour. The bout with the MRI machine broke her femur in two places, under the spot where the metal rod was secured. The team of agents replaced the old, iron based implant with a new titanium implant that could be scanned by the MRI machine. Marge's leg being broken would prove to be a setback in the CIA's experiment, but they would still measure any type of movement, if there was any, that Marge regained in her lower body.

Marge's surgery was finished up, and she was returned to the recovery area where the others lay in unconsciousness. The agents tended to the subjects. Each subject was peacefully resting while the stem cells inside began changing. They began replicating and taking on the properties of the surrounding spinal canal nerve cells. Beth and Dr. Cornelius were standing next to Marge's bed gazing down over her.

"Well, I'm glad that is over with, and subject M1's vital signs are strong," Beth said as she rubbed her left eye.

"Yes, that was quite a scare. Fortunately though, we have a great team assembled here to handle any emergency that might creep up," Dr. Cornelius said.

"Yea, let's hope we don't have any more of those mishaps though. God damn it, we can do better than that!" Beth shouted.

"Your right, your right, and we will," Cornelius said trying not to turn blood red again. There was an awkward moment of silence as Beth paced around the recovery room in frustration. As she paced, she stopped at each bed looking over each subject. They looked pale in the institutional florescent light shinning down from the ceiling.

Dr. Cornelius turned to leave the room and began walking towards the double door when Beth stopped him in his tracks.

"Wait. Dr. Cornelius," she said.

"What is it Beth?" He wondered.

"I...what..."

"Go ahead and spit it out Beth."

"What is going to happen to these subjects once the experiment is over? I mean, how are they going to go back to living the lives they had once before they were brought down?"

"Damn. Beth, I wish you wouldn't have asked that," Dr. Cornelius said as he tried to remain level headed. "What do you think will happen?"

"I'm hoping that they will be so medicated during this experiment that they won't remember anything," Beth said.

"You know we need them to be coherent enough to tell us what they are feeling," Dr. Cornelius said.

"What then?" Beth had to ask.

"They will be terminated," Dr. Cornelius said.

Marge's eyes flew open at that exact moment.

Chapter 25

JANICE AND VICK

"I'm only going to ask this one more time, how in the hell do you know about Jimmy?" Janice wondered in shock as to what connection Vick could possibly have to Jimmy.

"Ahhh. Janice. Jimmy and I go way back. I grew up in Charlotte too," Vick said as he returned to the table to talk to Janice.

"That's funny, because he never mentioned knowing a Vick," Janice said with an accusatory tone. "You two must not have been that close of friends if he never brought you up." Janice was coming off as a real bitch, and Vick became somewhat irritated.

"Listen, Janice, we were best friends all through elementary school. He ended up going to a different high school than me. We did lose contact for quite a while. But a few months ago, Jimmy became my friend on Facebook - you do know Facebook right?" Vick wondered.

"Yeah, I haven't been living under a rock," Janice said with a serious gaze.

"Well, yeah, he friended me on Facebook. He updated his status showing that he was single a few weeks ago. I knew that he was dating a Janice at the time, and I put two and two together. I just wanted to let you know that whatever happened between you two is not important to me. Jimmy and I don't speak often enough that I would feel that I would be disrespecting him if we date," Vick said.

"That's good to know," Janice said, "Jimmy and I don't speak anymore. The last time I heard from him he was in basic training for the Army and that was a while ago. He probably has graduated by now and working on a base or something."

"Yeah, I haven't heard from him for a while either. He hasn't posted anything lately on Facebook," Vick said as he twisted his face into a contemplative look.

"He probably has limited access to computers where he is now, who knows?" Janice said.

"Yeah, he's probably pretty busy doing whatever he's doing in the Army," Vick said, "Hey Janice, this may be an awkward time, but what do you say we plan another date now?"

"Well, um... that would be ok, I guess. What do you have in mind?" Janice wondered as she flipped her long black hair back out of habit.

"Have you ever been to Mangos on Ocean Drive?" Vick asked with a smirk on his face. He had many good times at Mangos. It wasn't so much the food as it was the women.

"Mangos? Yes, I've heard of it. That's the place where they have the strippers dancing on the bar, isn't it?" Janice wondered with a scowl on her face. It wasn't exactly what she had in mind for a next date.

"Well, they're not really strippers - the bartenders get up there too. The place is just plain fun and alive with energy. I just thought it would be a good time. Plus, the food there is really pretty outstanding. You have to try their chicken wings. One word. Awesome," Vick said as he nearly slobbered on himself at the thought of the Mango's Mambo chicken wings.

"Hmmm. That's a pretty rave review that you're giving the place. What the hell, let's go there," Janice said. Vick's good looks got the best of her.

"How about Saturday?" Vick asked.

"Saturday would be good. I can study during the day and then party my overworked, underappreciated, and unpaid ass off all night. I'm looking forward to it, really," Janice said.

"I've got you covered. I just want you to have a good time," Vick said.

"Thanks Vick. That is very thoughtful of you. I'm sure it will be fun," Janice said with a big smile on her face.

"Janice, I will call you on Saturday to work out the details," Vick said.

"Ok, Vick, see you then," Janice replied.

"Oh, and Janice, if this works out, maybe we can see each other again," Vick said.

"We'll see, won't we?"

Chapter 26

BETH AND DR. CORNELIUS

Marge tried to remain as motionless as possible. She heard what Dr. Cornelius said, but didn't quite understand what he was talking about or, even where she was at that exact moment. Her eyes darted around, and she looked to her left and saw the IV bag hanging beside her. After she got her wits back and the fuzz cleared from her head, Marge turned her gaze towards Beth and Dr. Cornelius. When she did, she got their full attention and the attention of two other nearby agents.

"Where the hell am I?" Marge asked visibly shaken and pale from the trauma.

"You're in the hospital; you've been in an accident," Dr, Cornelius said as the lies were about to flow freely from his mouth.

Thin curtains were drawn between the beds, and Marge was unable to see the others in the room.

"What happened?" Marge wondered not remembering much at all.

"You were in a car accident, just try to lay still and try not to move too much," Beth counseled as she stood beside Marge's bed.

"No, No, I can't...I don't remember being in any accident," Marge was looking at Beth with questioning eyes.

Dr. Cornelius thought that the propranolol might just be working to give her amnesia over her capture.

Marge threw the bed sheets towards the foot of the bed. She twisted her upper torso as if she was going to get up. She did not move.

"What? Oh my god! I can't feel my legs! What the hell is wrong with my legs?" Marge began to sob in short bursts.

"You've been in an accident which left you paralyzed," Dr. Cornelius said. "Your spinal cord sustained damage, and you are not able to walk," Dr. Cornelius said as he shot Beth a quizzical glance. He knew the story he was supposed to give to the subject, but he looked at Beth to see if she would react in regards to its believability.

"What? What do you mean I will not be able to walk? What has happened to me?" Marge was in complete shock.

"Just try to remain calm," Beth said. "We are going to make you better. We are going to get you to walk again. It may take some time, but with your help, it will happen."

"Where is my family?" Marge asked through her tears.

"Marge, I hate to be the one to tell you this, but none of them survived the accident. You were the only one," Beth was laying it on thick and piling it high. She anticipated that the subjects would want to know where their families were, and she had a unique lie for each subject.

"Oh my god!" Marge wailed after hearing this. "How could this be? How could this have happened?"

"Now, now, Marge, just rest. Just stay calm and rest a bit," Beth said as Marge turned her head on the pillow. Her tears created little wet spots on top of it. "I want you to try and get some sleep."

"How can I sleep when my entire family is dead?" Marge screamed out as Beth stood near her bed. Beth was doing her best to remain calm, but underneath she was in a panic. She was feeling all the pain that Marge was feeling, but did everything in her power to not let it show. This is just wrong she thought, but she pressed on as any well-trained troop would do.

"Marge, I am deeply sorry about your loss. You need to focus on you though. We want you to get better and be able to walk again. Just lay back and do your best to get some sleep," Beth said as comforting as she could. "Pretty soon we will move forward with your treatment. You will meet others that are in the same situation that you are experiencing, and we will all work together to heal you. Do you understand me?" Beth said trying to act more professional than motherly. She wanted to keep as much distance between the subject and herself as she could even though she found it extremely difficult.

"I just want to die," Marge said in a defeated tone of voice.

As Marge sat there sobbing, screams came from behind another curtain.

"My legs, I can't feel my god damn legs!" Carlos screamed in shock. "What the hell happened to my legs?"

Dr. Cornelius ran over to Carlos. He said, "Calm down, calm down, you have been in a bad motorcycle accident which left you unable to walk. We are going to begin treatment soon to get you back to where you were. We have already done surgery on you to begin the process to get you up and moving around on your own two feet once again."

"Motorcycle, I don't remember being on any motorcycle," Carlos said with a dumbfounded expression on his face.

"We were told that you were borrowing it from your friend. He brought you to the hospital after the accident," Dr. Cornelius said as a bead of sweat rolled down his forehead. "Just lay back and rest. We are going to work on getting you better real soon, but for now, you just need to relax."

Dr. Cornelius walked over to one of the agents standing to the side of the room. He instructed her to give the two awaken subjects a strong dose of morphine. She prepared the morphine and hung a bag of it on each IV pole; one beside Marge and one beside Carlos. Within minutes, they were sleeping.

"God damn it, that was close," Beth said through her frustrated, pinched lips. "I hope we can hold this network of lies together."

While Marge and Carlos came out of their comas and found sleep instead, Jimmy and Candice awoke with the same terrified reaction after finding that they could no longer feel their legs. Dr. Cornelius and Beth explained to each of them that they were in accidents that left them unable to move around as they were used to. Neither one of them remembered anything about how they truly came to have their legs rendered useless. This pleased both Beth and Dr. Cornelius.

After their initial shock wore off and the morphine was administered, both Marge and Carlos joined Jimmy and Candice in peaceful slumber. While they slept, Dr. Cornelius, Beth, and another agent stood near Marie looking at the ventilator move up and down. Unlike the others, who were taken off the ventilators once it was determined they could safely breath on their own, Marie was left on hers as none of the agents felt it safe to remove it yet.

"When do you think she will come out of her coma?" An agent questioned Dr. Cornelius.

"It was just good luck really that the others all came out of their comas relatively near the same time," Dr. Cornelius said. "We can only wait and see."

"We can't wait forever," Beth said obviously miffed over lack of anticipation on Dr. Cornelius's part. He should know what the others would do once they woke back up. "These other subjects are going to be cranky and impatient. They are going to want to begin the necessary steps to get them to walk again. We need to be ready."

"Beth, if necessary, we can begin the others on their physical therapy regimen and wait a little longer to see what Marie is going to do," Dr. Cornelius said in a conciliatory tone of voice in order to placate Beth's obviously frazzled nerves.

"I just think it would be easier if we have all of the subjects on the same page. Besides, wouldn't that skew the data if one of the subjects

163

doesn't participate in the same exact activities as the others? They each need to be subjected to the same treatment in order to measure their progress. That is the only way we can ensure accurate results," Beth was beginning to sound very condescending in her tone as she spoke to Dr. Cornelius and the other agent.

"I suppose you're right. Even though this is the first experiment of its kind and we are not sure what to expect in terms of data, I'm sure we'd be remiss if we were to let the others begin physical therapy and their exercise routine without all of the subjects beginning at the same time. We will just have to wait on Subject M2 to regain consciousness in her own time," Dr. Cornelius said as he paced back and forth. His pacing irritated Beth to the point she said something to him about it.

"Dr. Cornelius could you come back over here and stand still?" Beth said as she crossed her arms. "What is it that you need us to do now?"

"Just be ready to begin the rest of the experiment once all of the subjects have awoken. There are couple of cots up on the eighth floor that you two can rest on until the morning," Dr. Cornelius said as he did the best he could not to pace. He moved his feet back and forth a little but his eyes did not leave Beth's gaze.

"Oh, that should be a good night's sleep," Beth said as she rolled her eyes.

"You should be used to it by now," Dr. Cornelius shot back.

"I never get used to insomnia," Beth said with a scowl on her face.

"Well take your rest, no matter how bad, while you can; we have a busy schedule in front of us. I need you both to be ready for it," Dr. Cornelius just couldn't help himself and began pacing again as he talked.

"Who is going to be tending to the subjects tonight?" Beth asked.

"We have two agents that will watch over the subjects until about six in the morning. After that, we'll take control again. There will be an armed agent standing guard outside of the door in case someone happens to make their way to where they shouldn't be," Dr. Cornelius assured Beth.

"I want you to know that I am still uneasy about this whole thing. I mean, what we are doing here isn't exactly right," Beth said with her arms still folded and a look of worry painted across her face.

"Beth, Beth, Beth, I am not going to get into this with you right now. All that I will say is that you have nothing to worry about. This experiment will progress without any setbacks and will run smoother than you could ever dream possible," Dr. Cornelius told Beth with a shit-eating grin plastered across his face.

"You better damn well hope so," Beth said in return.

The seventh floor of the Louis Pope Life Center would normally have been quiet had it not been occupied recently by the CIA's diabolical experiment to find how stem cells can be used to cure paralysis. Now, it was a symphony of life hanging in the balance. Beeps, clicks, and the overpowering rush of air streaming through the tubes of Marie's ventilator filled the room. Two agents appointed to watch over the subjects fought against the much-needed sleep that filled their minds and bodies as they sat in nearby chairs.

Their dreams of big fluffy pillows and soft cushiony beds were torn asunder by a torrent of blood curdling screams. Screams that were every bit as startling as ones that would have occurred had they not been muffled by breathing tubes shoved down someone's throat. Marie had awakened. Marie had awakened in a tirade of anger and fear, of raw nerves startled to life by a jolt of pure adrenaline coursing through her veins. She swung her arms in her bed causing IV needles to be ripped out of her arm and hand. Blood trickled from her arms and splattered on the floor beside her bed. She grabbed the end of her feeding tube and ripped it from her nose, and she grabbed the ventilator hose and tore it from her mouth.

Marge, Carlos, Jimmy, and Candice were all awoken from their sleep. They sat up as best they could to determine what all the commotion was coming from their neighbor. They could not see past their drawn curtain though. Carlos peered at the two agents as they ran past his bed towards Marie's. They had a look of sheer terror on their faces.

"You! You motherfuckers!" Marie got the words out with much difficulty as she had a mouth full of slimy spit. She took a large gasping breath.

"You motherfuckers did this to me!" She screamed in absolute rage.

"Stay the hell away from me!" She yelled at the two agents that were trying to tend to the dripping wounds. They couldn't get very close as Marie was flailing her arms around.

"Calm down, Calm down!" One of agents shouted at her as he rushed a towel towards her. "You - you were in an accident," he stuttered while fighting to hold Marie down.

"This was no accident! You did this to me! I can't feel my legs because of you!" Marie screeched in fury.

The female agent ran over to a nearby cabinet nearly tripping on the way. She opened it, reached inside, and extracted a small syringe.

165

"Got it under control!" She informed the male agent as she ran back over to Marie's bedside.

"Is it a Benzodiazepine?" The male agent asked.

"Flunitrazepam." The female agent said.

"The same thing as Rohypnol - Ruffies?" he wondered.

"Yes sir, now hold her arm," she instructed. She lifted the syringe, jabbed it into Marie's shoulder, and forced the Rohypnol into Marie's body. Marie was out cold in a matter of seconds.

"I didn't know they made Ruffies in liquid form," the male agent said.

"You probably don't know a lot of things that we have access to that everyday people don't," the female agent said with a smirk on her face. "That was a very high dose we gave her. She'll be out for quite some time; probably a day or two is my guess. But right now, we need to call Dr. Cornelius."

"I will." The male agent said as he dialed the number for Dr. Cornelius.

"He is on his way down now, along with Beth," the male agent said as he hung up the phone.

While the two agents discussed Marie, the others in the room began to voice their concern.

Carlos asked, "What the hell was she talking about? What did she mean that you caused this?"

"Don't worry about that. The subj - I mean the patient here, Marie, is experiencing some extreme posttraumatic symptoms. She is just confused and angry about her unfortunate situation. She just needs some time to come to terms with her injury," the female agent said.

"I don't like this at all. I don't feel safe here," Carlos said.

"We are here to help you," the male agent was lying through his teeth even though they would be helping the subjects enough to get their results.

"Who is in charge here?" Carlos wondered.

"Dr. Cornelius is, he'll be here shortly," the male agent said right as Dr. Cornelius and Beth entered the room. Dr. Cornelius had a grave look of concern spread across his face. The male agent stopped Dr. Cornelius and Beth in their tracks.

"Follow me," he said walking towards the door. They entered the hallway.

"We have a slight problem here," the male agent said. "Subject M2 awoke just a short time ago. She was extremely agitated and was screaming that we did this to her. I don't think that she took to the

Propranolol. We gave her Rohypnol to knock her out until we can figure out what to do.

"That's a problem," Dr. Cornelius said while stroking his non-existent goatee. "Ok. For now, let's just keep her heavily sedated until we can figure out what to do."

"There's more," the agent said. "The other subjects are showing some concern over what M2 was saying. I tried to quell their fears, but I think that we are going to have some more explaining to do."

"Alright, I will go back in there and speak with them. Have M2 placed on morphine by the time she wakes up," Dr. Cornelius instructed as he opened the door and returned to his angry mob.

Chapter 27

JANICE AND VICK

Janice walked along Ocean Drive in the dark, sultry summer's night. Multi-colored lights flashed inside restaurants that doubled as nightclubs as a cacophony of electrifying music poured out onto the street. The palm trees lining the sidewalks gently swayed in the tropical breeze that careened through them. Janice loved South Beach and was excited about her date with Vick at Mangos. She walked a little further and saw the bright neon sign displaying a parakeet, and the restaurant's name adorning the top of the building.

Janice waited in a long line between rows of brown, wicker tables where patrons sat laughing and talking. The hostess was seating people as fast as the tables became available. While Janice stood in line, she observed the people around her. Scantily clad women were out in droves. Their beauty ranged, but there was certainly a higher percentage of gorgeousness that South Beach attracted. Model types with seductive curves were everywhere. There were also gangster types with enough jewelry on to fill a small store.

While Janice stood in line with her arms crossed taking in her surroundings, Vick was making his way over to the where she was standing. He walked up and greeted her with a big hug. Janice was obviously smitten with Vick. He was wearing designer jeans and a tight shirt that showed his great physique. His hair was neatly styled and his face freshly shaven. Janice took in the sweet smell of his Hugo Boss cologne. He was everything Janice could want in a man from a purely physical standpoint. Now, she thought, to learn a little more about his personality.

"Right this way," the hostess said to them as her breasts distracted Janice and Vick from their thoughts. Her breasts nearly leapt out from her low-cut black blouse as she made her way through the crowd.

Janice and Vick were seated at a table to the side of the bar, which was centered in the middle of the dining area. A salsa band played a rhythmic Latin song complete with congas and a voracious female vocalist. The patrons could barely keep themselves in their seats as the beats forced them to sway. A waitress came by and took their drink orders.

"I love this place!" Janice nearly had to shout to be heard by Vick.

"Come closer!" Vick said as he helped Janice scoot her seat nearer to him. Janice nearly fell off the chair as she hopped to his side. Vick grabbed her shoulders and his fingers accidently edged under her dress and bra straps. He jerked them back, and Janice's bra strap slid down her arm exposing a large area of her breast. She pulled the strap up and looked embarrassed.

"I'm sorry!" Vick said.

"You trying to make a move on me?" Janice joked.

"Maybe," Vick said with a large smirk on his face.

"Well, I may like that!" Janice said as Vick's smirk turned into an even larger grin. The waitress returned with their rum and Diet Cokes and placed them down in front of them. She took their food orders. Vick ordered the famous Mambo chicken wings and Janice had the BBQ chicken salad.

After Janice and Vick completed ordering, the Conga dancers made their way out into the main bar area. The women were dressed in brightly colored two-piece suits adorned with frilly accent threads. One female dancer's headdress stood high in the air like a rainbow-colored peacock while another dancer had a train that whipped back and forth as she swung her hips to the music. The male dancers wore black pants with red-layered tops trimmed in black. They all shook their bodies in a salacious display of metrical delight. Janice and Vick thoroughly enjoyed watching them perform.

After the dancers executed several numbers, the restaurant returned to a more calm state with softer music playing in the background. The food was slow to arrive but was placed in front of them as the last number was performed. They enjoyed their food and conversation until Vick put his foot in his mouth.

"What do you mean your last girlfriend was hotter than me?" Janice asked.

"Sorry, sorry, I just meant that she was a model. She was perfect. Not many other girls can come close to how beautiful she was." Vick said as his face turned three shades of red. He didn't think before he spoke. "You are very beautiful though Janice."

"You know what Vick?"

"What?"

"I'm going to let that slide this one time. But, you need to watch yourself," Janice said with a stern look on her face as she pointed her index finger at Vick.

"Again, I'm sorry. Of course, I'll pay for dinner," Vick said.

"Ok. Ok. Let's move on, shall we?"

"Yes, Let's do."

"Vick, I want to know more about what you're studying in medical school," Janice said as she leaned back in her chair a bit with her arms crossed. She still had a defensive demeanor after Vick's insensitive comment.

"Neuroscience," Vick said a little confused over Janice's question. "Why do you ask?"

"Yes, Yes, I know that you are studying neuroscience, but I am wondering what all that entails and how you apply it. I need to pick a specialty in law school and want to do so in the medical field - maybe medical malpractice. Can you tell me more about it?" Janice asked.

"Hmm. I'm not too thrilled about the medical malpractice area; but, if you want to sit in class with me or something like that, it would be cool." Vick told Janice but thought it was a peculiar request. He wasn't about to piss her off again though.

"That's not a bad idea." Janice said. "It would give me an idea of what type of material doctors are exposed to in medical school."

"Well, we are exposed to a lot. A snippet of a class doesn't give you a whole bunch to go on, but you may learn a thing or two." Vick said as he played with the remaining chicken wing lying on his plate. "I know the perfect class to sit in on though. It's a class dedicated completely to the central nervous system. It starts at 1 p.m. on Tuesdays and Thursdays. Are you available then?" Vick asked.

"Yea, actually, I only have two classes on Tuesdays and Thursdays. They are both in the morning. I could make it this Tuesday afternoon if that works for you?" Janice said and then took another sip of her rum and Diet Coke.

"I think that will work. Do you know where the medical school is?" Vick asked as he ran his fingers through his medium length blond hair and straightened his posture.

"Its downtown, over near 14th Street, right? I mean; it's where all the hospitals are?" Janice asked. She knew her way around Miami for someone who only has lived in town for only a few weeks. It was her visits to her aunt who lives there that allowed her to become familiar with some of the different areas of the city.

"Yea, it is. When you come to campus on Tuesday, park in the parking deck off of NW 16th Street. Then, give me a call on my cell phone. I'll come and meet you at the parking deck and then we can go together to the class. Try to get there about 20 minutes early so we can make it on time." Vick said as he pressed his leg against Janice's and placed his hand on her forearm. He was drawing her closer.

"Ok. Vick. I can do that." Janice said. "Well, I've got a busy day tomorrow, so I'm going to go home now."

"Sorry to see you go so early," Vick said. "But, I'll see you on Tuesday." Vick and Janice both stood up. Vick planted a deep kiss on Janice's lips.

"Very nice," Janice said. "I enjoyed that."

"There's more where that came from," Vick said with another big grin on his face.

"I'm sure there is. I look forward to more," Janice said as she turned, walked through the crowd, and disappeared around the corner.

Chapter 28

DR. CORENLIUS AND BETH

Dr. Cornelius entered the room to face Marge, Carlos, Jimmy, and Candice. If looks could kill, Dr. Cornelius would have been instantly vaporized.

"What is going on here?" Carlos demanded.

"Yea, what exactly are you planning to do with us?" Jimmy asked.

"Listen, each of you has experienced an accident which left you paralyzed. I'm sorry to say that most of your family members were killed in the accidents." Dr. Cornelius said. "The ones that survived were transported to different hospitals where they remain in a coma."

"Each one of us has had our family members killed?" Marge asked.

"Yes, your accidents were of a nature that each of you suffered the loss of your loved ones." Dr. Cornelius lied.

"What about our extended families?" Candice asked. "I mean, I have aunts and uncles in Atlanta that could visit."

"Your extended families are not allowed to visit at this time out of concerns for your health and our need to get you into physical therapy as soon as possible. Once we are well underway in your recovery, we will consider allowing your family members to visit." Dr. Cornelius said.

"I don't like this one bit. But, I want to get better," Jimmy said. "I want to be able to walk again."

"And you will. We have implanted stem cells into the areas where your injury occurred. They are growing inside you now and will become nerve cells if everything goes as planned. We need to get you on a physical therapy regimen as soon as possible." Dr. Cornelius said.

"When do we start?" Candice asked.

"Today," Dr. Cornelius said. "Once we get the fifth patient's cooperation, we will begin therapy."

"Wake her up," Jimmy demanded.

"In due time," Dr. Cornelius said.

"Wake her up now!" Carlos and Jimmy both shouted at the same time.

"Hmm. Hmm," Dr. Cornelius muttered to himself as he rested his hand under his chin as he stared at the ground. "I'll see what I can do."

Dr. Cornelius walked over to the side of Marie's bed. He said to an agent standing near him, "Dose her with Flumazenil. That should counteract the Rohypnol. Give her a strong enough dose to wake her up."

"She is going to be one toxic young woman," the agent said.

"Do it - now."

The agent walked over to a nearby cabinet and took out a syringe of Flumazenil. He walked back over to Marie and injected it into the vein in the back of her hand.

"It's done," he said to Dr. Cornelius.

"Good. Now we just wait for her to wake up. In the meantime, prepare to give her a high dose of Cinolazepam. That should keep her in a hypnotic state but allow us to put her through therapy."

"You said you wanted to use morphine before," the male agent said.

"Yes, but she may be too alert for that. I think Cinolazepam is the better choice."

"Ok. I'll have a dose ready," the agent said. "This girl is going to have more chemicals in her than Michael Jackson did."

"Well, It's the only way to be able to get her to cooperate."

Dr. Cornelius walked over to where Beth was standing. She had been waiting in the wing to see how Dr. Cornelius was going to handle the situation.

"Quite a mess we have on our hands, huh?" Beth said in a hushed voice.

"It's under control," Dr. Cornelius said. "I want you to get the therapists ready. Call them up and have them over at the gym in an hour and a half - we should be ready by then."

"I'll do it," Beth said as she walked out the double doors towards the office.

Several minutes later, Marie began to awaken from the effects of the Rohypnol. She was muttering something that wasn't quite coherent. Spit dribbled from her quivering lips onto the bed sheets wrapped across her lower body. She could barely hold herself up.

The male agent slid two tablets of Cinolazepam into Marie's mouth and put a glass of water up to her lips. She took several gulps and swallowed the pills without protest. She laid back and closed her eyes as the room spun around. After several minutes, Marie became numb to the things around her. She couldn't be understood when she spoke, and she lost some of her ability to move with dexterity but not to the point where it would become a problem during physical therapy.

Dr. Cornelius walked over to Marie and gave her a gentle shaking. Her head flopped from side to side and her eyes were glazed over. He asked Marie grab a pencil that he was holding in his hand. Marie reached out and swiped her hand beside the pencil missing it completely. She made another swipe and successfully was able to grip the pencil firmly.

"We are ready," Dr. Cornelius informed the other agents standing nearby.

A team of agents trained in physical therapy gathered in the gym adjoining the recovery room. Beth summoned them from their various lives and pulled them into the experiment. They will be instrumental in the progressive rehabilitation of Marie, Marge, Jimmy, Carlos, and Candice allowing them to walk again. The gym is equipped with state of the art equipment necessary to carry out the task of turning the subjects into ambulatory people once more. There are harnesses used for standing exercises, a Functional Electrical Stimulation (FES) bike, free weights, a body weight supported treadmill, and a Standing Ergometer used for trunk stability, muscular strengthening, and cardiovascular endurance.

While physical therapy by itself isn't sufficient to cure paralysis, the team will be implementing exercises that will stimulate key muscle groups that will help to promote walking. Rehabilitation exercises will also benefit the subjects through cardiovascular functioning, muscle mass development, managing pain, and lowering stress. Overall, it will help them keep their already svelte bodies in great shape.

The team of physical therapists prepared the gym for the subjects while Dr. Cornelius and several other agents were in the recovery room tending to the group.

"Ok, we are going to begin the first phase of your treatment now," Dr. Cornelius said to the subjects as he massaged his thick fake goatee. "You will be meeting with physical therapists who have designed an exercise program for each of you. This is an important component in you recovering your ability to walk again."

Dr. Cornelius stood beside a single black metal wheelchair he had rolled into the recovery room while each of the other agents stood by a wheelchair of their own.

"The first thing we need to do is get each of you into your wheelchair." Dr. Cornelius said as he moved from the center of the room over to Jimmy's bed.

"A fucking wheelchair? Are you kidding me?" Jimmy shouted at Dr. Cornelius. "I'm not getting in that god damned thing."

"You can't walk. This wheelchair is necessary to get you around."

"Mmmm," Jimmy grumbled in frustration. "I can't stand this shit, I fucking hate hospitals." He crossed his arms as if he were a pouting child.

Dr. Cornelius leaned over the side of Jimmy's bed until his face nearly touched Jimmy's. He stared at Jimmy with pursed lips and a furrowed eyebrow and said, "I suggest you allow me to place you in the wheelchair."

Jimmy met his gaze and nearly shouted, "I guess I don't have much of a choice, huh, asshole?"

"No. You don't."

Dr. Cornelius grabbed Jimmy by his left arm and pulled Jimmy up with force. Jimmy sat up straight in his bed and tore his arm from Dr. Cornelius's grip.

"I can handle this," Jimmy said with an eat shit and die look on his face.

"Well at least let me get the bed level with the wheelchair," Dr. Cornelius said while he pushed a button on the side of Jimmy's bed to lower it. He shoved the arm on his bed downwards which cleared Jimmy's path to the wheelchair. "Now slide over."

"This isn't rocket science Doc," Jimmy shot at Dr. Cornelius.

"I'm just trying to help you."

"Well, don't be dumb about it."

"You'll do what I say."

"Like hell I will."

"You'll do what I say or you will not improve your condition - you will never walk again," Dr. Cornelius said as Jimmy slid over and planted himself on the wheelchair. Jimmy turned around to face Dr. Cornelius. A look of terror came over Jimmy's face and a feeling of resignation filled his heart.

"Doc, you're right; I just want to get better. I just want to be able to walk again," Jimmy said as he hung his head. "Why did this have to happen to me?"

An agent pulled Candice in her wheelchair out from behind the curtain surrounding her. She looked at Jimmy and said, "You're not the only one to wonder that. We are all in the same boat kiddo. It sucks but, hey, we move on from here."

Dr. Cornelius chimed in, "That is the kind of attitude you need to make progress here. That type of thinking will get you back on your feet again - literally. We all need to keep a positive attitude and good things are sure to happen. Thank you subj..C...umm...I mean...Candice."

Dr. Cornelius nearly choked on his words. All of the agents were trying to avoid a major mess-up in the clinical setting. The protocols of the experiment for the CIA demanded that Jimmy, Marie, Candice, Carlos, and Marge be referred to as subjects - not as patients, and that is how the agents referred to them when they spoke to each other without the subjects present. The project also called for the subjects' names to be abbreviated to their first initials with either a one or two on the end depending on whether or not someone else had a name that started with the same letter. The purpose of this renaming was not only to make it more simple to read the detailed scientific reports being compiled but also to strip the data of all human sentiment that might fog the scientists' mind. Without personalizing the subjects, the scientist reading the report could concentrate on the hard facts.

Jimmy, Carlos, Marie, Candice, and Marge all eventually mounted their wheelchairs. Each agent pushed a wheelchair with a subject in it through the double doors that separated the recovery room from the gym. The physical therapists met them on the other side. Also waiting for them in the gym were three agents whose duty was to record everything. One agent had a camera, one was taping everything with a voice recorder, and one was to jot down notes as the therapy took place.

One of the therapists, Jane, approached Candice.

"Hello. Are you ready to begin your treatment, sugar?"

"Yeah. Only if it will make me walk again," Candice said with her arms crossed and a frown on her face. None of the five were exactly thrilled to be there trying to regain something that they had taken for granted most of their lives. They had to learn to walk twice: once as a toddler, and now, as full-grown young adults.

"Well, I want to place you in the Standing Ergometer," Jane said as she wheeled Candice towards the simple looking stick like machine.

Jane positioned her wheelchair next to the contraption.

"You're not going to torture me with this thing, are you - like your putting me into some medieval stretching rack?" Candice was only half kidding.

"Don't worry, this machine will help you with muscle strengthening, cardiovascular endurance, and you will learn how to stabilize your midsection. I will be holding you by the waist the entire time. Let your arms be in control as your legs follow their lead."

Candice grabbed the handles of the Ergometer and began to pull herself upwards while Jane gripped Candice's sides near her hips. She clumsily pulled herself towards the center of the machine until her body was positioned over the pedals below.

"A little help here," Jane said in the direction of a nearby agent. He ran over to the Ergometer where the two were doing their best to maintain stability and trying not to fall down. They weren't doing a very good job of it as evidenced by the wiggling back and forth of Candice's pelvis. The male agent shoved Candice's feet into the pedals and strapped them in place.

"Now move your arms," the agent said while keeping Candice from falling backwards. Candice began to move her arms slowly, and as she did, her legs followed along.

"That's it. You've got it. Now pull your arms a little harder," The agent said as Candice put more effort into dragging her weight back and forth while she strained against the resistance she was feeling. "Good, good. Keep your pace steady, you are doing really well."

"My back is starting to hurt," Candice complained as she was getting into a solid sustained rhythm on the Ergometer. She looked backwards at the agent supporting her while she rowed, but the agent had her head turned away from Candice. "I said that my back hurts," Candice said a little louder than before with apparent irritation in her voice.

"Push yourself through the pain, you are doing a good job," the agent said as Candice grimaced over the hurt. "The discomfort is temporary. You will not feel anything in just a little while."

"It is stinging where I was hurt, where my injury is, not because of this stupid machine, and these stupid exercises," Candice had tears in her eyes as her tempo on the Ergometer slowed.

"Oh, hang in there Shug, we'll get you some pain killers once we get back to the room," the agent assured Candice as she twisted Candice's hips back and forth. Candice was giving more resistance than before and the agent noticed.

While Candice continued to exercise, the team of agents responsible for documenting the subjects and their activities were using their various instruments to record every move Candice made. How she responded to the therapy, the therapist, the equipment, and the pain of her injury were all accounted for and were saved for future use. They were like vultures circling the fresh remains of a newly slaughtered rabbit, and they did not take an eye off of her for even a second. Candice was their prey, and these agents were hungry.

They also had the scent of the other subjects in their nostrils. The agents thoroughly prepared themselves for documenting Jimmy's, Carlos's, Marge's and Marie's activities once they were underway. They would be in for a shock, however, while trying to document Marie's progress.

Chapter 29

JANICE AND VICK

Vick stood at the entrance to the 16th Street parking deck waiting for Janice to arrive. He checked his watch on no less than four occasions, huffed in and out twice, and tapped his head against a nearby poll once. Janice was ten minutes late, and class started in just another ten minutes. Vick hated to be late to class, to work, and to any engagement that came his way. He thought that punctuality was a virtue and those who weren't on time didn't care about the matter at hand. Some, especially those that counted on him, admired his chronic need for promptness. Others found it to be irritating and obsessive.

Vick was just about to telephone Janice, but she whipped her car around the corner before Vick could press the call button on his cell phone. She quickly pulled her car past him and found a nearby parking space. She jumped out of her car and swiftly walked to where Vick was standing. Vick tried not to show his agitation with her and instead gave her a big bear hug.

He said, "Hey babe, where you been? We need to hurry to get to class before they start."

"Sorry, the traffic on 95 is horrible. I left forty-five minutes ago - you know I don't live but five miles away - and it still took a long time," Janice said as the two of them strolled towards the Schominger Research Quadrangle of the medical complex. They passed through the Quadrangle and entered the Clinical Research Building.

They crossed the front threshold, turned left, and made their way into a small classroom a few minutes late. The professor gave the two of them a dirty look as he took a pause from his lecture while waiting for them to take a seat. After an awkward and clumsy trip down the row of students to the vacant seats nearest the window, Vick leaned over and grabbed a Neurology textbook from his satchel. He whispered to Janice, "Here, follow along with me."

The professor continued his lecture, "during the early development of the vertebrate embryo, a longitudinal groove on the neural plate gradually deepens as ridges on either side of the groove, the neural folds, become elevated, and ultimately meet, transforming the groove into a closed tube, the ectodermal wall of which forms the rudiment of the nervous system."

The professor continued on the basic development of the nervous system. Vick thought that the material was of an easy enough nature that Janice could follow along well. It was early in the semester and the class hadn't progressed into the more complex aspects of the material yet to be covered.

After the hour of class had passed, Vick and Janice made their way over to the student lounge for a snack and some soda.

"So, what did you think of the class?" Vick asked with wonder in his eyes. "Did you like it?"

"It was interesting enough to keep me awake, and I understood most of it. It was a lot like the biology classes I took back in college. We covered some of the same things there, and I don't feel like I forgot a lot of that material. If I did go into medical malpractice, I think I would have a good handle on the substance that would need to be covered in the cases," Janice said as she ripped her muffin into small pieces.

"Hmmm. I wish you would have forgotten the material," Vick said flatly.

"Oh, don't give me that shit. You know there are some quacks out there that don't deserve a medical degree let alone be trusted with a patient," Janice said with a steely look on her face. She seemed to be posturing herself.

"Maybe, but there isn't a medical school in the US that you can just slide through without acquiring the skill to administer care to a patient," Vick said a little peeved at Janice's accusations. He didn't like feeling attacked, and he didn't like the idea that he may treat a patient one day for a disease that has no cure, and the patient would sue; or despite his best efforts to save a patient, there was some unforeseen complication beyond his control that caused the patient harm, and, then, that patient would sue. He hated the idea of needing to practice defensive medicine rather than tending to the true needs of the patient. It truly ran up healthcare costs considerably doing so.

"Yea, but just because someone gets through medical school doesn't make that person a good, competent doctor," Janice said with a steely look in her eyes and a pugnacious attitude to match.

"If you really want to get into it, there are some half-assed lawyers out there too," Vick said elevating his voice to the point that others around him were turning to look at the debate.

"Touché - you're right, and I think those lawyers who treat their clients poorly, and aren't competent, need to be taken to task as well. I'm just saying that despite the fact that a professional - or anyone - wants to do good, that is not always the outcome of their efforts," Janice was gnashing her teeth a bit as evidenced by the ripple of her jaw muscles. She found she did this when she was angry. She has been doing it a lot more lately, especially, after classes began.

"Yes, I know the old St. Bernard's proverb too: the road to hell is paved with good intentions; I guess the freeway to hell is paved with bad ones," Vick said as he finished up his diet coke. "Can we change the subject here?"

"We can. Just be aware that this is something you will have to deal with in your professional career. Hopefully, a patient will never sue you, but the reality is that nearly every doctor out there is sued despite his or her good intentions. It is a cost of doing business," Janice said between nibbles on her muffin bits.

"Well, they need to lower those costs. There should be greater caps on punitive damages against doctors," Vick said in a more subdued voice. The others in the room returned to their own business.

"Tell that to Grandma Mable who went into the hospital for surgery on her finger and left with one less leg than she brought into the place," Janice said. Vick almost burst out laughing but held it in while Janice cracked a smile.

"That's a major fuck up," Vick said with a grin.

"Yes, sir, that is, and Grandma Mable needs to be properly compensated for someone else not doing their job properly."

"Fine, you win - they should. God, arguing with a law student is like arguing with police officer after he discovered your loaded pistol on the seat next to you, sees the open container between your legs, and finds the dead body in the duffle bag in the back seat - you're basically screwed," Vick said trying to lighten the mood.

"You're screwed or I'm screwed," Janice asked in all seriousness.

"Shut up for a minute Janice, Just shut up."

"Ohhh we-

"Shut it," Vick said as Janice began to come down off the high she was giving herself. She just sat there staring at her muffin for a bit while trying to find a nice piece of it to fill her mouth.

After several minutes of awkward silence had passed, Janice asked Vick a question. She asked, "Could I see more of what you do? I mean - can I see the rats?"

"You have got to be kidding me. You want to see the rats?" Vick said with measured repulsion. The repulsion wasn't so much from the fact that Janice wanted to see the rats; it was the lingering tension between the two that he was expressing in his voice.

Janice felt he was giving her some attitude and resented it. She said, "God damn it, Vick, yes I want to see the rats. Is that a problem?"

"Wonder if I don't want to show you the god damn rats!" Vick said as he quickly stood up from the table. The several students in the lounge turned their eyes once again in Vick and Janice's direction.

Janice stood from the table facing Vick and shouted, "I want to see the god damn rats!"

Vick couldn't contain himself any longer. He reached out and grabbed the back of Janice's neck and laid a deep, deep kiss on her lips. Janice backed away a little and stared at him. She then grabbed the back of Vick's neck and returned the favor, but her kiss was even deeper and more passionate.

"Let's get the fuck out of here." Vick whispered into Janice's ear.

"Your car or mine?" Janice asked obviously aroused as indicated by the large bumps protruding from her shirt.

"Mine." Vick said as he grabbed her hand and rushed her out of the building toward the parking deck. They reached the car, and Vick quickly took off squealing the car's tires as he did. Vick nearly wrecked his car on several occasions trying to return Janice's kisses as they made their way to Vick's apartment.

Luckily, they made it to Vick's apartment unscathed and quickly ran up the steps and entered, slamming the door behind them.

Chapter 30

BETH AND DR. CORNELIUS

While Candice was busy on the Standing Ergometer, Jimmy was occupied with the free weights. An agent named Ralph helped Jimmy to complete several different exercises that focused on his arms and shoulders. Jimmy was using the heaviest of the barbells, fifty-pounds; he was already in excellent shape from basic training and breezed through most of the exercises that Ralph instructed him to complete. Jimmy worked out for nearly half an hour and became a little irritated for having to do the rudimentary exercises.

He asked Ralph, "Why I am wasting time doing upper body training; I mean, shouldn't I be focusing on getting my lower body in shape?"

"We'll get to that Jimmy. Right now, we need to focus on making your whole body strong, and we need to counteract the effects of you having to stay in your bed for such a long period of time," Ralph said as he guided Jimmy's arm as Jimmy lifted the barbell high above his head.

"I'm already in good shape. I was in basic training before this happened," Jimmy said still a little miffed that he wasn't making faster advancement towards walking again.

"Yes, but you wouldn't believe how much muscle mass is lost just after a few days of being totally inactive. Your upper body has to be in good shape to push yourself around in your wheelchair as well as complete other tasks. You are going to have an increased need for upper body strength now, and we want to make sure that you are up to the challenge," Ralph said as Jimmy placed the barbell back into its cradle on the rack.

"I guess you're right. I'm just wondering when these damn stem cells are going to kick in and allow me to walk again," Jimmy asked.

"It could take some time for the stem cells to grow into nerve tissue. There is the possibility that they may not grow at all if the surrounding tissues and fluids prove to be an environment that is not suitable for them. Only time will tell, in the meantime, we will be using every therapeutic tool we have to make sure that we are ready for the real possibility that the stem cells will undo the damage that has been done to your spinal cord," Ralph said as he pushed Jimmy in his wheelchair past Marge.

Marge was hanging from the harness suspended over the treadmill. An agent was pushing and pulling her legs back and forth in a steady gait. Another agent operated the treadmill to make sure that Marge and the other therapist weren't out of sync with the pace of the belt. Marge's face displayed discomfort as the therapists did their best to keep her on track. She was putting in maximum effort to maintain the balance in her upper body within the harness, but was growing increasingly tired and slumping a bit.

"Come on Marge, you can do this. We have a lot of work left to do yet, so we need you to try as hard as you can to keep up with the pace," Tabitha said to Marge in a deep voice. "You want to walk again don't you?"

There was a short, uncomfortable pause. "Don't you talk to me about walking again! You don't know what this is like; you already can walk," Marge shouted at Tabitha as she pulled on Marge's ankle. "You try getting your fat ass up here and see what you can do," Marge was livid. Tabitha began to blush from embarrassment.

"I'm just trying to help you Marge, and I am trying to push you. Don't take what I say personally. I want you to get better," Tabitha said as she tried to regain her composure. "We have a long way to go, and I need you to work with me, not against me."

"Ok. Ok. Let's just finish this stupid exercise already; I am exhausted," Marge said as she slumped even further in her harness.

"We'll have you back to your bed in just a bit. For now, just focus on keeping your back straight and feel the rhythm of the exercises in your upper body," Tabitha said as she continued to manipulate Marge's legs.

Fifteen more minutes passed, and Marge finished her exercises. She nearly fell out of the harness when Tabitha and the other therapist unzipped it to get her out. She shook her head from side to side as the agents placed her back in her wheelchair. Marge looked as if she had been hit by a freight train. The whole experience of being in what she thought was a hospital created a sense of anxiety and frustration in her that she had never experienced before and would never experience again. It showed in her puffy eyes and pale complexion. To her, it was maddening. She let out a guttural scream that roused everyone in the gym. Carlos and Candice turned their head quickly to see what had happened to cause Marge to scream like she did. Their respective therapists told them that she was just having a very bad time coping with her injury. Marie didn't so much turn her head as she did bob it towards the scream in a dazed and disoriented state.

While Marge was being whisked away to her room and being administered a sedative, Marie was surviving the effects of the

Cinolazepam. She was slow in her speech and was drooling on her shirt in regular intervals. She seemed almost as if she had been participating in a heavy night of drinking. An agent had her strapped into the functional electrical stimulation bike. Vibrating tingles of electricity were being introduced into her thin legs pulling at her muscles to pump up and down on the unusual bicycle.

The agent did her best to balance Marie on the bicycle and had to pull her up from a slumped position on more than one occasion. Marie's legs rotated around and around in a circular motion for nearly20 minutes. As she sat there, it was apparent to the agent that Marie was becoming more lucid. Eventually, Marie spoke to the agent. She did so in a soft voice.

"Wha?" She stammered. "What am I doin' here?" She asked while her head steadily dipped up and down, and she pointed a finger at nothing in particular.

"You are in rehab, honey," the friendly female agent said to Marie as she looked on with trepidation.

"Wha? Wha? Who? Who are you?" Marie asked the therapist but the therapist didn't have a chance to respond before Marie cut her off again.

"I...I know who ya are," Marie said still pointing a bent finger at the therapist. "You...you are the one who did this to me," Marie said.

Sheer panic strangled the therapist's heart. She leapt from her chair and tore off down the hall towards the recovery room where Dr. Cornelius, Beth, and two other agents were discussing the future plans for the subjects. She turned the corner near the recovery room and smacked the full weight of her body against the guard standing at the door. He flew backwards against the door and caused the lock to come loose from the catch. The wind was knocked from him. He stood there doubled over as the large agent tried to push him out of her way.

The guard grabbed the back of her scrub sleeve and tugged it with force. She tried to smack his hand away as she ran through the door that had been forced ajar.

He screamed, "Come back here!" He continued to pull at her sleeve as she slapped at him. "Come back here now you heifer!"

The therapist stopped and looked at him with wild indignation. She threw an elbow against his forearm causing him to lose his grip on her sleeve. She continued through the door to where the others stood.

The therapist was out of breath and tried to form words that wouldn't come.

"I..." She started.

"What is it?" Dr. Cornelius asked looking on with great concern.

"I...She," The therapist tried her best to get her words out but her need to breath got in the way.

"Ok. Ok. Take it easy. Take some deep breathes," Dr. Cornelius said as he placed a hand on the therapists back.

Several more seconds passed. Finally, the therapist was able to regain her composure.

She said in a slow and deliberate voice, "There is a problem." She paused to take a deep breath. "There is a problem," the stout agent said again. "Subject M2 is coming off her medication. She is starting to think again."

Dr. Cornelius's, Beth's, and the others' eyes got as big as saucers. Dr. Cornelius asked, "What is she saying?"

The large agent continued, "she is saying we did this to her."

There was a long prickly silence that grew more uncomfortable by the second as the agents all looked around at each other. Dr. Cornelius finally cried out, "Shit, shit, shit!" He quickly paced back and forth in a moment of irrationality and irritability.

He screamed at one of the male agents standing near him, "quick, get her some more of the Cinolazepam."

The agent quickly made his way to the cabinets alongside the recovery room. He opened one of the cabinets and searched around pulling different medicine bottles out and quickly replacing them. He moved on to the next cabinet and also pulled out several bottles one by one, read the label, and quickly placed it back in the cabinet. He eventually moved to a third cabinet, pulled out a bottle, read the label, and shouted at the others, "I found it!"

The agent peered down at the label that read Cinolazepam. He gently shook the bottle; there wasn't any sound, no rustling around of pills - nothing.

"It's empty," he screamed.

"Damn," Dr. Cornelius said trying to remain calm long enough to adequately access the situation. "How can we be out? We only gave her two doses."

"There weren't very many pills to begin with. The bottle was sample sized," the agent said as he eyed the empty bottle. He went back to the cabinet to see if there were any more bottles. After about a minute, the agent was unable to find any more Cinolazepam. He said in a defeated voice after slumping his shoulders and bowing his head, "There's none."

"Damn it to hell!" Dr. Cornelius shouted in the direction of the agent. "Well, we need to give her something to keep her from causing a problem. Just get in there and give her a strong dose of morphine until I can find something in the cabinet that will work."

The agent grabbed a syringe full of morphine and was prepared to give Marie an intramuscular injection. He ran towards the door. While he was running, the agent's foot caught the foot of the guard standing outside the door, and he fell hard to the ground. The glass syringe shattered in his hand and fragments of glass entered his palms drawing a copious amount of blood. The agent screeched in pain as some of the morphine entered the wound.

"Watch what you're doing!" the agent screamed at the guard. The agent became light headed from the morphine and clumsily sat down on the floor. The guard gave the agent a dirty look. He said, "fuck this," as he walked to a nearby bathroom to relieve himself.

Tabitha ran past the agent sitting on the floor. She had another syringe full of Morphine in her hand. Dr. Cornelius, Beth, and another female agent were following close. Tabitha made her way several feet down the hall to the doors to the gym when she heard the agent on the floor shout in somewhat slurred words, "goo luck ya faa bitch!"

Tabitha turned around and glared at the agent on the floor as blood from his hand pooled beside him. She said, "Yea, and good luck with your hand you skinny prick!" She stuck her middle finger up at him before returning her attention back to the matter at hand.

Tabitha saw Marie alongside the back wall of the gym. Marie was rolling her wheelchair over to a nearby emergency exit. Tabitha and the others quickly made their way past the exercise equipment towards Marie, and they caught the full attention of Marie who had shaken most of the effects of the Cinolazepam. She rolled her chair even faster to get away from the advancing agents.

She screamed, "Get the hell away from me!"

The agents were unperturbed as they made their way closer to Marie. One of the agents grabbed the back of her wheelchair so she couldn't roll any further. Marie threw her arms backwards and flailed them around. Her hand smacked at the agent's forearm as she continued screaming at them. The screams bounced around the gym that Carlos and Candice left minutes earlier. It was just Marie and the agents left to battle it out.

As one of the agents held the back of her wheelchair, another agent tried to immobilize her arms that were leaving bruises on the first agent's body. He held Marie in a bear hug; she tried to bite the agent's neck but failed to make contact with his skin since he bobbed his head backwards. She continued to let out ghastly screams.

"You did this to me! You motherfuckers! I will kill you!"

Marie's screams rippled through Tabitha. Tabitha was trying not to let her nerves get the best of her, but she found her hands to be a bit shaky. She seized the glass syringe full of morphine in the palm of her hand and positioned the stopper of the syringe in just the right position. She eyed Marie's arm looking for the spot where she would inject the morphine. Tabitha raised the syringe high over her left ear and slammed it down into Marie's soft skin. Marie shrieked in pain as the needle struck her muscle. Seconds later, the morphine introduced itself into Marie's veins and calmness gripped her body. She lifted her hand as if to hit the nearby agent but her attempt fell short. Marie mumbled something incoherently as she slowly dozed off.

"God damn it!" Dr. Cornelius shouted moments later at no one in particular as he paced the room. "What are we going to do about this subject? I mean, we can't continue to make progress on this experiment if this subject is going to be so uncooperative."

"We just need to find another drug to put her on," one of the male agents suggested.

"No, no, that won't work. We need to get some more Cinolazepam," Dr. Cornelius said staring at the agent.

"It could take some time before we can get it, being the weekend and all," the agent said.

"Well work on getting it here!" Dr. Cornelius shot at him.

Dr. Cornelius wheeled Marie back into the recovery area. Jimmy, Marge, Carlos, and Candice looked at Dr. Cornelius with unrelenting suspicion. Even though they could not hear exactly what Marie was screaming about, they did hear the high pitched squeals coming from the gym. Each remained calm, but the tension in the room was beginning to build. They would eventually want answers, but, for now, fear gave way to reason, and they knew to keep their mouths shut.

After Marie was safely placed back into her bed, Dr. Cornelius and Beth exited the room. The others were left with two male agents that would tend to them. The agents brought the group their dinner, which to everyone's surprise, was a well balanced and very tasty treat.

"Wow, I've never had hospital food that tasted like this before," Carlos said to the others through his curtain as he finished up his rotisserie chicken and braised spinach. "I could get used to this."

"It's pretty good isn't it?" Marge said as she placed her empty plate on the dinner tray angled over her bed.

"Yea, it is - kind of makes you..." Carlos trailed off.

"Kind of makes you what?" Marge asked.

"Never mind," Carlos stopped himself as not to look paranoid.

"No, tell me. Kinda makes you what?" Marge insisted.

"It kinda makes you wonder why people would complain about hospital food if it tastes like this," he said quietly as he looked down at his plate. "Unless, of course...we're not..." his voice trailed off again.

"Come on Carlos...that is your name right?" Marge asked.

"Yes it is...you must have heard one of the agents say it," Carlos said.

"I did...come on, though spit it out...unless, of course we're not what?" Marge demanded.

"Unless, of course, we're not in a hospital," he said. There were several moments of tense silence as Carlos's words hung in the air like a thick, black cloud of confusion.

Marge, Jimmy, and Candice all responded negatively to Carlos's comment.

Jimmy said," No, that's ridiculous, I mean look at this place. What else would this be?"

"I'm not sure, but witness how that girl over there is acting. I mean she seems to know something that we don't," Carlos said referencing Marie, who was sleeping, as his eyes grew wide with his harrowing thoughts.

"She's just in shock from the accident. She doesn't know what the hell she is talking about," Jimmy said to him.

"This is a hospital, plain and simple," Marge said, "They are trying to help us."

"I just don't have a good feeling about this," Carlos said. "I can't put my finger on it but something is wrong with the staff here. They seem a little off."

The agents were out of earshot from the others, as they were standing in the hall arguing over who was going to go pick up their dinner. Finally, one of the agents left and walked over to the elevator and got on. The other agent angrily tromped over to the bathroom.

"You're just anxious," Candice said to Carlos. "There is nothing to worry about. Just focus your energy on getting better."

"Ok. Ok, you're probably right," Carlos conceded. "I want to get out of here though. I don't like it here."

"None of us do," Jimmy said.

Chapter 31

JANICE AND VICK

Vick slammed the door to his apartment behind him as Janice, and he kissed each other feverishly. The corner of the coffee table caught Janice's leg, and she and Vick fell over the table and landed on the couch. They didn't miss a beat and continued kissing each other.

"Wait, wait a second," Janice said pushing away from Vick a little bit as she looked into his eyes.

"What?" Vick asked.

"This is a little fast, isn't it? I mean we really don't know each other that well," Janice said as she pushed away even more.

"I like you Janice," Vick said. "I like you a lot."

"Do you Vick?" Janice wondered as she stood up. "I don't want this to be some one night stand or just meaningless sex. I want to see you again."

"Ahhh, Janice. Don't worry about it. We'll still talk and go out if you want. I am not going to love you and leave you. Let's just enjoy this."

"I don't know Vick. There have been too many guys in my life that have broken my heart. I'm not going to let you be another one," Janice said as an apparent pain displayed across her face.

"Janice, we can talk about this later."

"No, we need to talk about this now."

"Alright Janice," Vick said in an agitated tone of voice as he sat upright. "I know you're the one who broke up with Jimmy. You have broken your fair share of hearts in your life; I'm sure of it."

"Well, I - I didn't like, I didn't want to be with them."

"Then, how is that any different from what your ex-boyfriends have done to you?" Vick asked. "Sometimes it just doesn't work out. You don't know until you try, and I think we should try."

"I guess, I guess you're right Vick. But, I'm tired of being hurt," Janice said as she plopped back down on the couch beside Vick.

"It's ok, Janice," Vick said as he wiped away a tear that had rolled down Janice's face. "It's ok," he said again as he gently kissed her cheek. He kissed her cheek again and gradually, tenderly kissed his way over to her lips where he softly pecked at them with his lips. Janice didn't return the kisses at first. Then, her defenses broke down. Within the minute, Janice and Vick were single-mindedly indulging each other with their loving kisses.

They adored each other on the couch for nearly 15 beautiful minutes, until Vick said, "Let's go to the bedroom."

"Ok," Janice replied as she and Vick got off the couch holding hands and slowly made their way through the door to the bed. Janice lay down on the bed as Vick began to unbutton her blouse. He pulled Janice's blouse off of her arms and his fingers made his way to the buttons on her jeans. He kissed her neck as he unbuttoned and unzipped the dark blue jeans.

A few moments later, Janice climbed on top of Vick. She moaned in ecstasy as Vick made love to her. The headboard violently smacked against the wall as their love making intensified. Several minutes passed by and, then, Vick curled his toes as he reached climax. Janice screamed out as she peaked. She screamed on each occasion.

Janice rolled off of Vick and laid beside him as he draped his arm around her. She was staring up at the ceiling when Vick asked her, "Was it good for you?"

"That...was amazing," she said with a large grin on her face. "You know, I could get used to that."

"I hope you do Janice. I hope you do. But, don't get too used to it, I don't want it to get old. We'll have to try new things," Vick said with an even bigger grin on his face.

"Well, let's not make any assumptions," Janice said moving a little closer to the edge of the bed. "I do want to see you again sometime soon."

"And, you will," Vick said as he placed his hand on Janice's flat stomach. "I want to see more of you."

Janice slid over a bit more and sat up. Normally, this would be the time where she would say her goodbyes and make a quick exit. Today, it was different as there would be no disappearing act on her part. She relished in the positive energy that was coursing through her body. Vick imparted a deep sense of sexual satisfaction in her with his attentiveness to her needs. Janice leaned over and picked her bra up and put it on. She also put her blouse and pants back on while Vick watched with unabashed adoration. Damn, he thought to himself, I have truly struck gold.

Vick slowly got out of bed and pulled on his clothes. He looked at the clock and noticed that he was late for his next lecture. He thought to himself that Janice taught him a class on anatomy that no professor could ever top. For once in his life, he wasn't concerned about the black hands that told the time.

Janice and he walked into the living room and sat back on the couch. Vick draped his arm around Janice as he looked into her eyes. She pulled back a bit but gave him a big smile. Something was alive in her. She felt her heart jump watching Vick intently as he reached for the remote control. Janice stopped his hand and placed it in her lap.

She told him, "I don't want this day to end. You are a great guy, and I want to see more of you."

"It doesn't have to end right now. I'm already missing my class. Why don't you stay for a while longer?" Vick asked. "I can start dinner for us in about an hour or two. Do you like chicken with garlic-mashed potatoes?"

"I'm missing my class too, but I don't really care - contracts are about as much fun as having a root canal," Janice said. "Yeah, chicken and garlic-mashed potatoes sounds good. Do you have any wine?" Janice asked as she stood up and slowly walked towards the bathroom.

"Does the spine have nerve cells?" Vick asked. "I'm going to be a doctor. We all have wine, or scotch."

"I bet I could drink you under the table, Vick," Janice said as she shut the door to the bathroom.

Vick shouted, "That sounds like a challenge to me!"

Janice shouted back, "Anytime, anyplace!" She emerged from the bathroom while the toilet was flushing in the background. She walked over to the kitchen where Vick just popped open a bottle of red wine. He already had a glass poured for her and handed it to her.

"It's a Pinot Noir," Vick said as he showed Janice the label. "It's from Napa Valley. It's got a very fruity bouquet and a robust taste for a Pinot. Swirl it around in your glass and take a whiff." Janice made circular motions with her bulbous red wine glass and stuck her nose in the opening. She breathed in deeply as she took in the aroma.

"Smells like wine to me," Janice said flatly.

"Oh, wow, we're going to have to get you educated on your wine. You're not like that with all your alcoholic beverages are you?" Vick asked with borderline disgust. He knew his wine.

"I know good vodka when I taste it," Janice said.

"Well, that's a start," Vick said. "Did you know that wine is actually named after the grape that it comes from? That there are over 5,000 varieties of wine grapes which - "

"Not now, just let me enjoy my wine," Janice said with a hint of anger in her voice. "Plus, I have something I want to talk to you about."

"Well, ok, what do you want to talk about then?" Vick wondered as he took another sip of his Pinot. He softened his stance by allowing his butt to rest against the counter.

"When can I see the rats?" Janice asked. She did so in a bashful way.

Vick stopped himself mid drink. He cocked his head to the side a bit and asked, "What is it with you and those damn rats?"

"I'm just interested, that's all. I haven't been to a lab before - not since high school. I want to see what you medical guys are up too. Would that be ok?" Janice wondered.

"You know I'm not crazy about letting a future malpractice lawyer in on the medical field; but since it's you, I'll make an exception," Vick said as he took a large gulp of wine. "I'll tell you though. It's not all that exciting, unless you like to see rats crawling around on their front legs or rats running around in circles."

"Believe it or not, I would be interested in seeing them. I'm all about learning right now," Janice said as she finished off her glass of wine.

"Well, get ready to be schooled."

Chapter 32

BETH AND DR. CORNELIUS

Physical therapy came early the next day. Jimmy, Marge, Carlos, and Candice were all awoken at six in the morning, fed a hearty breakfast, washed by the agents, and dressed in a new set of clothes before being wheeled off to the gym. The agents left Marie behind since she wouldn't respond to their attempts to wake her. The others were growing concerned over her absence and beginning to wonder how she was going to get better without participating in the physical therapy like they were. Candice was most concerned; Marie was, after all, her best friend, and Candice wanted nothing more than for Marie to be able to walk again.

"It's really starting to bother me that Marie is having such a difficult time with her accident," Candice said to Jimmy as she was lifting a dumbbell near him while he was being worked out on the treadmill.

"They keep drugging her so much, it's hard to tell what is going on in her head. She just seems to scream when she's not on something though," Jimmy said through gasps as an agent pushed and pulled his legs on the treadmill.

"I know. It's just weird that she keeps screaming when she's not drugged. It really bothered me when she first woke up and was shouting that the nurses and doctors did this to her. They don't deserve that; they're just here to help. I've never seen her act so irate towards anyone before. She's normally a sweetheart, and a horny one at that, might I add," Candice said through chuckles.

"That's a good thing!" Jimmy said as the agent increased the speed of the treadmill. "You'll have to properly introduce us once we get our shit together."

"Yea, that may be awhile though," Candice said straining from the weight as she curled the dumbbell. "For now, just concentrate on your legs and not your penis."

"Ha! You're funny one," Jimmy laughed.

While the subjects were training their bodies to increase the potential of their walking again, Dr. Cornelius and Beth remained back in the recovery room with Marie. They watched her closely as she slowly breathed in and out. Dr. Cornelius had a look of concern on his face when Beth turned to him. She asked him, "What do you plan on doing with her."

Dr. Cornelius replied, "We need her participation soon. She is already skewing the data as it is. Unfortunately, the Cinolazepam hasn't arrived yet, but we need to wake her up."

"You know that isn't a good idea," Beth said as she sighed. Dr. Cornelius turned his gaze towards her. He could tell that the pressure was getting under her skin; she looked like a bus ran over her. Beth's hair was disheveled, and she had large, puffy, black circles under her eyes.

"Why don't you go and get some rest," Dr. Cornelius suggested to Beth.

"You need me here to help deal with this situation, don't you?"

"No. I can handle it, just go lie down for a little while and take a nap."

"But it's only eleven o'clock in the morning; I don't need a nap."

"I know what time it is. You look like hell Beth, please go get some rest."

"Alright, alright, I will," Beth said as she made her way towards the door. She walked past the guard stationed outside in the hallway and made her way to the small cot adjoining the office. Once there, she laid down and quickly fell asleep.

Beth left Dr. Cornelius and Marie by themselves in the recovery room. Dr. Cornelius paced back and forth wondering what to do with Marie. He furiously stroked his invisible goatee as the edges of his lab coat flapped back and forth as he walked. He was startled from his thoughts when his cell phone rang.

"Hello, this is Dr. Cornelius."

"Dr. Cornelius, how are things progressing with the experiment?" Deputy Director of the CIA, Joanne, asked. She didn't even introduce herself first; she knew Dr. Cornelius would recognize her shrill, strong voice.

"Hello, Joanne," Dr. Cornelius offered. "Things are progressing as expected. The subjects have been in physical therapy for several days now and are making advancement in their recovery."

Dr. Cornelius paused for a moment and wondered if he should tell Joanne about Marie. Then, he thought to himself that there was a team of agents recording everything. He wasn't going to attempt to change the data, so he figured that Joanne would eventually find out that Marie, to date, wasn't participating in the study.

He began, "One of the subject's is giving us some difficulty. She may have some recollection of her capture. I don't think she took to the drug given to induce amnesia. We are going to wake-"

"What? What are you saying to me?" Joanne screamed. "I can't believe I'm hearing what I think I'm hearing. You mean to tell me that the project is underway, and we do not have all the subjects aboard?

"Yes, yes, Joanne. That is the case. We plan on waking her very soon to rejoin the others as soon as-"

"You listen to me, you, you little prick! You wake that subject immediately and have her in physical therapy ASAP. Do you understand me?" Joanne was livid. You don't get to be one of the directors of the CIA by being timid or a softy, and Joanne was neither; she could rip a new asshole in anything.

"Yes, Joanne, I will have her awake and participating in the study as soon as possible," Dr. Cornelius said in a hesitant and cowardly way. Joanne had backed him in the corner. He could try to fight his way out, but it would most likely cost him his job.

"It is unacceptable that the subject has not participated in the study up until this point. You know how sensitive and important this project is and if you fuck up this data, I will fuck you up! Is that understood?"

"Joanne, Joanne, calm down please, we are doing everything we can to make this experiment go according to plan. I want you to understand that there are a lot of variables here that we did not anticipate. We are making progress with the others though, and will eventually have everything in order," Dr. Cornelius said.

"You damn right you will, and it will be sooner rather than later," Joanne yelled before slamming her phone down. Dr. Cornelius winched from the noise before returning his cell phone to his pocket. He looked over at Marie lying in her bed. Her icy gaze met his; she had awakened.

Marie took a long and deep breath while never breaking her eye contact with Dr. Cornelius. Once her lungs were filled with all the air she could possibly hold, she let out a scream that could wake the dead.

She shrieked, "You son of a bitch! You are going to pay for this!"

Anxiety boiled up inside of Dr. Cornelius as he jerked his body towards the cabinets. He opened the cabinet doors and was staring at an array of drugs with which he was not familiar. He looked around for some morphine, a tranquilizer, anything that would quell Marie's rage. He grabbed for the drugs; he found a blood thinner, an anti-inflammatory, and an anti-rejection medication, but the morphine and Ruffies were gone.

Dr. Cornelius saw Marie jerking the handle on the side of her bed until it broke loose. She grabbed for her wheelchair and pulled herself onto it. Marie, still viciously screaming, gripped the IV poll sitting close by and smacked it hard on the ground several times. The base of the pole broke off creating a spear-like object. She wheeled her way over to where Dr. Cornelius was still overturning drug after drug looking for something that would knock Marie into a coma, or at least, a deep sleep.

Marie smacked the pole against Dr. Cornelius's side. He held his ribs and winced in pain. He screamed, "What the hell is wrong with you?"

Marie lifted the poll to hit Dr. Cornelius with it again. He stopped the poll in midair with his hand and grabbed at it. He tried to wrestle it away from Marie, but she wouldn't let go. She leaned over and bit at his hands. Marie bit the back of his hand hard enough to draw blood. Dr. Cornelius recoiled from the pain.

He stopped and looked at Marie who was trying to come after him again.

He said, "To hell with you!"

Dr. Cornelius took long and deliberate strides as he angrily made his way towards the recovery room doors.

He turned around as he was about to exit and shouted at Marie, "You aren't going to mess this project up any longer!"

Chapter 33

JANICE AND VICK

Vick and Janice made their way from Vick's apartment down to the parking lot where they got into Vick's car. They quickly exited the parking lot and merged onto US1 where they sat in traffic for what seemed like an eternity. Vick cussed at no less than six erratic drivers as they cut him off or drove too slowly. Janice did her best to make herself look presentable as she tried to fit her whole face in the reflection of the tiny vanity mirror attached to the back of the car's sun visor. Vick offered Janice a piece of Wrigley's spearmint gum to freshen her otherwise dirty mouth.

After nearly an hour, Vick and Janice arrived back at the parking deck adjoining the University of Miami Hospitals and Medical campus. They quickly exited the car and met each other in the rear of the vehicle.

Vick took a few steps toward the exit and stopped suddenly. He looked at Janice with a big smile on his face.

He said, "Janice, you were great today and I hope to see more of you."

"Thank you, Vick. You were not bad yourself, and you will see more of me. But for now, get me to those rats. I want to see what those little things are all about."

"I hope you don't fall asleep," Vick said as he and Janice walked into the courtyard in the center of several medical buildings. Vick stopped for a moment to greet a classmate that he knew. Janice stood by patiently until Vick introduced her. Vick and his classmate chatted about a recent break in on the medical campus. Apparently, someone had stolen several boxes of a Cinolazepam from the emergency room of the nearby Jackson Memorial Hospital.

After several more minutes, Vick and Janice said their goodbyes and walked into the entrance of a nearby building.

"Follow me," Vick said to Janice as the two of them made their way past the security guards stationed in the lobby.

"Hello Arnold," Vick said cheerfully as he waved to one of the security guards.

"Hi Vick," the guard replied not lifting her eyes from the small color television that was showing a rerun of *Family Matters*. Her tone and demeanor indicated that she enjoyed her job about as much as a dog enjoys being neutered.

Janice and Vick made their way over to the elevators and took one up to the seventh floor. They exited the elevator and walked a little way down the hall. Vick caught an evil look from a guy sitting in the hall with a suit on. The guy in the suit watched intently as Vick and Janice made their way down to the laboratory on the right side of the building. Janice was digging in her purse looking for a pen as she was walking and didn't notice the man in the suit. The two of them entered the laboratory and, as they did, Vick looked back to find the guy still glaring at him.

"Weird," Vick said as he turned on the lights to the laboratory.

"What's weird?" Janice asked as she placed her purse on top of a nearby counter. She was looking around the laboratory taking stock of what was in it. She noticed a skeleton hanging in the corner of the room as well as a large diagram of nerve fibers hanging in the front of the laboratory. She also noticed several cages, heard squeaking noises, and saw what she immediately identified as rats. She could tell something wasn't quite right with them.

"That guy in the hall, he was just staring at me," Vick said.

"What guy," Janice wondered.

"There is a guy sitting out there in his suit, way down the hall near the bathrooms, across from the elevators," Vick said.

"Maybe he likes you," Janice said.

"Ha, no, it's just weird that he's just sitting out there. I don't know what he's doing. I didn't think any of those rooms over there were even being used," Vick said obviously flustered.

"I wouldn't worry about it too much Vick. He's probably just a security officer or works for the building or something," Janice said while staring at the rats crawling around in the cage.

"What's wrong with these rats?" Janice wondered as she stared in disgusted amazement at what she was witnessing.

"They are paralyzed; their hind legs don't work," Vick said as he made his way towards Janice way who was standing next to the metal table supporting the rats.

"Why?" Janice asked.

"Well, as you know, we are doing stem cell research and our lab's objective is to get stem cells to grow and make these rats walk again," Vick said a little perturbed with Janice's naivety.

"How did these rats get paralyzed?"

"We, hit them with a 2 X 4," Vick said dryly.

"What? You have to be kidding me," Janice shrieked.

"Yes, Janice, I am," Vick said through a smile.

"Seriously, how did these rats become crippled?"

"Several of the scientists here made incisions in the backs of these rats with scalpels and then they separated the rats' spinal columns. They did so in a manner that would leave minimal scar tissue and also not damage muscle tissues and bony structures surrounding the separated area," Vick said as he spoke with his hands. Vick liked having an audience, even though it was a small one. Most of his time was spent in solitude or working with one or two other people in the lab. It was a nice change of pace to be able to explain what they were working so hard to accomplish.

"So, what is your role in all this? I mean what do you do here?" Janice said with a cocked head.

"My job is to monitor these rats for improvement in their ability to use their hind legs. After their spines were severed, stems cells were introduced into the area of separation. We are hoping they will grow, develop into nerve cells, and reconnect to the existing nerve cells. It is really a lot more complex than that and there are many variables that could prevent these rats from ever walking again," Vick said.

"How long ago were the stem cells injected into the spine?"

Vick thought that Janice was asking all the right questions. He replied, "two months."

"Two months? That seems like a long time. Have you noticed any improvement in the rats?"

"Not really," Vick said in a soft, almost inaudible voice. His discomfort was apparent as he swayed back and forth on his feet; he refused to look Janice in the eyes. "We expected to see some progress by now. We thought that the rats would gain some motility, but they haven't. We've been giving them drugs to help make the chemicals in their bodies a more favorable environment in which to grow. It doesn't seem like it's helping much though."

"That's too bad. I hope these little guys get better," Janice said staring through the glass of the terrarium.

"We haven't given up hope yet. They may get better. It's just a matter of waiting and seeing," Vick said as he pulled out an activity log located in the drawer underneath the counter where the terrarium rested. He set the log down beside the terrarium on the opposite side of where Janice was standing. He rested his chin on his hand as he watched the rats going about their business.

The rats pulled themselves around by their front legs as they ate, drank, and negotiated the obstacles placed in the terrarium for strengthening the rats' bodies. Most of the rats were different colors except two that were gray, one with a patch of white hair. They seemed subdued and more disinterested than a normal rat.

Janice bent over beside Vick as he scribbled notes down. She said, "Look at those pink eyes. They look like little beads you would find on a necklace or bracelet. I wonder what they are thinking behind those eyes."

"I guarantee you that it is nothing," Vick said as he turned his head to the side to look at Janice.

"You're probably right. If anything, they are wondering where their next piece of cheese is," Janice joked.

"It is outside my area of expertise, but I do know that in order to have thoughts and be conscious, you have to have self-awareness. I don't think that rats possess self-awareness," Vick said.

"I wouldn't be so sure of that. They feel pain, hunger, fear, and probably pleasure. That may give them a sense of self-awareness," Janice said.

"Yea, but they don't think like we think, I mean they're rats for God's sake," Vick was growing frustrated with Janice.

"That doesn't mean that we can treat them any way we feel," Janice said returning the irritated tone of voice that Vick was projecting.

"Oh Jesus, don't tell me that you are going to give me one of those animal rights, PETA, bullshit lectures," Vick grumbled.

"I should, but I'm not going to," Janice said backing off a little. She walked over to the side of the table and swished back and forth on her feet for a few seconds. Then, she asked, "What are you writing anyway?"

"I'm making observations on the rats' behavior. I'm trying to determine if there is any difference in their movements, especially in their hind legs," Vick said as he lightly touched a pen to the hind leg of one of the rats. The rat's leg began jerking violently.

Chapter 34

BETH AND DR. CORNELIUS

Dr. Cornelius turned his angry gaze from Marie and pushed the metal bar on the recovery room door opening it up. The guard was sitting on a chair outside of the door and quickly jumped to his feet. Dr. Cornelius reached for the guard's loaded pistol and ripped it from its holster.

The guard yelled, "What the hell are you doing?" He reached out for the gun but Dr. Cornelius already had it firmly placed in his hand.

Dr. Cornelius screamed, "Stand back."

The guard clumsily stepped backwards as he threw up his hands. He said, "Ok buddy, ok. You're on your own here."

"We've reached a point in this experiment that the use of force is necessary," Dr. Cornelius said as he placed the gun to his side. He didn't feel the need to hold the fellow agent at gunpoint since they were brothers in this game.

"We have an unanticipated problem with one of the subjects. You understand - isn't that right?"

"Yea, yea, whatever you say," the guard said as he took several steps towards the elevators. "I don't want any part of this."

"You know that you are bound to secrecy according to your obligations to the CIA," Dr. Cornelius said with a scowl displayed across his face.

"Of course, I know that," the guard said as the elevator dinged signaling that it had arrived. The guard boarded the elevator and made his way out of the building. His naked body would be found hour's later laying face down in a ditch.

Dr. Cornelius turned and shoved the right door of the recovery room wide open. He hurriedly made his way inside. Marie was still screaming.

"I'm going to kill you! You asshole!"

Dr. Cornelius grabbed Marie's arm and swung it behind her back pressing it firmly against her. He leaned in and his lips almost touched her ear. He held the gun up against her face with his left hand. Marie winced as the cold metal dug into her skin.

He said, "You listen to me you little whore. You so much as make one more sound the rest of the time you are here, and they'll be picking lead out of your dead ass for months. Do you understand me?"

Marie screamed, "Go to hell." Her words were muffled since her lips were distorted from the pressure of the gun smashed against her face.

"Maybe you didn't hear me. I said you will remain quiet until the end of this experiment or you will die. Do I make myself clear?" Dr. Cornelius said as spittle accumulated in Marie's ear.

"Fuck You!"

Dr. Cornelius raised the gun over his shoulder and smacked it across Marie's cheek. Moments later, blood trickled down her face. She groaned in pain as he raised the gun again to bring it down on her.

She screamed, "Ok. Ok, I will cooperate!"

Dr. Cornelius stopped his arm mid swing. He looked at her face and tears were streaming through the blood painted on her cheek. She hung her head as she sat in her wheelchair. Dr. Cornelius knew that he had gotten through to her.

Marie fell into a stoic silence. She sat motionless as she stared towards the floor. Her arms fell limp as drops of blood pooled on her bare leg. She knew better than to push Dr. Cornelius any further. The man had reached his breaking point and Marie didn't want to see what was on the other side of it. He had a crazed look to him, and it was anyone's guess as to what he was capable of now. So she sat there wondering what was going to happen to her and to the others.

Dr. Cornelius paced the room frantically. His white lab coat flapped back and forth as he made his way from one side to the other. He rubbed his hands through his thick, black hair wondering what he was going to do now. He was thinking about how to best proceed but felt the situation was getting out of hand.

He said to Marie with a firm voice, "Listen up. Here is what you are going to do." Dr. Cornelius stood over Marie. She refused to look at him.

"You are going to remain quiet about this. You will not mention one word of what has happened here to the others. Is that understood?" Dr. Cornelius's anger and frustration boiled up in his voice. Marie didn't say a word.

"The others are going to come back here, but they will not think anything is different about the situation. Do you understand me?" Again, Marie remained silent.

"I said, is that understood?" Dr. Cornelius pressed the cold steel of the gun's barrel against Marie's temple.

"Yes."

"Good. Now stay there and be quiet."

Dr. Cornelius calmed himself down and sat on a nearby chair. He glared at Marie wondering what he was going to do with her. He held the gun in his lap for several minutes shaking his head. He was at his wits end and looked like he could snap at any moment. Still shaking his head, he pulled his cell phone out of his pocket and made a call.

"Hello, Beth, come to the recovery room immediately," Dr. Cornelius said.

"But, I'm going through - "

"I said get here immediately!" Dr. Cornelius barked.

"Ok," Beth said as she hung up the phone. Within minutes, Beth walked through the doors of the recovery room. She noticed that the guard wasn't stationed at the door any longer. Then, she noticed the gun sitting in Dr. Cornelius's lap.

She asked, "What the hell is going on here?"

"The subject was being uncooperative as usual," Dr. Cornelius said.

"Why didn't you just try to drug her again," Beth wondered as she stood there with a confused look on her face. Her white lab coat was wrinkled and had several dirty splotches on it. She was in the middle of scrubbing some of the splotches out when Dr. Cornelius called.

"There was no time for that. I had to take matters into my own hands," he said. "Besides, now we can get a more adequate reading on the data since we will have this subject's full cooperation. Isn't that right?" Dr. Cornelius asked looking at Marie. Marie still refused to respond.

"I asked you a question," Dr. Cornelius said as he pulled the gun from his lap and extended it out in his hand. He closed one eye and looked down the barrel of the gun through the site. He could see Marie clearly through the little metal slit at the end of the gun.

"Yes," Marie responded quietly.

"Good," Dr. Cornelius said lowering his gun.

He told Beth, "Please go check the gym for the others."

Beth left the room and walked down the hall to where the others were engaged in Physical Therapy. She walked into the gym and noticed that Carlos, Jimmy, Candice, and Marge were busy completing their various exercises. She did not disturb them and instead decided to take a seat on the bench just inside the door. She folded her arms and slouched back on the bench. Her watchful gaze rested on each of them in turn.

Jimmy noticed Beth as she sat on the bench looking very angry. He wondered what she was doing there since he just saw her in the MRI room yesterday. Jimmy wondered why the MRI operator was so heavily involved in other aspects of their care. He never really worked for a hospital before, but didn't think that it was the usual way they did things.

Jimmy leaned over the functional electric stimulation bike and whispered to Carlos, "Hey, what is she doing here?"

"I don't know what Beth is doing," Carlos responded.

"It's just weird that she is always with Dr. Cornelius and then she runs the MRI machine too," Jimmy said.

"She's just helping him out," Carlos said. "Spinal Cord injuries must be her specialty. I wouldn't think too much into it."

"You're probably right, but she gives me the creeps sometimes. She's really weird," Jimmy said.

"Pay attention to what you are doing," one of the agents near Jimmy commanded. Jimmy gave her an eat shit look.

Jimmy, Carlos, Candice, and Marge continued with their exercises for several more minutes. Then, it was time for them to return to the recovery room for their lunches. As soon as they were loaded up into their wheelchairs, Beth grabbed Marge's wheelchair from the agent and lead her to the recovery room. The others quickly followed behind them.

Moments earlier, after hearing the approaching subjects, Dr. Cornelius shoved the gun into the elastic waistband of his underwear. The cold, metal barrel pressed against his groin. It felt uncomfortable jumping to his feet. He hopped side to side as he tried to reposition the gun in his pants. Within moments, the others arrived to the recovery room. Dr. Cornelius regained his composure as they filed in one by one.

"Welcome back," he said while grinding his teeth. He stood from his chair and walked towards Marie.

No one from the group responded. With the aid of an agent, each of the subjects was placed into their bed. They waited patiently as their lunch was set in front of them. Candice began eating right away. Carlos, Jimmy, and Marge didn't touch their food for several minutes since the workout left them exhausted. They wanted to regain some strength before digging into their meal.

Beth sat down in a chair near the recovery room doors. She didn't say a word. Her face was contorted into a miserable frown as she sat there with her arms folded. She was wondering how in the hell Dr. Cornelius was going to handle the situation. The other agents had exited the room.

Marie refused to be put into her bed. She continued to look at the floor in silence.

Dr. Cornelius asked her, "Marie, don't you want to get into your bed now so you can eat your lunch?"

"I don't feel like it," she said staring at the ground, "I'm not hungry for some reason."

Dr. Cornelius gasped a little while gazing at Marie and nearly broke out in a cold perspiration. He said with a nervous chuckle, "Marie, I think it would be a good idea for you to eat your lunch now. You need something to keep your strength up."

"I said I'm not hungry."

"Ok. Marie. Suit yourself," Dr. Cornelius said. He passed a little gas due to his nerves being so frazzled. The others didn't notice. Dr. Cornelius walked over to where Beth was sitting and took a seat. He looked over at Beth and shook his head. The others didn't see him.

Marie lifted her head and looked around the room. The curtains around the beds were rarely drawn anymore since the subjects had become accustomed to each other.

She began, 'You...you all aren't." she trailed off.

Dr. Cornelius lifted his eyes towards Marie and fear gripped him.

Marie said, "You all are not safe here! You have to get out now!"

Chapter 35

JANICE AND VICK

Janice asked Vick, "Why is that rat's leg jerking like that?"

"Reflexes," Vick said, "nothing more than reflexes. I wish I could say it was because the rat felt something, but it's just an automatic response. The rat didn't feel a thing."

"That's too bad," Janice said. "Maybe stem cells aren't the way to go. I mean, if it has been this long with no improvement in their ability to walk, maybe it's just not going to work."

"It's really too early to tell, Janice. This is the first batch of rats on which we have tried the experiment. Only time will tell if it is going to work. After several more weeks, if there is no improvement, then we'll probably have to find alternatives to the stem cells or try a different method of implanting them with a different combination of drugs. That's what we do here though. We are conducting experiments, which don't have a whole lot of precedents," Vick said.

"I guess you're right," Janice said. "Hopefully, you'll find the cure for these little guys someday." She walked over to a skeleton standing in the corner of the room. She picked up the arm of the skeleton waist high and dropped it. She did it twice. "So, this is what we look like underneath all of our layers?" Janice asked.

"Yup," Vick said.

"Kind of makes you wonder, huh?" Janice asked.

"Wonder what?"

"Where we came from and where we're going." Janice said. "What we are doing here."

"I wouldn't think about it too hard Janice. That's something science has yet to answer. If, it is science at all."

"True." Janice said. "Very true. I guess I just wonder sometimes what the purpose of life is. I wonder what my purpose here on Earth is sometimes. It could make you crazy thinking about it too much, though. People dedicate their whole lives trying to find the answer to that question, and they never find it."

"You just have to believe in something. You'll find the answers to the questions you are looking for with a little trust. Whether its trust in a higher power, trust in science, trust in the government, just trust something, and the answers will come." Vick said.

"Trust in government - that's a stretch," Janice said with a big smirk on her face. "Trust the government, and you'll get burned every time."

"I suppose so." Vick said while maintaining his focus on the rats.

"What do you believe in Vick? I mean, what do you trust?" Janice asked.

"I mostly trust in science." Vick said while shifting on his feet a little bit. "Look at these little guys here. They need help and healing. They are going to get that through the answers science provides."

"Yea, but some people would say that prayer and faith have healing powers too," Janice said.

"Maybe, of a different sort," Vick said. "There are some things science can't explain, I'll agree with you there, but seeing is believing to me. It is to most scientists."

"I bet your rats don't feel that way. Science isn't really doing them any good right now," Janice said. She mumbled it again as she turned away from Vick. Janice sat on a nearby chair and brushed her fingers through her long brown hair. She sat quietly looking over at Vick.

Vick shot Janice a harsh glance. He groaned, "We're doing what we can. There is a hell of a lot of red tape and politics that go into my line of work, you know."

"That's unfortunate."

"That's life."

Janice hung her head and stared at the table deep in thought. She sat there for a few seconds wondering if she had crossed a line with Vick. She didn't care though, because she knew there were others out there that felt the same way. There were people whose life had been turned upside down by some medical condition and there wasn't anything that science could do about it.

A few more minutes passed in silence and then Janice asked Vick.

"Well, what do you say we get out of here?"

"Wait," Vick said. "Don't you want to know where we get the stem cells from?"

"You just take them from the rat somehow don't you?" Janice asked.

"Kinda. Here follow me. I'll show you the umbilical cords."

Chapter 36

BETH AND DR. CORNELIUS

Again Marie shouted to the others, "You all are not safe here! Get out while you can!"

Carlos, Jimmy, Candice, and Marge looked around the room at each other. They didn't understand what had gotten into Marie. Again, she was acting like what they thought was an unstable personality.

"What are you talking about?" Marge asked with a startled look on her face.

"The Dr. is a fak-"

"Marie, come now Marie," Dr. Cornelius abruptly interrupted. "Don't mind her. She is in need of medication." Dr. Cornelius said. He wheeled her away from the others into a room to the left of the gym. He shut the door behind him and pushed her midway into the large space.

"I told you to remain quiet." Dr. Cornelius said to Marie as he pulled the gun out from his waistband and pressed it into the back of Marie's head. Marie winced in pain as the barrel dug into her skin. Dr. Cornelius dug the gun in harder.

"Do you want to live?" He asked her.

There was nothing but silence. "I asked you if you want to live." Dr. Cornelius said as the metal pressed hard against her neck.

"Your god damn right I do!" Marie shouted. Her face was in a knot of rage.

"This is your last chance you little whore. If you cause one more problem for me, your life is over," Dr. Cornelius said. "You will participate in the remaining Physical Therapy without any disruptions."

Dr. Cornelius pushed Marie back into the room where the others sat with blank expressions on their face. Carlos, Marge, Candice, and Jimmy watched attentively as Dr. Cornelius and Marie made their way over to Marie's bed. The others didn't know what to think about her; they entertained the notion that she was coming unraveled or just couldn't deal with her injury. Carlos was growing increasingly concerned over Marie's behavior. He was also growing more suspicious of Dr. Cornelius and Beth, because his gut was telling him something just wasn't adding up.

An agent entered the recovery room with the subjects' lunches. He set a tray down at each of the beds and walked back out of the door. Beth and Dr. Cornelius looked on as each subject slowly lifted the lid off of their meal. Carlos shot the two of them a glance that radiated mistrust. He stared at them for several seconds as the steam from the broccoli edged around his face. Eventually, his eyes moved to view the plate.

Carlos ignored the others as they ate except he looked over at Marie a couple of times. He noticed a bruise on her face and wondered how she got it. He sat in silence for the rest of the meal wondering how he went from his former life in Manhattan to his current situation and wondered how and when he would get out.

Candice and Jimmy poked at their food and took a few bites.

"This ham is horrible," Candice said spitting some of it out onto the plate.

"Yea, it is really bad, and it's got a weird color to it," Jimmy said. "What gives doc? What happened to the food? It used to taste so much better."

"Eat what you are given," Dr. Cornelius said with an angry look on his face. "I guarantee you that the food is the best choice to aid in your recoveries. The dieticians know what they are doing, and they have worked hard to ensure that you are given a combination of nutrients that will work to maintain your health and strength."

"But it tastes like shit doc." Jimmy replied.

"It's all you're getting!" Dr. Cornelius shot back.

Jimmy looked down at his plate. He hadn't eaten since breakfast, which was a less than spectacular assortment of eggs, fruit, and burnt toast. The eggs were cold and the fruit seemed gushy and overripe. By now, Jimmy was starving and wanted to eat something, so he did his best to eat the meal in front of him. He gnashed down on the ham and pulled a chunk off with his teeth. He cringed as he chewed the tuff and sinewy meat. He took another bite and threw the ham back onto the plate.

"This just tastes awful doc," Jimmy said as he shook his head in disgust.

Dr. Cornelius ignored Jimmy's criticism and instead walked over to the side of Marge's bed. Marge was sitting upright in her bed in silence. She hadn't touched her food. She had an irritated frown on her face and had her arms crossed.

"Why aren't you eating your food?" Dr. Cornelius asked her. "You didn't eat your breakfast either. I need for you to eat."

"I'm not hungry," Marge was seething.

"You need to eat to keep up your strength."

"I said I'm not hungry. If you are so worried about it, then you eat it."

"Marge, it is important that you eat if you are going to get any better. You need food to help your chances of walking again," Dr. Cornelius said.

"I'm not getting better! None of us are getting better!" She shouted.

Candice put down her fork as her eyes glazed over. She yelled at Dr. Cornelius, "Yea doctor! When are we going to improve? It's been two months now and nothing!"

"She's right!" Jimmy said.

"Come now everyone. This just takes time. Your situation has and will continue to improve."

"When doc?" Marge shouted.

"Your physical therapy has created significant increases in your muscle mass surrounding the areas that will regain feeling first. You continue to build strength and balance. Everything we have gotten back from the lab indicates that each of you is in good health."

"Yeah, doc. That may be the case but none of us are any closer to walking again. I can't feel a thing in my legs. I want to get better!" Jimmy shouted.

"You will, Jimmy. In due time, your situation will improve."

Jimmy, Marge, Carlos, and Candice finished their meals and sat in silence. Marie still refused to eat. The tension in the room was thick as each subject wanted more answers about their conditions and Dr. Cornelius. Marie's behavior was alarming to the others to say the least, and the thought that she knew something that they didn't was on the forefront of their minds.

The others knew Marie's accident caused her psychological trauma, as they felt it too, but no one else seemed to have as much of a problem with their condition as her. They wondered if her psychotic ranting had something more behind it than just anxiety and pain. The others wondered if there was some other reason that she was acting the way she was, if she knew something more.

After the subjects were fed and well rested, they were led to the gym for another round of physical therapy. This time, the therapy was conducted under the watchful eye of Dr. Cornelius; Marie reluctantly participated. She actually pushed herself to get through the exercises and for the first time thought that she may need to keep up with the routine if she was ever going to get better. She thought this despite the fact that she knew Dr. Cornelius had other plans for them.

Each subject took his or her turn on the exercise equipment, and each one had their exercises documented by the team of agents assigned to do so. The agents' recorded every move of Marie, Marge, Carlos, Jimmy, and Candice. There weren't any loose ends left open to chance. Should a subject so much as blink it would be recorded.

A new activity was introduced into their routine. The subjects formed a circle and a ball was thrown back and forth between them. This activity was used to build more upper body strength and to cut some of the boredom from the day. At first, Marie, filled with anger and hatred towards Dr. Cornelius, refused to participate just like she did in all the other activities. She sat with a large grimace on her face and her arms crossed. Dr. Cornelius flashed Marie the gun sticking out of his waistband when the others weren't looking. Shocked and frightened, Marie quickly found the will to participate in the new therapy.

After the activity ended, the subjects all returned to the recovery room. An agent tended to each subject. The agents administered medications given to promote a favorable environment for the stem cells to grow. They were also bathed and their clothes changed.

The subjects were permitted to read from an assortment of pre-selected magazines and books. Television was not permitted as the CIA was aware that there were several stories running on the national news about the disappearance of Marie, Carlos, Jimmy, Candice, and Marge. After each subject read, it was time for lights out.

The next morning the subjects awoke and ate another lackluster breakfast. Afterwards, it was time for a periodic MRI examination to determine the growth of the stem cells. Dr. Cornelius picked up the phone and called Beth.

Beth twisted in her cot as the cell phone rang beside her. She rubbed her eyes while the ringing stung the frazzled nerves in her head. The last time the cell phone rang it was her abusive husband calling. They had a heated argument over her absence and over the children. He berated her for being so neglectful of her family. In a rage, she nearly threw the cell phone against the wall but regained her composure before it happened. Hesitantly, she picked up the annoying little phone and placed it to her ear.

With a scratchy, irritated voice, Beth said, "Hello."

"Hello, Beth." Dr. Cornelius said into his cell phone. "I need you to come and help me take the subjects down to the MRI room now."

"I'll be there when I can. I need to get dressed first," Beth said.

"I need you down her now!" Dr. Cornelius shouted.

"I said I'll be down there when I can!" Beth shouted back and hung up the phone. Beth shook her head as she pulled on her clothes. There was no time for a shower. She was rushing as she pulled up her pants and grabbed her lab coat. She pulled on her shoes. She grabbed one of the two badges that were sitting in the drawer of her desk. She thought she was grabbing her fake hospital badge. The badge she grabbed would throw the experiment completely off course.

Chapter 37

JANICE AND VICK

Vick lead Janice through a door adjacent to the laboratory they were in, which opened up into another smaller laboratory. Sitting on the counter was an assortment of lab equipment including a centrifuge and various beakers. Beside the counter was a deep freezer used to store specimens. Vick walked and stood beside the deep freezer before opening the door.

"Look at this," Vick said as he reached his gloved hand holding a pair of tongs into the deep freezer. He pulled out a small, glass vial that fogged up as it reached the warmer air of the laboratory. There was a small label on the side of the tube which had something written on it.

Janice walked over to where Vick was standing and bent closer to take a better look at the vial.

"Subject 1," she read from the label. "What does that mean?"

"It's one of the rats out there. Subject 1 is the brown rat. If you didn't notice, they are all different colors except the two gray rats. Each subject is identified by its color. Subject 2 is the gray rat with the white streak. Subject 3 is the black rat."

"Oh, I see. Why don't you just give them names?" Janice asked.

"It's because we are trying to keep the scientists from thinking the rats are pets; it keeps the objectivity," Vick said.

"Hmmm, I guess that makes sense," Janice said turning away a bit. "So, what's in the vial?"

"It's subject 1's umbilical cord," Vick said as he gently shook the vial to bring the umbilical cord into view better.

"How do you get the stem cells from it," Janice asked while intently staring at the vial.

"Shortly after the rats were born, scientists here took samples of blood from the umbilical cords of the rats and held them in a test tube. They were kept frozen until the time we introduced them into the bodies of the rats after they became paralyzed."

"How do you know that they will become nerve cells in the rats?" Janice asked.

"The stem cells from the umbilical cord have the potential to differentiate into several types of cells within the body. With any luck, they will eventually take on the genes of the nearby cells and start dividing into those cells. It's sort of complicated, but that's the basics of how it works." Vick said as he slid the vial back into the deep freezer.

"Could it work in humans?" Janice asked.

"Well, yes, it can and does work in humans. There are stem cells that live in the body and replace damaged tissues all the time," Vick said.

"Wonder if humans that are paralyzed like the rats out there. Could it work for them?"

"It could, but the umbilical cords would have had to been saved a long time ago for someone to use it later in their lives. There were very few places that actually froze umbilical cords until recently. It just wasn't a popular thing and just a few clinics scattered around the United States actually had the technology and foresight to freeze the umbilical cords," Vick said.

"I see. Hopefully one day they'll be able to cure it."

"Hopefully."

A tense silence filled the room as Vick rearranged some of the equipment on the counter. Janice watched as the muscles on Vick's forearms twitched under the weight of the Bunsen burner. She walked over and stood behind Vick. She took her hand and placed it on Vick's shoulder rubbing it a bit. Vick turned around to face her and arched his eyebrows a bit wondering what she had in mind. Janice leaned in and gave Vick a kiss on the lips. She kissed her way down his neck while rubbing his hairless stomach with the hand she snuck under his shirt.

The kissing intensified; then, Vick grabbed Janice's shoulders and spun her around pressing her against the counter. They continued kissing while Vick lifted her onto the counter. Suddenly Janice began pulling away from Vick's kisses. She turned her head sideways as Vick continued kissing her cheek.

"Shit," Janice said holding the sides of Vick's head in her hands.

Vick stopped kissing her and looked at her with a quizzical look on his face. "What's wrong?" He asked.

"Sorry, but I have to pee," Janice said as she hopped off of the counter.

"You're right, shit," Vick said as he reluctantly stepped away from Janice. He turned away from her, and they both walked back out into the main laboratory. Vick sat on a nearby stool as he looked at Janice walking towards the door leading out into the hallway.

He said, "Turn left and the bathroom is all the way down the hall on the right, across from the elevators."

"Ok. Thanks. I'll be right back."

Chapter 38

BETH AND DR. CORNELIUS

Beth made her way up to the recovery room. She exited the elevator and walked towards the recovery room doors. On her way, she attached what she thought was her falsified identification badge to her lab coat. She walked through the doors and was greeted by Dr. Cornelius.

"Hello, Beth." Dr. Cornelius said. "Are you ready to take the first patient down to the MRI room?"

"Yes sir, I am," Beth said.

She walked over to Marge and helped one of the agents place her in her wheelchair. She rolled Marge over to the MRI room and completed the scan. Beth and Dr. Cornelius looked over her results and, within less than thirty minutes, Marge was back in her bed reading a magazine.

Beth also completed scans on both Jimmy and Marie, and they too were sitting in bed reading while they waited for everyone else's scan to be completed. It was Carlos's turn to have his scan done. Beth walked over to Carlos. She gently let the arm down on his bed and began to slide him over to his wheelchair. Carlos accidentally knocked over the water on the stand sitting next to the bed. The water spilled all over the bed and covered his legs and face.

Beth ran to get a towel from a nearby counter. She made her way back to where Carlos sat drenched with the water. Beth began sopping up the water from Carlos's face and legs. As she did, she bent over Carlos. Carlos noticed her cleavage sticking out from the top of her blouse. He ogled her breasts for several seconds and thought how nice they were. Then, his eyes made their way from her breasts to Beth's badge. He read the badge, which said, Dr. Beth Jernigan, CIA Special Operations.

Carlos was filled with a near panic. He jumped back in his bed and knocked over his IV pole. The pole crashed down on the floor with a series of loud clanks. Carlos looked at Beth who was staring back at him with a perplexed expression on her face.

He raised a pointed finger to her badge and said, "You liar! Who the hell are you?"

Beth looked down at her badge.

"Ahh, shit," she said. She looked at Jimmy and the others, and they all had a look of deep concern on their faces.

Jimmy asked Carlos, "What's going on?"

Marge also asked, "What's happening?"

Carlos let out several gasps as he tried to balance himself in his bed. His face was red as fire as he continued pointing at Beth.

"Her badge!" He screamed.

"What about it?" Marge asked.

"It says...It says CIA Special Operations on it!" Carlos said chocking on his words.

"I told you so." Marie said in a calm and cool voice sitting in the corner with a smug look on her face.

"Shut up!!" The others shouted at Marie.

"What the hell is this?" Candice asked. "Some kind of sick joke?"

Beth did her best to hide her mistake. She thought about ripping the badge off of her lab coat and hiding it but thought that may be too obvious. She needed to think of something quick, but her nerves were getting the best of her. She stumbled back from Carlo's bed a bit and rubbed the back of her neck with her hand as she looked at the angry mob sitting around the room.

Several agents were working nearby and had a look of severe apprehension on their faces. Three of the agents walked from the counter where they were working towards Beth and the others

"I..." she began. "Yes, yes that is right. I am with the CIA Special Operations Unit. All of the staff here is with the CIA. We are just here to make sure that everything is going well with your treatment. We are interested in the results and want to make sure that your progress is recorded accurately."

"That's a lie!" Marie shouted. "They did this to us! I remember everything."

Dr. Cornelius was mortified. He gave Beth and an evil look as he made his way to the center of the room.

He said, "No that's not true. Marie here is quite delusional and suffering from post-traumatic stress disorder. She doesn't know what she is talking about."

"I know perfectly well what I'm talking about. I was at a nightclub with my friend Candice here, and we were abducted. They used some machine on our backs to cause this to happen."

"That's quite enough out of you Marie. Beth, why don't you administer Marie her medication, take her to the room next door," Dr. Cornelius said as Beth jumped into action. She made her way over to Marie's wheelchair and began pushing her towards the door.

Jimmy shouted, "Why are you taking her away? Why can't you just administer her medication here?"

"Her medication is in the other room and so are the cups for water she needs to take her pills," Dr. Cornelius said. "They will be back soon."

"Don't take her anywhere!" Carlos shouted. "We want some answers!"

Jimmy also screamed out, "What the hell are we doing here?"

Carlos picked up a book lying nearby and threw it at Dr. Cornelius hitting him in the arm. The agents standing on the sides of the room moved in closer to the group but still remained out of sight from the others.

"I told you already. We are here to ensure that your recovery goes as anticipated. There is really nothing more to it. We are trained to handle any medical issue that you may have," Dr. Cornelius said.

"Bullshit!" Carlos yelled. "We want out of here now!"

Candice cried out as well. She said, "You have no right to keep us here. We don't want to be here any longer!"

"Come now. You need to stay here so you can get better, so you can walk again," Dr. Cornelius said.

"We want out of here now!" Marge screeched. She threw a magazine towards Dr. Cornelius that fell short before hitting the ground. Jimmy picked up a pack of rubber gloves sitting on the nightstand next to him and chucked it towards Dr. Cornelius. Each continued to yell at Dr. Cornelius as Beth stood gazing on the angry group.

Dr. Cornelius marched over to where Beth stood and said, "This has gotten totally out of hand; we need help."

"Do it."

"You all leave me no other choice," Dr. Cornelius said. He circled his finger above his head pointing at the group while the agents standing nearby looked on. Three agents moved into the center of the room. Once each one of the agents took a position in front of the subjects, they withdrew their gun from its holster. Dr. Cornelius also pulled his gun that was now placed in his holster.

He said, "Ok. Now do you understand how serious I am? You all will participate in this experiment or each and every one of you will be dead. Do you understand?"

Marge gasped as she fell into a scared silence. The rest of the group also tensed up and didn't say a word. They sat there, shocked, over what had just happened as the agents held their silver guns in their direction.

None of them could anticipate that this would occur and had no idea how to handle the situation.

Jimmy spoke up after several tense minutes had passed. He said, "You can't do this to us, and you can't hold us hostage like this. We are not animals; we deserve better treatment."

Marie said, "What have we done to you to deserve this?"

Dr. Cornelius had a flat expression on his face that revealed no emotion. He said, "You all are here to participate in this experiment in order for the government to get the data we need to one day improve the lives of millions of people. You all had what we need, and we took it. You're part in this experiment is not open for discussion. You will be guarded for the remainder of your time here and you will not give us any more trouble. Do I make myself clear?"

There was no response from the group.

Dr. Cornelius said again with an agitated voice, "Do I make myself CLEAR?"

Marge replied through a gush of tears, "Yes, yes you do."

Everyone else also agreed with Dr. Cornelius except for Carlos who remained silent. He sat with his arms crossed as he stared blankly at the agents that had surrounded them. He was fuming over the dreadful situation he was in and wanted to lash out against the agents in every way possible. But, for now, he did what he was told to do since the drawn guns made it hard not to go along with Dr. Cornelius's plans.

After several more minutes of tense silence, several agents arrived with trays of food for the subjects. The trays were placed in front of each one of them, and they began to eat, with the exception of Marie who sat quietly staring at Dr. Cornelius with a defeated expression on her face.

Dr. Cornelius said to her, "You need to eat your food. You need your strength to perform your best during the physical therapy."

Marie replied, "I'm not hungry."

Dr. Cornelius yelled, "You need to eat!"

"You eat it you asshole!" Marie shouted. She picked up her tray and threw it against the floor.

Dr. Cornelius quickly approached Marie. He bent down beside her and whispered into her ear. "You'll be sorry you did that."

"Fuck off."

Dr. Cornelius lifted his gun high behind his head and slammed it down on Marie's face. Blood splattered across the room as the others gasped in horror. Marie groaned in pain while holding her cheek.

Dr. Cornelius said, "Let that be a lesson to each of you. This is not a game. I expect your full cooperation throughout the remainder of this experiment, and I'm sure you'll get the point or I can help you get the point."

Carlos, Marge, Jimmy, and Candice sat in shock while Marie nursed her wound. Marie was using her bed sheet to stop the bleeding from the gash on her face. There was a large bloodstain that had collected on the sheet that continued to grow by the second.

Jimmy spoke up, "Aren't you going to help her?"

"She did this to herself by being a pain in my ass. She has been nothing but a pain in my ass from the beginning of this experiment. She'll learn to cooperate or that wound she has now will look like a scratch," Dr. Cornelius said. "Now finish up your meals."

The group ate the remainder of their meals as the bleeding from Marie's face stopped. She eventually ate her dinner as well under the direct pressure of Dr. Cornelius and his firearm. Afterwards, several agents tended to the hygienic and medical needs of each one of the subjects. They were cleaned and administered their medications.

Then, each agent placed one of the subjects into their wheelchair. They were all carted off into the gym where they began their regular regimen of exercises. Jimmy was sitting next to Carlos on the electrical stimulation bike while the therapists were talking at the side of the gym. Jimmy leaned over to Carlos.

He said, "We need to do something about this shit we're in. They can't just hold us at gunpoint like this; it's insane. Who knows what these bastards will do next."

"You're right. What can we do though? We're in a pretty tough situation here and I don't know if we can get away from them," Carlos said.

"We need to try and get the gun from one of the agents when they least expect it," Jimmy said as he strained on the weights beside Carlos.

"When are we going to be able to do that?" Carlos said.

"I don't know. We'll just have to look for the opportunity. We'll have to distract them at some point so one of us can just yank the gun from their grasp. Maybe when they have us surrounded in the recovery room and aren't paying attention, perhaps," Jimmy said.

"Yea, but will they get close enough where we can do that?" Carlos wondered.

"Your guess is as good as mine. We'll just have to wait and see what they do," Jimmy said.

"Ok. Well I hope it doesn't take too long; I'm sick of being here. I'm sick of being under the control of these fools. It's inhumane how they treat us, like we're some sort of animals or something."

"I know what you mean, lord, do I know what you mean," Jimmy said.

The group continued their exercises for another thirty minutes before returning to the recovery room for an hour of rest. Once there, Marie as well as Candice fell into a deep sleep induced by medication. Carlos eventually dosed off too, but Jimmy remained awake for a while reading a magazine he found near his table. He flipped through the pages mostly looking at the pictures while the agents sat in chairs on the side of the room watching him dose in and out of consciousness. Eventually, he joined the others in a peaceful slumber.

The subjects were all sleeping when Dr. Cornelius came into the recovery room. He looked them over and seemed pleased that they were out cold at the moment. His gaze turned toward the agents as they either sat in their chairs or lined the back of the walls in the recovery room. He looked at each one in turn and pointed his finger towards the room adjoining the recovery room. They each got up and made their way through the doors as Dr. Cornelius shut off some of the lights and followed them into the room. There was a lot to discuss.

Chapter 39

JANICE AND VICK

Janice exited the laboratory with a big smile on her face. She was thinking to herself how lucky she was to have met a guy like Vick. He was smart, funny, and sexy as hell; and hopefully, they could see each other for quite some time to come. He was everything that she wanted, and she wanted more of him. She thought that they were a match made of fairy tales and legends, but she didn't want to seem too overeager to be by his side. She wanted to leave a little bit of mystery and something for Vick's imagination. She didn't want to be that girl who was overly needy or too clingy, because she thought that would just push him away. But, that wasn't part of her nature anyhow and not something that she really needed to worry about.

Janice made her way down the hall towards the elevators. She peered through the little rectangular glass on the doors to her left and saw a laboratory much like the laboratory where Vick was still working. She looked to her right at the little red fire extinguisher hanging inside the little square box and thought to herself that she didn't want to have to use that anytime soon.

She saw a sign hanging in the hallway for the restrooms but didn't find the doors anywhere. Janice looked around a bit and couldn't see the doors hiding behind the small wall that protruded into the hallway. She looked for a few more seconds and saw a set of double doors near where the restroom sign was located. She wondered if those doors lead to the restroom and gently pushed on the metal bar to open them. The doors didn't open on her first push, so she tried again pushing a little harder, and still they wouldn't open. Growing frustrated at the lack of cooperation from the door, Janice thrust her arm hard against the metal bar and slammed the door with her hip.

The doors cracked open a bit and she was able to peer inside. The room was dimly lit and she couldn't exactly make out what she was seeing at first. She took a few steps into the room and noticed people lying in beds. She saw the IV poles and heard the heart monitors intermittently beeping. Janice was gripped with a near panic, as she had no idea what she had just walked into. She didn't know that the building had patients inside and didn't know what they were doing there. She nearly wet herself at the sight. Janice turned to walk away from the scene and placed her hand on the door to open it. Light from underneath the door illuminated Janice's face.

Janice heard someone shout out, "Janice?" She turned to see who it was but didn't recognize the voice.

"Janice is that you?"

Janice took a few steps towards the voice. She still couldn't place it and asked, "Who is that calling my name?"

"It's me, Jimmy."

"Jimmy? You mean my Jimmy? What the hell are you doing here? I thought you were in South Carolina."

"Shhhh. Keep it down, Janice. Yes, it's me."

Carlos awoke from his sleep moments earlier. He asked, "You know this girl?"

Jimmy replied, "Yes, we dated until a few months ago."

Janice saw a light coming from around a door near the recovery room. She could see through the small glass pane that there were people in the room. Janice crouched over a bit and walked closer to where Jimmy was lying. She got alongside him, and Jimmy grabbed her hand and pulled her close enough to where he could reach his hand around her head. He pulled Janice close to his ear and in a loud whisper he told her they needed help.

He said, "Janice, we are being held her by the CIA."

"What?" Janice whispered in disbelief. "Are you delusional?"

"No, Janice. The CIA crippled us and is holding us here against our will. They won't let us leave, and they are holding us at gunpoint," Jimmy said getting spittle in Janice's ear.

"Oh my god, oh my god," Janice said on the verge of hyperventilating. She stumbled backwards a little bit but regained her footing. Her eyes were as wide as golf balls as she stood there in shock.

Janice asked, "What do you want me to do?"

"Call someone to help us Janice -" Jimmy said as his voice trailed off. He could see from the look on Janice's face that she saw something. Jimmy turned to where Janice's gaze was focused and saw the door to the room where the agents were located crack open a bit.

Janice turned and began dashing towards the exit as the door adjoining the recovery room swung open fully. Dr. Cornelius entered the room first and saw Janice running towards and then through the exit.

Dr. Cornelius shouted out to Janice, "Hey! Stop right there!" It was too late though and Janice was able to run down the hall and duck into one of the empty laboratories. Dr. Cornelius and several other agents ran into the hall after her, but they didn't see which laboratory she went into.

Dr. Cornelius instructed the others, "Spread out and check each of these rooms."

Each agent took a laboratory to check. One of the agents walked into the laboratory that Janice had run into. Within seconds he came back out into the hall.

He said, "She's gone."

Dr. Cornelius walked over to the laboratory door. He glanced inside to see a window cracked wide-open leading to a fire escape. He stuck his head outside and saw a large crowd of medical students strolling about the courtyard below.

"Damn," Dr. Cornelius said. "This was a major fuck up. We can't have this anymore." He paced around the laboratory examining what was in the room as the agent looked on. Eventually, he and the others made their way back to the recovery room.

Several tense minutes passed. Then, a cabinet door underneath one of the workstations gently swung open. Janice uncurled herself from the fetal position she was in and extended her legs so that her feet touched the ground. She pulled herself out of the cabinet and stood up. Janice quietly made her way over to the door and peered into hallway. Noticing that no one was there, she opened the door wide enough to stick her head into the hallway.

Janice made her way to the laboratory where Vick was. She walked inside and didn't see him at first but heard the faint humming of a machine. She walked over to the little side room and saw Vick through the door using the centrifuge. She gently tapped on the door and motioned for him to kill the noise.

Vick looked puzzled but quickly shut the centrifuge down. Once it had stopped he opened the door and walked into the laboratory with Janice.

He asked her, "What's wrong?"

Janice replied, "A whole hell of a lot."

Chapter 40

BETH AND DR. CORNELIUS

Beth's cell phone was incessantly ringing when she, Dr. Cornelius, and the others entered the recovery room. She pulled it out of her pocket and looked at the phone number and name displayed on the phone. The caller was her husband, but Beth didn't feel it was a very good time to take a personal call. She switched the phone to vibrate but the calls kept coming. She eventually turned the cell phone off; however, seconds later, her second cell phone, the one her husband was never to call because it was for business use only, began to ring.

"Ahh...Damn ," Beth said as she rolled her eyes. "Excuse me while I take this call; it's got to be important."

Beth made her way into the laboratory adjoining the recovery room where they just had a meeting. She shut the door behind her, which made a dull thud noise that echoed throughout the recovery room. The ringing of the phone was like throwing kerosene onto a fire, because it aggravated Beth's already frazzled nerves.

She picked up the phone and chided her husband with intense anger. She said, "Listen here, I'm in the middle of something very critical. This better be really fucking important!"

"Don't you talk to me like that you bitch!" Her husband was dealing with a little bit of anger himself. "Do you have any idea what it is like to be what I would consider a single parent?"

"Boo hoo," Beth said, "Why are you calling me?"

"We're finished Beth."

"What do you mean we're finished?" Beth wondered.

"Well, in two ways really," her husband said.

"What are they?" Beth asked.

"Number one, I want a divorce," her husband told her.

"Ahh. This is not a good time to talk about this," Beth said flatly.

"We need to discuss this as soon as possible," her husband said.

"Ok. When I get time, I will call you to discuss this with you, Ok."

"Fine Beth," her husband growled.

"Ok. What is the second way we're finished?" Beth asked.

"You know how you've been cheating the IRS for so long? Well, they have sent a criminal investigator out to the house on several occasions to go through our financial records. They wouldn't even let me send the records in because they suspected that the financial data that you have is bogus. How does that sound honey?"

"Fuck!" Beth screamed.

Ok. Ok. Breathe, Beth, breathe, she said to herself. "Ok, dear, let me get home, we'll sit down and talk about this. We'll have a nice family dinner and you and I will discuss how we are to handle our future."

"Well hurry, I don't know how much time we have. I'm sick of this shit Beth," her husband said as the line went dead.

Beth hung her head as silence enveloped the room. Tears made an appearance in her eyes but were soon cut off as anger seethed through her body. Beth nearly screamed, but her cries were muffled, interspersed with heavy breathing. She threw her head back and stared at the ceiling letting the emotion stream through her body. She gazed at the little holes in the ceiling tiles and began to count them. Eventually, her head cleared a bit and her nerves settled while a listless calm took over her raging anger.

She stood there focusing on the ceiling tiles while her mind wondered about what her life had become. Beth felt out of control and needed to regain composure before returning to meet with the others. The seconds ticked by and turned into minutes before she was ready to return. She readied herself to face Dr. Cornelius and take whatever punishment her and the others would have to endure. She turned to walk into the recovery room and took two steps.

"No. No. No!" Beth shouted out. Something inside her snapped, and she decided right then that she would no longer be the pawn in this nightmare her life had become. Dr. Cornelius, her husband, her children, and the rude asshole in lunch line who took the last turkey sandwich would have no more control over her. They would not be the source of so much pain and anger; she would take back what belonged to her, and she would do it in a big way she decided.

Jimmy, Carlos, Candice, Marge, and Marie all returned to the recovery room where they were able to get some rest. Their hopes to fall asleep where soon dashed as Dr. Cornelius and the rest of the agents also walked into the recovery room shortly after the others had returned. It was apparent that Dr. Cornelius was pissed off as he paced around the room.

He said with a grumble, "We can no longer have any situations like the one we just had. We need to be on full alert for anyone that may try to compromise the security of this project. Two agents will be stationed outside of the doors as well as one stationed on the elevator."

"It's a little late to be thinking about security now," one of the agents said with a sarcastic tone of voice.

"No, it's not," Dr. Cornelius said staring at the agent with a scowl on his face. "We still have a long way to go on this project, and we will be successful obtaining the results for which we are looking. I spoke with Joanne, the Deputy Director, and assured her that the project is moving forward as planned."

"It isn't going as planned," one of the agents said.

Dr. Cornelius walked over to the agent and slowly withdrew his firearm from its holster. He lifted the gun into the air and brought the butt of the gun down on the agents face. The agent grabbed his cheek and stumbled backwards in shock.

Dr. Cornelius asked the agent, "Is the mission going as planned?"

The agent pulled his hand away from his face as blood trickled down his neck. He said, "Are you crazy?"

Dr. Cornelius walked back over to the agent and brought the butt of his gun down on the back of the agent's head.

"Is the mission going as planned?"

The agent looked at Dr. Cornelius with a combination of disbelief and shock as Dr. Cornelius brought the gun up above his head again. The agent reached for the gun in his holster and pulled it out. Dr. Cornelius reached out with his free hand and ripped it from the agent's grasp. Dr. Cornelius now held two guns, one in each hand, as he pointed them at the agent.

Dr. Cornelius said, "I asked you a question. Is this mission going as planned?"

The agent looked terrified. He said with a quivering voice, "Yes...yes it is."

"Good," Dr. Cornelius said. "Now let this be a lesson to all of you. As far as anyone knows, at the CIA or elsewhere, this mission is progressing without any complications. Isn't that right?" One by one, the agents agreed with Dr. Cornelius.

"Now, let's get back to business. I want each of you here to watch out for any suspicious activity. If anyone tries to enter this room without authorization, you have my permission to draw your gun and shoot if you need to," he said.

While Doctor Cornelius spoke, Jimmy eyed one of the agents standing near him. The agent kept brushing up against the side of his bed, and he didn't have a jacket on. Jimmy could see that the agent's gun was sticking out from under his arm nestled in its holster. The agent had his back turned to Jimmy while he bobbed from side to side listening to Dr. Cornelius's rant.

Jimmy reached out to try to grab the gun, but the agent moved away and walked closer to the center of the room. The agent blocked Dr. Cornelius's view of Jimmy as Jimmy recoiled backwards from his failed attempt. Jimmy looked over at Carlos who was staring back at him, and he nodded at Jimmy with approval as he sat up in his bed with his arms folded.

Dr. Cornelius circled the room giving each agent instructions on what was expected of them for the rest of the project. He moved from each agent one after another, as they sat there in silence listening to what he had to say. He had the look of determination on his face and believed that they were making real progress on accomplishing their goals. The team recording the data for the project was analyzing the preliminary results and found that subjects were following the protocol for the project as well as could be expected. The CIA was fulfilling the objectives that the Deputy Director had set for them.

Dr. Cornelius finished giving one of the agents his instructions for completing the project.

He asked the agent, "Please get me that clipboard over their on the counter, I want to show you something."

The agent turned and walked towards the counter. He passed to the left of Carlos who was staring intently at him. As the agent walked past, Carlos could see the butt of his gun sticking out from underneath the agent's jacket. Carlos thought to himself, it was now or never. Carlos reached out his hand and grabbed the butt of the agent's gun.

The agent gasped in disbelief as he grabbed Carlos's forearm with both hands. Carlos squeezed down as hard as he could on the gun as the agent jerked Carlos's forearm away from the agent's jacket. Carlos's arm jerked back while holding the gun, and the agent's holster tugged hard against Carlo's pull. Carlos heaved the gun again as the agent fumbled to grab the gun as well, but the agent only managed to grab Carlos's wrist. Carlos braced his other arm against the railing on the bed and yanked with all the force his body could exert. The straps securing the gun in place snapped loose and Carlos rushed to position the gun so he could fire it, but the agent quickly grabbed the barrel of the gun. The agent tried to wrestle the gun out of Carlos's grip, but Carlos held on tightly and never lost control of it.

Dr. Cornelius and the other agents were panicked. They quickly withdrew their guns and pointed them at Carlos and the other agent. They sat there for what seemed like an eternity waiting to see who was going to get the gun.

Dr. Cornelius shouted, "Everyone hold your fire."

Beth readied herself to reenter the recovery room. She had no idea of the struggle taking place between Carlos and one of the agents. She withdrew her gun and was geared up to take out the next person she saw. She was furious and wanted out of the place as quickly as possible. She walked toward the recovery room and kicked the door with her foot while holding her gun straight out in front of her. The door slammed against the wall of the recovery room as she made her way inside.

Beth was shocked to see that the others had their guns pulled as well. She noticed Carlos and the other agent struggling over the gun to her left as she entered the room. Beth was shaking as her nerves were getting the best of her, but she held the gun in place as she pointed it first at Dr. Cornelius then the other agents.

She screamed out, "All right you mother fuckers put down your guns!" Dr. Cornelius and the others turned and pointed their weapons at Beth.

Dr. Cornelius said, "Beth, you don't want to do this. We need you to be on our team. We need your help to finish this operation."

Beth said, "The only thing that is going to be finished is you. Now get down on the floor you asshole!"

While Beth and the others squabbled back and forth, Carlos and the agent continued to struggle over the gun.

Carlos screamed out, "Let go!"

The agent shot back, "Hell no!"

Carlos reached out with his left arm and pushed the agent as hard as he could. The agent stumbled backwards and caught the corner of a nearby chair and fell over it landing flat on his butt. He turned to look at Carlos who was now pointing the gun at him.

He said to himself, "damn."

Carlos now pointed the gun at Dr. Cornelius while keeping a watchful eye on the agent who continued to sit on the floor. He cocked the trigger back as he looked down the sight at Dr. Cornelius.

Jimmy, Marge, Candice, and Marie sat in complete silence unable to believe the situation that was unfolding in front of them. They felt outnumbered as only Carlos had a gun, but knew that Beth was on their side. They knew that she had had enough of the situation and was trying to leave this place. It was Dr. Cornelius who had to worry.

Carlos screamed out to Dr. Cornelius, "Are you ready to die now?"

Dr. Cornelius responded, "What is it you want from me?"

"I think I'll take one of your eyes and part of your twisted brain with me as a souvenir, after I blow them out of your head," Carlos said.

"We can talk this out," Dr. Cornelius said.

"The time for talking is over. You don't deserve to live after what you've done to us."

Marge asked, "Why did you do this?"

"It is my job," Dr. Cornelius said.

"No. Why did you pick us?"

"You all had what we needed," Dr. Cornelius said.

"What's that?" Marge asked.

"You all are physically fit, young, and resilient enough to endure the protocols of this experiment, and - " Dr. Cornelius trailed off.

"And what?" Marie demanded.

"And, you all were some of the first ones to have your umbilical cords preserved, which we needed to harvest the stem cells."

"You did this to us for our umbilical cords?" Candice asked.

"Yes."

"Well, we'll see if they can patch up your head with your nut sack doc," Carlos said.

"Wait. You all need us to get better; you need us so you can walk again," Dr. Cornelius said pleading with his hands.

"We'll go to a real hospital!" Marge shouted as the others agreed.

"You shoot me and the agents here will shoot you all. Isn't that right?" Dr. Cornelius said looking to the agents for agreement.

One of the agents looked flustered and unsure what to do. After several minutes of deliberating, he turned his gun towards Dr. Cornelius and held it firmly in place. He said, "I can't deal with this shit anymore. It's time for you to die."

Another agent turned his gun towards the head of the agent holding his gun towards Dr. Cornelius. He said, "I wouldn't do that if I was you."

Carlos couldn't care less if the agents shot each other. He knew who he did want to die though as he held his gun towards his intended target.

He said to Dr. Cornelius, "Say goodbye."

Chapter 41

BETH AND VICK

"What is it Janice?" Vick asked as Janice quickly fanned her face with her hands. Janice was panicked and whispering, "Oh my god," over and over again.

"Calm down Janice. What's the problem?"

"Jimmy - I, I saw Jimmy just now."

"What? Where was he?"

"He's in one of the rooms down the hall with a couple of other people!"

"That's kind of weird, but why are you acting so panicked? What's the big deal about that?" Vick wondered.

Janice tried to regain her composure as she continued to fan her flushed face. She said in a hurried, high-pitched tone, "He told me that he's being held there by the CIA. He said that they crippled him and are holding him hostage."

Vick's face lost all of its blood and turned white. He asked, "You have to be fucking kidding me, right?"

"I don't think that he would go through all this trouble for a joke - Vick."

"Holy hell, what are we going to do?" Vick wondered.

"Well we need to call somebody, obviously," Janice said as her face began turning from a rose color to a more normal, peachy color.

"Who do we call about this? I mean, if it is the damn CIA is doing this, then who knows who else could be involved," Vick said.

"I don't know. Maybe we should call the police or the FBI," Janice said.

"Hmm, I guess we don't have many options. We could call Rambo or the Terminator."

"Funny Vick - It's no time to joke."

"Well, I'm thinking we should call both - let them sort this out," Vick said.

Janice picked up her rectangular, silver, I-phone and quickly punched the keypad with her fingertips dialing 911.

The operator answered the phone with a surly and dismissive tone as she asked Janice, "This is 911, please hold?"

Janice couldn't believe what she just heard.

She screamed into the phone, "Hold please? Are you kidding me, you want me to hold when people's lives are in danger? This is what I pay taxes for, you stupid bitch!"

She listened to the phone's receiver, but all that she heard was dull, intermittent static as the operator had already put her on hold. At first, Janice thought that she might be tending to someone else, but she quickly changed her mind and came to the conclusion that the operator was probably eating her ham and turkey sandwich with extra mayonnaise or filing her overly long and crocked nails. She sat there for what seemed like an eternity as Vick looked on in shocked amazement.

He said, "You mean to tell me that she put you on hold?"

Janice turned her angry gaze from her cell phone towards Vick. She said, "Yes can you believe the nerve of this girl?"

Vick turned up his nose and said, "No, I really can't. That is some crazy bullshit."

After several minutes of Janice and Vick stewing in their irritated resentment, the operator returned to the phone.

She said, "911, what is your emergency?"

"I can't believe that you put us on hold!" Janice shouted into the phone as she looked over at Vick. Vick shook his head in agreement, but knew the operator wouldn't be too happy with Janice.

Janice began to talk but heard the phone click and then go dead.

"She hung up on me!" Janice shouted.

"Ok, Janice, let's calm down. We need to get this call placed as soon as possible. I know it's frustrating, but just hold your tongue the next time you call and maybe someone else will help us," Vick said in a soothing and caring voice.

"You're right, but I just can't believe that happened. I'll call again and see if I can get through to someone else," Janice said as she touched the numbers for 911 again.

The phone rang five times before a different operator answered the phone and said, "911, hold please."

"You have to be kidding me!" Janice shouted at the phone.

"Calm down Janice, calm down, I know it's ridiculous, but let's get this reported as soon as possible," Vick said.

Several excruciating minutes passed and finally the smoky voiced operator returned to the phone.

She asked, "911, what is your emergency."

"Finally," Janice said as she tensed up anticipating that the operator might cut her off again. These public service workers were so unpredictable she thought to herself.

Again, the operator said in a louder, more agitated voice, "911, what is your emergency?"

"We need help here! We are in a laboratory on University of Miami's Medical Campus," Janice began as she looked over at Vick and shrugged her shoulders indicating that she didn't know exactly where she was.

"We are in the Lois Pope Life Center," Vick mouthed to Janice almost inaudibly. Janice forwarded the information to the operator and then told the operator that they were on the 7th Floor of the building.

Janice continued, "There are several people being held hostage on the floor in a laboratory near us, and they are being held there by the CIA."

"Excuse me?" The operator said.

"You heard me right, the hostages are being held by the CIA," Janice said, "What are you going to do about it?"

"Is this some sort of prank call, because if it is I'm goin-"

"This is no prank call! This is real! They have been injured by the CIA and are being held against their will by them! Now, what are you going to do about it?"

"Well, I can't - I don't think -"The operator was having trouble grasping the situation.

"Excuse me?" Janice said.

"Well, I will notify the Miami police first off," the operator said, "I think the FBI should be notified as well. I'm dispatching the police right now."

"Yes, I think that is a good idea. How long do you think the police will take before they arrive?" Janice questioned.

"It should be a matter of minutes. Please remain on the phone while I call the FBI as well," the operator stated.

"Ok. I will," Janice said.

The operator clicked over to another line and fumbled through her electronic rolodex for the number to the local branch of the FBI. Several minutes passed before she finally located the number for them. She placed the call to an agent and explained the situation to him. The FBI agent was mortified but assured the operator that they would send out several agents to investigate the situation. The operator clicked back to the phone line where Janice was waiting.

"Ok, I have notified the FBI, and they should arrive shortly," the 911 operator said with her raspy voice, as she took a deep breath. In all of her twenty years working for Miami-Dade's 911 operations center, the operator had never fielded a call anything like this one. All of her training and all of her stoic, detached emotions went straight out of the window as she nervously contemplated the map of the city shining brightly on the computer monitors before her. She could pinpoint where the closest police units to the Lois Pope Life Center were located and could see that there were several units heading towards the Medical Campus. Seconds later, the operator suddenly lost her focus on the map before her when she heard a shrill, blood-curdling, scream on the other end of the line.

"Hello?" The operator said into her headset. "Hello?" She said again.

Someone yelled into the phone, "You tell anyone about this and you are fucking dead!" and the call was disconnected.

A CIA agent, who quietly snuck up behind Janice and Vick while they were on the phone, cornered them.

"What the hell do you think you are doing?" The agent asked as he held out his gun in their direction.

Janice and Vick just stared at each other in horror.

"Come with me," the agent said as he grabbed Janice by the hair pulling her up from the floor where she was sitting. The agent jabbed the gun in Vick's side, and they all made their way to the recovery room where the others were waiting.

Chapter 42

BETH AND DR. CORNELIUS

The situation in the recovery room was deteriorating rapidly and the tension was substantial enough to cause a person of lesser health to sustain a heart attack. Three guns were pointed at Dr. Cornelius's head while three others were pointed towards the subjects. One agent had his gun drawn and had it firmly positioned to give Beth a fatal chest wound. Each was ready to pull the trigger and commence unloading their first round of bullets when the recovery room doors flew wide open.

An agent pushed Janice and Vick into the center of the room where they clumsily fell to the floor and came to rest at the feet of Dr. Cornelius. Dr. Cornelius looked down to see the terrified faces of two people he did not recognize.

He looked over at the agent and asked, "Who are they?"

"I found them in one of the laboratories down the hall. This is the girl that tried to escape from us earlier. I found her placing a call to someone about our operation - She needs to die," the agent said with an angry expression emblazoned across his face.

"No! No! No!" Dr. Cornelius shouted as he stomped around in a circle like a little child.

"Who did you call? As if I need to ask," Dr. Cornelius questioned.

Neither Janice nor Vick responded.

Dr. Cornelius got next to Janice's ear and stuck the barrel of his gun in it. He bent down, placed his mouth near Janice's temple, and shouted, "You better hope that the police do not show up here!"

"Leave her alone!" Jimmy shouted. Dr. Cornelius ignored him and continued to badger Janice asking her who she called.

A single gunshot rang out and the sound reverberated around the room. Dr. Cornelius could feel the air from the bullet ruffle his hair as it whizzed past him within inches of his head. He tensed up and turned around to see Carlos eyeing him while a small amount of smoke waffed into the air from the silencer on the end of his gun.

"You heard Jimmy. Leave her alone!" Carlos said.

Dr. Cornelius stared at Carlos with panic in his eyes. He left Janice's side and made his way over to Carlos and, once he neared Carlos's side, he pulled his gun back and slammed it hard against Carlo's face.

He bent over and said to Carlos, "I should kill you right now."

"Do it." Carlos challenged.

"You're on my list." Dr. Cornelius said as he walked back over to where Janice and Vick sat. He summoned two of the agents over to him.

He said, "These two need to be separated. Take this one here next door and dispose of him."

Janice screamed out, "No. Don't take him!" But the agents were already poised to take action.

The agents grabbed Vick by the back of his shirt and drug him to the room attached to the recovery room. Once there, the agents beat Vick viciously as he pleaded for his life. After the agents rendered Vick unconscious, one of the agents grabbed a syringe filled with hydrogen cyanide from a nearby cabinet. He walked over to where Vick lay motionless and quickly injected it into Vick's neck. Vick jumped back to consciousness, momentarily, and clutched the insertion point while gasping for breath. Within a few agonizing minutes, Vick was dead.

The agents made their way back into the recovery room and announced to Dr. Cornelius that they had carried out his request.

Dr. Cornelius said, "Well done. The both of you." He turned to face the others who, with the exception of Carlos, sat in shock over what had just happened.

Dr. Cornelius continued, "Let this be a lesson to all of you! This is not a game. If you continue to fight me, you too will die!"

Carlos remained unfazed by Dr. Cornelius's threats and held the gun steadily pointed in Dr. Cornelius's direction.

Dr. Cornelius and another agent slowly walked towards Carlos with their guns drawn. As they neared Carlos's bed, Dr. Cornelius felt something poking him on his butt.

Beth shouted, "How does this feel you motherfucker?" She pulled the trigger of her gun and discharged a bullet into Dr. Cornelius's rear end.

Dr. Cornelius shrieked out in pain as blood quickly rolled down his pant leg and stained his lab coat. He fell to the floor holding his backside as the blood puddled around him. He tried to roll over to face Beth but the pain was too intense. After writhing on his stomach for several minutes, Dr. Cornelius came to rest on his left side while holding the wound on his rear.

Dr. Cornelius dropped his gun moments earlier, and Beth leaned in to grab it but quickly retreated when she heard a gunshot from behind her. She immediately fell to the ground and rolled to one side dogging a bullet that dug into the floor near her ear. Another shot rang out, and Beth rolled to her other side and jumped up. She began running towards the door when she heard a third shot ring out.

Beth looked over her shoulder as she passed through the recovery room doors and saw that the last shot had hit her shooter in the back of his head. The agent's limp body fell to the floor with a thud as Beth entered the vacant elevator. Another agent had killed him.

Carlos still had his gun drawn and was alternatively pointing it at the two agents holding their guns towards him. One of the two agents pulled the trigger as a third agent dove for the gun taking the shooter down with him. The bullet hit Carlo's IV bag causing it to burst and splatter a white fluid around the room.

Carlos fired his gun at the remaining agent standing. The agent fired back at Carlos as the bullet from Carlo's gun entered the agent's chest piercing his heart. The bullet exited the agent's back and penetrated the wall behind him. The agent stumbled backwards and slammed into the wall leaving behind a trail of blood as he slid along the wall to the ground.

The agent's bullet clipped Carlos's ear taking a chunk from it. The bullet ricocheted off of the metal plate securing the oxygen nozzle, and entered Marie's temple. Marie gasped out in shock and pain but quickly grew silent and; within seconds, her lungs filled for the last time.

Minutes earlier, several squad cars from the Miami police department arrived on the Medical campus. They were instructed not to use their sirens or flashing lights, as they did not want to draw attention to the situation they knew nothing about. The cars sporadically took positions around the base of the Lois A. Pope life center near the loading dock. A short, burly man with a thick, gray mustache, named Sergeant Hawkins, exited his cruiser and walked over to one of the other police cars.

After hacking several times, he said to his fellow officer sitting inside his cruiser, "I'm not quite sure what's going on in there. Dispatch said something about the CIA being involved in this."

"Yea, I heard the dispatcher too but couldn't quite believe it. We weren't trained to handle this type of situation," the handsome officer replied. "What do we do now?"

"We wait." Sergeant Hawkins said. "Go tell the others that the FBI is on its way too. We need to see how they plan on handling the situation, whatever it is. We'll likely be playing second fiddle on this one and providing back up."

The handsome officer walked over to the other officers and one by one apprised them of the situation. Sergeant Hawkins saw a lot of them shaking their heads in disbelief as the officer spoke. There were several people gathering around the edge of the street wondering what the police were doing there.

Ten tense minutes passed before the fist FBI agents arrived on the scene. They drove up in a Chevy Suburban with dark, tinted windows and a large antenna sticking up from the rear of the vehicle. They slowly pulled into a spot adjacent to Sergeant Hawkins's police car while the others looked on. A second vehicle following closely behind pulled up next to the first vehicle.

The driver's side door to the first Suburban flew open and a tall man in a navy blue suit exited the vehicle. He was wearing black sunglasses that he removed from his face as he neared the officers. His gait was purposeful as he strolled up to the group.

The FBI agent asked the officers, "Who's in charge here?"

"I am," Sergeant Hawkins said moving in closer to the agent. He extended his hand towards the agent to give him a handshake. The agent looked down at Sergeant Hawkins's hand and turned away.

"I'm in charge now. Do you understand?" The agent asked.

Sergeant Hawkins hesitated for a moment and a look of disgust was apparent on his face. He said, "Ok, yes, we understand. You, the FBI, is in charge then."

Sergeant Hawkins paused for a moment before asking, "So, what do you want to do about this situation?"

"I have no idea." The agent said.

"Yea, that makes two of us."

"I believe that the first thing we need to do is secure the premises. We need several of your men to make sure that no one enters or exits the building," the agent said.

By this time, the other FBI agents made their way from the vehicles over to where the others were standing. All the police officers had also exited their cars as well forming a rather large group of law enforcement officials. Sergeant Hawkins informed several members of his team to stand guard at the main entrances to the Lois A. Pope Life Center.

The tall FBI agent continued, "We are unaware on which floor the CIA, and its victims are located as the 911 operator did not provide that information. I believe the best way to obtain their whereabouts is to form teams of two to search each floor."

The FBI agents and the police officers paired off forming teams of two. The teams consisted of one police officer and one FBI agent. The teams made their way over to the entrance to the Lois A. Pope life center, but several officers remained near the police vehicles to secure the area, as the crowd was continuing to grow.

The teams entered the building at the same time. The tall FBI agent made his way into the building first. He approached the security guards sitting at the lobby's front desk and pulled out his badge. The guards looked on in shock.

The tall FBI agent said, "FBI, we need your full cooperation to secure this building. Are you aware of any unusual activities that may have gone on here?"

"No." One of the guards said. "We received a complaint that there was some loud pounding noise coming from one of the floors, but we determined that it was one of the professors demonstrating compound fractures on a skeleton. The medical school formally reprimanded the professor. But that was over a week ago."

"Right." The tall agent said. "Please make sure that no one enters or exits this building. Is that understood?"

"Yes." The guards responded in unison.

The teams made their way over to the elevators and boarded them. Each team got off the elevators at one of the floors. There were not enough teams to cover each floor so the team that got off last was instructed to cover the remaining two floors. After a couple of minutes, the elevators were empty.

The team on the second floor came across several people working in a laboratory. Surprising, they thought, since it was a Saturday and the building was mostly vacated. The workers were instructed to make their way to the lobby and remain there. The officers couldn't be sure that the workers were not somehow involved in with the CIA, but they would sort that out later. They were mostly concerned with finding the victims, and those people immediately surrounding them.

Several of the other teams found more people working in the building. And like the others, they were instructed to find their way into the lobby and remain there. There were about twenty people in all in the lobby not counting the police officers. The scientists were wondering what was going on. Several of them thought that the law enforcement agents were there in response to the noises that they heard on one of the floors moments earlier.

Dr. Cornelius grabbed at his rear as he writhed from side to side while laying face down on his stomach. Blood was spilling onto the ground near him since it over saturated his soaked and tattered pants. He reached out to grab the side of Carlos's bed, but Carlos smashed his hand with the butt of his gun. Dr. Cornelius screeched out in pain as he fell back onto his stomach like a wounded sea lion. He grabbed at Carlos's bed again, but Carlos took his fist and struck Dr. Cornelius across his face knocking some of his teeth loose.

Carlos screamed out, "You better stay down you sack of shit, or I will kill you!"

Dr. Cornelius shouted back, "Do it!"

"You stay down, or I will do it!" Carlos said.

"Kill him!" Candice yelled.

Dr. Cornelius reached up to grab Carlo's bed again but his reach came up short. His attempt was slow and weak; it was apparent that he was exhausted and about to faint from his massive blood loss.

"I want him to live," Carlos said to Candice.

"Why?" Candice shrieked out. "Why would you want that evil, horrible man to live? How could you after what he has done to us? Look what happened to my best friend! My sweet Marie! He needs to die, and I mean NOW!" Candice's voice was a mixture of sobs and fury. Tears filled her eyes as she pleaded for Carlos to end Dr. Cornelius's life.

"No." Carlos said. "That would be too easy. That would give him what he wants. He needs to suffer for the rest of his life for what he has done to us. He needs to be locked up to rot in his own filth and feel the pain that he has caused us."

"I'd rather see his insides. But, if you think that would be better, than suit yourself," Candice said as she calmed down a bit. Her hair was matted and tangled mess and her clothes were disheveled and dirty. Her face was a portrayal of sleepless nights, as large bags and oily, wrinkly skin glistened under the institutional fluorescent lights.

All of the subjects showed singes of wear, with the exception of Marie, whose pale skin and blue lips signified that she had crossed over into a different realm altogether. But Carlos, Marge, Candice, and Jimmy were fighters whose souls had been pushed to the limits, but they have fought back from the depths that some could not survive. They have conquered untold misery and pain, but they continue to push forward so that they may see brighter days.

Each one of the subject victims felt that the worst of the situation was behind them. They thought that the gun violence was over and there weren't any more threats from the CIA agents. Dr. Cornelius was wounded and incapacitated, and he teetered in and out of consciousness, as he lay sprawled out on the floor. The two other agents looked like they had had enough of this situation. The only reason that they didn't just high tail it out of there was that their sense of duty as law enforcement officers weighted on them. They didn't want to be fugitives from the law, but felt that it would be better that they face whatever consequences may come their way.

The crowd in the lobby of the Lois A. Pope Life Center continued to grow as the Miami Dade police and the FBI found more people on each of the floors they searched and sent them down on the elevator. The crowd was growing noisier as they questioned the authorities over what was going on and why they were being held there. Several times, someone from the group tried to make their way outside, and each time someone did, they were not allowed to leave. After this had happened to more than one person, someone from the group began yelling at one of the police officers.

"Why are you holding us here?" A short, fat woman in a lab coat bellowed out as she shook her fist at the officer.

"Calm down, calm down," the police officer said to her and the others in the group. "You will be informed of the situation once the information becomes available to us. For now, just hold tight and remain calm."

"Remain calm? Remain calm? We came here to work today and the next thing we know we are being pulled out of our labs and being held against our will, and you are telling us to remain calm? I don't think so!" The burly women screamed at the officer. She began to push at the officer's arm as she tried to make her way to the exit. The officer tried to pull her back away from the door, but the burly women broke away from the officer's grip. She continued toward the door fighting against the officer's pressure to remain in place.

The burly women pushed her way through the crowd towards the exit. Several officers standing next to the exit tried to block her from leaving. The burly, fat women shouted, "out of my way! You can't keep me here!" She pushed a little closer towards the officers.

Thwack! There was the sound of metal on metal as one of the officers slammed a handcuff against the burly woman's wrist. Thwack! There was another jarring, tightening noise as the officer slammed the other end of the handcuffs against the nearby metal handle of a door to one of the exercise rooms.

The burly women screamed out, "you can't do this to me! I have rights! I want to speak to a lawyer now!"

The officer completely ignored her as he walked over to contain the crowd looking at the burly women.

He said, "Let this be a lesson! Not one of you is going anywhere!"

Someone in the crowd threw a wood and metal business card holder sitting on the security guards' desk at one of the police officers standing nearby. The holder struck the face of one of the officers causing him to bleed. As the officer held his face, two of the other officers ran over to the offender and subdued him, and they placed handcuffs on the scientist.

The scientist wrestled with the officers for several minutes but quickly realized his defeat. The crowd was becoming increasingly violent, as they wanted explanations as to why they were being held there against their will. The officers explained nothing and simply tried to reassure the crowd that they would be informed of the situation once more information was available. Their words did nothing to placate the crowd's nerves. The police officers and FBI agents watching guard over the crowd knew very little of the situation and they secretly prayed that someone would give them the answers that they needed.

The FBI agent and Miami-Dade police officer exited the elevator on the seventh floor of the Lois Pope Life Center. They slowly made their way down the right side of the hall and stopped at the entrance to one of the laboratories across from the bathrooms. The police officer carefully peeked one eye into the small plane of glass on the door. He did not see anything of interest besides some jars containing body parts floating in formaldehyde. There were no people in the laboratory; the only life was movement coming from some rats scurrying about their cage.

The FBI agent and police officer turned their attention to a second door on the right side of the hall, which also came up empty. They backtracked down the hall a bit and stood against the wall with the double door entrance to their right. The police officer was about to stick his head around the corner to take a look in the window, but he noticed his shoe was untied. He leaned over to tie it, and as he did, the black baton attached to the back of his belt came unloose.

The baton fell to the ground with a loud thud. It rolled in a half circle and hit the double doors. The noise got the attention of everyone in the recovery room, with the exception of Dr. Cornelius who could think about nothing other than the pain he felt. There could have been an elephant stomping around outside and Dr. Cornelius wouldn't give it much of a second thought.

However, the others in the room were startled from the fear that enveloped them. For a moment, they just sat there with their eyes trained on the door. One of the remaining agents spoke up.

He said, "Shit. What was that?"

"I think someone's out there," the other agent said. "We don't have much time."

"What do you want to do?"

"I don't know."

"You all are finished!" Jimmy screamed at the agents while Dr. Cornelius continued to fade in and out of consciousness.

"I think we should fight!"

And at that moment, the doors flew wide open, and an FBI agent and police officer entered the room with their guns drawn and surrounded the CIA agents. Several more FBI agents and police officers exited the elevator and quickly entered the room with their guns drawn as well.

"Right on time guys!" Marge said with sarcasm dripping off each word.

"Shut up!" One of the FBI agents shouted at her.

"Now you are going to do as I say," The tall, head FBI agent said more towards the CIA agents than the subjects.

"You are going to slowly place your weapons on the ground."

One of the CIA agents cocked the trigger of his gun.

"You're not taking me anywhere," he said defiantly while taking a step towards the FBI agent.

"Boy, I told you to put your weapon on the ground! Now!"

"Not a chance." The agent said. He pulled the trigger to his gun releasing a bullet that struck one of the police officer's shoulders standing behind the head FBI guy. The police officer fell to the ground as the others looked on in disbelief.

There was a combination of 12 law enforcement officials in the room - five police officers, five FBI agents, and two CIA agents. The police officers and FBI agents unloaded round after round into the daring CIA agent. The sound was deafening as it bounced off the walls of the recovery room. Smoke was beginning to fill the air as the guns continued discharging their death metal.

"Hold it! Hold it!" The lead FBI agent said to the others, waving his hands furiously. The shots ceased. The CIA agent was left a bloody piece of Swiss cheese; he was unrecognizable.

The other CIA agent in the room had thrown his gun on the ground minutes earlier. He laid face down on the floor with his arms stretched high above his head.

"I surrender! I surrender!" The agent kept screaming again and again, trying to avoid ending up like his partner.

Sobs could be heard around the room as Marge and Candice were on the verge of a breakdown. They couldn't believe what they were going through, and they just wanted it to be over with.

"Take him into custody!" The tall FBI agent screamed at one of the other agents. "Call the paramedics immediately.

EPILOGUE

Beth left the Lois A. Pope Life Center in a frenzy of confused emotions. She jumped into the government issued Crown Victoria and sped down Highway US1 until it became Interstate 95. She needed to get away from that place quick now that she was a fugitive and found herself on the other side of the law. "How could this have happened to her?" She wondered out loud.

According to the trip odometer, Beth had traveled 75 miles when her husband called.

She answered the phone. "Hello," she said through anxious huffs.

"Hello, Beth. Where have you been?" Her husband shouted. "We have been waiting for a week to get some kind of contact from you. What is going on?"

"Nothing. I'm on my way home. I'll see you soon. Tell the kids that I love them, and they will be with their mother shortly."

Beth made it home in just less than five hours. Her husband and she fought for quite a long time, scaring the kids. Her children seemed distant and untrusting towards Beth. She tried to talk to them, but they were too frightened from how their father had treated them for so long. The fighting didn't help matters either. Beth assured them that they would be fine and a nice family dinner would help matters.

That night, Beth fed the family their last meal, ever.

The paramedics arrived on the scene minutes after the shootout took place. They rushed up the elevators and through the recovery room doors. The paramedics pushed several stretchers in front of them, each holding a defibrillator pack on it. The first paramedic to arrive on the scene was mortified. There were usually bad days and worse days for what you would see as a paramedic; this day was one of the worst.

After they took in the initial disgusting view of the room, the paramedics got to work. They first tended to Dr. Cornelius, doing their best to stop the blood loss from his massive ass wound. Two of the paramedics did their best to remove the bodies from the room, including Marie's.

Candice was in tears as they pulled Marie's body onto the stretcher. "That was my best friend," she said to one of the paramedics. "I am going to miss her so much!" She screamed.

The paramedics tended to the subjects' particular needs. Jimmy was given some water to fight the dehydration that set in over the course of several days. Carlos's ear was tended to and, eventually, patched up with medical tape. The paramedics gave Candice a dose of morphine to alleviate some of the pain she was experiencing from her injury.

The FBI agents began to question the subjects about what they had seen, but no one was in the mood to talk about it. They remained silent as they were questioned. After trying for a few minutes, the FBI agents decided that it would be best to find what they were looking for after the subjects were in a better situation.

The agents asked for the phone numbers of the subjects' immediate families, and the families were called, with the exception of Carlos's. Carlos did not want his family to be involved in his predicament at this point; he thought it would be too hard on them. So, he waited as the others' families were called.

The paramedics transported the subjects to the nearby Cedars Medical Center where they were wheeled through the emergency room doors and taken into separate rooms for the physician's evaluation. Carlos insisted on staying behind as he demanded time for himself to sort through what he wanted to do at this point. The FBI agents agreed to let him stay as long as they had a number where he could be reached. He gave them his mother's cell phone number but said not to call her for a day or two. He needed to contact her first and explain the situation to her.

The emergency room physician on staff heard the subjects' stories and was shocked and mortified by them. He ordered MRI scans to evaluate the current status of their injury so he could make his determination as what to do next with them.

Candice, Jimmy, and Marge were eventually taken to their own, private rooms where they were administered medication and fluids. The nurses tended to them, gave them baths, and changed them into fresh clothes. They were allotted time to relax and watch some television.

Candice was watching CNN and heard a story about a missing person. The reporter on the screen said that the missing person's name was Carlos Montenegro. It was the same Carlos that was one of the subjects with her at the Lois A. Pope Life Center. Candice became so upset that she shut the television off and threw the remote control on the floor.

After several hours, the subject's parents began to arrive. Marge's parents arrived first. They had tears in their eyes at the sight of her. They asked her, "What happened to you?" She said, "You wouldn't believe me if I told you."

They kept on questioning her as to her whereabouts. She was missing for more than three months. Eventually, she told them about Beth and Dr. Cornelius and what had happened to her. Her parents were both mortified and upset. Jimmy's and Candice's parents arrived as well. Marie's parents also made the trek to the hospital and crumbled after learning the fate of their daughter. They had to fly from different places of the country and were exhausted from the trip. Each of them had the same reaction when they learned the horrible truth about where their children had been.

The subjects remained in the hospital for several days where they were treated and then released. They made the long trip home to their respective cities where they rested a few days before beginning rehab again. They returned to their lives scarred and fractured but adjusted themselves the best they knew how. They would meet each other again for the trial.

Dr. Cornelius was treated at the Cedars Sinai medical center as well. He was eventually released into FBI custody and held in a federal prison. Dr. Cornelius's superior was also detained as well as all of the remaining CIA agents involved in the experiment.

After several months of confinement, a trial was held. The trial attracted international attention, as this was a government conspiracy to rival anything conducted in past. The trial was held at the federal courthouse in Washington, DC where media vans lined the streets for nearly a mile on both sides.

After several grueling weeks of testimony from Candice, Jimmy, and Marge, all of the agents were found guilty of violating nearly twelve federal laws. They all were sentenced to life in prison where they remain today.

Carlos never made it to the trial. The FBI was never able to get in contact with him. Several attempts to subpoena him yielded no results. They tried different methods to locate him but were unable to do so.

After the paramedics took the others to the hospital, he remained in the empty recovery room where he sat in his wheelchair deep in thought for nearly an hour. He was stoic and distant, but he eventually decided to call his mother. He assured her that he was fine and would eventually return home to see her.

After he hung up the phone, he grabbed the side of his wheelchair and pushed. He raised himself up a little and then reached out for the IV pole, and then, pulled himself up. He took a step forward, and then another. He lost his balance on one occasion but quickly steadied himself. He then, slowly, walked out through the recovery room door, through the lobby exit, and vanished into the cool night.

Hello, please consider donating to one or both of the causes listed below to cure paralysis.

To Find a Cure for Paralysis

www.gofund.me/Cure-Paralysis

and/or Contributions for Nick's Medical Expenses

www.gofundme.com/Nick-Med-Expenses

Many Thanks,

Will

Made in the USA
Columbia, SC
10 February 2023

11595706R00139